THE WIND AND THE RAIN

Martin O'Brien

"Every man's life ends the same way. It is only the details of how he lived and how he died that distinguish one man from another."

Ernest Hemingway

"The driving people of the Gypsies ... remained a harmful foreign body in German culture. All attempts to tie the Gypsies to the soil and to get used to a sedentary lifestyle have failed.

Even draconian punishments could not dissuade them from their erratic life and their attachment to unlawful acquisition of assets. Despite multiple mixing, their offspring have become Gypsies again with the same characteristics and habits that their ancestors already possessed."

Alfred Dillmann, 1905 Gypsy Book, Munich Gypsy Centre

FAREWELL LJUBLJANA

Monday, 24 June 1985

A man with a bubbling white scar across half his neck tells me we need to leave now. He speaks to me in French and his voice has a texture reminiscent of the sound of walking on crushed stones.

"You must hurry," the man next to him says. He is also speaking French.

Five minutes earlier I had been in bed in fitful sleep, dreaming of being trapped inside a burning coffin. Each time the flames touched my body I would wake up with a start and check my bed wasn't on fire. I would settle down, drift away and the cycle would repeat. In the middle of one of these fiery dreams Dad woke me up and said I had to leave my home. He told me these men were going to keep me safe because of what I did.

"I don't understand," was all I could answer, momentarily puzzled. The post-sleep amnesia faded and I remembered what I did and this all began to make sense. My stomach lurched as I stood up and I took a few seconds to allow my insides to settle.

I dressed as if someone had switched my mind and body to autopilot mode. I put on white denim shorts and my favourite t-shirt, my blue one with the Rocky III poster with Rocky Balboa and Clubber Lang printed on it. I went to the bathroom and after relieving myself I looked in the mirror. My eyes were stinging, tears streaming down my pink cheeks.

"Please Ana, hurry now," Dad poked his head into the bathroom, "We have already put your luggage in the car."

"Where's Mum?"

"She's in the kitchen, she's making you some food to take with you,"

I headed downstairs which is where I first clearly see the two men who had barged into my bedroom telling me to go to their car. They are stood in the open doorway at the front of the house. They are both older than my parents. The man with the neck scar is big and menacing with dark eyes, the other guy is small and wiry, ghostly white hair with a kind face.

I walk past them to go to the kitchen to see my mum. The younger, brooding one grabs my left arm with his giant, hairy hand. I push him off and I can only weakly whisper: "Mum". He stares at me but I refuse to break his gaze despite my watering eyes.

The man relents and releases my arm. He allows me to enter the kitchen but he looks around at the other man with a look of severe annoyance. I don't care. Mum has her back to me and is packing all kinds of foods into a brown bag. I say her name again but she doesn't turn around.

I walk up behind her and put my arms around her waist and lean my face on her warm shoulder, her sobbing echoes around our basic kitchen.

"I'm sorry Mum," I say quietly.

She doesn't speak or turn around. She simply hands me the bag and continues sobbing. It could be the saddest experience of my life. It is due to me that this bizarre scene is unfolding but it isn't my fault and to be truthful I am not sorry for what I have done. I turn round and head to the front door where my father is waiting for me. He doesn't know what to do with his fidgety hands.

"What time is it, Dad?" I ask, the sun has not risen yet but there is a hint of the morning beginning to brighten. The outline of the other houses and satellite dishes in the neighbourhood have a strange dark orange glow.

"It's half past four, princess,"

"Where are they taking me?"

"They will keep you safe, they are good people,"

"The big one hurt me," I show him my arm which has a dirty red tint to it where the hefty oaf grabbed me. Dad doesn't look at my arm. Instead, he cups my face in his hands.

"He is trying to protect you. We can't protect you here now. They will look after you,"

"I still don't understand, when will I come home?"

"I don't know, my sweet princess, I don't know. You need to be strong," He is in tears now. My tears have ceased, the shock taking over my body. Dad is forcing himself to speak again. He is struggling so much, witnessing it is making me so uncomfortable. In the distance I can hear the faint sound of sirens.

"We love you," he finally says and pulls his hands away from my face and stuffs them awkwardly into his trouser pockets, "You...you need to go now with these men. They are family,"

Dad stares at his feet. A shattered figure shivering despite the warmth. An arm gently touches my shoulder from behind. I turn and it is the menacing man again, startling me. I see the white scar gouging a line around half of his neck. I shift my gaze to his dark, large eyes. He doesn't say anything this time but guides me out of the house and into the back seat of a rundown car. The siren sounds are rising in volume. A voice inside my head is shouting that they are coming for me.

It's a typical mid-summer night in Ljubljana, with its unrelenting, stifling humidity. The darkness makes it difficult to make out any of the features of our house, save for the little chimney. I don't want to leave my beloved home in Bežigrad. The light from the open kitchen door illuminates us and all I can see is my father with his head still bowed. My mother hasn't come to the door, resulting in a pain I can barely describe. A withering sense of loss that makes my whole body ache.

The younger man drives the car away from my house, where I have lived since I was six years old. An ominous feeling grows telling me that I won't see the tiny place again. An immediate wave of nausea strikes my belly but I force myself to hold it in, I have to be strong like my dad said.

The noise from the police cars sounds scarily close by. I sit in the middle seat in the back and force myself to look straight ahead. I glimpse at the rearview mirror and the younger man is looking at me. Examining me might be a more accurate description.

"We're heading west, which way from here?" the menacing man asks me in French, maintaining his scrutiny of me, "Quickly, please,".

"You need to head south towards the train station, then on to the main road which is called Tivolska cesta. Then follow that and it should go round the city centre and take you right onto Tržaška cesta. Follow that and you're out of the city."

"Back towards Sežana?"

"Yes, is that where we're going?"

"We have friends there who can help us,"

The car trundles past Tivoli Park and another wave of nausea sweeps over me. Mum and Dad would take me there when I was younger. I loved running through the tall trees pretending I was a soldier, using a sturdy branch as a machine gun. We'd always end with an ice cream at the cafe near the tennis courts. Vanilla for Dad, strawberry for Mum and chocolate for me. The longing for ice cream is even stronger than the need to see my parents.

Before I can prevent it, the tears start flowing gently down my cheeks. My sobbing increases in intensity but I try not to make any noise so the men don't see me. Finally, as the long road takes me away from my town I regain a tiny portion of my composure but the tears won't stop. This is so annoying! Come on Ana, be strong right now!

"Are you OK back there?" it is the old man speaking now, the voice of a smoker, grizzly and deep, "are you comfortable?"

"I'm fine," is all I can say, if I start talking now I will break down like a stupid child.

"You should be comfortable, you are riding in a Fiat Argenta. This is one of the finest examples of Italian automotive engineering. Reliable, yet with the grace of Gina Lollobrigida,"

I remain silent. I don't know anything about cars.

No one in my family owns a car, never mind a top-notch Italian vehicle.

"My name is Janko and my friend here is Gunari," the old man has turned around now to look at me. The sun is beginning to creep above the fields and I can see his face. He must be seventy years old, he has bright blue eyes and very white hair. His finely lined face reminds me of Dad's leather chair at home.

"You are safe here with us but we need to get out of Yugoslavia today. How far is it to Sežana, Ana?"

"I don't know, I think it's about eighty kilometres,"

"Good, we should be crossing the border by about seven hopefully. Can you understand our French?"

"Yes, I studied languages at school - it's what I wanted to do at university," I find myself speaking this without realising that is one thing that won't be happening now. Stomach-churning guilt about what might happen to my parents attacks my insides, sizzling acid around my belly.

"Will my mum and dad be alright?" I say. The old man holds his gaze at me.

"They have made a brave decision for your sake Ana. They will be fine. You need to start thinking about yourself Ana. You have some big choices to make in the next few days that will define you for the rest of your life."

The journey to Sežana passes by like I'm starring in a film, unsure of where reality begins and ends. The sun is intense, a grubby blood orange hanging in the early morning sky. The trees that line the road make it appear that we're on a rail and not a road. We pull off the main road and head into the town of Sežana next to the Italian border.

"What time is it?" the menacing man, Gunari asks the old man, Janko.

"Half past six," comes the response. Gunari begins to speak but then stops himself.

Sežana appears to be a very pretty town, it even has palm trees. The car has pulled up in a side street behind another car, this time a rusting gold Jugo.

"There they are," Janko says. Gunari exits the car and walks to the driver's side window and is speaking to someone. About two minutes later he comes back to the Fiat.

"We follow them to the border, they have sorted our exit papers for Yugoslavia."

"I don't have a passport," I say, completely puzzled at the thought that we are about to leave the country. Who on earth are these two men I have ended up with?

"Our friends have arranged for us to pass Yugoslav customs," Janko replies, "And you happen to be the duty-free gift that we picked up on our trip," Janko laughs and I am even more baffled.

"But how will they let us into Italy, won't the border guards stop us?"

"Italy is no problem, corruption is ingrained into their culture. Yugoslavia is a little more complicated," Gunari says, "We need friends who know the border guards here as they won't allow people they don't know through without passports."

"Understandable, you never know what kind of undesirables try that kind of thing," Janko says.

"Don't worry Ana, try and get some sleep,"

Gunari looks around and actually smiles at me, he even looks like he means it. I am actually very tired and whatever adrenalin has kept me awake until now is ebbing away.

A VENETIAN ROMANCE

Tuesday, 25 June 1985

I wake and my head hurts. A real pounding through my forehead, my brain is surely leaking vital brain-juice. The smell is unfamiliar and I realise I'm still in this car with the two strange men. Two odd men with their incessant chat about nothing!

"Fiat manufacture the best cars in Europe. It's a fact, Gunari, an indisputable fact," the older man, Janko, is in the driving seat now. Out of the window, I can only see grey road, low grey barriers and loads of railway tracks out of the left window, to the right scruffy concrete buildings and cranes.

So this is Italy?

It looks damp and washed-out, the opposite of where I'm from in Yugoslavia.

"You talk rubbish Janko, you've barely driven anything else,"

"I don't need to. It's as good as the day I bought it,"

"You bought it last year,"

"Are you crazy? I've owned it for eight years. I had that red Trabant before that, remember? We got it off that guy for three hundred marks, what was his name?"

"I have no idea. I try to forget as many of your friends as I can,"

"The anarcho-syndicalist from Brussels? Portuguese Pierre? I'm sure it was him. Or it could have been his brother..." Janko says. I look at Gunari and he is shaking his head.

The Argenta continues rumbling along the road. A huge train catches us up on the left-hand side and the traffic is intense. None of this is helping my sore head. The only surprise is the train is green and not another shade of grey.

"Where are we?" I sit up and poke my head between the front seats. It's a wall of grey cloud out of the front window too.

"Ah, our little *Dornröschen* awakes," Janko looks around, "My sleeping beauty, we are in Mestre,"

"Where is that?" I say the word 'Mestre' in my head, rolling it around. I then try to say it out loud, repeating the word.

Nope, never heard of it.

"Well," Janko again turns towards me, I wish he'd concentrate on the road, "Imagine you have a horse. At the moment where we are right now, you could describe that as the horse's arse."

A horse's arse? This old man is crazy. Outside of the car, the factory windows are beginning to fall behind us and we heading out onto a bridge. There is a thick, light grey mist hanging over the traffic which leads me to assume that we are over water. Janko and Gurani are smiling at each other.

"I don't understand anything you say, Janko," I say, still nonplussed.

"Wait a few minutes," Gurani has decided to speak at last, "and you'll see the face of the prettiest horse in the world,"

"You two are mad, are we off to your secret island?" They both laugh and I am even more confused than ever. Last night we were supposed to be off to Italy, are we now in Albania? If the situation wasn't so ridiculous I would be scared but in all honesty, I'm excited.

"What time is it?" the fog is beginning to lift as we head towards land and the sun is breaking out of the whitening clouds. On the left are some prettier buildings that look like apartments and I can see some little bridges with high steps at their bases which would surely be more efficient for pedestrians if they were flat. What boats would travel down these little streams?

Janko swings the Fiat into a nearby multi-storey car park and parks in one of the nearest spots to the entrance. He parks up and says "We're here,"

We all get out of the car and the men stride purposefully away out of the car park. I have to break into a little jog to catch up and maintain pace with them. We walk around a corner and a wave of noise hits me, then the aroma.

I have never seen a busier place in my whole life. A large flat expanse filled with people and a ridiculous number of buses and coaches. There must be thousands of people here, more than I've seen before in one place. I can hear all kinds of languages - Italian, English, Russian. There are tourists taking photos and old men shouting and selling newspapers as though it was a competitive sport. Buses are constantly whizzing past and I can hear drilling too. I can see at least six different construction sites going on all over the place.

The distinctive smell reminds me of the swimming baths where I would try to hold my breath and rush past the pools of standing water in the changing rooms. Is this the smell of islands? Why would an island smell differently to normal land? It doesn't smell like this when you walk over the Triple Bridges back home.

I realise I'm stood right next to Gunari and he has his arm around my shoulders. Janko joins us and stands in front of us with arms in a welcoming gesture. He spins around like a circus ringmaster.

"Ana, please allow me to welcome you to the jewel of the Adriatic, the floating city, *La Serenissima...* Venice!" Janko flamboyantly calls out. I look up at Gunari and he is smiling down at me.

"I've never seen anything like it," I say.

"This is Piazzale Roma, it can be a bit of a shock to the system," Gunari replies.

"There are so many people here, I'm surprised the island doesn't sink,"

"Come back in a few years," Gunari says.

"Do you like ice cream Ana?" Janko says.

"I do," I reply.

"The best ice cream in the world is found in Italy. Let's get you some lovely Italian *gelato* and we can have a chat,"

The buildings are tightly compact and the little rivers are everywhere. At every bridge, I stop and watch the boats pass under. A dozen tourists also do the same at every crossing. Many of the boat drivers are singing or shouting abuse at their mates on the banks who respond in kind.

"Those boats you see everywhere, they are called a gondola, or *góndoła* if you're a native Venetian. The locals are very proud of their language here. Many common words everyone uses in Europe originated from here: casino, lotto, ciao,"

Janko begins to start saying "Ciao!" to people walking past, many of them reciprocating. Others seem baffled by his exuberant behaviour. He is clearly a strange old man. I'm not sure why he's hanging out with the mean lump, Gunari.

Yesterday I was cooped up in my room running the past couple of days constantly through my head. Now I am walking around a city I had read about in encyclopedias. Venice has a ruined beauty that I find captivating with its crumbling houses and the tight alleyways between the buildings. You could lose yourself here and never be found which I currently find a very alluring idea.

The three of us are sat outside a cafe on a huge plaza. Unsurprisingly it is extremely busy here too. Tourists are milling about taking photos and local youths are congregating around a statue in the centre of the square. It is disorientating being amongst so many people. Janko tells me this place is called Campo Santo Stefano, I am eating ice cream but the two men are drinking coffee.

"How old are you Ana?" Gunari says.

"I'm eighteen years old, I'll be nineteen in December."

"And what did you do?" Gunari says.

"Don't you know?" I reply, reading him for signals. He is as inscrutable as ever, his unnerving eyes don't shift from mine. All I want to do is carry on eating this delicious ice cream. I chose the pistachio flavour. I've never had it before but the taste is a nutty delight.

"I want you to tell us what you did and we can explain why we had to take you away,"

"I did what I felt was right,"

"We don't doubt that, *Schatzi*. Tell us what happened three days ago," Janko says.

I examine both men but their faces are impassive. I finish the last of my ice cream, put the spoon down and I tell them my story.

"My dad moved us to Ljubljana when I was a little girl as he wanted a better life for us. We used to live in a little village in the east of Slovenia near the Hungarian border called Mostje. That's where I was born. Dad found it hard to find work in the local area. He used to travel to Maribor occasionally but it was so far from home. Finally, he got a job as a bus driver and we moved to Ljubljana. So we moved to the big city, to a little house not far from the train station.

Dad always pushed me to educate myself, he said education is my passport to a brighter future. I've always worked hard at school, I had to work harder than other kids in my year. And all because I'm Roma. Roma kids are automatically put in the bottom classes in Yugoslavia, it's what they do.

I like going to school and learning and I was good too. I was easily the best at my school in languages and I enjoyed history lessons too. I chose all the language options - French, German, Italian and Russian. I even did extra classes in English on top and my dad paid for a tutor too.

Even when he had spells out of work he paid for Mr Asanović to come round. Mr Asanović said I was his best student and that if I kept going at it I could get a top job. He said that Europe and the world are changing and that being able to speak a few different languages will help me.

At my school most of the teachers were good but our head of year, Mr Mijatović, hated Roma kids. I heard him once tell a lad in my class, Roman, that he was a 'typical thieving gypsy'. He said Roman had stolen Dejan's dinner money but he hadn't done anything, it was a girl called Alina. I saw her take it. She did it after we came back from the morning break and I saw Alina taking her hand out of Dejan's coat pocket. She caught me looking and she ran off.

I said "Mr Mijatović, I saw who took the money,"

He looked at me and said, "No one likes a telltale Ana, especially when we know you're defending him because he is your cousin,". I said he isn't my cousin and he laughed. Can you believe it? The teacher, he laughed at me for telling the truth. He didn't believe me because of my background. I never once saw him give any praise to a Roma child. We were always being called into his office for things we hadn't done.

None of the other teachers even stood up for us or told him he was wrong. I suppose that's how it is done in Yugoslavia. I decided to keep my head down and not engage with the teachers unless it was to do with school work. I was desperate to get out of school and go to university.

I knew if I worked hard I would get the grades and if I did well I could even go to the University of Belgrade. That was my dream and I was determined to earn a place to go there. You know I love the Rocky films? I used to watch them all the time, they always used to show them on television on an evening and Dad would let me stay up late to watch them.

My life was like the training bits, they call them

a montage. Rocky does all the training and you only see little bits of it but you believe it all. You know that he wasn't taking the easy way out but he pushed himself every day. That was like me, I studied so much. You've heard me, you know I speak excellent French. It's the same for German and English. I love watching American movies. My dad takes me to the Vič cinema in town to see a film every month.

By the time it came to my exams I was confident that I would obtain the grades I needed. I applied for the best universities in the country and I was hoping I could win a place on a great course. And you know what? I did it. My marks were ace.

Then I started getting the rejection letters. The universities kept turning me down. The last one was Belgrade four days ago. And that was that. I didn't know why it happened so I went to school three days ago to see Mr Mijatović. I was in his office with my mum and my French teacher was there too, Mrs Jarni.

"You see Ana, certain eligibility criteria need to be fulfilled. Unfortunately, you didn't meet the criteria,"

"But my marks are better than everyone else's on the course. Marko Robić is going to Novi Sad to study French and Italian and I'm better than him. Is it because he is a boy?"

"Of course not, the Yugoslavian education ministry doesn't discriminate on lines of gender, there are other things to consider,"

"What am I not understanding?" I was choking up, "why can't I go to university?"

"Mrs Bihari," he dismissed my questions and turned to my mum, "you must realise that this is a sensitive area. This country is built upon unity through diversity. Slovenes need to be represented at the major schools else we will be dominated by the Croats and the Serbs. We need top class Slovenes working for the public good. A broad church will ensure the future of our nation,"

My mum eyed him in a strange way. She simply stood up and said "Come on Ana, we are going home,"

"But mum," I said, looking at Mrs Jarni to offer some support. She was looking at the floor. What a pathetic coward.

We left the school and we were walking down the pavement on the way home. I was unable to stop crying and I was walking a few steps behind my mum.

"Mum, what's going on? Nothing is making any sense,"

She stopped, turned around and placed her hands around my face.

"Ana, you are old enough to understand how the world works. I won't hide this from you. Simply, you are not going to university because you are Roma. There is no other reason. Only because your blood is Roma blood,"

"But my grades? I worked twice as hard as everyone. How can that not be good enough?"

"For our people, nothing will be good enough. These people are full of loathing, not only for the Roma but for everyone else in this sorry excuse for a nation. Actually Ana, it is more fear than loathing. They fear everything because it is all built on sand. But our blood is strong Ana. We will get through this together."

We walked home in silence holding hands.

The way my mother spoke to me told me there

was nothing we could do about it. Always the guilty. To be judged on nothing. To be Roma is to be guilty by default.

So, I thought, as I'm already guilty I could take out my anger on someone who deserved it. I wasn't thinking clearly. I mean, my life had been taken away from me. That's how I felt. It's how I still feel. It's more a sense of loss now, rather than anger.

I was heading home from the shop a couple of days ago and I saw him. Mr Mijatović. He was walking down the street with his granddaughter holding hands. This pretty little red-haired girl in a white dress holding a teddy bear and babbling to herself.

As we approached each other he caught my gaze. And he smirked. My fists were balled up ready to punch him on the nose. Time seemed to slow and as we passed he sneered at me. Like I was a stray dog, not one of his best students. I was livid. I went home and stewed in my room. I shouted at Mum to keep out of my room.

By the evening, I was even more upset at what had happened in the last few days. I decided to take action. He had destroyed everything I had hoped for so it seemed only fair to destroy everything he had.

I was laying in bed but I couldn't sleep. The anger had a hold on my thoughts that I can't explain. I checked my watch and it said it was past midnight. I got up, put on my clothes and left the house. At first, I walked around Bežigrad and my brain kept telling me to hurt him as he had hurt me.

I knew I couldn't damage him in the same way. He had the power and the money and the big house.

That's when the idea struck me.

I should burn down Mr Mijatović's house.

So I went down the road to the petrol station on Dunajska cesta. I bought two jerry cans and filled them with petrol. The woman who served me looked bored and didn't even question why a teenage girl needed two cans of petrol in the middle of the night.

My mind was clearer than it had been since I was told I couldn't go to university. I knew where he lived as it was right by my school in nearby Šiška. He lived in a big house with its own garden, rather than in one of the big apartment blocks that surrounded it.

The house possessed a couple of balconies on either side, the house was painted white. I walked through the open front gate towards the front door.

The night was still and very warm. I was sweating from lugging the cans across the city. I can see now that I've caused so much trouble but at that point in time, it felt like the most righteous thing I could do.

So I started pouring petrol over the front door and the window ledges. When I was done I stood there and realised I had no way of actually setting it alight. I must be the worst fire-starter in Slovenia!

And then, and then it's one of those things you think is natural at the time but when you look back on it, it's madness. On the bench next to the front door was a pack of matches. On the pack of matches was the logo of *Zveza komunistov Slovenije*, the local Communist party. It felt like an omen. It was proof that I was doing the right thing.

I picked up the pack and pulled out a bunch of matches, struck them against the pack. I looked at the flame for a quick second then I threw the matches against the door. They hit the door silently but they were very effective. The door caught fire and began to creep around the edge of the frame.

At first, I could only stand in the same spot, after a minute or two the heat and the noise of the flames against the wood began to rise and become unbearable to be near. So I walked back home and went to bed.

I even managed to fall asleep. In the morning I went down for breakfast and told my mum what I had done. She didn't say anything, I laid my head on her lap and she stroked my hair. It was hard to tell how she felt. She didn't seem angry, she seemed almost resigned about it.

I sat out in the garden for the rest of the morning and my Dad finally came back from his early shift. I heard him talking with Mum, I zoned out of listening to the conversation. My state of mind was placid and a funny lightheadedness kept me calm.

Eventually, Dad came outside and sat with me on the grass. He wrapped his arm around my shoulders and we simply sat there for a long time. How long? Who knows, maybe a couple of hours.

He didn't say anything to me. I don't think he could find the right words to say. That day I tried working out why. Was he ashamed of me? Was he proud of me?

He remained quiet and then said he had to make a phone call. I presume that was you guys. He must have had your number next to the Ghostbusters in his address book.

Then a couple of days later I wake up to you guys abducting me and taking me for ice cream in Venice.

ANGELS IN FLAMING FIRE

Tuesday, 25 June 1985

"What happened to the teacher?" Janko asks, then motions to the waiter requesting the bill.

"The last I heard was that he is in hospital at the moment. His wife too. I don't know if they survived or not." I reply. In yesterday's newspaper, I read that the police believe the perpetrator could be tried for attempted murder. It's very strange seeing yourself in the newspaper and knowing that you will soon be known as the 'alleged suspect'.

It's hard to grasp what will happen when they find out it was me. The media and the police will be swarming all over my parents' house. I hope Dad doesn't lose his job because of me.

"Come on Ana," Gunari says, dropping some lira on the table, "let's go for a walk to clear your head."

"Did I do the wrong thing?" I say, astonished by his non-reaction. An almost imperceptible smile crosses his lips.

"You did what you thought was the right thing. Only God will be able to judge you when the time comes,"

"I'm not sure I believe in God," I reply. God has never been anywhere near my mind to be honest.

"That's because you were educated by those

godless communists," Janko advises in a rather admonishing tone.

"Do you ever feel that you're part of something bigger, Ana?" Gunari asks and keeps his eyes focusing on me despite us walking around the packed Venetian streets.

"I don't know, it's not the kind of thing I think about,"

"Sometimes you take a path, not knowing which direction it will take you. I rely on God to guide me down the righteous way,"

"Does He talk to you?" I ask. Gunari ponders the question for so long he may have forgotten I am here. Or he's having a private chat with God checking it's alright to answer me.

"No, he doesn't talk to me. Sometimes I...when I'm on my own I enjoy going for walks and I talk. To myself," Gunari finally says. Janko looks at me and winks, and I stifle a giggle, "It helps me gather my thoughts, it clears my head and I can feel His presence sometimes and it makes me feel tiny. And overawed too,"

I'm not sure how to respond, I can't believe this big, scary man could be scared of someone you can't even see. I look at Janko to see his reaction, he moves towards me and puts his left arm around my shoulders

"You will soon see Ana," Janko whispers to me, "the world is bigger than you can ever imagine. And the people inhabiting this world are capable of things that you can scarcely comprehend,"

"I know there are bad people around,"

"We're talking about people who are indescribably bad. Gunari and I disagree on the nature of these people and on the definition of evil. But what we don't disagree on - and what your parents are in full agreement of - is on how to deal with bad people,"

This conversation is weighing me down, I'm struck by the memory of my first swimming lesson when the water crashed over me and I would panic. I learnt then to focus and to conquer the rising anxiety. But I'm struggling now to push away this gnawing emptiness.

Clearly, Janko and Gunari sense that I'm at a low point, they seem to be able to read me and that is unnerving me. Venice could be the most beautiful place I've ever seen, decaying but with a sense of history that seems to emanate out of the buildings and bridges. It is almost an entity in its own right, that all the people could disappear and the city would thrive without them.

We continue to walk over bridges and across the city when we come out on a huge square which somehow seems to contain even more tourists per square metre. Collonaded, austere buildings surrounding the square and at the end of the square must be the biggest church in the world.

I automatically walk towards it, entranced by its majesty. It pulls me in and I'm helplessly enthralled. The powerful lower section draws your eye but it's the dome that sends my head spinning. Rising out of the immense structure, it is surely God himself piercing through the blue sky.

The castle in Ljubljana was always my favourite building but this is something else. A building has never stirred my belly in this manner before. I could be in love. I don't know how long I remain in its hypnotic presence, it could be minutes, it could be millennia.

"What you see before you is San Marco Basilica," Janko appears behind me and lays a hand on my neck, "People call it the Church of Gold because of the gold-tinted mosaics,"

"It's like nothing I've ever seen before," I reply, unable to take my eyes away from it.

"Personally, I prefer San Geremia, but it is an iconic church, I'll grant you that Ana. It's stood there for a thousand years, you can't imagine it can you? Building something like this basilica in those days."

"Can I go inside?"

"Of course, Gunari will show you around,"

"Are you not coming in?"

"No, I need to have a rest after all that walking. I'll wait on the bench here for you both,"

"OK Janko," I turn round and spot Gunari a few yards away, "Hey Gunari, will you come into the church with me?" He nods and we cross the square to enter the church.

We walk through the giant gates and I make a noise, halfway between a sigh and a yelp. Even Gunari takes an intake of breath, he makes the sign of the cross as we enter so I copy him and do it too.

"I've never seen so much gold," Gunari says, eyes raised to the ceiling. Janko was right about the gold mosaics. The intensity of them is incredible. I crane my neck to look at the stories in the windows lining above the ring of the dome. Men on a mission from God.

I wander around the church trying to take it all in. The amount of time and money to create this structure. Janko is right - it is unbelievable.

The people that built this must have been so committed to the project. I can't get enough, I want to stay forever. I know it isn't possible but I'm positive nothing can hurt me inside here protected by the saints on the walls and the massed pilgrims of the Christian world.

For half an hour I inspect every part of the church, fascinated by the artworks and the scale. I look for Gunari and I see him near the altar knelt down in prayer, I approach him and I see his eyes are shut, I'm a bit uncomfortable watching him and I don't want to interrupt.

So I wait for a few more minutes and then I decide to sit beside him, I close my eyes and try to process everything that has happened in the last day or so. The witching hour departure from Yugoslavia to arriving in Venice. Is any of this real? What does the future hold for me now? I've never felt such a sense of dislocation. Being of Roma descent means you are often treated as the outsider. It's always something you are conscious of but will this feeling remain forever?

"Are you ready, Ana?" Gunari pokes my arm and startles me. I laugh and nod at him.

We exit the basilica and Janko is stood waiting for us. Janko smiles at us both and raises an arm to usher us to where we need to go next.

"This is the Doge's Palace now on your left Ana," Janko's guided tour has restarted, "Venice was an independent republic and the Doge was the big boss. Hundreds of years ago they had a great trading empire and they had one of the most powerful navies in the world. Eventually, the Turks took most of their possessions away and the city became part of the Habsburg empire who also ruled where you're from Ana,"

We turn the corner and I can see an island in

front with a church on it. Janko once again reads my mind:

"That is San Giorgio Maggione over there, it was founded as a monastery. That was over a thousand years ago too. A lot of famous people have been there since that time like Barbarossa and Cosimo de' Medici. A couple of hundred years ago the monks were expelled and it became a military base,"

"There's a lot of history in Venice," I say, impressed by his knowledge.

"That is true. Venice is a crossroads of cultures. East would meet West thanks to its trade links. However, it's not all beauty here. In 1692 the government here offered an amnesty to galley slaves to hunt gypsies. To hunt! Can you believe that?"

I stare at Janko to see if he is joking but I can tell from his face that he is telling the truth. He raises an eyebrow at me and I don't know how to respond. Janko sets off again and Gunari and I follow him.

We stop around the back of the Doge's Palace and loads of people are gathered looking at a small bridge traversing a canal. One end goes through the palace and the other end into the building opposite.

"Why is everyone looking at the bridge?" I ask. It's only a small bridge and doesn't look very special.

"It's one of the most famous bridges in the world even if it's quite small," Janko replies, "It is the Bridge of Sighs,"

"That's an odd name. Why is it called that?"

"They would take prisoners from the palace over the bridge to the prison cells. There are a couple of little windows you can see there. The prisoners would be able to gaze out at the beautiful city one last time and that would be it - thus the Bridge of Sighs.

"You know about a lot of things Janko,"

"I'd hope so at my age. You can't have enough knowledge, princess,"

"Yes, I suppose," An odd form of compassion for the prisoners touches my thoughts. I bet some of them will have been innocent and then had their liberty taken away. No more freedom for those people. What about me, will I ever be truly free?

"Ultimately, they were on a path from the palace to the prison," It's Gunari who is speaking now, "They saw the lagoon but they would never see it up close again. That was their fate. All of us are on a journey Ana, yours is now different from what you thought it would be last week,"

"I have to admit to being very scared," I reply, Gunari can be so heavy sometimes, the whole world seems to be weighing me down. I prefer not being so honest with people I've only recently met but I can't help myself.

"Don't be scared Ana, 'For He will command his angels concerning you to guard you in all your ways'"

"Are you saying you and Janko are angels?" I ask in a manner somewhere between incredulity and silliness.

"Something like that Ana," Janko says, "And you're our little angel-in-training,"

"Time for some food now, I think," Gunari adds, "We can tell you a little bit more about God's plan for you,"

Dusk has enveloped the city by the time our starters arrived, I chose vegetable soup to warm me up as it has gotten a little chilly. We are sat outside at a restaurant on a large rectangular piazza. The blockiness of the low rise buildings that surround the square reminds me a little of back home. Janko informs me this is the Campo Santa Margherita.

"Our people came originally from India fifteen hundred years ago," Janko says, prodding his antipasti elements around his plate with his fork, "Did you know that Ana?"

"Yeah, I guess so,"

"There are many myths about our people, and many of them come from us. In the end, we are travelling people. We don't write down our history and we love a tall tale. Nothing bonds people more than good conversation.

"Being Roma is difficult in the modern world with its borders and ideologies. We have passed from land to land over the last thousand years, we are people of the earth and we have every right to roam over this planet."

"I live in a house, my family don't travel around the place. Although my dad drove a bus," I say, I'm not sure where Janko is going with this.

"Humans don't like people who don't look or act in the same way as themselves. That is the history of our species. Violently suppressing the lifestyles of others. It is a stain on humanity. Our people have probably been more discriminated against than any other in history. This isn't to debase the suffering of other people but ultimately part of our identity is in resisting this prejudice. To be Romani is to know suffering, to know what is like to be on the bottom rung of every society we appear in,"

"Why though, I've never hurt anyone, all I wanted was to attend university. It's not a crime," The tears are welling again which is annoying. I cannot face crying again. I only want to eat my soup.

"No it's not a crime," Janko is as serious as I've seen him, "It's disgusting and you have our full sympathy. Gunari and I have a deep aversion towards people who pick on the vulnerable. Denying an education and a chance of betterment to a young girl by abhorrent politicians and cynical bureaucrats is wrong. You are not alone, in Austria last year a mayor of a small town incited locals to burn down a stall selling vegetables by the side of the road run by a Roma family,"

"Why would they do that?"

"The owner of the grocery store in the town centre was the brother of the mayor. The family stall was taking business away from the grocers. Rather than compete for business legally by selling better produce or lowering prices or however business people act in civilised places they hatched a plan to simply set fire to the Roma family's stall."

"So what happened, did they do it?" I say and Janko grimly smiles. I glance at Gunari but he is watching people walk past the restaurant, or at least pretending to watch them.

"Of course they did. They planted stories in the press about the food making people ill and that they were overcharging non-Roma. It was lies. The mayor eventually gathered four men and they travelled to the stand one night and burnt it down. They treated them as people would handle a wasps' nest in the garden that needed exterminating.

"The morning after, the owner - a man and wife

called Tomáš and Cecilia - saw what had happened. Everything was burnt to a crisp. That was it, their little chance of providing a good living for their children was destroyed by callous bigots."

"They should be punished," I say, my voice rising and making me angrier than I am about my situation, "It's awful. They can't get away with it,"

"They didn't," Gunari interjects.

"Why, what happened? Did the police get involved?"

"Of course not," Gunari replied, "One of the men who burned down the stall was actually a policeman. Instead, Janko and myself paid the mayor a visit after a brief arsonistic stop-over at his brother's grocers shop. We sneaked into his house when his family was out, found him in his study drinking scotch. We confronted him, his face was a picture. I pulled a knife out of his my pocket and held it to his throat,"

Janko added:

"And I calmly informed him about the unfortunate accident that had befallen his idiot brother's shop. I also informed him that if we ever hear of any discrimination in this town towards a single member of the Romani community then we will be forced to murder him. And his brother. And potentially anyone else directly connected to the abuse of our people,"

For the millionth time in the last forty-eight hours, my world begins to shift on its axis. God knows what angle my poor brain is at now.

"You two," I say, "You....what...you burned down the shop and attacked the mayor?"

"Yes," Gunari replies, "It was the least we could do,"

"Very proportionate, I would say," Janko adds.

"I can't…" there's nothing I can say. Nothing quite seems real now.

"Do you think we are in the wrong Ana?" Janko has laid his hand on to my wrist, holding my soup spoon.

"What can I say? If I say no, will you throw me into one of the rivers here?"

"Oh Ana," Janko lets out a belly laugh, "Of course not. And they are canals, not rivers,"

"We know this is a shock," Gunari says, "Ultimately, you need to know who we are and we don't want to lead you on,"

"You're vigilantes, like Mad Max?"

"Roma people don't hold power in any of the countries we reside in, Ana," Janko says, "Our people are not police chiefs or mayors. You'll find no Roma judges or prime ministers. We aren't newspaper editors or television news reporters. We don't possess an army of thousands or a navy full of gunboats."

"So what are you? Are you terrorists like those guys who hijack planes?"

"We never attack innocent people. Ever,"

"How do you know? That vegetable seller may have made the whole story up. Have you considered that?"

"Of course we considered that on our way to see the family," Gunari this time is speaking, "Then we met a man with his livelihood ripped away from him, his wife barely in control of her body, repeatedly having fits and three innocent children caught in the middle,"

"Don't make me sound like I'm such an awful person for asking," my voice this time does raise towards a shout, "You know exactly what I'm saying,"

"We know Ana," Janko replies, "We wouldn't insult your intelligence. The fact is, we can't afford to make mistakes. That would undermine the work we do. There aren't many of us Ana."

"Who do you work for?" I say.

"We work for ourselves, and for you, and for all the Roma in the world. We don't have a manager or a sergeant or a capo. For centuries there has been an organisation that has stood up for the rights of our brethren. Fighting back when we can; to impart justice on those who oppress us,"

"I've never heard of this so-called organisation," This must be some sort of Western European practical joke.

"You're still a child Ana, in the grand scheme of things," Janko says, "As you age, the community would have made you aware of our work. You wouldn't have been told much at first, only that if there was ever a grave inequity committed against you, then potentially we could help."

"Ana," Gunari looks at me, and I can see actual tears in his eyes. Upsetting me appears to have actually upset this brutish man, "We took you from your home because we want you to join us, to be part of our organisation. We know it's not the life you hoped for, but it's better than the life you would have had in a Yugoslav institution,"

"You want me to join you? I don't even know the name of this outfit," I say, dropping my spoon in the soup with a satisfying splosh.

"We don't have a name - our enemies have called us many names but they usually end up calling us bandits or worse. Our philosophy is to strike as stealthily as the wind and wash away their filthy sins like the rain cleans the streets of blood,"

"The wind and the rain..." I say and I have to confess the name does sound rather compelling, "Restoring the natural order,"

"Exactly," Janko says.

"Are you completely sure you've picked up the right person?"

O FORTUNA

Thursday, 19 December 1985

I slam the telephone receiver down. The cheap plastic base cracks from the impact. My hands are shaking. It is not due to my failing body on this occasion but from rage.

"Albert, Albert, everything will be fine," Paul had told me, minimising his grandson's actions while I struggled to maintain my composure. I have a tendency to avoid anger as much as possible, I do not believe anger is a productive emotion but today I cannot banish it.

My word, Paul angered me on that telephone call. He probably won't realise the extent he has riled me. Understanding the emotions of other people is not one of his skills.

His grandson's behaviour defies rational explanation. What a stupid, stupid boy. And Paul himself isn't much better off on the intelligence front. What brains they possess could together fill one normal person's head with ample room to spare. I'm not sure if Paul is stupid or deliberately disingenuous. He pretends to be dimmer than he actually is while conversely not being half as clever as he believes he is.

I despise the Christmas period enough without receiving vexatious telephone calls from old acquaintances. Never have I succumbed to the juvenile antics of decorating my home with trees or other ridiculous paraphernalia. I used to be astonished at normally right-thinking men tarting up their houses like an Italian bordello every December.

Eventually, I realised that people will fight to maintain these pitiable traditions. It can be very difficult to sever individuals from their religious or cultural habits. I learned to accept what I could change and not worry about the things I couldn't. The top brass was obsessed with the reclamation of the festival because of the Jews. I was never swayed by their hysterical claims about the Jews being responsible for breaking the world-liberator on the cross. I simply could not understand the irrational preoccupation with Christmastime.

For myself, the easiest thing to do was simply to avoid all contact with people for about three weeks and stay at home with enough scotch to keep a whole infantry division on the move for a year. From the first of January onwards, I could then deal with people shorn of their superstitions and forced familiarity.

I must confess that the only thing I miss at this time of the year is the snow. Whatever stresses I carry, I could always alleviate them by virtue of a brisk walk through the wintry streets of Rothenburg or Bamberg. In my opinion, there is nothing that makes me feel more German than admiring the snow-covered roofs on the perfectly proportioned houses, smoke billowing out of the chimneys. An image from a tin of biscuits doesn't do it justice. There is nothing like the real thing.

In my eyes, it is the pinnacle of civilisation - the German people's mastery of nature allied with our craftsmanship and community. I cherished those moments when I would take a walk in the snowy streets and return home and head to my study. The fire would be raging with flames so captivating you almost wanted to touch them. I would attain a pure joy simply by sitting in my reading chair in front of the fire, playing some Gramophone recordings by Schumann and allowing the warmth to embrace me I was never a fan of Wagner like a lot of my friends. Too much bombast in place of melody for my tastes. Happiness is sipping a fine scotch as the *Piano Concerto* engulfs you.

Nowadays, I am increasingly afflicted by waves of melancholy that can last for days. My appetite disappears and my consumption of scotch increases. Melancholia must be one of the symptoms of old age to go with the constant aches in my knee joints. Oh, how I wish I was in my little apartment in Bamberg with the view of the old town hall and the river.

But I'm not in Bamberg. Where I am now, all I see is grey clouds and miserable rain. I walk on the streets and hear people moaning in their grating, discordant language. My arms are tingling again, this infernal wet weather is going to be the death of me.

I must have been standing for a good ten minutes following the phone call from Paul. He has an answer for everything, the fat *Labertasche*, I have so little respect for him and his idiot children. I want to pick up the telephone receiver to slam it back down again but I refrain from permitting myself to do this. I will not allow the anger to poison my system.

I need to sit down so I grab the decanter next to the telephone which is only a quarter-full and sit in my chair by the window. Thankfully, a glass tumbler is also on the table resting on today's copy of *Die Welt*. I take the top off the decanter and I pour a solid measure of

Chivas Regal into the glass. It's strange, pouring a drink is one of the few things that makes the shakes in my hand disappear. The shakes have worsened over the last couple of years and the doctors here don't have any answers. They prefer taking money from rich housewives and prescribing happy pills rather than investigating my problems.

Even by the window, there isn't enough light to read despite it being midday. I am loathed to switch on the light at this time of day. I would like to take a walk but I'm still tired from trudging to the news-stand an hour ago. That phone call has irked me, the sheer brainless idiocy of that boy Horst. I won't be able to calm down for the rest of the day, I am sure of it.

It's funny the way these matters resurface after so much time. All the things that are happening now in Germany are barely in my mind at all. My thoughts of my homeland are mainly taken up with remembrances of the past, of my glory days in my twenties. The days when people respected me for my achievements and my knowledge. The times when hundreds of people would follow my instructions and address me in the correct manner.

Snap out of it Albert! I can now add nostalgic musings to my melancholy. What a feeble excuse of a man I have become. An old man hiding in a nondescript place wallowing in memories from decades long past. Melancholy and nostalgia, the Phobos and Deimos of the elderly man.

As I have withdrawn from life it could be said that I have empowered Paul to take charge. Paul is not a man of ideas or instruction. Maybe it is time for me to become a man of action again. To enforce my will on the weak-minded fools obsessed by jocularity and laziness. One last comeback like Dietrich von Bern? I chuckle at the thought and down my drink.

It is unlikely that I can remain here. There is a good chance that following Paul's conversation certain people will begin to feel they can find me. I doubt they will discover my location because of the precautions we have in place.

However, it may be time to leave again. A nagging sense in the back of my head that has stood me in good stead in the past. I am sure leaving is the best idea but at my age, I am not confident I am able to do it again.

The phone call could be seen as the final argument to convince me to leave here. In all honesty, I won't mind if I need to leave, the people here are vacuous cosmopolitans with no morals. It's time to prepare.

CHRISTMAS IN SAVOY

Tuesday, 24 December 1985

Today has been the first day since we arrived at Janko's cottage in snowy Savoy that the longing for my parents has almost overwhelmed me. My cosy bedroom induces cloying claustrophobia, aided by the heavy duck down duvet. I peek out of the covers at the clock on the wall at the foot of my bed which states it is seven in the morning.

I quickly jump out of bed and dress into tracksuit bottoms and a t-shirt. I lightfoot my way across the hallway and out of the front door. Forty metres ahead is the lake, sugar-frosted with a layer of ice. The temperature must be minus ten but I'm glad of the bracing air and the dearth of wind.

The beautiful, chalky lake is entrancing and I dip my right foot in, easily breaking the thin layer of ice. The water makes me gasp but I hold my foot in as long as I can. I'm tempted to take off my clothes and jump in but Janko says I should only take one full-body ice bath a week.

I decide that two dips in two days won't kill me and I slip out of my clothes, take eight deep breaths and then bomb into the water. I gasp as the exhilarating cold envelopes my body and immediately reduces my body temperature. The coldness thrills me and I start laughing at the sheer madness that is me wallowing in this random lake in France.

I pull my arms out of the water and examine the bruises dotted along each arm like filthy brown smudges. The bruises are painful all across my body but at long last, I am beginning to notice my muscles develop and my body evolve from a skinny teenager into that of an athletic woman.

My toned body is becoming my shell, my protective layer against homesickness. A year ago today my family celebrated Christmas together in Ljubljana. It's no exaggeration to say that was a lifetime ago.

A year ago I was a quiet girl helping my mother put up the decorations on the Christmas tree. I would take over from Dad putting the figures in the nativity scene, his clumsy hands knocking over the three wise men making them look like a bunch of village drunks. My Dad would pretend to be annoyed at this and then pat me on the head as I told him I would sort it out.

Now I'm running eleven kilometres five or six days a week, swimming three days a week, lifting and chopping logs five days a week, sparring seven days a week with Gunari. Occasionally I even cook a hearty home cooked dinner for Janko and Gunari.

In all honesty, Christmas last year was more mundane than when I was a little kid. At seventeen, it doesn't mean much, a festival for kids and the religious. Yet, the thought of my dad lighting the yule log on Christmas Eve in our toasty-warm front room makes my belly swirl. The same ripping hole in my gut I felt on the morning I was taken away by the two men.

I have been surprised at how easy the acclimatisation to my new life has been. Gunari told me that exercise is good for the brain and the body and he's right. My thoughts have been lucid and clear-cut. The self-discipline that I applied to my studies has now swapped over to my physical regime. I have enjoyed running different routes around the hills and lakes and the changing of the seasons. The first beautiful snow-fall coincided with my first week of running ten kilo-metres.

My body is beginning to numb now, a sure sign that I've been in the water for long enough at this tem-perature. The icy water is healing my bruised body, I dip my face in the pool. The bruise below my left eye stings and I pull my head out of the water.

In yesterday's one-on-one combat training, Gun-ari had whacked me full across the face after I failed to duck one of his punches. He knocked me down and I must have lost consciousness. In what seemed to be the very next moment, he was handing me a cup of coffee.

"There's whiskey in it," he said, his face stonily impassive.

I couldn't speak, my whole head was still ringing, bright sparkles in my vision. I took the mug and sipped at it.

"My hand travelled a fair way there Ana, you should have seen it coming,"

"I know," was all I could say and the tears were welling in my eyes, more from the deadening sense of failure rather than the actual blow.

"All it takes is one drop in concentration and you're dead. You know this Ana. The last week you have been slacking,"

"I haven't,"

"This isn't an argument, I'm not engaging in a discussion about each individual point I make. I'm stating facts,"

"I didn't see it,"

"And next time you will do. Your improvement has been rapid since you came here but I won't tolerate a drop off in performance,"

"I'm sorry, Gunari,"

"Don't apologise. Learn."

I continued to sip at the coffee, tolerating the burning of the top of my throat and enjoying the queerness as it travels down my chest and warms my insides.

"Every time you train," Gunari took the cup away from me, sat on his haunches with his eyes barely twenty centimetres from my face, "Remember why you are doing this, if you remember the hurt and the prejudice every single day you will need no more motivation. It's what I do every day."

Gunari stood up and began to walk back to the cottage, he turned back to me and said:

"It helps with the penance too. Our actions compel us to silence. The Lord tells us that silence eats our bones away. The responsibilities are a burden but if you embrace that responsibility it helps day-to-day."

Gunari's ominous pronouncements would sound absurd from Janko. From Gunari, the Old Testament has burst back to life and is repeatedly smashing my head in. I'm sure one day I will see him stoning a blasphemer outside the back door.

"I'm not sure I'll ever be ready," I replied.

"You will, Ana. But it will take time and discipline, which is what we have at the moment. You can look at this as a vocation. In a few years, you may even be glad of these times,"

"What, you clobbering me around the chops? I remain very sceptical of that Gunari,"

Gunari laughed and walked back into the house and left me nursing my aches.

I'm shivering a tremendous amount, I need to get out of the water. As I spin around I see Gunari wearing his running clothes at the edge of the lake holding a towel. He nods at me, places the towel down and sets off around the lake for his morning jog.

I doggy paddle back to shore and exit the water. It's even colder than inside the water so I wrap the towel around me and scamper back to the cottage and back inside where I sit by the fire.

Janko is also up and about and sat in his tattered red chair with a cup of coffee in one hand and a plate with toast and jam in the other.

"Help yourself Ana, I've made a bit too much hot bread,"

"Thanks," I say and begin buttering some toast, "I'll head to the shop afterwards, do you need anything?"

"Only the newspaper, princess. You know how I like to keep myself abreast of current affairs in the world,"

This conversation is now a ritual. I ask Janko if he needs anything from the shop and he replies with a remark about his love of the news. It has become a reassuring aspect of my time here in Savoy.

I finish my toast, change into jeans, t-shirt and a big furry white parka I found last month in the back of one of the wardrobes. The walk to town is a couple of miles uphill, most days I try and jog it but this morning

I amble absent-mindedly. Snow-dipped trees escort me along the well-paved road.

No traffic passes by and with it being the festive season the chances of a vehicle passing me by have reduced to almost zero. I stick to the centre road marking and try to line my steps up with the non-painted sections.

My low-tempo steps are virtually the only sounds I can hear. I spot a couple of pine martens burrowing around in the muddy snow-sludge at the side of the road but that is the only other sign of life. I can see why Gunari likes living here by the lake, a sense of peacefulness simply washes over me when I walk to town.

The town itself is called Criément, not far from Chamonix and the borders with Italy and Switzerland. It is more of a village in all honesty but compared to life at the cottage it is a bustling metropolis. The silence remains as I pass by cottages on both sides of the road. I can see the shop in the distance and the "Ouvərt" sign is lit up. I'm not even sure how a neon sign can have the letter 'E' dangling upside down and remain lit up but it does gladden my heart each time I see it.

I enter the shop and wave at the shopkeeper, a man with a tremendous comic-book walrus moustache called Xavier. The man is called Xavier, not the moustache. I don't think he has named his 'tache. He waves back cheerily.

I walk to the counter and see his face turn from cheer to concern.

"Everything OK, Xavier?" I say,

"I am well young lady, but what about you? Your face?" he replies. I realise now that the heavy bruising around my eye will look shocking to strangers. A sign of my otherworldly existence I now inhabit. I raise my hand up to the brown mark on my cheek.

"Oh yeah, I'm OK. I've been doing some boxing training,"

"Hmm, girls shouldn't box," Xavier says, disbelief etched around his eyes.

"Why not? I like it,"

"It's not ladylike, you could hurt yourself,"

"Don't be so old-fashioned Xavier," I say, giggling, and start shadow-boxing in front of the counter, "It keeps me in shape. I'll be ready to take on Clubber Lang soon."

"Who? Does he live around here? Lang, you say? Sounds like a German name to me," Xavier now looks completely nonplussed, "You're crazy, young lady. How is Janko? I do worry about my older customers when it comes to this time of year,"

"He's good, thank you. He told me you would be open today even though it's the day before Christmas. I thought you would be closed."

"I only open in the mornings for the next few days, you would be surprised how many people forget things. I've got a couple of the papers in that Janko ordered,"

Xavier handed me the Swiss daily *Neue Zürcher Zeitung*, the British *Sunday Times* and *Le Monde*, a French newspaper. I hand over twenty francs and with the change, I buy myself a bottle of Orangina to drink on the journey home.

"Goodbye Xavier, have a lovely Christmas," I say. popping my hood up on my parka in the doorway.

"See you soon Ana, enjoy the rest of the festive

season,"

Instead of rushing home I sit on the bench outside the St Symphorien church to drink my Orangina. Fair play to the French, they know how to make a nice soda. It's much nicer than the Cockta I would occasionally drink when doing my homework.

I glance at the French newspaper and it has some boring news about politics. The English one seems to be more of the same. The Swiss one has a story about some scandal-ridden politician trying to avoid resigning and a story about some stolen artwork being found in Germany which might be worth millions. Shame I didn't find that on my walk to the shop.

I set off back towards the cottage, downhill this time so a very easy journey. I check in my jacket pocket and touch the first weapon that Gunari gave me last month, my tiger claw.

As well as the strength training Gunari has been teaching me how to use weapons. He's not trusted me with a gun yet but we have been using a variety of weapons used around the world. My favourites have been the Japanese shuko which is a claw-like weapon which you wrap around your hand. The iron claws rest on the palm and you can rip a man's face off with ease. Gunari taught me that it's also an effective defensive weapon which can counter a knife attack.

The instrument that I have practised with the most is the bagh nakh, from an Indian word for 'tiger claw'. Janko told me that it is an old Roma weapon from the days before our people migrated West.

It is quite similar to the shuko in that it is a claw weapon. Instead of the claws resting on the palm, they nestle against the underside of the fingers, akin to having talons.

Much of the training is not to do with striking but in using the body to generate the momentum used to perform stealth kills. Gunari has shown me how to balance and move with the grace of one of those Romanian Olympic gymnasts. He said in boxing it is the movement of the feet rather than the hands that often proves decisive. I would suggest it is equally important not to be punched in the face.

Many days I have headed to the shop spinning around and swiping at imaginary enemies. I have to remember to leave the bagh nakh in my pocket when I go into the shop. The last thing Xavier needs to see is me slicing open the bags of pasta on the shelves.

The gradient of the road increases and the downhill walk becomes even easier. Two weeks ago I went on my first assignment with Gunari. Sadly I didn't even have the chance to use my tiger claw but I did see the potential power we hold.

HEARTS AND MINDS

Tuesday, 24 December 1985

I see the pine martens again frolicking in the snow. Tiny little creatures that are so vulnerable to nature. Predators wanting to kill and eat them. The weather conspiring to freeze them or drown them. The fragility of their lives. The fragility of all life.

Three weeks ago and as usual Janko was sat in his chair and commentating on whatever articles he was reading in the newspapers. No one listens to him but he seems to enjoy narrating the day's current affairs. Suddenly he jerked out of the chair. Gunari, who was sat at the table cleaning his pistol snapped round.

"What's up Janko?" he said, "Are you ill?"

Janko is waving his copy of *Le Progrès* and pointing at something on one of the pages. It was a tremendously comical image. His cheeks were red and he was spluttering.

"Jesus, Janko," Gunari said, "Calm down and tell us what you've read," Janko looks at us both and then almost turns off an internal switch, calming immediately and re-taking his seat.

"There is an article in this newspaper today about a man aiming to be elected as the new mayor of a town called Meyzieu, close to Lyon," Janko said, once more waving the paper above his head from his seated position, "He has pledged to, and I quote, 'deal with the recent infestation of gypsy thieves' in the commune."

"Infestation," I said, "Like flies?" I looked to Gunari who nodded.

"The wonderful new mayor has blamed a spate of stolen cars in the area on a group of Roma who have moved to a camp near the Grand Large reservoir. There are other quotes but I'm not reading them to you, I'm too angry,"

Janko stood up, waved the paper around one more time and walked out of the room with it. Gunari turned towards me and said:

"Well, Ana. This could be your first chance to see what we do,"

Two days later, Gunari and I set off on the road to Lyon in Janko's battered Argenta. Janko remained at the cottage. We arrived at the Roma campsite at lunchtime and we were welcomed by four of the men from the camp. One of the men embraced Gunari in a way that suggested they had known each other for a while.

The camp was in a state of disarray, out of the twelve or so caravans and motorhomes a couple had been burnt out. The smell of oil and smoke lingered in the air. The camp itself was in a car park in the middle of an industrial estate. A couple of young boys ran past me playing tag. Aside from the four men we were walking with, other adults were talking to each other in hushed tones and periodically looking at us.

There was a palpable tension, you would have to be emotionally crippled not to be able to sense the bubbling anger. I was immediately conscious of being far, far out of my depth. These people were looking to

Gunari and me for answers. I kept my head down as we walked up to a sparkling new motorhome parked at the back of the lot parallel to the wall of the warehouse behind.

The six of us walked in through the back towards a table that seats four people. Gunari and I parked ourselves on one side and two of the guys sat opposite. The other two guys; one a rat-faced young man of about twenty-five and a man who could have been his father stood up squarely behind the seated ones.

"Gunari," the man nearest the window said, his eyes betrayed his lack of sleep. Dark marks ringed his eyes and edged down his nose, "It's been a long time,"

"Yes, far too long Jean," Gunari reached his hand out and the man gave it a quick, yet warm squeeze, "What happened to the caravans?"

"Last night, after we spoke, a couple of men turned up in the early hours and petrol bombed us,"

"There were children in the caravans," the bald, intense-looking man next to Jean blurted out angrily, flecks of spit flying from his mouth, Both men are at least in their fifties, "Can you believe it? We woke up when we heard screams. What a scene, God only knows how many bombs were chucked at us,"

"Did everyone escape?" Gunari asked.

"Yes, we managed to rescue everyone," Jean gestured to the men behind, "Gabrielle, Mondine's mother and Tony's grandmother, she suffered from the smoke. We took her to the hospital this morning and she is still there."

"Bastards," the younger one, Tony said.

"Why don't you two go back to the hospital and check on her? I can sort out everything here," Jean said.

The two men eyeballed me suspiciously and then left the vehicle. I could sense Jean's gaze on me and I was reluctant to lift my head up.

"This is Ana," Gunari said, "She is working with us now, Jean,"

"She's very young," Jean replied, "and scrawny,"

"I can hear you," I said, frankly pretty annoyed that this man was talking to me as though I didn't exist. I stared at Jean but he refused to even respond in kind.

"I hope this one is reliable," Jean said. I turned to Gunari and I saw he was unimpressed by the remark.

"We sow the seeds Jean, we never know if the seed will prosper," Gunari said.

"I know, I know. Remember that unchecked pride consumes humility." Jean said and Gunari opened his arms in resigned acceptance. I have no idea what they are talking about.

"Things here have heated up, we plan to leave very soon no matter what actions you take Gunari. My cousin's teenage son was beaten up by these...fascists. His eye-socket was fractured. It is not safe for us here," Jean said.

"OK," Gunari nodded, "If you wish, that is your choice. I am not here to tell you what to do or not do,"

"The candidate is a man named Ginesty. He runs a delivery business in Lyon but his headquarters are near here. I believe the people acting on his behalf are his employees, he is known for taking on former convicts and using them to intimidate councils into selecting his firm for contracts,"

"Does he have a family?" Gunari asked.

"No, he isn't married. He cultivates an image of the playboy. He's always being photographed in the newspapers with young models on his arm. All that money and all that pride, flaunting his immorality with unmarried girls,"

"Well, we'll try and find him tonight, I've got his address. We will come to see you tomorrow morning to confirm our plan,"

It was time to leave so I headed out without saying anything and got straight into the car. Gunari said his goodbyes to Jean and joined me.

"I don't think he looked at me once," I said. I didn't want to say anything to Gunari but I couldn't hold it in.

"This is how the community can be Ana, all over Europe. Many of the older generations will only deal with men,"

"It's disrespectful,"

"I agree but you can't change peoples' beliefs overnight,"

I didn't want to continue this conversation so I remained silent until Gunari asked me to check the map to find the grubby mayoral candidate Ginesty's house. It took some time to find as he lived in the suburb of Brotteaux in the north of Lyon. I marked the street down for later as we were about to head to a speech Ginesty was giving at a community centre in Meyzieu. The area was run down and bore more of a resemblance to some of the toughest estates in Belgrade than the image of France that I held since I was a child.

It was a mild early evening and a large crowd had turned out to hear Ginesty speak. A quick head count showed there must have been over a hundred people there. There was a boisterous atmosphere and on a couple of occasions earthy chants rose from the crowd.

A large hoarding is visible at the back of the stage with *Les Françaises aux Les Français!* written on it alongside a large Front National logo.

The crowd was composed wholly of white people. Some of the people had angry faces and I began to notice a few people eyeballing Gunari and me, the two dark interlopers. Ginesty was ten minutes late coming on, Gunari told me this was a standard tactic for politicians to keep people waiting and to help build the atmosphere.

Another ten minutes passed and the crowd swelled even further. More songs could be heard around the crowd. "France for the French" was being bellowed by the younger members of the crowd. The atmosphere suited a football match rather than a political speech.

Ginesty finally appeared from behind the hoarding with a fist raised in salute. The crowd erupted into almost animalistic shouting. Ginesty stood at the lectern with his arms out drinking in the adulation, a cross between a resurrected Jesus and a deeply untrustworthy second-hand car salesman. The roar of the crowd barely ceased as Ginesty tried to calm them down. His black hair was slicked back and he was wearing an expensive suit. I have to say he definitely looked the part of a politician. He moved to the microphone and the noise only slightly decreased.

"Friends, please, I don't deserve this welcome," Ginesty said, his false humility was blatantly obvious to my eyes. He was clearly loving the attention and he was grinning, possibly in surprise at the reception. Eventually, the shouts and songs finally faded away and Ginesty addressed the crowd.

"Thank you all for taking time from your busy

lives to come here and listen to me. I am greatly humbled by the sight of so many concerned citizens. But I'm not only humbled I am also very disturbed. I am disturbed that so many people feel so appalled by the state of our once-great country. A nation of heroes. A nation that gave rise to Napoleon, that allowed Victor Hugo to write great novels, for Rodin to sculpt his masterpieces.

"A nation that spawned the writings of Voltaire, Sartre and Rousseau that now spawns graffiti on trains saying 'Kill the cops' or 'Arab power'. Has our nation sank so low that this has become acceptable?"

The crowd responded with a unanimous shout of "No!". Ginesty's tone is cynical rather than angry. His reasonable tone contrasts with the ferocity of the crowd making his points appear more legitimate.

"You may not know this but I moved to Meyzieu only three years ago. I arrived in this wonderful town after I was forced out of my home following the riots in Les Minguettes. My parents moved there after the war and set up a little bistro hoping for a peaceful life. However, years of abuse at the hands of foreigners sent them both to an early grave."

"None of that is true," Gunari whispered to me. He barely averted his eyes from Ginesty, "His parents are both solicitors who have lived in Guillotière all of their lives," I'm guessing Janko helped to supply this information.

"I know you feel betrayed by the profligate socialists in the Élysée Palace. I know all you want is to feel safe in your homes and on the streets, I know all you desire is for public transport services that are on time and not vandalised with Arabic muck. And I agree!

In fact, I don't quite understand why these things aren't at the top of the agenda for the bigwigs in Paris."

Ginesty's voice started to morph from reasoned teacher to a loudmouth spitting venom. The crowd were devouring every word he said.

"If you vote for me in two weeks as your mayor I guarantee I will do everything in my power to make all of your lives better. You are the backbone of this country, you are hard-working French people who pay your taxes and abide by the law.

"I will ensure you can walk to the shops without being accosted by gangs of youths speaking filthy *verlan* slang. I will ensure you can catch a train without the fear of being pickpocketed by a team of teenage gypsy thieves. I will ensure you can visit your friends and family without African pimps trying to sell you an hour with one of their contaminated black whores.

"For too long, Lyon and France have been a soft touch led by liberals and depraved homosexuals. The city is a cesspit of immigrants bringing with them crime and disease. And all they want is handouts. I say no, no, no!" A huge, primal roar erupts and reciprocates the shouts of "No!" and both Gunari and I flinch.

"Do you want Meyzieu to be the new Vénissieux? Full of gangs of youths burning cars and smoking drugs? The police standing idly by whilst these deviant cultures infect our beautiful heritage. What happened there will be on your doorstep in the near future.

"The time is right. I say it is high time that we remove the undesirable elements from the city of Lyon. Let us start with the Arabs! Send them back to Algeria where they can indulge in their backward Islamic customs as much as they want. Next, we will search every one of the *traboules* in the city amidst the rubbish and the rats and round up the gypsies and send them back to India. We have no need for their filthy traditions of theft or incest here.

"This is France, do you hear me, foreigners? This is the nation of Vercingetorix and Charles Martel, of Joan of Arc and Charles de Gaulle and they didn't rest until they had ejected the foreigners from our land. The land of the free French!"

The noise was unbearable. From every direction, I could hear remarks about Arabs, blacks, gypsies and Communists. Gunari gently nudged me and nodded his head towards the exit. We made our way out past snarling faces. Luckily people were so caught up in the emotion of the speech they were oblivious to two of their enemies sidling past them.

We made it to the car which was parked up opposite the community centre and remained there until the speech ended barely five minutes later. People filed out of the centre and conversation was ablaze amongst the attendees. After a few minutes, we saw Ginesty stood outside chatting to an elderly couple. As he spoke a young blonde girl who can't have been much older than me appeared at his side.

She was so pretty it was barely believable. Simply clapping eyes on her beautiful face and confident demeanour made me conscious of my clumsy old spinster appearance. It's funny how someone as beautiful as this girl could fall for someone who has spent the past half an hour spewing hate-filled shit out of his mouth.

A couple of tough looking security types also joined them and after a long animated conversation, the old couple sloped off into the night presumably to waffle on about thieving gypsy kids. Ginesty and the blonde girl walked down the street away from us and his two heavies followed.

"Let's drive to his house and wait there, we won't be able to get close to him now," Gunari said. He drove off towards the city of Lyon and it took us half an hour to arrive there. Ginesty's claims that he lived in Meyzieu were clearly nonsense as his place was in one of Lyon's leafy suburbs.

He lived in a modern low rise apartment block on the Boulevard des Belges opposite a large park. As we sat in the car on the street outside his block devising a plan, I spotted him. He was swaggering down the street towards us dressed in jeans and sports jacket animatedly chatting to a young man. I nudged Gunari who grunted.

The two men entered the apartment block and the foyer light flashed on automatically. Through the window, I saw the two men climbing up the stairs. As they were going up Ginesty suddenly slapped the young man's bottom. His friend turned around towards him and smiled. Ginesty then stood level with the young man and they began kissing in a very intense manner. I was shocked at the window shenanigans and in truth, I wasn't sure I actually saw that.

"Did I actually see that?" I said to Gunari.

"Yes. Yes, you did," he replied. Gunari was smiling.

"What are you smiling for?" I asked. Gunari didn't respond to the question. Instead, he beckoned me to follow him out of the car. I glanced up at the top window and I saw the two men entering his apartment.

"Have you got your camera?" Gunari asked. I

opened the back door and grabbed my Polaroid One-Step that Janko had bought me for my birthday in October. I had been snapping photos with it for the last two months. Gunari led us through the gate to the apartments then turned to me and said:

"How are your climbing skills?"

"I've climbed the occasional tree," I replied. I raised my eyes up to the third floor where Ginesty lived.

"Do you want to go up and take a look at what is happening in there?" Gunari said and I nodded and straight away began pulling myself up to the first-floor balcony. Luckily it was a modern building with loads of ledges to grab on to.

I clambered to the first storey with ease, then stood on the balcony wall and leapt up to the next level. Again, this was straightforward. I needed to get to Ginesty's floor above but I had to avoid making any noise or being spotted. The level I was now stood on ranged over two windows. On the floor above, the mezzanine only covered the left-hand window where the living room was situated. The right-hand window, probably the view from a bedroom, had no balcony.

The light was on in the left-hand window but not the right-hand window so it was most likely they were still in the living room. I decided to go for it and climb to their level. Once I was up there I could devise a plan, or hide.

I jumped and grabbed the balcony wall and pulled up my head up to look in. I saw Ginesty pouring a couple of drinks from a glass decanter. Ginesty walked over and handed his young friend a glass. My arms began to slightly ache but the pain vanished when I saw

Ginesty strip off to his white underpants. His companion slid off the sofa and was on his knees where he took off Ginesty's pants and started doing things to him. The kind of things that I've never witnessed on my time here on earth.

This was easily the most surreal moment of my life, hanging off a balcony in Lyon watching two men kissing and touching each other. I pulled my right leg up onto the deck and hung on there like you would cling to a ship if someone was trying to hurl you overboard.

One of my arms was now free and I started taking snaps of the now naked couple. They were engrossed in their nude adventures, so I threw myself over the wall onto the cold floor. I slithered over to the living room outside wall where I managed to stand up.

For the next twenty minutes, I took more photos and saw things that I can probably never unsee. I checked the photos and they were very clear, probably too clear for the sensitive amongst us. I sneakily leapt over the balcony and scrambled down to see Gunari.

"Come on, let's go," I said and handed the Polaroids to Gunari.

"Top work, Ana," Gunari replied. He was cycling through the photos and grinning.

In the morning, we returned to the camp and met up with Jean again. We were sat in the motorhome. The conversation meandered for an hour or so as Gunari and Jean talked about friends, most of whom it seemed had died from a variety of awful illnesses or perplexing accidents. During this time I don't think Jean looked in my direction once.

Gunari finally told Jean that we had some information he may be interested in. Jean raised a quizzical eyebrow and I tossed the Polaroids across the table.

Jean was fascinated by the extremely graphic pictures of two men engaged in rather vigorous explicit acts. One of the photos clearly showed the face of a handsome middle age man kissing a young lad who didn't look much older than me.

"Oh, this is exactly what we need," Jean smiled.

"And there was me thinking we might need to burn down a warehouse or two tonight," Gunari replied. This was easily the most jovial mood I had seen from Gunari.

That night we returned to Ginesty's apartment. Almost identically to last night, we saw Ginesty walking along the street with a young lad. It may even have been a different boy from the night before. We exited the car and followed behind them towards the apartment block entrance. Ginesty even held the door open for us as we followed him inside. His realisation that something was amiss occurred as we followed him to the top floor. Gunari had already noticed that there was only one apartment up here.

Ginesty turned around and came face to face with Gunari's pistol.

"My God," he said calmly. Gunari pointed towards his door and Ginesty unlocked it and the four of us entered.

"I don't need to tell you," Gunari whispered, "If you try anything stupid, I will blow your brains out with immediate effect,"

Ginesty nodded and led the way into a large living space with an amazing all-white kitchen attached.

He sat down on an off-white leather sofa and told his friend to sit on the chair opposite. I noticed the youngster had pissed himself and tears were rolling down his cheeks. He looked at me and I smiled sympathetically despite the situation.

"You are making a big mistake," Ginesty said, his composure returning although his face was covered in a layer of sweat.

"This isn't a Hollywood film, Mr Ginesty, so keep your mouth shut." Gunari barked at him. Ginesty flinched and his demeanour visibly went from cockily composed to utterly terrified. I glanced at the young lad and he was struggling to cease crying.

"Listen, I can get you some money or anything else you need," Ginesty begged. He actually clasped his hands together, submitting to Gunari. It looked false, a piece of acting by an insincere politician.

"I don't need anything from, you lowlife. I have heard about the wicked crimes you are perpetrating on the Roma community here in Meyzieu. I am visiting you to tell you that you need to cease your bigotry and violence against my people,"

"Of course, of course. I only said those things as it's what people want to hear. You know what the people around here are like?"

"Mr Ginesty, you can drop the false modesty. I know you and I know how you operate. Sycophancy, duplicity and insinuations will not work with me and our demands are not up for negotiation." Ginesty dropped to his knees with hands pleading with Gunari. Yet again, I remained wholly unconvinced by his performance.

"You will no longer make any public remarks

about, or discriminate against, the Roma community. You will no longer instigate, or support any acts of violence upon the Roma community. Am I clear?"

"I promise I won't, I promise,"

Gunari started to walk away and I kept my eyes on Ginesty, a smile creeping on his lips as the pretence began to peel away.

"Of course," Gunari turned around again to face Ginesty. "If every single one of our demands isn't adhered to, the copies of these photographs will be sent to all of your employees, all of your potential voters and your friends and family,"

Gunari threw down the photographs and Ginesty examined them. His face was rigid. He seemed to be staring through the photos and through the floor straight into the bowels of his own personal hell. Finally, he forced his head up to look at us in the doorway. He simply nodded his head in broken defeat. His boyfriend stretched over and laid a hand on his arm which Ginesty lamely batted away. Gunari picked up the photos and placed them back in his coat pocket.

I opened the door and Gunari and I left. The strangest wave of tempered exultation came over me, it was hard to explain. Vastly energised, yet hollowed out.

"I felt sorry for Ginesty at the end," I said to Gunari as we sat back in the car, and then rushed to the second part of the sentence "I know he was an awful man and he deserved it,"

"Don't lose that humanity Ana," Gunari said, surprising me, "No one is all good and nobody is all bad. This is a man who has continually made decisions to make himself more powerful or richer by exploiting others. In the grand scheme, he isn't the worst person we have dealt with. However, his behaviour needed to be corrected,"

"I hope he doesn't hurt his boyfriend, he only looked about my age,"

"Yes, I agree. I don't think he will hurt him. I wouldn't be surprised if the boys he picks up are the only people he treats like human beings. Yet, these are the ones he keeps hidden from the rest of his life," Gunari started the car and pulled away from the kerb on the journey back to the camp.

"Funny world we live in," I say. A man can be taken advantage of simply by threatening to expose his relationship with another man. If the man's friends and the voters didn't mind that he was in love with a man what would we have done then? I am about to ask Gunari when he cuts in:

"Oh, your Christmas gift is in the glove compartment,"

"It's a bit early, isn't it? Christmas isn't for another few weeks," I said in an admonishing tone while simultaneously hunting around the glove box like a maniac, "Where is it?"

"It's the envelope there," Gunari pointed vaguely in the direction I was already looking in. I spotted a white envelope amongst the debris and saw it had my name neatly written on it by Janko. I exclaimed an "Ooh!" and opened it, pulling out a ticket for the upcoming Rocky IV film!

"Wow Gunari, did you know that it's already been released in America? Here in Europe, we have to wait until January. He's fighting some big Soviet guy called Ivan Drago,"

"Oh yes? I bet he's no Rukeli Trollmann," Gunari said.

"Who?" I replied blankly, "Is he in the film?"

"No, he was a great German boxer in the Twenties and Thirties of Sinti descent. He fought for the German title against Adolf Witt in 1933, the Nazi authorities gave it to Witt at first until there was an outcry as he had been outboxed by Rukeli. Janko claimed to have seen the fight when he was a boy but I think the chances of that are less than me living on the moon next year,"

"What happened then?"

"The officials stripped him of his title then made him fight someone else and pressured him to lose. By the time the Second World War began he had been sterilised for being of Sinti descent and packed off to the Eastern Front. Ultimately he ended up murdered in a concentration camp by a criminal who he had beaten in a boxing fight."

"That's an incredible story," I said.

"He was only thirty-six when he died, what a life he had. He was my hero growing up even though I never saw him fight. Even in boxing, gypsy fighters have to do twice as much work to earn a win,"

We returned that night to the camp to drop off the photos and explain what had happened. Following that, we returned to Janko at the cottage. In the subsequent three weeks, images from the trip to Lyon have been at the forefront of my thoughts.

The rabid response of the crowd to Ginesty's speech scared me as much as the sight of young Roma kids playing amidst burning motorhomes sickened me. For some reason the image that stuck in my mind was Ginesty's face as the world he knew crumbled in an instant. All it takes is one moment and the fragility of the life you construct is exposed as a house of cards. It took us one evening and some commando photography to end a politician's career.

THE DEATH OF MARTIN BORMANN

Wednesday, 25 December 1985

"You'll never guess who lived here before me Ana?" Janko is sat in his favourite chair, in the midst of lighting one of his favourite French cigarettes, a Gauloise. He claims they have the flavour of a Parisian street cafe in late May. I am sat in front of the roaring fire eating my Christmas Toblerone. It's so hot sat here I am sure my whole body is melting. It feels tremendous.

"No, Janko," I say, humouring him, "Someone famous, I bet?" Janko cackles and takes a big drag on his cigarette. He exhales and smokes rises around him reminding me of a elderly Native American chief regaling the younger Indians with some buffalo-related tales.

"You could say that," He sits there in the chair, a pensive look crosses his face and he continues to smoke. Janko and his dramatic pauses may be the death of me.

"Are you going to tell me before the New Year? Who was it?"

"Have you heard of Martin Bormann?" Gunari intercedes from his seat at the kitchen table.

"The Nazi? Yeah I've heard of him, why would he live in Savoy? Unless it was before the war?"

"No, it wasn't before the war," Janko has finally come back to life, "It was after the war, not too long after. Ha, he thought he had escaped justice,"

A harsh look appears across Janko's face, the sudden change from his kindly face is shocking. Janko stubs out his cigarette, lights another immediately which is against his normal habit and re-focuses back on me.

"Bormann was one of the worst of the Nazi leadership, and let's be fair, that says a lot about your character doesn't it? He was an avid hater of pretty much everyone who wasn't Martin Bormann. Not only the Roma or Jews, but Catholics, Slavs, you name it - he instigated a policy of discrimination against them. From the beginnings of the Nazi party he was there, and not only in a political role. He was directly implicated in some pretty unsavoury incidents including slicing the throat of a suspected informant."

"How did you end up buying a house off him?" I say, I hear Gunari snort a rare laugh in the background.

"What? Are you soft between the ears?" Janko says, chuckling out loud, "I think if he knew that I was living here now he wouldn't be very pleased.

"He was there until the bitter end when Hitler and his wife killed themselves in his bunker in Berlin. Bormann escaped with some other high-ranking Nazis allegedly holding Hitler's last will and testament. Despite the Red Army bombarding them they somehow managed to cross the Spree and escape.

"A very good source informed me that an infantryman who was there accompanying them said that this group of Nazis all split up and agreed to meet in Salzburg at an agreed location. Bormann, against all odds, made it out of Germany alive.

"Oh, Germany was imploding. It was stricken, a violent mess. After the war it was..." Janko's voice trailed off, his sad eyes moistening as he looked out upon the ice-blue mountains beyond the lake. It was decades ago and I could see it was a deep struggle for Janko to tell me what happened. He brought his eyes back to me and smiled kindly, wiping a tear away from his eye. He continued:

"You wouldn't believe that people could actually live in such a devastated, benighted place. Whole districts that were there when I was a boy had simply vanished. Vanished. I lived in Munich as a teenager and it was a wonderful city full of centuries of history. But it was now a shell of a city.

"Bricks, rocks and bombed out tanks were scattered all over the place. People simply stood around in the streets, their homes had probably been destroyed. Barefoot children were wandering aimlessly around. Their mothers most likely killed in the Allied bombing or raped by the Red Army and their fathers killed on the Eastern Front. It was now a nation of zombies. They didn't think it was real, that such a difference in five years could be possible.

"The funny thing was that I was numb to the sheer amount of death and bodies that I had seen over the course of the conflict. But I was much more affected by the destroyed buildings. The brilliance of humanity that could craft such a beautiful city full of stunning churches and palaces yet could also generate hatred and violence that facilitated its destruction. The revulsion I felt was similar to when I travelled to Frankfurt to rescue a friend a few years earlier and I saw the conditions our people were being forced to live in.

"During the war, I had been recruited by a fellow called Věštec, from thé Czech part of Austro-Hungary. His name meant "Oracle" and he had actually named himself this. He genuinely thought he was blessed with supernatural mental powers. A strange man, as Gunari would also attest, but also one of the bravest men I have ever encountered.

"Luckily for me, my German accent turned out to be a tremendous asset," Janko chuckles to himself at this, "I sounded more Bavarian than most of the SS and with my fair hair and strong build I could pass as a native German. Yes, I possessed thick straw-blond hair in those days which may surprise you, Ana.

"At the end of the war, we heard about an American army captain, William Marek who had Roma roots. His father was of Moravian Protestant stock and his mother was a Roma from what is now Poland. It was a risk to speak to him but we knew he was involved in army intelligence. Věštec set up a meeting between us.

"You have probably heard of Odessa, the city in the Soviet Union, but it was also the name of an organisation that helped Nazis evade justice and flee to South America where they would be protected by corrupt regimes.

"Well, Bill Marek had an idea. He had a couple of contacts who worked in art dealerships across the *Sprachraum*, the German-speaking parts of the world: Switzerland, Austria and Luxembourg. The escaping Nazis were financing their global jaunts by desperately selling the artwork they had looted off the Jews across Europe. It wasn't altruism and ideology that enabled their departures but Rubens and Michelangelo.

"One of the dealers in Salzburg was Jewish. He

had hidden his identity and was willingly fencing art, it was his guilt that prompted him to speak to the Americans. Luckily, Bill knew the dealer and a plan began to take root.

"I had been in and out of Germany all the way throughout the war. Věštec, me and our other team member, an old chap called Mircea would travel around the country and the sights we saw meant not only did we understand the depravity of the Nazis. But it meant we also knew we could convince others to believe that we were Nazis too. I was selected to be a sheep in wolf's clothing.

"I was planted to work with the art dealer. Isaaksen was his real name but he changed it to Smith before the start of the war. He sold off the family gallery in Berlin and opened an antique and art shop called 'Cooper and Smith's Fineries' in Salzburg and he passed himself off as a South African art dealer.

"During the war Nazis, including some very high ranking ones, would come to his shop for advice regarding artwork that they had looted, mainly off the Jews. He would advise on the value and history of each piece and secretly would attempt to discover the provenance of them too. He would build rapport with the Nazis and try to find out where it had been 'liberated' from,"

"That could have caused him a lot of trouble," I say, enraptured by the tale.

"Oh yes, definitely. But Smith, as I had to call him, was very charismatic. He charmed everybody, they wouldn't have guessed he had Jewish blood. He wasn't tall but had broad shoulders and blonde hair, we could have been brothers. The perfect Aryan specimens, he called us: the gypsy and the Jew. He was an excellent reader of people and he knew exactly how to deal with each customer. He disarmed them with charm.

"And all the while he was teaching me about art while I worked as his assistant. I would spend my days with him at museums and galleries in Salzburg, Munich, Vienna, Prague. You name the place and we spent time there. He would visit local Nazi leaders and rich businessmen and he would facilitate sales of the artwork.

"I was soon picking up a massive amount of knowledge, both of art and of the Nazis and their industrialist enablers. None of them realised that Smith was making an incredibly detailed log of the artwork and the connections related to them. It was funny, Smith frequently predicted the Nazi regime wouldn't last five years. That was in nineteen forty-one when he first said it.

"Nowadays, the narrative is crystal clear with the benefit of hindsight. But you don't understand fear until you've lived under the Nazis. Every day I was scared I would be exposed as a Roma. Smith never showed fear but I know he was driving himself insane with dread. Some nights we would drink a bottle of Scotch whiskey and talk about life like it was our last night on earth. He was only about forty at the time but he seemed so knowledgeable about the world.

"The scale of the Nazi advance was incredible. Smith was, in a manner of speaking, quite admirable of their achievement. He said if he didn't own the shop he would have thought that they were an unstoppable force. But the avarice and self-serving nature of the

Nazis he had been dealing with since he moved to Salzburg convinced him that the moment they suffered a setback they would collapse.

"We were hearing updates from officers who had been on the Eastern Front and this only reinforced his view that the Nazi state was on the verge of collapse. We were hearing the truth about what was unfolding in forty-two in Stalingrad from the officers and comparing it to the propaganda they were pumping out in the Reich. It was bullshit and the high-ranking Nazis knew.

"By forty-four, we had gleaned snippets of information about an organisation called Odessa. Smith was now a regular at parties hosted by the top Austrian Nazis. After the Sicily landings, Italian fascists began to depart for South America, especially Argentina. Many of the Italians already had family there. Apparently, some of the Italians began helping some German friends to flee also.

"With the connections made with sympathisers in South America, the Nazis began to forge a partnership where they would be able to move to the Americas. It was small scale at first with low ranking officers fleeing but after the fall of Mussolini, some of the famous names you may recognise from your history books started to make discreet inquiries. And how did they pay for their escape?"

"I don't know, the looted paintings?" I reply.

"Exactly, princess. And it turned out that I was at the beating heart of the operation."

Janko lights yet another Gauloise and his eyes betray a reflective gaze.

"A German called Reutlinger was behind the ratlines out of Europe. To this day, I barely know anything about him despite my research. The first time I saw him was in forty-four and he was dressed in the uniform of a Sturmbannführer. The more I look back, the more I am convinced he was not SS,"

"What do you think he was?" I ask.

"Gestapo perhaps, maybe something else entirely. The Nazis thrived on secrets and secret organisations, sometimes it felt like a game. Almost as if they enjoyed the surreptitious nature of their work with no regard to the damage they caused. And if they lost the game, rather than shake your hand - they would simply kill you.

"One day in April forty-five Reutlinger arrived in the shop in Salzburg. For the first time, he looked panicked. He had received instructions to sell some paintings as quickly as possible as a few Nazis were looking to escape. He told us this with no hint of subtlety or precaution. He straight out supplied us a few names of the Nazis involved and the artworks they were prepared to sell. Smith would make copious notes about the artworks which I still have to this day. This was only weeks before everything collapsed and the Germans lost the war.

"Bormann was selling a painting that was locked up in a bank in Luxembourg. Vincent van Gogh's now legendary *Painter on the Road to Tarascon*. Other Nazis possessed some truly priceless artwork. We discussed a plan and we realised that to keep our cover we would only be able to take out one Nazi. Bormann was the biggest bastard on the list so he was our pick.

"Bormann was planning on leaving his wife and moving to Argentina. The plan was for Reutlinger to take him from a safe house somewhere in Austria to a cottage the Nazi Party had obtained in Savoy thanks to the pliant Vichy regime. Our humble abode here, need I say any more? We arranged to bring the money over to Savoy. Smith would obtain the painting in Luxembourg and telephone the cottage to inform us we had it in our possession.

"The drive to the cottage was probably the most nervous I have ever been in my life. Most of our missions prior to this during the war were sabotages. We would blow up bridges and telephone exchanges. The only time violence was used was when we would threaten people to provide information. And most of that threat was implied. A couple of times on the drive I had to tell Věštec to stop the car so I could be sick. I tried to pretend it was carsickness.

"We wound our way through the mountain roads and I couldn't shake the queasy feeling in my stomach. Before that point I embraced danger, you don't engage in as many fights as I did in my life without a certain sense of recklessness. But this time, all I could think was this was my end and I wasn't ready to die. I knew Reutlinger was a dangerous man, and now he was on the run and potentially erratic.

"There was still light snow flurries despite it being the middle of spring. Věštec kept telling me that he had seen what was going to happen, he knew both men would die in a few hours. I didn't respond, I was sure two men would die but I was ninety-nine percent sure it would be the two of us being buried in shallow graves on a French hillside.

"Věštec drove us up near to the cottage, he got out and went off to prepare his part of the job. I moved to the driver's seat and guided the car up to the cottage.

The sun was setting over the cottage and the mountains were tinted a beautiful shade of red. At least if I was going to die it would be in the nearest thing to paradise I had laid eyes on.

"I parked up and fought against a panic attack. I couldn't bring my hands off the steering wheel. I spent too long in the car, a suspiciously long time before I could gain the confidence to get out and meet Bormann and Reutlinger.

"I spent about an hour in their company, it was the longest hour imaginable. I attempted a couple of conversations but they were both so edgy I didn't want to push them too far and I was sure that every time I spoke my voice cracked. Eventually, the telephone rang, I almost ran to pick it up, I answered and Smith confirmed he had the painting.

"'Good luck, my friend,' Smith said to me and I hung up the line. I told Bormann and Reutlinger that we had the painting in our possession. I handed over twenty thousand Swiss Francs to the two Nazis. I was convinced Reutlinger would shoot me in the head at this point but he didn't. He told me where to leave the keys to the cottage and then they both left. Perhaps I didn't factor in that these two men were even more terrified than I was, they wanted to abscond from the cottage more than I did.

"Bormann had perked up now he had the cash to escape. His joy would last barely a few minutes. They packed their cases in the back of their car outside and drove off. Seconds later the car exploded, a massive roar echoed around the valley. Christ almighty, you wouldn't believe how loud it was, I was sure they would have heard it in Hamburg. Věštec had set the car bomb off to perfection. We both waited in the cottage overnight and I hope I never endure a night like that again. Věštec was also incredibly nervous, the size of the explosion was truly epic. We were awake all night expecting a bunch of Nazi soldiers to arrive but they never did.

"The day after we locked the house up and rolled the burned out car containing the crispy corpses of Bormann and Reutlinger into the lake. Sadly the money had also been incinerated but twenty thousand francs was a worthwhile investment in punishing a man like Martin Bormann. We headed back to Salzburg feeling euphoric. Finally, we were gaining revenge for the crimes perpetrated by the Nazis,"

"That is an incredible story Janko," I say, utterly captivated by the tale, "and the public has no idea who killed him,"

Janko looks thoughtful and we both stare at the painting on the wall of a sad-looking man in a blue suit carrying his painting equipment along a parched path lined with trees.

"People outside our community believe Martin Bormann killed himself, or the Soviets did it. Our people know that his blood was let by Roma. That is all that matters."

"Is this the painting Janko?" I ask. Surely this can't be a priceless painting hanging on the wall of this rustic cottage in the middle of nowhere. I turn my head from the painting towards Janko and I see he is smiling contentedly.

"Yes, I returned to Salzburg to see Smith who kindly allowed me to hold on to the painting in case we needed funds for our work. Smith moved to Israel after the war and I never heard from him again. I've read virtually every book written about Israel and I've never seen any mention of Smith or Isaaksen,"

I stand up and walk towards the wall, piercing white sunlight is striking the painting and I can see it in all its glory. So this is a Van Gogh masterpiece. I have barely given it a second glance, simply accepted it an image of a man walking along a path by surrounded by bright yellow and green fields.

As Janko said the painting is about an artist and I can see he is burdened with multiple cases and canvases. The artist himself casts a dark shadow but the trees accompanying him cast colourful shadows that bounce off the cobbled road.

It's hard to tell what the painter is thinking about as his face is so impassive. He is situated in the middle of the painting so I can't discern if he is eager or hesitant to reach his next destination.

The painter is stuck between two places. Am I being arrogant in thinking that I feel a certain parallel with my life? I can't go back and I'm wary about moving forwards. In the distance of the picture lies a town with mountains in the distance. Can the painter not simply forget the path he is walking and head back home?

A LEAF IN
THE WIND

Wednesday, 25 December 1985

"I was born on a farm, I don't even know exactly where. Can you believe that Ana?" Janko is telling more tales following our Christmas dinner, "A farm in Czechoslovakia, somewhere on the road from Plzen to Munich. My father was helping to build a barn along with some of his cousins. We moved a lot when I was a boy, a traditional Romani life. The borders didn't mean much to us, everything was still in flux after the Great War. I didn't know what a Habsburg was then and to be honest I barely do now!

"History is a strange thing. When you've been in the middle of major events you simply don't realise it. People look back on these points in time and say they define an era. But when you actually live it, these moments are your day to day life. Wars, currency collapses, revolution - that was our normal. And when society is in turmoil, that is when our people face the most danger.

"I was six years old when I first saw a man being killed. We were in... I'm not sure, I seem to remember it was in Austria, somewhere along the border with Germany. That's another thing, with time certain details slip away and not only the little things. Sometimes, the major details, the catalysts, they simply drop out of your memory like soap suds bursting. It could be the brain trying to keep you sane.

"My father and I were in a busy market town, he was there hoping to sell a horse to a local man. Across the road from us was a bank and a man was arguing with a bank clerk. It appeared to me that the clerk was escorting the man from the building. It was noisy in the town but I could sense the tumult growing louder and louder. But it wasn't the noise that grabbed my attention. It was an electricity that started pulsing through the people walking around doing their daily business.

"They started looking towards the man who was becoming more and more irate. His suit was tatty and his shoes were falling apart, the clerk was dressed in an immaculate suit but his hair was ruffled and he had a look in his eye that I had never seen before. I know now what the look meant. It was disgust. The bank clerk was disgusted by the human being in front of him. A man who clearly possessed nothing except his pride.

"Both men were shouting at each other but were now looking around and they realised there was a crowd developing around them. The poor man became more agitated, he started bellowing at the top of his voice and began pushing the bank clerk. The clerk kept his bearing, his composure began to return to him. And then, seemingly out of nowhere, from the crowd, another man appeared and I saw the gleam of a knife. He looked at the clerk and a wordless moment passed between them and he stabbed the poor man straight in the middle of the chest.

"I was twenty yards away and I saw it all. When he pulled the knife out I could see blood splash back over him like flicked paint. The stabbed man simply stood, the crowd went quiet and then erupted, one man threw a wild punch at the attacker who then started swinging his knife to make some room and then he ran away.

"A couple of people made half-hearted sprints after him and the bank clerk had retreated inside the bank and locked the doors. People were looking after the man, my father went over to help but was shooed away by a doctor who was on the scene.

"The blood was spreading out over the cobblestones as I went to hold my father's hand and we simply watched as the life drained out of him. The doctor then informed the onlookers that he had died. It was almost as if the crowd was one organism and they were his next of kin. Housewives broke down in tears and some of the men who were there began to bang on the doors to the bank. A policeman also appeared and began to ask the congregation questions.

"My father then took me away, we walked the four or five miles back to where we were camping in total silence. I would usually be chatting away constantly but all I could think about was how small, how insignificant the actual stabbing was. The tension preceding it had been noticeable but the act of violence seemed as mundane as buying a loaf of bread. The emotions of the crowd that day and the finality of the murder have probably lived with me longer than anything else in my life.

"I can't remember my own father's face as vividly as I can that man lying in the street. His eyes watering in pure fear, enveloped by the realisation that his life was ending there in a street outside a bank by some rickety market stalls, killed by a man he probably didn't even see or know,"

Janko picks up a cigarette but instead of lighting it he puts it down. He then walks to the drinks cabinet and pours a brandy each for the three for us and drops some ice in each glass. He hands the glasses around and I mumble my thanks, as does Gunari. Janko takes his seat and sips his drink.

"Our family mainly moved around Bavaria and my father would trade horses and horse equipment. He made good money in those days too. In the twenties, not many people owned a car. They were good times for us in Germany at that time. Occasionally we would be abused in the street by drunkards but that was generally as bad as it got.

"I had been training to become a prizefighter from about ten years old which was handy as that was when things began to take a downturn for the Roma in Bavaria. The Great Depression hit, people stopped spending their money, especially when it involved handing money over to 'filthy gypsies', as people started calling us.

"By the time I was fourteen in thirty-three, going into urban areas alone was dangerous for Roma. Gangs of militiamen would be prowling the roads looking to attack Roma and other undesirables. Not just Nazis either, Nationalists, Communists, you name them - they would beat the hell out of us given the opportunity.

"On a weekly basis, I'd end up having a scrap with someone, usually after a day at the market where we would be selling furniture. My dad was good with woodwork and had built carriages for horses, then moved into making tables and chairs. People would turn up and start hurling insults at us.

"I was so wild at that age, I remember one man who must have been in his fifties casually calling us 'mongrels' in the same tone as he would be if was asking to borrow a newspaper. I leapt across one of our tables and floored with him one punch to the temple. My father was furious with me and to be honest it was a big mistake.

"More and more people would turn up each day and make life intolerable for us. We were pretty much the only Roma family that was living in the town. My mother wasn't well so we simply couldn't keep moving around.

"It seemed every few days I would have a confrontation with some bigot or other. Most of the time it was verbal abuse but occasionally it would descend into a fight. One on one, I was never beaten - they didn't realise I was fighting for my family, to the death if needs be. They were foolish, but when they had a group of them together they were also very dangerous.

"One time near Christmas in thirty-four, my brother and I were hauling our stock back on to our carriage when a group of five or six big blokes turned up. Full of Christmas spirit, you could say. They tried picking on my brother who was a bookish sort. They pinned him up against the carriage and one of the guys gave him a hard punch to the stomach. He keeled over and they tried pulling him back up.

"I had to step in, and I knew this would come back on me, but I went for it. I ran in and punched one guy from the side. He wasn't expecting it and I could feel his cheekbone disintegrate over my knuckles. The guy went down hard, the other guy holding up my brother was frozen but a fat chap grabbed me from behind.

"I easily used my boxing skills to ebb in front and then step away and hit him with the sweetest, cleanest jab on his nose. He went down too. Then my own head started spinning after another punch from God-knows-where landed on the side of my chin. One more crack above the temple put me down. I screamed at my brother to run. He was stood stock still, and I shouted again telling him to get the hell out of there.

"Next thing I know I was waking up in the middle of the street, the remaining stock had been destroyed and the carriage too. I was in an incredible amount of pain. A couple of ribs were definitely broken, as was my nose and probably my jawbone. I managed to stand up, it was now late evening, I looked up at the clock at the town hall and it said nine o'clock.

"It took a couple of hours to walk home and my mother gave me a massive hug when I arrived back. Despite the pain, it was the best hug I've ever had. My brother tried apologising but I told him he had to run. If they could do that to me, they would have snapped his weedy body!

"Finally, at the start of nineteen thirty-five, my parents decided to travel to the Sudetenland in Czecho-slovakia and live there instead of Germany. The growing impact of the Nazis was becoming intolerable. Civil society was being hollowed out, the remilitarisation of the armed forces and the discriminatory policies were in full swing.

"As you know, the Nazis would annex the Sudetenland before World War II. Nothing much changed immediately for my family but I had already left. My genes were urging me to roam. I left my family and visited friends and family in Germany before the war began. I was careful and never interrogated or captured,"

"Did you ever see any of the camps Janko?" I say, fearful of the answer, even though I wasn't even there.

"I did, young girl, I did," Janko's face returns from the dreamy look he had shown during the tales of his childhood and darkens. A shadow quickly passes over his face, barely perceptible, but I'm certain I saw it.

Janko pulls himself out of the chair, makes his textbook groaning sound and heads towards the drink cabinet and pours himself another brandy. He gestures to me asking if I want another one. I shake my head and keep watching him. He pours one for Gunari who has remained silent during Janko's stories. Gunari downs his brandy and then announces he is off for a run and leaves the room. Janko sits back in the chair and continues sipping his brandy.

"Strangely enough," Janko says, "It was before the Second World War. Before the world witnessed what the Nazis had accomplished," Janko snorts at this.

"Before the war?" I ask. I was sure the camps were set up during the war.

"Yes, before the actual war officially started. For the Roma, the war had already begun. Before I had joined our movement, word had spread that the Nazis were 'hosting' a camp for Roma and Sinti people. It was near Frankfurt in Germany. Dieselstrasse was its name,"

"I've never heard of it Janko," I say. Everyone has heard of Auschwitz, Dachau or Buchenwald. Not this one.

"No, I suppose people haven't heard of it. It

wasn't strictly a death camp, thousands of people were shipped to Auschwitz for extermination. Extermination, it sounds bloody awful, doesn't it? I'm sorry Ana, where was I?"

"The camp in Frankfurt,"

"Oh yes of course. I had heard that a cousin of mine that I played with as a young boy had been placed there. So I headed there one evening in late thirty-eight with a crazy idea about liberating him. The camp was near to the river and we could hear the buzz of people before we reached it. It was lightly guarded but I was very careful.

"People were living in vans, families were packed into vehicles in numbers you wouldn't believe. Removal vans! Can you believe that Ana? Being forced to live in trucks while trigger-happy young soldiers prevent you from leaving,"

"This was before the war and it wasn't news at the time? If it came out surely the war might have been prevented?"

"Unfortunately Ana, there are many reasons why this wasn't the case. To be honest, it was bigger than our people. The tectonic plates of geopolitics were in motion. Once Hitler attained power, conflict was inevitable,"

"So were the Nazis killing people at this camp?"

"No, not at first. They basically wanted Roma to be herded away from the general population. Adults were still allowed to leave the camp during the day, and children were allowed to attend school until a local government order was brought in to stop that kind of thing.

"I managed to find my cousin Peter and I spoke to

him through the fence. I passed him some money which he used to bribe a guard to allow him to leave. Peter said he knew a man that his father had told him about who may have some work for us. It took us over a year but we finally located Věštec and Mircea.

"Peter departed to find his family in Munich but I never saw him again. I was recruited to work with the organisation and we began performing guerilla actions in Germany. We returned to the camp two years later, we actually sneaked in despite the guards and spoke to some of the captives. That's when we discovered that a doctor was working at the camp and conducting, oh Ana, how do I even describe it?"

Janko's hand is shaking and he places his drink on the table beside the chair.

"Who was he?" I ask, the words appalling me to my core.

"His name is Albert Tremmick, the Exterminator of Dieselstrasse - that's what he was nicknamed by the newspapers during the Nuremberg Trials. Of course, he never faced justice. Jesus, in the years after Ana, we have been close a few times. It wasn't until after the war that we realised the major role he played in Nazi human experiments"

"So what happened to him? Is he still alive now?" If only he was near me now, I would easily kill the man. Janko looks at me with a bemused face.

"Where is he? I wonder that quite often, *Schatzi*," Janko's eyes narrow, he looks at the Van Gogh, then back towards me. There is a shimmer in his eye.

"Ana, Ana, Ana. There is something on the tip of my tongue and I am sure it has something to do with you,"

"I don't know where he is," I say. Janko roars with laughter, stands and paces around the front room.

"Oh, Ana. Why are my bells ringing? You could be the key to the biggest puzzle of them all,"

"I doubt it, Janko," I watch him stride around the room picking up papers, putting them down, lifting up folders and flicking through the contents.

"Let's start from the beginning, always the best place to start. Yugoslavia, is that the link? What do you think, Ana?" I start laughing at this daft inquisition.

"I only heard about this man half an hour ago, I can't tell you where he is living now Janko, stop being silly. You kidnapped me in Ljubljana and we ended up in Venice eating gelato,"

"In Venice! That's it!" Janko slams his hand onto the table. I jump at the noise.

"What is?" Even I am beginning to be enthralled by his enthusiasm.

"I'm not sure," Janko shrugs.

My enthusiasm immediately wanes. Janko walks to the bureau and picks up the newspaper I had purchased earlier today.

"Where did we eat that day?"

"It was at the big, long square,"

"Campo Santa Margherita," Janko scrutinises the paper for a few more seconds, a small smile creeps on his lips and he turns to face me.

"Go and find Gunari. Tell him we may have caught something in the breeze,"

I bound to my feet and run out of the cottage where I spot Gurani stood by the lake in his running clothes. I jog over to him, he glances in my direction upon my approach.

"Everything OK?" he says, his creased face somehow finds another worry line to add.

"Yes. Janko has found something. He said to come and get you,"

"I would have been back in the house soon, no need to worry,"

"It's about Albert Tremmick,"

As soon I say his name, Gunari stares down at his feet for a few seconds, then abruptly walks off to the cottage and grabs my hand to hold on the way. Am I supporting him, or is it the other way around?

Back in the cottage, Janko has been digging through his boxes of files. Gunari walks over to him and quickly says something in German to him. They both turn to look at me, it's all very odd.

"What's going on guys," I say, trying to act lighthearted, "Is there a problem?"

"No, of course not, Ana," Janko says, "We are discussing whether you are ready for the next step,"

"What's the next step?"

"Investigation," Janko says.

"Followed by possible termination of the sinner," Gunari says in a manner easily twice as apocalyptic as his normal proclamations.

"There's only one way to find out," I reply, steel in my response. Janko beckons me to the table where he and Gunari are eyeing the documents he has spread out. Today's newspaper is placed in the centre of the table, I examine it and something triggers my brain.

"The stolen art in Germany from the newspaper. It has to be that,"

"Indeed Ana, oh my," Janko says, "I was reading the story earlier and it didn't click. That's why we need young heads like you around here,"

I examine the article in the newspaper and it's all very strange. Health inspectors in a suburb of Munich were checking a butcher's shop as part of their normal rounds. It seems they were exceedingly thorough and spotted a locked cabinet. The owner, a young man named as Horst Beckermann, told the inspectors that the cabinet was only for staff documents and nothing to do with hygiene.

The assessors grew suspicious of the man and they informed him that they had permission to access any part of the premises. Beckermann reluctantly opened the safe, the article states he was actually crying. Inside were a few papers relating to the staff but also inside was a rolled up painting.

In itself, this wouldn't have been odd but due to Beckermann's demeanour, they asked him a few questions which he bounced away. They called the police who came down and Beckermann told them the truth. That his grandfather had asked him to temporarily place the paintings in a safe place. Beckermann had been immediately doubtful, having heard of recent tales of looted Nazi artwork being discovered. He presumed the health inspectors were actually police which was why he was acting so strangely.

"So, how is this painting linked to the doctor?" I ask, nothing in the story mentions anything about him.

Janko is shuffling papers around on the desk and then picks up a tattered notebook. The cover is brown and from I can see the pages have turned brown too. It looks at least ten thousand years old.

"What is that?" I say. Janko chuckles at the face I am pulling.

"This book," Janko is thumbing through the pages of the notebook, "contains all the secrets that Smith and I managed to note down in our time in the shop,"

"So you know where all the stolen Nazi art is?"

"Oh, I wish Ana. No, but it contains detailed information about which Nazis had links with certain artwork. Hopefully, this book will help us to...ah, this is it," Janko stops talking and scrutinises the book.

"Is it there Janko?" Gunari whispers. Janko looks at Gunari and nods. Gunari steps away from the table and sits down on the sofa nearest to the fire.

"What does it say?" I ask.

"According to the list, it is a painting by Canaletto of the Piazza Santa Margherita. The name of the person who was asking for an estimated value was 'Tremmick, Albert'. We left the section describing his rank as blank. At that time we weren't aware of how significant he was. And the date was November nineteen forty-four,"

"Anything else, no contact information?"

"No, nothing else but it doesn't matter. The investigation can begin now." Janko is looking out of the window, his face as old as I have seen it.

"The Israelis will be looking for him too," Gunari is smoking a cigarette, a rare relapse for a man who quit eight years ago, "They will be as desperate as us to find him,"

"That's true," Janko sits back down in his favourite chair opposite Gunari, "We won't rush Gunari. No, we will plan and then we will find him,"

"We need to go to Germany, he's already an old man,"

"So am I but I will not plunge into this in a hasty manner. I'm not losing him again," Janko bangs his hand down on the table next to him which again startles me. I wish he'd stop doing it.

"I'll contact Boris to look into the grandfather. Do we know who he is?" Gunari says.

"I don't think so but he must be closely connected to Tremmick. Tell Boris that there can be a maximum of zero mistakes. I believe that if he catches a smell of a trace that he will vanish,"

"He might have already disappeared," I say, knowing that's what I would do in his situation.

"Perhaps. We can deal with that if that is the case. However, I would guess that he will stay where he is,"

"Why?" I say, "Everyone will know what he has done,"

"He will stay because that is his job. Old grandfather Beckermann is the soldier that remains in Germany. He will be the one who orchestrates everything from there and deals with what needs to be done there,"

PROMETHEUS

Tuesday, 31 December 1985

Joachim is due to pick me up from Munich-Riem airport to take me to see that flabby fool, Paul. It has been nearly five years since I last encountered Paul. He has become such a worrier as the years have worn on. Phoning me directly two weeks ago was a serious breach of protocol. The protocol is in place for precisely these reasons. But to call me again two nights ago was taking things too far.

What an infuriating individual. It may be time to cut him loose from my life. It falls upon me to deliver a few home truths later and I have to decide whether to tell him it is time for him to retire. His son is a much more dependable man, the reports that he files are diligent and very well written. He must have inherited that side of his personality from his mother, God rest her soul.

It is biting cold in Munich. The temperature must easily be minus fifteen if you factor in the abrasive wind searing my face. I should have worn a thicker jacket but I'm used to wet winters now and I forgot about wearing the right type of coat. All the other people outside the airport are dressed appropriately, unlike me. Everyone is rushing around trying to race home for New Year celebrations. That reminds me, those blasted fireworks will be going off all night too so I won't catch any sleep.

The last time I was at this airport was forty-five

years ago. Forty-five years later and I can remember every detail of that evening, the first time I ever had the honour of meeting Dr Josef Mengele. The weather on that night was very similar to this evening except there were intense intermittent flurries of snow to accompany the ice cold wind but I was much more prepared back then, protected from the elements in a big fur coat and winter boots.

Dr Verschuer had asked me to meet Dr Mengele to discuss some of the plans we had prepared. We wanted to take Mengele away from active service and for him to lead our research into preventable illnesses that were hampering the war effort, especially on the South-Western Front. Our research was at an important practical evaluation stage and we all felt that progress was imminent.

The airport was almost deserted, there were virtually no flights at all with it being the eve of the New Year barring a couple of military planes taking supplies East. A bunch of exhausted soldiers were sitting around on the floor quietly chatting with their corporal and passing around a bottle of *Doppelkorn*.

Josef Mengele arrived and was apparently in fantastic health, his toothy grin beaming as we hailed each other and embraced warmly. It was strange meeting someone whose papers and research I had pored over for the last couple of years. We had corresponded by post for more than two years without ever meeting face to face.

"Dr Mengele, may I say what a pleasure it is to finally meet you," I was jabbering like a schoolboy asking a girl to the May Day dance, "Please, let me take you inside and we can grab a coffee and some cake,"

"I haven't eaten cake in months," Mengele replied and began laughing, "Albert, take me with great haste to the cakes!"

We headed inside and the solitary girl behind the counter of the cafe was resting her elbows on the counter in a derisively unprofessional manner. According to her badge, her name was Helga, I had conversed with her earlier but I was not impressed by her stand-offish demeanour. I introduced Mengele to her as one of Germany's most distinguished scientists and she barely acknowledged him.

I remember how furious I had felt at the time being undermined by a silly little serving girl. If Dr Mengele wasn't there I would have severely reprimanded her for her brazen attitude. Mengele didn't seem troubled by her behaviour so I allowed her insolence to pass this time and ordered our refreshments.

We took our seats in the deserted airport lounge and swapped stories of the war. I explained to Mengele that much of the work I had been doing at Dieselstraße was inspired by his studies. My examinations of skull shapes had brought potentially interesting results. I was convinced that there were certain characteristics that could definitively highlight the racial group they came from. Mengele told me how much he missed doing practical experiments. I passed on the offer from Verschuer to work at a new facility we were setting up but Mengele was unable to accept.

"I'm going to the Eastern Front in two weeks," Mengele told me, for the first time his face betrayed concern, "By all accounts, I appear destined to be posted to Ukraine,"

I didn't reply, by Mengele's voice I could tell that

he wasn't going to be persuaded to apply for a transfer. I didn't push him either. Instead, we told stories about our youth, both of us hailing from beautiful Bavarian towns about hundred kilometres apart. Mengele was originally from Günzburg and I grew up in Ansbach.

We talked for hours even after the serving girl finished her shift and went home. The two of us were alone barring a few dozen soldiers who were lying down and snoozing all around the arrivals area. Two of the great minds of the Reich discussing ideas and inspirations, rivalry and reason. We were engrossed in conversation as the clock ticked past midnight and the beginning of a new year. The world was ours.

"Dr Tremmick?" a voice knocks me out of my thoughts. I mumble something and it takes a few moments to process where I am. Back outside a barren airport freezing to death.

"Oh, you must be Joachim?" I say. A man of about twenty years with a handsome face and thick winter coat stands in front of me. Luckily for him, there is only a small hint of his father's looks in his puppy-dog eyes.

"Yes, Doctor, please let me help you with your luggage," I only have one small carry-on case but Joachim takes the bag and places it in the back of a black BMW. Joachim opens the door on the passenger side but I decline and take a seat in the back. Thankfully it is very warm inside and the numbness that was beginning to creep into my fingers has been kept at bay.

It is a shame it is too dark to be able to see anything of note on the journey into the city. The gloom only adds to the feeling of despondency that is creeping through my body. It is only when we reach the Maximilianeum, rising out of the ground half-castle and half tree-house, that I finally recognise where I am. It has been decades since I last visited the Bavarian capital, the village of a million people that I used to call home. It wouldn't be an overstatement to say that it was the place where I became the man I am today.

The car continues along leafy Maximilians-brücke and memories of Oktoberfest drinking parties spring to mind. The graduation party in thirty-six will always be number one. I must have drunk fifty steins of beer that day and eaten God knows how many kilograms of *Weißwurst*. I was sick for a week after that day but it was worth it. We were the cream of a nation on the rise. Ten years later half of my friends had perished in the war, fodder for the unstoppable Nazi machine which wasn't as unstoppable as it first appeared.

I remember my best friend Marcel, an avowed anti-Nazi when we first met as undergraduates. Both of us were sickened by the book burning in thirty-three. What a welcome to university life that was watching thousands of library books in flames with students dancing around the fire like primitive pagans. Marcel was disgusted but I managed to pull him away from a confrontation with some of the arsonists, the situation being incendiary enough.

Throughout our time at university anyone holding anti-Nazi views was treated initially with good-humoured pity. It didn't take long for this to develop into unconcealed contempt. Marcel withdrew into his studies as I did also, only joining the party in thirty-five under pressure from the head of the faculty. I was rather ambivalent to the rise of the Nazi party, I found a lot of their uptight pomposity ridiculous but the economic successes were impossible to ignore. From the beginning of my time in Munich, there was a stark difference than at the end of my time. There was a change in peoples' mindsets, money was flowing and pride in being German was evident.

In nineteen forty-three I discovered by a quirk of coincidence from Mengele that Marcel was a tank commander and had been killed in the battle of Kursk. I had known a few opponents of the Nazis who were purged in the years following our graduation. I expected Marcel to be one of them, not leading the battle from the front. It is strange the way these things turn out in the end.

Joachim has parked the car outside a run-down bar. He turns around and with a lift of the eyebrows indicates that I need to go in there. A couple of guys in overalls and bare arms are stood outside the door talking in thick Bavarian accents. I push my way past and they barely move for me. Ignorant peasants.

Inside the entrance, through a fug of stale smoke, a bunch of old-timers are talking about the latest football match. I spot Paul at the bar and he gracelessly steps down off his chair to greet me.

I inspect him and I immediately observe his lack of self-discipline exemplified by a huge belly that hangs over his trousers like a bag of loose potatoes. He is gargantuan now, what a difference to the first time I met him bearing a resemblance more akin to that of a garden rake than a human. A desperate, craven creature starving and eating straw and mouldy apples. By the looks of him, I don't think he will need to buy next year's calendar.

"Have you heard those old guys over there talking about football, Albert?" Paul embraces me warmly but I barely reciprocate, "1860 play in the Bavarian league now, can you believe it? And Bayern are favourites for the national title! These guys don't have a clue. Hey guys, Ai! Ai! Ai! Super Bayern!"

The old-timers respond with some very personal insults at Paul. Did this man compel me to travel here so I could listen to him engage in a slanging match with some porcine men over football, of all things?

"Paul, sit down," I say. He obeys my command and sits down again at his spot at the bar, embarrassment covers his red face.

"Sorry Albert," Paul says, holding an apologetic arm up, "It's been a long time since, ah, you know. Michaela, two beers please,"

I don't want a beer but I don't say anything. Simply meeting up is too much of a risk, however I need to ease Paul out of my affairs and a face-to-face meeting is the only way he will listen.

The haggard bar woman places two large Löwenbräu glasses down in front of us. Paul is ogling her breasts without any hint of subtlety but she doesn't seem to mind or care. I glare at Paul which at first he tries to ignore but after a couple of minutes, he finally cracks.

"Oh Albert, stop staring at me, I'm not a child,"

"No, neither of us are children Paul. What are you doing about Horst? He has caused us a major issue,"

"What can I do?" Paul replies, "The damage is done. He knew nothing and his honesty overcame him,"

"Jesus, Paul. Your grandchild is a law unto himself. He requires a firm hand which you are incapable of delivering."

"I'm sorry, what else do you want me to say. Do you want me to grovel?" Paul suddenly leaps off his chair and kneels down like a Turk pretending to kiss my feet.

"Stop it, you stupid man," I say. My patience for his drunken tomfoolery is at its limit, "You are on your final warning, Paul. One more mistake and you will no longer work for me,"

Paul sits back down on the barstool, takes a big swig of his beer and nods. He can't maintain eye contact. He is obedient and he knows I have him in the palm of my hand.

"Can you explain why your grandson acted in the way he did?" I ask Paul who begins licking his lips.

"I did not tell him anything. I only followed your instructions. You said that the fewest people who know the truth the less chance of any mishaps,"

"But we have had a mishap, haven't we? If Horst knows nothing of our work why did you leave the painting in the safe at the shop?"

"I am never going to be able to give you a satisfactory response Albert. I'm not engaging in these stupid conversations," Paul is now sulking and he downs his beer and gestures to the barmaid to give him a refill.

"Oh, so are you in charge now Paul? Do you dictate the content of our conversations now? You forget the past very easily,"

"I don't think you will ever stop bringing this up. I think you enjoy holding that against me. Maybe it's all you are holding on to,"

"What do you mean by that?" I say, perturbed by Paul's attitude.

"It doesn't matter," Paul drinks again and waves a

dismissive hand.

"Paul, I have to be strict and you know why. All I ask is that you follow the proper channels for reporting anything. That is all I ask."

Paul nods at me and carries on drinking his beer.

SPRINGTIME IN BAVARIA

Tuesday, 29 April 1986

Gunari has been gone for too long, way too long. He claimed "I'll only be ten minutes" but this has now stretched to over an hour. The sun is out but it is chilly sat outside at the cafe. I would prefer to venture back inside but I agreed not to move from where the spot I'm sat at.

What if he doesn't come back? After nine months of what some people may term captivity, this is the nearest thing to freedom. Munich is easily the most imposing city I've ever seen. We once visited Belgrade on a school trip when I was twelve years old but the buildings in the city centre cannot compare to the grandness of this German city.

Gunari left over an hour ago to meet with Bavarian Boris.

Bavarian Boris is a man who is neither a Bavarian - he is a Slovak - nor actually called Boris as his actual name is Adam. Janko and Gunari both told me completely differing stories regarding the origin of his name. Which confirmed to me that it is almost one hundred per cent certain that neither of them knows how he obtained the nickname.

Boris is not Roma but a Slovak nationalist and a fervent anti-Nazi. And anti-Communist too it must be said. He was sentenced to prison for subversion during the Prague Spring but managed to escape and ended up in West Germany working to overthrow the Communists from abroad.

Gunari says he is easily the best in Europe at digging information up. It made me wonder if he actually has a ranked list of information-digger-uppers in a folder.

This digging quite often would involve searching through peoples' trash giving him another sobriquet of Boris the Bin Raider. Gunari wouldn't tell me how many Marks he paid for his services but I saw him take a lot of money out of the safe before we departed Savoy.

There is still no sign of Gunari so I order another coffee. Ten Marks it costs, what a scandal! If Gunari has disappeared I realise that I have spent the last of my money on that coffee. What would I do if I am on my own?

Back at the cottage, Janko would give me whatever I needed but I never received any pocket money or allowance. In fact, the more I think about it, this could be a form of slavery. I may have to contact the United Nations about this situation. It's over seventy minutes now and I am beginning to worry. I contemplate venturing to the train station to find Gunari but I decide against it.

There is a certain surreality about my situation. I am not employed nor in education but within reason, anything is available to me. If I need new clothing I ask Janko and he will give me money to head to the shops. All my food is taken care of. In many ways, it could be seen as the life of a soldier. Which makes sense considering the enormity of the challenge we face.

For the last three months, Janko has been devouring as many old Nazi records as he can. He travelled to Berlin and London trying to find out who old man Beckermann is. All he found was that his first name is Paul. There are apparently no records of a wartime soldier by that name. Or Gestapo. Or any part of the military that he could search for.

The man is a ghost. Obviously, during the war, he was known by a different name. Nothing Janko has looked for has provided a clue or an answer. I suggested that maybe Beckermann is Tremmick which Janko considered as plausible until he saw a photo of him sent by Boris. Beckermann is a corpulent, five-chinned man who is also around two metres tall. Tremmick is about fifty centimetres smaller and of a rather petite, almost womanly figure for a man, according to Janko.

My training has carried on unabated. I can now run a daily fifteen kilometres with barely a problem. Gunari has stepped up the combat lessons and I can feel the power in my arms now which is a big help when it comes to using the axe to chop the wood for the fire.

I have put on twelve kilograms in less than a year but it is all muscle. There is barely a shred of fat on me, although I was a scrawny kid anyway so visibly I can't see the difference. Gunari, on the other hand, is quietly proud of my toned body and the impact of his training regime.

We arrived last night in Munich and checked in to a cheap hotel opposite the central train station. Luckily we have a room each so I spent my evening relaxing in the bath. I never thought it was possible to spend an evening in the bath but with a technique of letting out the tepid water and topping up the hot tap with my toes, I managed to bathe for a good two and a half hours. I went to bed a contented, shrivelled lobster-woman.

Breakfast was eaten at the hotel and the taste of the eggs nearly prompted a hail of vomit whilst the bacon teetered on the border between inedible pig scrapings and actual cardboard. When I found out it cost fifteen Marks I almost threw one of the baseball-like bread-rolls at the hotel manager.

Gunari and I ate a more edible brunch at a cafe by the fountains on Karlsplatz and at midday, he departed to meet Boris at the main train station. That was a good hour and twenty minutes ago now. I'm pondering using the phone inside to call Janko and ask his advice when I spot Gunari lumbering towards me.

He is walking over the main road with his brown leather jacket thrown over his shoulder. Other people eye him cautiously as he walks past, he possesses a definite sense of impending mayhem. I wave to him and he nods at me and beckons me towards the U-Bahn station over the road. I grab my rucksack and hop the fence to join him.

"What took you so long?" I ask as we start heading down the steps at the U-Bahn station.

"He wasn't there when I arrived. I waited to see if he would show up but he didn't. I looked out for people who might be aware of our meeting but I couldn't see anyone,"

"He wasn't there? Why not?"

"I don't know, maybe he was being cautious. Luckily we prepare for these situations. I took a walk for half an hour and then headed back to the station to the lockers,"

"I was worried about you. I thought you'd been

kidnapped by Boris, the Bavarian Bin Raider,"

"Not this time. We have a locker key that we use if we need to pass on important knowledge. I checked the locker and bingo!"

Gunari passes me a manilla file, he points at my rucksack and I place the file in there.

"Have you looked at it yet?" I say.

"Not yet,"

"Where are we going?" we are now in front of a map which Gunari is inspecting with all the solemnity of Gorbachev deciding whether to press the nuclear codes and wipe out Washington.

"I want to take a look at him,"

"Isn't that risky?"

"Boris was being careful, there will be no problems for us. Now which way to the butcher's shop?" I pull out my notebook and find the address. Janko has also jotted down the nearest U-Bahn station.

"It's the U3 or U6 line, to...let me see... to Giselastraße station. Do you know it?"

"It's on Leopoldstraße, it's a very busy street. A lot of street life for us to blend into,"

"Come on then Gunari, there's a train in two minutes,"

We speedily pass through the bare, utilitarian corridors and leap onto the train with seconds to spare. The map above the door informs me we are three stops along. I hope Gunari knows what he is doing by visiting the Beckermann's butcher shop.

We depart the train and a few gangs of university students bound off the train chatting boisterously to each other. Exiting the station I see a traffic-filled boulevard lined with tall trees. It is early afternoon but the streets are lively, people milling about and Paulaner beer trucks doling kegs out to the busy nearby bars. Summer has reached Bavaria and it is a very pleasing place to spend a day.

"Which way?" I ask.

"It's over the other side of the road," Gunari nods towards the crossroads on a diagonal.

"Oh, I can see it," I say, the butcher's sign is falling apart so it now states -ECKERM-NN METZG--R-I. Those missing letters would drive me insane if I worked there.

"There is a bar opposite, let's buy a drink and see what is in the file,"

We take a seat, Gunari pops on a pair of sunglasses and I start laughing.

"Is that your disguise?" I say as a waiter approaches us.

"The sun is shining in my eyes," Gunari pleads and then he notices the waiter, "A beer for me please,"

"Could I have orange juice?" I ask in halting German. The waiter nods and heads inside to the bar. I gaze over to the butcher's shop and notice a steady stream of customers entering and leaving the shop. Clearly, the discovered Nazi treasure hasn't impacted the business too much.

The waiter returns with our drinks and places them carefully on the table. Fresh orange juice in a tall glass for me and a foaming glass of Löwenbräu beer for a gleeful Gunari. As the waiter walks away to serve the customers next to us, I pull the file from my rucksack and begin reading the documents.

"There's not a great deal here," I say, despondency creeping over me. It contains a few photographs and then one sheet of paper with typed notes.

"Quality above quantity Ana, that is the key," Gunari takes a sip of his beer leaving a foamy moustache above his top lip, "It may take only one piece of information for us to move forward,"

"Paul Beckermann, age unknown, birthplace unknown. That's a good start," I re-read the biography that Boris has written.

"Come on Ana, tell me it all,"

"The shop opened in summer 1947, by Paul Beckermann and his brother Horst. It appears that Horst is another ghost. No details could be found about him either,"

"So who is he I wonder," Gunari says, in a rhetorical manner, "I would guess that it is not his brother,"

"It's two years after the war, it would be likely that he also resides in Germany perhaps?"

"Quite possibly. Go on Ana,"

"The shop doesn't appear to be a front. It is a popular shop in this neighbourhood and from what they found, none of the Beckermann family has been in trouble with the police. In fact, they are well-respected members of the community and the local business forum. Paul Beckermann lives in a small flat on a nearby street and rarely leaves the house. During the surveillance, he would go for a drink at a local tavern called Michaela Bar on two evenings a week,"

"Interesting, go on,"

"It says here that he usually sits at the bar on his own and doesn't talk to anyone except the bartender, the eponymous Michaela, a busty blonde of about forty years," I look up at Gunari, "Boris enjoyed this research I think,"

"It does sound quite tantalising, but I don't think

it helps us. Is there anything else in there?"

"On the first of the month, he drops a letter in the post box at the post office on Kurfürstenplatz at around four in the afternoon,"

"Every month?"

"According to Boris, four months in a row,"

Gunari whistles and takes off his sunglasses. He rubs his eyes and takes the paper from me.

"Excellent translation Ana," he says and I can feel myself blushing with pride, "I think this could be the clue we are looking for,"

"How would we intercept the letter?" I say.

"I'm not sure, he is taking the letters to the slot in the wall of the post office so it won't be exposed like a postbox in the street would be,"

"It's two days away from the first of May, his next drop will be soon," I say.

"We should take a walk to the Post Office and find out a bit more," Gunari leaves a few marks on the table and stands up, I take it as a sign we are leaving so I neck my juice giving me a minor brain-freeze and put the file back in my rucksack.

It is a short walk through clean streets and plain apartment blocks towards the post office. Kurfürstenplatz is a dull square with a few trams chugging through the streets, it is filled with road traffic too.

We head to a corner bar and once again sit outside where Gunari orders another beer and I choose an apple juice this time. I check the time and it is now half past three.

"What are we looking for?" I ask.

"Probably a vehicle arriving to pick up the letters from the box,"

"When will that turn up?"

"I have no idea, the shop closes at five so I'm guessing before that. Unless they come in after hours then we could be waiting here for the rest of the day,"

"You might want to hold back on the beers, otherwise you might see two vans instead of one," I say. The sun has dropped low in the sky behind the buildings opposite which makes keeping an eye out quite difficult as it is pretty much blinding me. I decide against asking to wear Gunari's master spymaster sunglasses.

After months of training, it is exciting to be on a mission. Seeing the students earlier larking about at the U-Bahn station left me with mixed feelings. The sense of youthful camaraderie highlighted what I had been deprived of yet, on the other hand, my body tingled due to the sheer exhilaration of acting like a real-life secret agent.

Gunari repeatedly told me during training that there is no better experience than the lessons you learn on the job. There is no way of recreating the adrenalin rush but also the pressure of working out a practical solution with time running out. At this point, it is almost like being full of energy but having to hold off from expending it. It is the ultimate feeling of anticipation.

At about half-past four a yellow van pulls up outside the post office. Gunari nudges me even though I spotted it first. I try to act as naturally as a person trying to act naturally would do - looking at my watch and stroking my hair.

"Stop playing with your hair," Gunari says, "I can't concentrate,"

The driver pops out of the van. He is defined by

a huge beer belly and messy hair, he looks old but on closer inspection may only be around thirty years old. Instead of heading to the wall and taking the post, he walks into the post office. A couple of minutes later he departs with two sacks of mail, which he carelessly hurls into the back of his van.

The big lump pops back into the driver's seat and the van trundles away keeping pace with the tram alongside it. We both watch the van as it disappears from view, once it has vanished Gunari whistles lightly.

"So how do we see the contents in that letter?" he asks, I look at him and notice he was asking rhetorically as he is looking far off into the distance.

How do we obtain the letter? We can't touch the fat old man and we can't break into the post office either.

"The only way I can see that we grab that letter is…" I say and Gunari turns to face me, "…well, it would be to intercept the letter after it's left the post office and arrives at the sorting office. Is that where it would end up?"

"Yes Ana, that sounds right. Let's have a think about it tonight and we can work out a plan for the next letter. I'll give Janko a telephone call and update him,"

Gunari drops more money on the table and we take a slow walk back through the city towards the hotel. It is a warm, heavy evening and the two of us are silent, contemplative of our next actions.

LAST TANGO IN BUENOS AIRES

Wednesday, 30 April 1986

Our plan is settled upon for tomorrow and Gunari and I have gone to a local bar near our hotel for a few drinks. Gunari says it is the best way to relax before a big occasion. There is a satisfying buzz about the smoky bar, different languages and ages mixing together. Gunari is telling me about the time they nearly captured Albert Tremmick in Argentina.

"I remember the passports we used. My passport claimed my name was Florian Marchand. Janko was Honoré St-Juste. It's funny how you remember the details. He still buys some of his magazine subscriptions in that name. The whole flight across from Paris it was all I could do to stare at the passport and memorise the details: Born in Paris on the third of June nineteen-thirty. Even now, when someone asks for my date of birth I'm often at a loss to remember which is mine, and which is Florian Marchand's.

"It was not only my first time on an aeroplane but it was for Janko too. I could tell he was nervous at Orly airport. Travelling around Europe at the time was easy if you knew the tricks of the trade. But transatlantic flying was a different matter entirely. Even knowing how to behave at an airport was a baffling experience,"

Gunari begins to laugh, a hearty chuckle of times

gone by. There is a pleasing hubbub in the bar and I am actually enjoying listening to Gunari's story. His mutterings of doom have been replaced by the tales of a man who has lived an interesting life.

"I can imagine you two in the airport lounge surrounded by pilots and chic air stewardesses," I say, joining with the laughter and enjoying the bitter first sips of German lager beer.

"You should have seen us, Janko had bought a brand new tailored suit, he never tired of telling me that it was tailored by a man called Ermenegildo Zegna. He said he was the best suit maker in Italy and that he exchanged it for some German wine and Black Forest ham he had in his car. You know what Janko's stories are like.

"At Orly, they didn't even glance at our passports, simply waving us through on to the plane. It wasn't until the late sixties that hijackings became relatively commonplace. This was still the 'Golden Age of Flying'. I wish I had savoured the experience rather than looking at that bloody passport. It was only a small airport but it was spotlessly clean and it felt so modern.

"Janko was in love with every air hostess who walked past, especially a little French-Algerian girl called Amina. Every time I looked at him he was regaling her with some invented story about his fake business. She actually seemed quite charmed by him. I was a bag of nervous energy. I drank about ten vodkas on the flight but I couldn't relax.

"We arrived at Ezeiza airport in Buenos Aires and I had not slept or rested the whole journey. I woke up Janko to tell him we arrived and he told me, 'I'm staying on the plane and marrying Amina'. Remember Ana, this was my first mission. What you probably feel now, that was me in nineteen-sixty. My sense of humour didn't stretch to allowing Janko to marry air hostesses. I gave him a quick punch in the guts and told him to get moving.

"We approached passport control and I genuinely thought I was going to piss myself or feint. I approached the Argentine officer and he simply beckoned me through. I don't think he actually looked at my passport or me. I could not believe it. Janko was waved through too and when he caught up to me, he looked at my face and my sweaty shirt and started laughing like a drunken horse,"

"What was Argentina like?" South America seems such a long way away. All I know about Argentina is beef and Diego Maradona.

"Neither of us spoke any Spanish and to be honest I think we were overwhelmed by the place. It was so...so grand, Europe was still rebuilding at that time but Buenos Aires looked like the future. They have a main street in the centre of the city that is enormous. Double the width of the Champs-Élysées, I would say. At first, it seemed everyone was dressed up and the cars gleamed."

"Was everyone rich there?"

"It was strange, the day we arrived we saw a big demonstration outside our hotel which was being dealt with pretty brutally by the police. We spent about a week there and every day we were witness to some form of civil disturbance. Yet, the city was beautiful and lots of buildings were being constructed. There was money in the city but also desperate poverty. It was an inequality that was often very stark. Quite literally next door to a glorious mansion would be a square kilometre of shacks crammed with poor families.

"It took us a few days to gather our bearings with the size of the city and the culture shock. By the fourth day, we were ready to put our plan into action. Back in Europe, we had found out that Tremmick was working under an assumed name as a doctor at a private clinic in Buenos Aires so Janko had an idea. He decided that we would work as pharmaceutical representatives and we would attend a huge conference that was being held in Buenos Aires. We knew Tremmick's firm had passes to attend the conference so we planned to offer him a great deal on drugs and arrange a private meeting to close the deal.

"Janko spent a small fortune with a local company to arrange the stand, the paraphernalia and some young Argentinian girls to work for us. We wanted it to look as professional and as glamorous as possible. I have to confess our stand advertising FrancoPharm, our made-up company, looked superb.

"Janko had not spared anything to make it look convincing, he had paid for one of the larger booths next to Bayer on one side and Johnson & Johnson on the other side. Would it be enough to tempt Tremmick?

"His clinic, which we later found out he owned in its entirely, was a popular destination for a certain clientele. He was using a pair of Argentinian brothers as a front thus the name of the company was *Clínica del Hermanos Hernández*. It was styled as a high-end private medical centre catering for expatriates. Again, it was only later we found out it was mainly for reconstructive surgery for former Nazis and other fascist pigs. And boob jobs for their wives,"

"Did they attend the conference?" I ask. Gunari prepares to answer, then stops to buy us two more beers at the bar even though I've still got over half of my lager remaining. He brings the beers back and recommences the tale:

"Oh yes, he was there and he wasn't lying low. He was wearing a cream linen suit and these ridiculous Jackie Onassis sunglasses even though we were indoors. The two brothers were following him around like lapdogs and we could tell the way this relationship was structured. Perhaps it made us complacent, we thought his arrogant manner would betray him. The more I look back on it, the more I feel like he was a man who had lived a charmed life and his arrogance was part of his genetic make-up. I don't like saying this due to his crimes he has perpetrated, but it is what made him so successful.

"He wandered around the stands like a little Mussolini, his minions picking up samples and showing them to him and he would dismiss them with a wave. He gravitated towards our stand where he saw one of our girls holding a leaflet. Tremmick started chatting to her in a very sleazy way. He invaded her personal space and was touching her arm. I could see the girl was uncomfortable. Janko told me not to say anything.

"Eventually the girl said if he had any questions to speak to us. The young girl had no idea. I mean, we didn't have time to send her on a training course, did we? Janko and I braced ourselves for coming face to face with a monster. It had been sixteen years since I had seen the man,"

"You had met him before?" I am incredulous at this. Gunari's face clouds over, his beery redness disappears from his face.

"Yes, Ana, on a freezing morning in January nineteen forty-four, at Auschwitz camp,"

I look at Gunari, a silence suffocates the atmosphere. I can see he wants to talk but his voice catches and he looks deeply into the bottom of his beer glass. My eyes implore him to continue if only to break the soundless barrier between us. If he doesn't speak soon I fear we may never converse again. Gunari looks back up at me and I bear witness to moisture at the corner of his eyes.

"It was the face of evil, Ana. I swear it," Gunari again looks down but only for a second before he looks up and holds my gaze again, "I don't think until that point I had faced the real darkness of the soul. The previous year I had been held at a detention camp near Berlin called Marzahn. that was nothing compared to arriving at Auschwitz."

"I didn't know you were there, Gunari,"

"Oh yes, one day at the French camp they chose my mother and father and their parents, along with all my brothers and sisters and my grandfather. They put us on a train along with other Roma families and we travelled to an unknown destination which we later found out was Marzahn. It wasn't easy there, oh no," Gunari runs his hand along the large scar on his neck.

"We were held there for a few months before they announced we were moving. We didn't know where. If we had known, would we have been able to change it? Probably not.

"The morning after we arrived, they lined up all

the Roma children including myself and we were inspected by the guards and some of the doctors. It was very cold and I was dressed only in a light shirt and trousers with no shoes. They went across the line checking on us like we were cattle. I was at the end of the line and eventually, this little, wiry man dressed in full medical whites was eye to eye with me. Considering I was only ten years old or so I didn't know if he was very small or if I was big for my age.

"He eyeballed me but unlike the others who looked at the floor, I held my gaze. I was in no mood to back down. His breath smelt like scotch even though it can't have been later than nine o'clock. He broke off eye contact and tried touching my ear. I batted his hand away and I felt a wounding pain in my kidneys. One of the guards had rammed his rifle in my back so hard it made me cry immediately. I couldn't halt the flow of tears, the shame of it now disgusts me.

"I looked at Tremmick and I saw a little smile develop. I knew that this man in front of me was a dangerous individual. The things I witnessed over the next few months would only confirm it. He treated people like animals yet he was the one with zero humanity.

"Sixteen years later I had come full circle. He approached our table where myself and Janko were casually leaning, I expended more energy on keeping my legs standing upright than in any of the boxing fights I had been in. He walked over to us and the first thing I noticed was that the same smell of scotch as he exhaled. The memories washed over me, I had tried to block it out of my mind but I couldn't. I was back amongst the stench of burning and death. Somehow I stayed standing.

"Tremmick spoke to us in German to which we both played dumb, Janko especially. He inquired about our stock in staccato French, his accent would have been funny if it hadn't been for the context. I informed him that we were selling cut-price anaesthetics which piqued his interest.

"He looked at me in a queer way and I am sure he was staring at my scar on my neck. I was sure he recognised me but I couldn't see how that could be realistically possible. After a few more questions we had tempted him into a possible sale and arranged a meeting with him and his colleagues a day later.

"We had booked out a private room at the Café Tortoni, a beautiful Parisian-style bar, not far from Avenida del Mayo. Our plan was simple, or so we thought. A little demonstration of our merchandise. Tremmick would lean in and we would stab him with a syringe and inject him with a little bit of his own medicine - sodium cyanide. We felt confident we could take on his goons and then we planned to escape by ferry to Uruguay and then back to France,"

Gunari starts chuckling and realises his beer glass is empty so he heads for another refill. My head is beginning to spin. Whether this is due to the booze or tonight's revelations it's hard to pinpoint. Gunari returns with two more steins filled with beer for us both. I neck the remains of my second and take a sip from the fresh glass. It is excellent beer, fair play to the Bavarians.

"We set up the room at the back of the Café Tortoni with a few samples on a table. We placed seats at the front with the two on either side of the central one set back a little bit. Janko thought that would serve two purposes: it would make Tremmick feel like the most important man in the room and it would give us a tiny bit more time to apply the fatal dose."

"But you might not have been able to escape from there, was it busy?"

"Yes, it was always busy. Ultimately as long as we killed Tremmick we didn't care if we didn't make it out or not. You may call it a suicide mission and you may be right."

"Did he show up?" I ask.

"Yes, but he was an hour late. He showed up in the room as we prepared to pack our stuff up and leave. We were all set to think of a new plan. He came in and wished us a good evening in Spanish.

"We gestured to Tremmick and the two Hernández brothers to sit down and they did so in the expected way. Tremmick looked edgy and I could see he was staring at us.

"'Are you not taking a seat?' he asked us in French. Janko and I had failed to place chairs down for ourselves. In our planning, we had become too caught up in worrying about everything that we missed something basic like that.

"'Oh' Janko said, 'We prefer to do business standing up, here why not take a look at what we have in stock?' Tremmick began to lean over the table. I was waiting behind with one hand under the table holding the syringe.

"Only a little further and I would have plunged it into his neck but he sat back in his chair and said 'No business will be completed today'. Janko and I swapped looks and then one of the Hernández brothers leapt out of his chair for Janko. Tremmick ducked away and ran out of the door.

"Janko was grappling with the brother when I stuck the syringe in his neck. He went limp straight away. At the same time, the other brother tackled me around the waist and took the wind out of me. Janko punched him a few times and pulled him off me.

"I gathered my bearings and we delivered a hiding to him knocking him out. We rushed out of the room into the main bar where the commotion had caused the band to stop playing and for the patrons to see what was going on. We caught a glimpse of Tremmick running out.

"A couple of goons were blocking our path so I had to deal with them with some old school boxing lessons. A few people tried grabbing us to prevent us from leaving but Janko smashed a wine bottle and attacked anyone who came near us. We managed to escape outside. We couldn't see where he had gone. The streets were busy with people and traffic and the Piedras metro station was next to us. He could have gone anywhere.

"We didn't know what to do so we headed back to our hotel, we packed up our stuff and caught the ferry to Montevideo in Uruguay, which took a few hours. We laid low for a few days and didn't read anything in the newspapers about the incident so we flew back to France."

"That is an amazing tale Gunari," I say, "I can't believe it. You should write a book,"

Gunari shakes his head, drinks his beer and says "The publisher would probably turn it down as too farfetched,"

"I hope tomorrow is less eventful," I reply and

take a big gulp from my beer. Gunari simply smiles.

SPECIAL DELIVERY

Thursday, 1 May 1986

Munich Town Hall shoots out of the ground towards heaven like mutant stalagmites. I can't avert my eyes from the sheer grandness of the building. We are sat out at a cafe in a big square, which Gunari has been telling me is called Marienplatz. The huge town hall leers over dominantly, highlighting my insignificance.

I order a glass of white wine, Janko's tip was a Silvaner, a Bavarian local wine. He may be a mad old chatterbox but he knows his wine. I spoke to him an hour ago by telephone when I confirmed the plan that we were proceeding with.

"It's high risk," he said.

I contemplated a snappy Arnold Schwarzenegger comeback like "If anything, it's low risk for me" but instead I replied with, "Yeah, maybe,"

I can't believe this plan will work. The hours of discussions about subtle ways of infiltrating the German postal service have come to nothing. Subtlety will take a back seat this evening.

"Right I'm off to pick up the van," Gunari stands, stretches and places a hand on my back, "I'll pick you up outside the huge white church, you can't miss it when you exit the station. Any issues when I arrive we leave immediately and think of another plan,"

"It might be too late by then," I say. Gunari nods and walks off to the Marienplatz U-Bahn station. I wait until he disappears before finishing my wine and following the same route to the U-Bahn station.

The platform is thronged with people, jabbering tourists, bookish students and pent-up workers mingling together. I can feel my pulse racing and I try to perform some breathing exercises which isn't easy especially when some spotty youth spills some of his currywurst sauce on my arm. I give him a death-stare and he becomes immediately apologetic.

The train stops at Odeonplatz station, my stop is the one after. The train fills up with even more people, including what appears to be half of the student population in West Germany. The clumsy sausage spiller nearly repeats his mistake so he tries moving away through the crowded train when he knocks into someone else who actually lectures him on his inability to stand still and eat his sausage.

Despite the journey lasting only a few minutes it seemed to me to last a good fifty-five minutes. The warmth and smell of curried pork pieces are making me feel sick. The train pulls up at the next step and I look out of the window to double-check we are at Universität station.

Heading out of Universität station, over the road stands an incredible white stone church. The brightness of the stone dazzles me against the rich blue sky. It stops me dead in my tracks and a man bundles into the back of me.

"Oh sorry," he says apologetically despite it being all my fault, "You're not the only person I've seen that happen to," and the man walks off smiling to himself.

I guess this is the church Gunari said he would pick me up from. I walk across the road and the sign outside confirms it is St Ludwig church. I check the time and I notice I have half an hour to kill so I decide to take a look inside.

Compared to the busy St Mark's in Venice, this church is a haven of tranquillity. Despite the city buzz outside, it is completely still in here. I am conscious of my trainers squeaking when I walk even though it appears that I am the only person in here.

The church is wide and very high, light is beaming in through the windows but I can't see any stained glass. The ceiling is painted blue which makes me feel even more serene. At the far end is an altar with a huge painting at the back. God is sitting on his clouds while below angels are lifting some people up to heaven whilst demons are grabbing and scrapping down below. The sheer scale could be aptly described as biblical. The time it must've taken to paint astounds me.

I exit the church, shielding my eyes from the dazzling sunshine. I put on my sunglasses quite literally at the moment Gunari pulls up in a red, Opel van with more scratches than your average zookeeper.

"Let's go," he says, rather needlessly considering the first part of our plan is to go. I jump in the passenger seat and Gunari manoeuvres the van back into the busy early afternoon traffic.

"Everything all set?" Gunari asks.

"Yes, I've got the map and the other bits and pieces. Is this van going to hold up? It's falling apart,"

"It's the best that a thousand marks can buy with twenty-four hours notice. It might not achieve Janko's high standards but it should fulfil our needs," Gunari is buzzing, and I have to say, so am I. We are meandering through traffic approaching Beckermann's apartment but adrenaline is coursing through my veins. I need to keep this together.

We pull over the road from Beckermann's and our timing is good. Too good, some might say as we need to pull away almost immediately. The fat man comes out of his apartment building's door, makes a cursory look in both directions and starts waddling towards the post office right on queue.

Beckermann is a genuinely huge figure, despite his age and slight hunching of the shoulders he still towers above everyone else on the pavement. He is dressed in a simple grey cardigan and black trousers. He holds the letter in his left hand and he is holding a cigarette in the other.

"Describe the letter Ana," Gunari says. I pull out my recently purchased and calibrated Bresser binoculars and line up Beckermann from our position in the traffic thirty metres behind him.

"Standard manilla envelope, it looks A4 size,"

"What about the writing, can you see it?"

"It looks...it's black writing and quite large. He's moving too much. Wait, wait. I can see the city on the address, it's in big block capitals," I keep staring at the bewitching envelope hypnotically swaying and filling my field of vision. And then it's almost like someone whispers the solution in my ear, "It's Berlin. It's Berlin, Gunari!"

"Can you see any more?"

"I can't see anything else, he's moving his chubby arm too much,"

"It narrows it down, do you think you would recognise the envelope again?"

"I think so,"

"I hope so, Ana. Right, let's head to the post office,"

Janko speeds up and overtakes the traffic and a few minutes later we are outside the post office on Kurfürstenplatz eating chewy *kürtőskalács* that Gunari bought in a Hungarian bakery earlier today.

"Where did you buy the van?" I ask. It's after five o'clock and the post van is clearly late, I'm sure it's made up of seven different vans haphazardly welded together.

"A friend of Boris's. I think it may have seen a little nefarious action in the past. He said it won't be traced back to the owner. Are all our things back in your rucksack?"

"It's all in there,"

"He's here, make sure your seat belt is on, champ,"

Gunari is right, the garish yellow van has pulled up outside the post office. The scruffy van driver hops out and he might have actually had a hair cut. Perhaps there's a girl in the post office that he's trying to impress. Little does he know that this evening's shift is destined to be one he would prefer to forget. Although he may gain another story to impress his sweetheart.

Finally, after an interminable wait of over ten minutes (maybe he does have a fancy woman in there after all), the van driver exits the building, tosses the sole mailbag from the post office into the back, closes the doors and enters the driving seat. Within seconds he begins to pull away.

Gunari keeps pace with the van and maintains a position right behind him, there's no real need to keep a great distance. The last thing the van driver will be expecting is two Romani lunatics chasing him around the streets of Munich. I check my map against the road and I don't think we are too far from where our plan should culminate.

Gunari gestures to the right which is the BMW factory so we prepare to pull off the road. As expected, the van driver pulls off Georg-Brauchle Ring towards the Olympiastadion. Sneaky van driver hopes to shave a vital minute from his journey again. Unfortunately, today's circumvention will be coming to an abrupt intervention. Gunari follows him around the junction and towards the car park.

On our left the rising metallic canopies of the Olympiastadion roof tower over us like giant circus tents. The van driver sticks to the road on his cheeky short cut back to the depot. Gunari pulls right on to the huge car park parallel to the driver's road and rapidly accelerates.

I look across and the van driver is maintaining his speed, he hasn't noticed our van hitting a much faster pace with the occasional rows of trees separating us. Gunari has lined up our paths for convergence. The van driver is unaware that we are now heading straight for him.

"Brace yourself, Ana,"

Christ, I'm braced like you wouldn't believe.

Gunari cuts the wheel even sharper and prepares for impact. Finally, the post van driver notices us but it's too late. I catch a glimpse of his incredulous face but a moment later everything becomes noise.

The crunch of metal sounds sickeningly loud. The post van crunches and sadly spins away in a slow-motion arc across the tarmac.

Our van is stopped abruptly and Gunari and I both are flung forward. Luckily the seatbelts hold out and my only injury is when my right arm flies out to protect myself and cracks against the dashboard.

From the violent noise of the impact follows the post-crash quiet. I look at Gunari, he is in a trance. I nudge him with my left arm and it takes him a few seconds for him to come back to the general vicinity of planet earth and, more specifically, the Olympic Park in Munich.

"OK?" he says finally.

"Staying alive," I say, "Come on, let's find that letter."

We both escape out of the car and I can see the front of our van is a crumpled mess. Shit, this was a big accident.

I'm wary about checking the van driver. Is he injured or angry and out for blood?

I inch towards his door and Gunari heads to the back of the van. The back doors are hanging off which should help us.

The van driver is slumped in his seat, blood is careering down his nose from a wound above his eye. He looks conscious but out of it. I knock on the window and all he can do is move his arms, he doesn't look towards me so I forget about him and head to the back.

Gunari is already looking in the first sack of mail, rifling through with careless abandon.

"Slower," I shout, "It was the last stop so it'll be in this bag. Sort it carefully and catch the right one, OK?"

"Yeah, yeah, I know. Here, you take a look."

I start checking the letters one by one. Manilla

envelope, A4 - there are quite a few in this sack but it doesn't take long for me to spot the one we need.

"This is it," I say lifting the letter like it is the Holy Grail, I hand it to Gunari, who eyeballs it suspiciously. It's not a bomb Gunari, for the love of God.

"Are you sure Ana?" Gunari is face to face with me. I can hear nearby sirens.

"One hundred per cent. Put it in my rucksack and let's get out of here,"

Gunari points me towards the far end of the car park, away from the stadium. We jog off towards the dual carriageway, there is an underpass I can see which will take us to the other side. I turn around and see two policemen running after us about three hundred metres away.

"Hurry!" I shout to Gunari, despite him being ahead of me and a much faster runner despite being over three decades older than me, "Police!"

We burst out of the underpass and a garish tangerine coloured apartment block is on our right. Gunari shouts for me to follow him. We continue along the path taking us past more apartments. We run over the road at a big junction barely acknowledging the traffic and run past people playing tennis on clay courts.

I could run for hours. Talk about reaping the benefits of my training regime. Unless the police chasing us are former fifteen-hundred metres Olympic finalists they won't be catching me. Apart from the fact that I don't know where I am. I'm relying on Gunari's knowledge of suburban Munich and I hope it is up to scratch.

We fly past another much smaller stadium and into another car park, I hear distant voices telling us to stop. No chance of that. I spot the U-Bahn station sign and Gunari hurtles down four steps at a time which I attempt to recreate. I stumble on the last step and fall over again bumping my sore arm and knocking the wind out of me. I am lying on the floor of the platform with my head by the bottom step. I open my eyes see the two cops at the top of the stairs and I fear this is the point where my adventure ends and my prison sentence begins.

NEXT STOP BERLIN

Thursday, 1 May 1986

I hear train doors clanking open. A huge hand hovers over me and grabs me by the scruff of my t-shirt. It is Gunari who pretty much drags me on to the train as the doors close. The train begins to pull out of the blue-tinted station as the policemen arrive downstairs.

I rest my clammy forehead on the window and I make eye contact with one of the police officers as we move out of his jurisdiction. I give the policeman a cheeky wink and he looks bloody furious as he bangs on the train windows as we pull away. I turn to check on Gunari who is sporting the most tremendous grin I have ever seen.

"That was closer than I anticipated," Gunari says, the sweat pouring down his face reminds me of a craggy cliff-face in the middle of a rainstorm.

"It's definitely not leather jacket weather. That was your big problem," I reply.

I sniff my armpits and I immediately regret it. Luckily there aren't many passengers on the train to be repulsed by my malodorous body. I lean against the doors for support. Although I was confident of outrunning the cops, I don't fancy doing it again when we get off the train. I try to take as much air in as I can as the train trundles through the city.

After two stops trying to regain our breath, we disembark at Rotkreuzplatz station. Thankfully, there are no police around so we amble the short walk to Donnersbergerbrücke S-Bahn and catch the train back to the main train station.

We step off the train and enter what looks like a big greenhouse. There are a lot of passengers and we attempt to merge in with a large group of middle-aged couples as we head down the platform. Luckily no one checked for tickets on the train and no train station staff are waiting on the platform.

Near the exit, I spot four men in green tunics who appear to be on guard. I nudge Gunari and we de-merge from the group and head to one of the tobacconist stands where we peruse the magazines.

"What shall we do?" I say, worry creeping over me. I can't face going to prison and being deported to Yugoslavia. The excitement of the mission has now given way to panic.

"Calm down Ana," Gunari says, pointing at a magazine aimed at aviation enthusiasts. He takes off his leather jacket and places it on the floor, "Let's walk through normally, right past them,"

He must be mad. Gunari turns to me and winks and we both turn around and head towards the exit. Gunari aims for the middle of the policemen and he apologises as he slices through the group. The police allow us through and I almost hear my stomach lurch to the floor as we pass.

We keep walking and cross the road. I daren't look around in case the cops are waiting for me to do so. It might be their signal to chase and arrest me. We walk around the corner and I can see our hotel a hundred metres away.

Finally, we arrive at our hotel. The hotel manager nods curtly at us and I say "Good evening!" about four times as loud as any normal person would do. A man reading a newspaper in the lobby looks up at me and tuts so I blow him a kiss. Gunari presses the lift button and the doors part within a second.

In the lift, I close my eyes. I have a terrible premonition that when the lift doors open a dozen armed police will be pointing their guns at me. I hear the doors divide and I am frozen to the spot.

"Come on," Gunari says. I open my eyes and there is nothing in front except a painting of a fairy-tale castle emerging from a snowy forest. I exit the lift and trot to catch up with Gunari. I already have my key ready to open the door.

I enter my hotel room with Gunari close behind me. I flop onto my bed, lie out like a starfish and close my eyes.

"Hey, this is no time for sleep," Gunari's voice has never sounded more infuriating. I open one eye and tell him:

"I'm not sleeping," I can't even be bothered explaining that I could do with a few minutes to gather my thoughts following our kamikaze antics and journey back to our hotel worrying that any of the cops would pull us in.

I spring back up and sit on the edge of the bed.

"So," I say, "Are we taking a look at the letter?" Gunari looks at me, begins to speak then holds a finger up and stops himself. He walks off to the telephone near the window and dials a number which sounds like it contains about thirty numbers too many. Gunari holds the phone to his ear. I'm not sure if he realises he is still holding his finger up on the other hand.

"Janko!" Gunari exclaims excitedly, "Janko, my friend, the mission was successful and we are now in possession of Paul Beckermann's letter,"

I can hear chatter babbling out of the earpiece from my spot four metres away. Janko sounds unsurprisingly in high spirits too.

"Ana, put the kettle on," Gunari says to me and his pointy finger has turned to a wavy finger directing me towards the kettle. Funny time to have a cup of coffee. I walk to the kettle which is empty. I take it into the bathroom sink to fill up with water before placing it back on the base and turning it on.

Gunari is holding the letter and I realise that Gunari isn't fulfilling a great thirst but is going to steam the letter open. I've seen enough spy films to recognise this classic technique. I look in my rucksack and take out the Polaroid camera. Gunari looks at me and winks.

I bring the freshly boiled kettle over to Gunari and say "Hi, Janko!" near the phone. Gunari holds the envelope over the kettle while managing to lodge the phone between his ear and shoulder. I help him out by grabbing the envelope and gently peeling the flap back.

"Carefully," Gunari whispers.

After a minute or so the flap separates from the body. I open the envelope and pull out a sheet of paper with two columns. It has been typed up on a typewriter, presumably by Beckermann.

The left-hand column is a list of random six-digit numbers, the column on the right is numbered from one to thirty-one - surely relating to the amount of days in May. There is nothing else in the letter, Gunari informs Janko.

"Janko has asked the address," Gunari says, even though I'm so close to the phone I can hear him myself.

"Michael Schwarzer, Apartment 8, 87 Sebastian-straße, Berlin,"

"Is that West or East Berlin?" I'm not sure if Gunari is asking Janko or me.

"I don't know," I say and it appears Janko isn't sure yet either. Gunari holds the line and I can picture Janko pulling out his Berlin street guide. A few minutes pass and finally I faintly hear Janko's voice say 'West Berlin'.

"Right, OK. I'll call you before we leave Munich. We'll see you in Berlin," Gunari hangs up the phone and looks at me, "Kreuzberg, West Berlin,"

"Is it easier for us to get into West Berlin?" I ask, confused about how part of a city in the middle of East Germany could be part of West Germany.

"I don't think anything is going to be easy from now on Ana,"

"Have you been to Berlin before?"

"Many times when I was younger, the last time was a few years ago but that didn't end so well," Gunari looks down at his arm and I notice he is looking at the tattoo on his inner right arm. Four letters spell out the word NURI. I consider asking Gurani what it means but I decide against it now. I think he will tell me in his own time.

"We will leave tomorrow, Boris should be leaving a car outside for us. I'll take the letter and reseal it. We can post it tomorrow at the station. Try to go to sleep now Ana," Janko takes the letter and heads back to his room.

I doubt I'll be sleeping after the day I've had. I hope the postman is OK, he looked in a bad way when we left him. His girl will miss him tomorrow at the post office too, I would imagine.

The man might not be aware but indirectly he is ultimately helping us to remove a pernicious influence from society. I have no idea who Michael Schwarzer is but I know he is helping protect a Nazi who performed vile experiments on children.

Gunari returns to his room to speak with Janko. I put on jogging bottoms and leave the hotel to go running. Two hours of blasting my way around the clean streets and the English Gardens helps clear my head. I return back to the hotel and slump my exhausted body into bed.

MESSIAH

Thursday, 1 May 1986

My joints are relishing the sweet relief resulting from the arrival of this spell of warm weather. The pain in my knees has been the worst I can remember over the last couple of weeks. On Monday morning, it took me over an hour to step out of bed and stumble the short journey to the bathroom. Each step was agony, pains shooting up from my heel and splintering like thorny tree-roots across the backs of my thighs.

Every time I placed a foot down on the floor, I was unable to hold the pain inside and I cried out. About halfway to the bathroom, I was in tears, a throw-back to being a silly schoolboy. Tears of shame on top of tears of pain. When I finally reached the sink I stared at my reflection in the mirror.

A tired old man stared back. A man with leathery, tanned skin, sharp red jagged lines interlacing my eyes and a sweaty pock-marked forehead. An old man who can barely hold a glass of water without spilling some of it over the sides due to the shakes. If only there was something I could do about these damnable tremors.

The last doctor I visited in the summer was an embarrassment to our profession. At no point did he make eye contact with his patient or actually listen to a word of what I was telling him. He would sit there nodding, looking at his notepad and then he prescribed the same ineffectual medicines exactly like the last doctor.

I sat there as compliant as any typical ageing valetudinarian. This young clown had no idea that my medical skills far exceeded his limited knowledge. I craved knowledge about some new and effective treatment. The doctor had clearly not read *The New England Journal of Medicine* since he graduated. I maintained a dignified silence rather than hectoring him on his shortcomings. It wouldn't achieve anything. Perhaps it is time to contact Karl and ask him to prioritise trials relating to my worsening condition.

Thankfully, the weather has finally taken a turn for the better. Since my travails on Monday, the pain has subsided so much that it has taken me by surprise. I have gone for a couple of long walks around town after which I felt much more clear-headed and healthy. In my opinion, a lot of issues that elderly people suffer could be alleviated by regular exercise. If only the pain was more manageable I would take a long saunter around the streets every day.

After the effort of flying to Munich to meet Paul in that grotty bar, life has now settled down again into a similar pattern. Maybe I was too hard on Paul regarding his grandson and Paul's subsequent breach of convention in twice telephoning me at home. Nothing suspicious has occurred despite my extensive checks.

I will probably send Joachim home too in the next few days. There isn't much point in him being here with me although the help with carrying my shopping will be missed. He's an honest man, not many brains but he possesses robust morals which I respect. Not many young people have that kind of selfless attitude these days.

As I wallowed in pain over the winter, my mind was fixated on the belief that the Israelis would send a team over to kill me. Thoughts of those degenerate pigs coming to my home and shooting me in the head crashed around my brain. Every day I double-checked every lock, peeked behind every door and investigated all the potential hiding places in the house. I would stare out of the window for hours scrutinising everyone. After weeks of doing this, every single person appeared suspicious to me. It was hopeless. I was hopeless. In March, Joachim arrived to keep an eye out.

I asked Paul for help which I was loath to do after our conversation in Munich. He always acted as though he was my keeper or my manager. His tone was frequently condescending and overtly paternalistic. He never seems to understand, he is my subordinate.

I first met him when he was a lowly Gestapo officer cowering in a barn days before Warsaw fell. Paul and a colleague had been ambushed by Polish nationalists outside Katowice and he had somehow escaped and made his way towards the camp where I was working. I was in the middle of an evening walk when I heard spastic coughing from behind a wall. I was young and fit then and I easily clambered over the wall. As I landed I saw a man in a filthy dark suit. I instinctively edged backwards. I studied the man: a pathetic, scrawny creature begging for food.

"Who are you?" I demanded. I must confess to being a trifle scared by the man in front of me. Desperate people can be very dangerous to interact with.

"I am German too," the man responded, I anticipated reedy sounds to emanate from his bloated, cracked lips but there was a rich timbre to his voice, "I am starving. Please sir, do you have anything that I can eat?"

"Who are you?" I repeated, keeping my voice level. The wretched man couldn't answer and keeled over onto his knees and then sideways on to the floor. If it was a theatrical scam that he was performing he was very convincing. However, I could tell the man was genuine so I told him I had food back at my home.

I walked the short distance back to my quarters outside the camp with the man hanging off my right arm. Luckily the route home was deserted and no one saw us. I heated some of my leftover *Pichelsteiner* stew from the night before and gave it to the man. I warned him that he should eat very slowly. The man ignored my instructions and after a few mouthfuls he ran off to the bathroom to vomit.

He returned and apologised. The man adhered to my advice and ate the remaining stew over the course of the next hour. I ate and said nothing but simply observed him. His skin was drawn over his skull like it was two sizes too small for his head. He bore an uncanny resemblance to a lot of the inmates at the camp. In his desperation, I held him completely in my power.

The man offered to wash up but I rejected his gesture and told him to rest. After I completed the dishwashing the man was asleep in a chair. I let him sleep and in the morning I cooked some eggs and toast for us both. I telephoned into work to say I was unable to come in today and I spent the day talking to my visitor.

I learned his name was Paul von Reichardt and he was a scion of Bavarian royalty. His family had pledged allegiance and significant sums of money to the Nazis very early in their rise to power and had been well rewarded. Not only had they kept their ancestral home but Hitler himself had promised them vast tracts of land in the Caucasus after the war.

Paul became a Gestapo officer with a little bit of help from his father and had been operating in Poland. Paul was unable to tell me what he had been doing, whether that was because of official secrecy or due to personal shame I still don't know. As the Polish uprisings began, Paul and his colleague were caught quite literally napping. They were on a stakeout of a potential high-ranking army turncoat when the two of them fell asleep.

They awoke to the sound of gunfire on the streets of Katowice, their car was being used as cover by gunmen. The gunmen were surprised when the two Germans exited the car beside them and immediately began running away the moment they heard Polish voices. The rebels shot at the two Gestapo agents but missed every shot.

Thus over the next seven days the two men walked as far from the city as they could get. As they woke on the fourth morning, Paul's colleague decided to head for the German border and Paul headed south. Paul was nearly caught twice that day by roving patrols of Polish militia.

Eventually he arrived in the town of Auschwitz where he finally saw German soldiers. He was so embarrassed by his condition and scared that our boys would shoot him he continued to hide in peoples' gardens across the city scavenging for food.

I allowed Paul to stay with me as the war ran its course. With the help of a Jewish forger inside the camp, I had new documents made up for Paul and gave him the new surname Beckermann. Dispatches came through that Paul von Reichardt had been killed in Katowice due to documents found in the streets. Paul did not bother to correct them, he had contacted his father who knew the truth.

As the war and my departure drew near Paul surprised me with a gift. In the looting of the Jewish ghetto in Warsaw he had raided the house of an elderly jeweller. Upstairs in the attic, he had discovered a couple of paintings. As he saw the pictures on the wall, the jeweller lost his composure and tried attacking Paul who shot the man in the head. Paul pulled the paintings off the wall, rolled them up and smuggled them back to Bavaria.

Paul arranged for the paintings to be delivered to me and he asked me if I could find out who the artists were. I said I knew a man who could tell us everything about the artworks. Luckily for us both that I did, as it would shape the next four decades of our life.

I moulded Paul in to the man he became and now he has the temerity to speak to me like I am a senile old relative. Short memories breed ingratitude. I'm not surprised. If I have learned anything over my long life it's that men are weak and predisposed to selfishness and egotism. At times, I think this affliction may have infected me.

Paul suggested that I may need some support so he sent his grandson over from Munich to help out. Thankfully it wasn't the idiot boy Horst, who caused all this panic in the first place. Joachim is a strong specimen, not tall but very muscular. A fine example of Bavarian manhood. The two brothers are like chalk and cheese. They remind me of the Hernández boys that aided my South American business ventures. Federico is like Joachim, quiet and resourceful. Sadly Miguel was a mirror image of Horst, a huge liability. Horst inherited his grandfather's shit-for-brains, Miguel inherited his old man's drinking problem.

Major Sebastián Hernández was a brave man, a career soldier serving as a close advisor to the Argentinian President Agustín Justo. After President Justo passed away in forty-three, Sebastián became the contact for Odessa agents in Germany. After my arrival in Buenos Aires three years later he became a very good friend to me. He set me up in a house in Quilmes living with his daughter, a pretty little mother-of-one called Gabriela.

Poor Sebastián passed away weeks after we set up a business together in nineteen fifty-three. I was using my adopted name of Alfonso Hermann. At first my little pharmacy struggled for business as I tried to get to grips with the language. My rudimentary Spanish seemed to bear no resemblance to the Rioplatense dialect I would hear in the *villas miseria*. My only regular customers were German immigrants, none of them aware of what and where I had escaped from.

I ended up caring for Sebastián's three children after his wife also died in the late fifties. By nineteen-sixty I had opened up a clinical research centre where a lot of major American and German pharmaceutical companies requested my expertise. I named the business after the two boys (their sister Gabriela had moved to Spain a year earlier to marry a naval officer who was surprisingly willing to take on an unmarried mother) and thus *Clínica del Hermanos Hernández* was founded.

Life was good and I had left the basic flat in Quilmes and moved to a wonderful apartment in Recoleta with a view over the cemetery. The two Hernández boys were exceedingly loyal and honest. Federico was an excellent business companion with a nous for negotiation. Miguel offered little apart from brute force and a pleasing ability to source attractive women who could accompany me to meals and other social events.

I miss those days, living the high life in Buenos Aires. For a long time I almost felt Argentinian, my Germanness began to peel away. Especially with the two embarrassing governments in the fatherland. East German puppets of the Russian Communist *untermenschen* and the West German American lapdogs. To be German was to be defined by humiliation and subservience to other powers. By contrast, Argentina was a nation of progress and opportunity. I was successful in business allied with a home life that would make most Germans jealous.

And all it took was one week and the new life I had single-handedly created, was over.

My cautious nature saved me in Buenos Aires from those two maniacs at the Café Tortoni and their pals who tried and failed to capture me as I fled the city. My new life ruined by nefarious Jewish secret agents. Well, I certainly had the last laugh. It was very sweet to outfox the most cunning, low people in all of the world. It was such a shame that Federico had to lay down his life for me but it proved his true loyalty.

I have grown to believe that I possess an innate sense, an instinct to spot danger. Sometimes I can't put my finger on it but eventually the realisation strikes and I can evade trouble. This extra sense has stopped me saying the wrong thing, or making bad life decisions and occasionally has handily prevented murderous attacks upon my life.

I remember those final days in *la reina del Plata* back in nineteen-sixty as clearly as anything that has ever happened in my life. The bustle of the conference hall, the hairless man from Pfizer trying to sell me a new antibiotic they discovered. I stood fascinated, not by his sales pitch, but by his lack of eyebrows. He didn't look real to me and in the end he walked off ashen-faced when Miguel made a crude remark to him.

The two men escorted me around the hall and at every stand I could feel the eyes of representatives from all the major firms wanting to speak to me. They knew Alfonso Hermann was the most respected medical researcher in all of the Americas. I was curious when I saw a stand next to the big Bauer presentation for a firm called FrancoPharm.

I had never heard of the company but this wasn't too much of a surprise as a lot of European firms seemed to be coming from nowhere and taking market share. The stall looked very professional and they had the most beautiful girls handing out their marketing paraphernalia. It was Miguel who actually led us over to them to speak to, he was as entranced as I was by the raven haired women.

I saw the two men who were in charge. One was a smartly dressed man with greying hair. He looked clearly like he was the boss. This assumption was confirmed when I examined the other man. The second man was easily two metres tall and in tremendous physical shape. His face was a hard, cracked portrait. He was dressed in a suit but he had the look of a man who was rarely attired in that manner. He was lounging on a table and he stood to attention when I approached. That was a good sign that he was acknowledging my importance.

"Good morning," I said to them both in German. The two men looked confused. The older man told me that they are French and don't speak German. I found that strange considering the importance of German firms in the pharmaceutical industry.

We engaged in a stilted conversation in which all I managed to take away was that they were selling exceedingly cheap anaesthetics. Federico asked them a few questions about products and they replied with knowledgeable answers. But there was something about the big man that troubled me. He occasionally would touch the jagged white scar that ran all around one half of his neck.

Somewhere, a bell tingled in my head. Had I met this man before? I could not recall meeting such an imposing monster but the thought continued to eat away at me.

We arranged a meeting with the two men from FrancoPharm. I explained my concerns to the Hernández brothers. Federico was sceptical of my thoughts and the more he talked, I became increasingly convinced that I was imagining things. We worked out that this company could help cut our annual drugs costs by more than thirty per cent, a huge saving for the company. I simply asked the brothers to be mindful that we could be walking into a trap.

A day later, Miguel drove us to the historic centre

of the city in his sparkling new Kaiser Carabela. He boasted that simply by owning this car, no woman on either side of the River Plate would be able to resist him. Federico responded with some jokes but I remained silent. A profound sense of foreboding rose in me, my blood felt like it was expanding in my veins as an early warning sign.

Miguel had arranged for a couple of watchers to be sat in the main bar area near the stage which was reassuring. We parked up near to Plaza del Mayo and walked up Avenida de Mayo to the meeting. My disquietude would not be dispelled and I told Federico that I think we should cancel. He squeezed my shoulder and told me that nothing bad will happen to me tonight.

We stepped in to the Café Tortoni and it was very busy. Every table was full and the waiters were weaving their way around the tall brown columns serving drinks to the well-dressed clientele. I had only been here a handful of times. If I wanted to impress a lady companion I would normally take her to Café La Biela. She would usually be won over when I would introduce her to famous racing drivers such as Froilán or Fangio. If she was of a more literary persuasion, I would discreetly point out Borges and Casares arguing by the window seats.

Federico nodded to two men sat underneath a group of portraits. The sight of two burly men in our corner helped ease my nerves somewhat. In a bar so busy it seemed nonsensical that anyone would attempt to do anything crazy in here. But I had heard a few tales about what the Israelis were capable in the last few years. A crazy plan would not necessarily be ruled out.

One of the managers informed me that we were being awaited in the barbers' area. I walked through the bustling bar until I saw the *'Peluqueria'* sign. From the fug and the music of the main bar the barbershop doorway was clear yet I could feel my lungs compressing.

I entered knowing something was amiss but not realising that something was the end of my life in Argentina.

THE DARKEST VALLEY

Friday, 2 May 1986

Sleep arrived quickly which is no surprise after a day spent crashing vehicles, running away from the police and steaming letters open like a smelly James Bond. I check my watch which states it is seven in the morning. I feel refreshed and jump out of bed for a shower. I hope the postal worker is bearing up after our little incident yesterday.

After a quick breakfast, Gunari and I check out of the hotel and head towards the main train station. Gunari tells me we are hiring a car as it should make border checks a little easier as we head to the Eastern bloc.

We go to the Sixt counter and Gunari arranges the important stuff. After a short wait, we are informed our car is outside the station. It is a pea-green Audi 80 in immaculate condition. I'm impressed and Gunari seems suitably happy.

"Can I drive?" I ask hopefully.

"Yeah OK, can you actually drive?" Gunari responds.

"No," I say, feeling deflated.

"I'll drive,"

"Good idea,"

It takes time for us to fight through the rush hour morning traffic but eventually we are out of Munich and soon flying through the green Bavarian country-side. According to the speedometer we are travelling around two hundred kilometres per hour. This is surely the fastest I have ever moved. At this rate we will be in Berlin by midday.

We pass Nuremberg and we hit our first patches of traffic and we are forced to slow to a rather more pedestrian one and forty kilometres per hour. It is strange as it seems much slower now Gunari has eased off on the accelerator even though we are cruising at a very high speed. Gunari is in a world of his own and I can see his tattoo on the arm bearing the letters NURI holding the steering wheel. No time like the present to find out what it means.

"What is Nuri?" I say.

Gunari laughs at this and I can feel myself blushing and hating myself for it.

"Why is it funny?" I say to him crossly, "You're always looking at that tattoo. What does it mean, is it a French word?"

Gunari continues to chuckle and I briefly contemplate jabbing him in the ear. As I ponder whether to perpetrate this fully deserved assault he looks round at me and smiles.

"Nuri isn't a thing, she was a person,"

"What? A person, a female person? Who was she?"

"She was someone who Janko and I were both very fond of,"

"You both knew her, how come?"

"Because she was your predecessor,"

Once again, Gunari has delivered a knockout one liner. He's more clinical than Apollo Creed when the mood strikes him. My predecessor? Why have I never even thought about who came before me? Maybe I was arrogant enough to believe that I was the special protégé of these two men.

I dare not ask what happened to her because the potential answers scare me. Does her absence explain the sadness that lingers around Gunari like a faint shroud? Nuri, who was she? I'm not sure how I broach the subject. I choose my usual 'tactless Ana' way.

"Were you in love with her?" I ask. Gunari is taken aback by the question.

"What makes you ask that?" he replies.

"You have her name tattooed on your arm, why would you do that otherwise?"

"It's not about love Ana, it's about the memories of someone who meant a lot to me,"

"I'm not sure I believe in love," I say it absent-mindedly but the point stands.

"You love your parents I'm sure,"

"Not that kind of love, the love which make you do stupid things and lose yourself," I am blabbering and I wish my mouth would close up and not reopen, "You know, the love you see in the films, or when Janko talks about his car,"

"I didn't realise you were such a romantic, Ana," Gunari is grinning again and the urge to bop him rises again in my brain.

"Forget I said anything," I say, turning my head away and allowing the scenery to wash over me. Gunari starts speaking in a very low voice.

"I won't lie to you Ana, the line of work we do makes that kind of emotion very hard to find. And…and you know there is a phrase from a famous Englishman?

He said it is better to have loved and lost than to never have loved somebody at all. It's not a theory I subscribe to, Ana,"

"Why not?" I'm still staring out of the window, I can't bring myself to look at Gunari after that statement. Gunari continues driving but I know he isn't ignoring me but is weighing up his answer. One thing I appreciate about him is the respect he has for the people he speaks to. He would prefer to say nothing rather than lie.

"Love makes you fearful. I learned that at an early age. Fearful of what you could lose in one single moment. The glory of love can be offset by a life mundanely taken away in a second. It can be hard to bear,"

"Is that what has made you so religious?" I notice Gunari is fingering his rosary with his non-driving hand.

"My family were always extremely observant of our Lord, but I can't deny my faith has been strengthened by the tests He has sent to me. It is written that the Lord is close to the brokenhearted and He saves those who are crushed in spirit. If that is true Ana, then I know that when I pass from this earth I will be comforted in eternity by God,"

I don't reply to this but Gunari speaks in response as though I have spoken.

"It brings me tremendous solace. I have seen things and done things in this life that I wouldn't wish on any God-fearing person. I've endured unimaginable loss but I will fight the good fight until my dying breath,"

"I feel bad that I don't believe in God," I say and Gunari smiles again, which lightens my mood.

"You're a good girl Ana and it doesn't matter. He believes in you."

I'm not sure I agree but I refrain from commenting. Gunari is right in that this isn't a normal life for anyone. Especially a teenage girl who had never left Yugoslavia and is now chasing old Nazis around Europe while in desperate need of a haircut.

I have never been one for those kind of urges. I buried myself in my books and avoided most situations where talking to boys was involved. And the boys never bothered with me anyway. Whether that's due to my background or haircut I suppose I will never know.

Now I'm living at a remote cottage in the middle of nowhere with two men old enough to be my grandfathers. I seriously doubt I'll be meeting Tom Cruise or Harrison Ford while I'm splashing about nude in the lake.

"We don't take pride in what we do. Pride is a sin, vengeance is a sin. That is why we take the necessary steps so the rest of our people can live without sin."

"So what we do contravenes the bible?" I say, puzzled at Gunari's statement. It sounds to my ears like a massive contradiction.

"It says in the bible: 'Beloved, never avenge yourselves, but leave it to the wrath of God, for it is written, 'Vengeance is mine, I will repay, says the Lord.'"

"That still sounds like a contradiction." I say.

"I prefer to think that we are working on behalf of the Lord. It's the only thing I can do Ana,"

"What if God isn't too impressed with your behaviour?" I say, half-jokingly. Gunari sighs deeply.

"Ultimately we have to protect our people and do the Lord's work on earth. As long as our people know who took certain actions and why they did it, then that is all that matters. If I can meet my maker knowing I did what I thought was the right thing, it's all I can offer. I hope God will forgive me but I am ready for the consequences if not."

It explains why Gunari seems to bear the weight of the world on his shoulders. He genuinely believes he is doing God's work on earth. That's quite a responsibility. Especially, if God takes a dim view of Gunari's action then he won't be spending his eternity in the place he wants.

"Did Nuri believe in God?" I say.

"I don't know. Maybe at the end she saw things a little bit clearer," Gunari says.

MONSTERS

Friday, 2 May 1986

I wake up with a start. Gunari has been poking my ribs, either to wake me up or simply for his general amusement.

"We are only about six kilometres from the border Ana. Remember you are my daughter and we are off to visit our grandfather in West Berlin. I don't think they'll talk to you though."

"OK Dad," I reply and we both laugh, I crane my head to see across the lanes of traffic and speeding up behind us are two bright yellow Deutsche Post vans, I point them out to Gunari.

"Ha, look Ana, the post office have sent two vans to chase us down before we escape!" This cracks us up even more as we laugh hysterically.

"Maybe he didn't have any insurance," I say.

"Or Bavarian Boris has another package for us!"

Our laughter continues until we reach the border where we are waved through the West German border after only a cursory glance at our passports. My passport is in the name of Anna Orchon, born in Clichy-sous-Bois. The date of birth matches mine so it is easily memorable.

Our car rolls slowly up to the East German border guards. For once I don't have any nerves. I hope this complacency isn't a prelude to six years in jail for illegally entering the country.

A young border guard, handsome but gaunt, approaches. Gunari winds down the window and hands over our passports.

"Where are you heading to?" the guards says and leans his head in to take a closer look at us.

"To West Berlin," Gunari replies, "My father lives there. I am taking my daughter to see him for the first time,"

I grin inanely at the guard. Or is an inane grin my normal smile? The guard has had enough chat and stamps our passports, hands us our visas and tells us we must arrive at West Berlin by the end of the day. Gunari nods and we set off again

I examine the DDR stamp which has a cute little car in one corner. It's funny having your first passport and that passport also being a fake one. It is like I am leading someone else's life. Is there an Ana who remains in Ljubljana completing her studies and hoping to work at the United Nations in New York as a translator? I hope so.

I'm sure it has been Janko's influence but I have started looking at the cars in the places we go. From the scooters and Fiats of Italy to the Audis and Volkswagens in Bavaria. As we travel through East Germany, the heavily forested road edges are the same but the vehicles look completely different.

Faded paint jobs seem to be the fashion here and it seems every second car is a boxy Trabant. They make the Yugo shine as an emblem of modern engineering. Our sparkling Audi 80 is speeding past most of the traffic and is attracting a lot of stares.

We are making good time so we stop at a service station outside Leipzig for some lunch. The sun is shining so we sit outside and it feels very warm. I am enjoying having a nice bask. Gunari brings over a couple of plates of pork schnitzel and some coffees.

"Janko's plane arrives at eight this evening, we will pick him up, it's a long drive from here and we have another checkpoint to cross later. Try and sleep for a bit Ana on this leg of the journey,"

"I'm not tired, I want to find that man in Berlin,"

"All in good time,"

This service station is busy with truck drivers and young families. A few policemen stand around their cars looking very bored and clearly unaware that I am wanted by the authorities in two countries.

"How did you find Nuri? Did you kidnap her like me?" Gunari fires me an icy glare until he realises I am joking.

"She was from Yugoslavia too, maybe there's something in the Balkans water that turns out girls like you both,"

"Was she my age?"

"No, but I wish we had found her earlier. We might have saved her and her mother from a lot of pain. She had the hardest of starts in life. Her mother gave birth to her in the Jasenovac concentration camp in what was then the Croatian puppet state during World War Two,"

"Oh my, that is a tough break," the word 'Jasenovac' in Yugoslavia is synonymous with utter dread. Even though I don't know the details of what went on there every schoolchild in the country knows that it is a stain on our country.

"The Ustaše regime stood out like a terrible beacon in the Second World War for their crimes against humanity. Which tells you a lot about them considering the abuses perpetrated in that conflict. Her father was shot in the head when her parents first arrived at the camp. One bullet in the temple in front of her mother.

"Every male that day that arrived at the camp suffered the same fate. Over thirty men exterminated like flies because they were Roma, or if they were Serbs or Jews. And they called us subhuman. The only positive was that within a few weeks of giving birth her mother managed to escape with her after a big revolt in the camp.

"Her mother, Denisa, made it to Belgrade, which had been liberated a year earlier by Tito's partisans. Denisa brought her up in an apartment block near the train station but unfortunately that wasn't the end of the turmoil for their family."

"Why, what happened?"

"She met a man when her little girl was about five years old. Another Roma who had escaped from a camp in Hungary. He turned out to be a very aggressive, angry man with violent tendencies.

"For the next eighteen years he would beat both Denisa and occasionally little Nuri. Finally, Denisa asked a friend for help who put her in touch with us. Janko, Věštec and I travelled to Belgrade in the summer of sixty-eight. They lived in one of those huge tower blocks in the suburbs.

"Denisa's face was purple from bruising. Nuri too, had bruises on her arms. Anger was rising up in me and I think Janko could sense it too. He has always been able to keep his emotions under check compared to me. However I knew he would be burning up inside.

"The wife-beater refused to allow us to take

Nuri away. He was under the mistaken impression that we were some kind of country fools who would walk out and leave the women there. It's not often that other Roma underestimate us but this guy was something else. He was only a small man but his ego was enormous. He squared up to Věštec, who was taller than me and looked like Rasputin. Věštec simply floored him with one punch. He collapsed unconscious and we carried his body down to our van. Janko brought along Nuri too.

"We drove to a lake about twenty kilometres from the city. By this time the piece of dirt had woken up, luckily I had tied his arms up with rope. He began to mouth off so I punched him square in the mouth and teeth and blood began to dribble from his gaping mouth. He was shocked at the treatment he was receiving. It took all of my energy not to kill him in the back of the van.

"Janko told me to ease off and wait. We reached the lake and hauled his body out of the car and threw him on the ground. He could barely make any sense when he spoke but we could tell he was begging to be let go. Unfortunately for him, this was one situation he couldn't escape from. Janko pulled out his Glock and prepared to shoot him when he stopped and asked Nuri if she wanted to do it.

"Without saying a word she took the gun off Janko, her stepfather tried scrambling away until Věštec kicked him in the ribs with immense force. He kneeled and pleaded with Nuri to allow him to live.

"Again, with no words spoken, she aimed the gun in between his eyes and pulled the trigger. His head exploded but she continued to hold the gun in the same spot. Janko put his arms around her and took the gun away whilst Věštec and I tied up the body and tossed it in the lake,"

"Wow, she didn't hold back," I can't even begin to imagine what went through her head as she pulled that trigger.

"On the journey back to her apartment Janko explained who we are and asked her to join us. Nuri accepted immediately and when she arrived back home she spoke with her mother, gathered her belongings and came back with us,"

Jesus, what a life Nuri had experienced. What I have experienced is nothing in comparison. An imposter in a world I can never understand. Nuri shot her abusive stepfather in the head to earn her position, all I did was a silly, impulsive act of revenge.

"It is a reminder Ana, that we have monsters in our own community," Gunari maintains his eye on the road as we travel north towards Berlin. I am beginning to feel uneasy about our trip to the divided city.

"When was Nuri's first mission?" the airport coffee tastes barely of coffee. It's pretty much dirty, hot water. Janko's flight is due to land any minute now from Geneva.

"A few months after we took her back to Savoy. We knew that a lot of former fascists were living in Spain. The Franco regime was providing asylum to prominent members of the Ustaše command,"

"Didn't they have the Nuremberg trials after the war?" I can't believe they would allow such people to carry on with their lives after what they had done.

"Not for the Croatians," Gunari replies and takes

a sip of coffee, grimaces and continues:

"After the war, many of the former Croatian leaders were killed by Serbs, Montenegrins, Yugoslav Communists, disaffected Croatians. I'm sure you know what it's like being from where you're from. The leader of the Ustaše, Ante Pavelić fell out with his own head of the concentration camps, a man called Vjekoslav Luburić. Luburić formed a rival Croatian nationalist organisation after the war. Pavelić was assassinated by a Montenegrin in Madrid, possibly aided by Luburić.

"By the late sixties, most of our targets had been terminated by various groups. However, word reached us that Luburić was living in Spain, with wife and children, playing happy families.

"This was a man who had raped and sexually mutilated women, sanctioned multiple massacres and held overall responsibility for the Croatian death camps. I say these words to you Ana and it doesn't seem real. What people can be capable of is truly astonishing. This man, without doubt is one of the worst I have dealt with in my time on this earth.

"He would turn up at concentration camps and personally execute one prisoner. At another camp he introduced prisoners infected with typhus in to the rest of the camp to hasten the others' demise. He ended up living in a little village in Spain not too far from Valencia and spent his time writing romanticised, Nationalist shit about his homeland. A man without remorse, we naturally thought it would be good for Nuri to come face to face with a man who potentially killed her father.

"Nuri and I travelled over on the ferry from Genoa to Valencia in April sixty-nine. A two man job,

Luburić wasn't in hiding and we found his address with ease. From our research he didn't have any bodyguards but he was close to the local police.

"We arrived in Carcaixent, rather a dull place and not very pretty. Nothing stood out about it, mostly rows of plain white houses with very little greenery. It didn't take long to find out where he was living. It transpired that a lot of the locals were latent left-wingers who didn't publicise their leanings following the civil war. They were pretty eager to give us the information about Luburić's house. One couple also said if needs be we could stay at their house if anything goes wrong.

"I found his house which was a large red-brick building and the name he was using: Vicente Pérez García. It was five in the morning and the streets were deserted. We broke into his house and hoped he wasn't awake yet. It turned out he was awake but he was sat outside on his patio eating his breakfast.

"We sat at the kitchen table waiting for him to finish his breakfast and come back into the house. Nuri was frozen still like an ice sculpture. She was holding a Spanish police baton she had stolen the previous day. Frozen, not in fear, but in concentration. It concerned me how much of a natural she was. The demons that she carried with her could probably have never been exorcised.

"Eventually we heard footsteps walking through the house. Nuri lifted the baton and as Luburić entered the kitchen she swung double-handed and hit him square in the nose. He collapsed to the floor. I thought he might die from the force of the blow, it was the sweetest strike I have ever witnessed. Even now, when I think about it, it makes me flinch.

"He spoke in their language. I'm not entirely sure what was said but Nuri told me later he said that he was prepared for this moment but didn't expect it from a woman. Nuri smashed the baton over the top of his skill and he lay prone on the floor. She hit him one more time and Luburić could now barely speak.

"Nuri then pulled out the weapon that she had been carrying in her bag. She told me later that it was called a *srbosjek* and was used by the Ustaše in the camps, the word meant 'Serb-cutter'. She placed the leather strap over her hand and the long knife protruding from the bottom of her hand.

"She sat him up and went behind his back. She pulled the *srbosjek* in to his full view and whispered something to him then violently tore it across his neck. His throat was ripped apart and blood poured everywhere. Nuri stood looking over his dead body while I washed the baton and threw it in to a nearby garden.

"She didn't hesitate, did she?"

"No, she was remorseless. Like I said, her lack of compunction scared me. Taking a life is incredibly difficult, no matter how bad the person is, but she never hesitated."

What an astonishing story. I've been utterly engrossed by it. I realise that this is the first airport I have ever been to so I decide to take a walk around the arrivals hall here at Berlin Tegel.

The airport is busy with people, taxi drivers are milling about. Loved ones are meeting up with their friends and family. I walk to a large window at the end of the long Arrivals hall. I decide to check out the planes to take my mind off Nuri.

The sun has nearly set and I can only just make

out some of the logos on the planes out of the window: Pan-Am, Air France, British Airways, TWA. Maybe one day I will fly on a plane. Fly off to somewhere exciting. I could visit the great cities of America or the Great Wall of China, places where the scars of my past aren't so prevalent.

I walk back to meet Gunari and take a seat again at the cafe. Almost immediately I see Janko is heading toward us. I wave at him and Janko smiles.

"Good evening Ana," Janko says, "I hope you've managed to get through today without mindlessly crashing into any vans?"

KNOWLEDGE
IS POWER

Saturday, 3 May 1986

It takes me a few moments to realise where I am. I stumble out of bed and notice I'm still wearing my jeans and t-shirt from yesterday. I open the curtains and catch my first real glimpse of West Berlin. Following our late arrival at the hotel in West Berlin, sleep arrived quickly for me and I'm now ready for what today will bring. I sniff my armpits which is a decision I soon regret. I could do with a wash.

The drizzle of the last few days has receded and the sun is blazing down on the big junction where our hotel is situated. Huge signs advertising Mercedes-Benz, Graetz Radio and the Kranzler Cafe shimmer as they hug facades in the sunshine. People are milling about and in homage to the weather the local men are eschewing coats and young women are wearing miniskirts and summer dresses. The weekend traffic is bustling and the pavement cafes appear to be doing a fine trade.

Since I left Ljubljana, I have seen places that I realistically never expected to clap eyes on at my age. The canals of Venice, the lakes of Savoy, the grand buildings of Munich. In some ways I am very lucky but in other ways I wonder if this is a life I should be leading. I feel like an otherworldly presence. A girl on the periphery of living in these places but outside of it as though I'm looking at postcards.

Hearing about Nuri and her travails has upset me tremendously. I can't shake off the feeling that I'm masquerading as a...what? I don't even know how to describe what I do. Following obese old men around German cities and then organising car crashes with innocent postmen. Is this what my parents wanted for me?

Guilt builds inside of me but I have to push it away. I am not the one who should feel guilty. Gunari is right; describing traumatic events paints only a veneer of reality. It's when you take the time to process what drives a man to order the rape of a teenage girl based purely on her ethnicity that you understand the enormity of the power a single person can indiscriminately wield.

I can see why Gunari holds his faith so dear. One man may hold immense power but in comparison to God it is nothing. Gunari believes he is on a mission from God which provides him with his strength. But, what of Janko? I don't think I have ever heard him speak of God during my time with the two men.

He has a sense of right and wrong as rigid as Gunari. Could it be that humans have an underlying moral code that doesn't require a belief in a deity? If so, what causes some people to break that code?

I don't have the answers and I am hungry so I make an executive decision to have a shower and meet the guys for some breakfast. It is refreshing to take my clothes off since I have been wearing them for over twenty-four hours.

The shower blasts out water which feels divine splashing against my body. I steadily raise the temperature to a level which almost burns my face off. A quick dry off and I throw on faded black jeans and a black t shirt. I skip down the stairs three at a time and enter the quiet hotel restaurant. Photos of bustling Berlin before the Second World War line the far wall.

I'm too late for breakfast, Gunari tells me, which I can only answer with a long, low wail. They are both sipping coffees and they seem to be under the mistaken impression that my lack of breakfast is amusing. I pour a coffee and hope it will stave off my impending death from starvation.

"What's the plan for today?" I ask, the coffee is actually very tasty which makes a change from my experience of Germany. The Germans could benefit from hiring some Italian *baristi* to help them with their coffee issues.

"Today, *Schatzi*," Janko replies, "We will investigate our link that you helped us discover. I will be doing some research on Michael Schwarzer. His name hasn't rung any bells for me, nor for Gunari," Janko looks towards Gunari who continues:

"We have an address so we should be able to obtain some rudimentary basics but it may take a while to discover who he is. I will be organising what we need once we know who we are dealing with,"

"What do you need me to do?" I ask.

"We need you to visit his address and find out about his place," Janko says, "Tie your hair up like the Berliner girls and buy some sunglasses. You can get as close to his door as possible. It's not the end of the world if he sees you, I'm sure you can think of an excuse if he does." Janko winks and hands me a stack of Deutschmarks.

"OK, no problem," I say.

"Maybe buy yourself some food on the way if you're hungry too," Janko says and both men laugh. I simply shake my head at these two daft men, "Will you be alright travelling around the city on your own?"

"Of course I will. I'm more concerned about you two clowns getting lost on the U-Bahn," They chuckle again and I make my excuses and leave the hotel.

Outside, it is even warmer than I expected. Summer has arrived, make no mistake. The smell of hot German sausage hits me straight away and I see not five metres away a girl selling bratwurst in bread. In all my life, I have never wanted to eat a sausage so much. I hand over 4 marks and within two minutes I devour the bratwurst. It's not as good as the *čevapčiči* I would occasionally gobble down back home but it certainly filled a hole.

I contemplate buying another sausage as I wander across the road to the Kurfürstendamm U-Bahn station. I catch sight in the distance of a tall, ruined church at the end of the road. The roof has been blown apart, presumably in the war. It reminds me of something from Krull which my parents took me to see at the cinema for my sixteenth birthday. I'm hoping the Beast and his slayers don't start coming out of the entrance and hunting me down. That would ruin a lovely day.

I spot a newspaper kiosk outside the U-Bahn station and buy a city map which includes the transport system in this divided city. I open the map and notice that some of the stations pass through East Berlin. I ask the shopkeeper if I can travel through these stops but he tells me they are *Geisterbahnhöfe*, or ghost stations. Unless I misheard him completely with my rudimentary German.

It takes about half an hour and two transfers to end up at Moritzplatz station. The dirty yellow trains are quiet at this hour on a Saturday morning. I see the sign for Moritzplatz and I am one of a handful of people still on the train. Due to the Berlin Wall, the line ends here.

Schwarzer lives a block away from Moritzplatz itself, a diamond shaped plaza beyond nondescript-ness. Faded grass in the centre of the roundabout surrounded by scrubland and fenced-off construction sites with no actual construction taking place. His apartment is on Sebastianstraße which if my map reading skills are up to scratch should be a couple of streets away off Prinzenstraße.

There is a lack of people around, I check my Casio watch which informs me it is eleven in the morning. It's a Saturday so people won't be at school or work. Everyone must be having a sleep in. I head along Prinzen-straße and almost immediately I am confronted in the distance with the Berlin Wall. A thrill rushes through me at seeing the Wall. One of those things that we were taught about at school and here it is in front of me. The visual representation of the barrier between East and West.

The schools in Ljubljana were not very ideological and the teachers struggled to provide coherent answers as to why it had been built. I could sense the dryness as the teachers stated that the wall was there to protect the East Germans from Western aggression. It seemed pretty clear even as a schoolgirl, that it was there to prevent East Germans leaving.

It sounds strange but as I approach the wall it

doesn't seem as big as I was expecting. I assumed it would be twenty metres high blocking out the sunlight but it is barely three or four metres tall. There is a checkpoint too but I can't see any guards. Presumably the West German guards aren't fighting off folk from trying to enter the DDR.

I walk towards the wall and realise the buildings on Sebastianstraße actually face the wall. I am searching for number eighty-seven so I turn right before I head through the checkpoint and accidentally end up in East Germany. I locate number eighty-seven which is a corner building and was probably quite a grand apartment building before the wall was constructed literally five metres away. That must have put a real dampener on the value of the building.

The graffiti-covered wall curves away from the building down the bisecting road, which according to the sign next to me is called Luckauer Straße. I contemplate taking a Polaroid of the building but decide against it; instead I amble casually over to the main door. I examine the names on the intercom and I spot "8 - Schwarzer, M.A.". Found you, Mr Schwarzer!

I ponder waiting around to see if anyone leaves but the streets remain deserted barring the odd Berliner Pilsner truck passing by. Janko told me about how sometimes the best place to hide is in a crowd, telling me that people sometimes struggle to see the forest for the trees.

The thought struck me that if I do gain access to the building I am going to stand out a mile. A tanned, dark haired foreign girl walking around a quiet, run-down Berlin suburb. I decide to head back to the hotel so I walk back towards the checkpoint taking out my camera to photograph parts of the wall so anyone who does see me will think I'm a curious tourist and not a mad, Gypsy avenger.

As I set off down the street, a blond-haired man of around forty or fifty years old is walking the opposite way. As we pass each other he glares at me so I hold his gaze. I need to break this habit of out-staring people. We nearly end up turning round as both of us are determined to maintain the stare-off. Finally I stop performing my convincing owl impression, breaking the gaze and carry on walking down the street. At the end of the road, I turn around and see the blond-haired man entering number eighty-seven. He doesn't look around but walks straight in. What a strange man. There is a distinct possibility that I have been engaged in eyeball activities with Schwarzer.

I consult my map again and work out it is about six or seven kilometres back to the hotel so I decide to walk it. Summer is almost here and the feel of the warm sun on my skin is tremendous. I arrive back at the Moritzplatz roundabout, check my map which advises that if I follow Oranienstraße it should take me to Checkpoint Charlie, the famous border crossing.

Oranienstraße is yet another unremarkable tree-lined road which helps me gather my thoughts. I wonder what Janko and Gunari's plan will involve as we still don't know what the relevance of the codes are. Janko believes they are daily codes but at this point we don't know if Tremmick calls up Schwarzer or the other way around. Or there could be another middleman that they both liaise with.

It takes about a quarter of an hour to reach the checkpoint and in all honesty it's not radically different to the Prinzenstraße checkpoint. How different was I expecting it to be? At the end of the day it's a checkpoint. It's unlikely hordes of East Berliners will be trying to pass through on a weekend lunchtime.

In the foreground I see the 'You are now leaving the American Sector' sign and behind that the 'ALLIED CHECKPOINT' sign with the American, French and British flags that I have seen on television before. In the background is a large white watchtower. I can see the East German guards walking around holding firearms.

It is a reminder of the power of borders. If one girl tries crossing that border without consent that guard up there will be obliged to shoot her. It is quite scary to contemplate the authority over life and death that a young lad in a watchtower holds. How would a twenty-three year old man deal with returning to his wife and young daughter knowing he had to shoot a desperate person in the head simply for trying to move from one part of their city to another? Do the people who give these orders feel anything for the poor kids who have to carry them out?

For the remainder of my journey back to the hotel I struggle to remove these thoughts from my brain. The arbitrary nature of holding a human life in your hands. I'm not naive and I know that is why we are here. To find Albert Tremmick and kill him. I keep walking and push the thought that I may need to murder this man out of my head. It's now eight in the evening and it is still very warm outside but Gunari takes us inside a French bistro on Kurfürstendammm, or Ku'damm as I am hearing locals and Janko call it. Luckily it is air-conditioned inside but the interior is a bit grimy and dim for my tastes. Janko orders a bottle of wine from the menu while Gunari and I investigate the menu.

"So, Ana. How was your day out?" Janko asks after the waiter has handed over the wine and provided us with three glasses.

"His house has a view of the Wall ten metres away. He is flat number eight, which looking at the numbers is on the top floor. It's a very quiet neighbourhood."

"What about police?" Janko asks, looking out of the window thoughtfully, "Or even border troops,"

"There is a checkpoint a couple of minutes away, I didn't see any guards but I'm guessing they are there very close by,"

"This probably rules out a snatch, eh Gunari?" Janko says.

"Yes, I would agree," Gunari replies. Both men look dreamily in concentration. I can almost see the cogs turning inside their brains.

"So, who is he?" I ask, breaking the reverie.

"Not who we were expecting Ana, that's for sure," Janko says, "We thought he may be military of some description or at least an explicit link with the armed forces. But it wasn't the case,"

"No?" I can tell Janko is enjoying this moment of disclosure as he always does, the big drama queen.

"No, firstly we checked the land registry as we thought it may be social housing considering its location. It turns out that the apartment is owned by a private medical company called Internationale Medizinische Forschungsgruppe, or IMFG. A very vague title meaning International Medical Research Group.

"They are a Swiss company. Probably because of

that I barely managed to find any filings about them. They have a German subsidiary which lists Michael Schwarzer as the Chief Executive and Paul Beckermann as secretary. Again, I couldn't find anything that actually describes what they do. The only thing I noted was a linked director with a farm machinery company called Karl Mengele & Sons - the man's name is Horst Beckermann"

"Paul's elusive brother," I say.

"Indeed, but it also turns out that the house on Sebastianstraße is not Schwarzer's registered address."

"Oh, no?" I say, once again wilfully bearing Janko's dramatic pauses.

"Oh, no indeed, he lives with his wife in a lovely apartment overlooking a park not too far from here in Schöneberg. Three children too, from a previous wife but they don't live in West Germany, they are in America."

"How do you know that?"

"I had a chat with the man who runs the bakery below his apartment, very talkative man. I told him I was an old friend visiting from Hamburg. He said Schwarzer went through a very messy divorce due to him having an affair with his secretary. Who he then married as he is such an honourable man."

"He sounds very charming," I say.

"The problem is we don't know the connection between them all. Did Beckermann know Tremmick during the war. Or maybe in Argentina?" Gunari says.

"What about the codes, what do you believe they are for?"

"There was only one envelope from Beckermann, so he wasn't posting anything to Tremmick. I would hazard a guess that he also receives a letter from Tremmick too each month. Again, I would guess that Beckermann will call up each day and state the word that matches the code."

"That does seem likely," I say, "So what is our plan?"

"Tremmick is probably aware that people will be on his tail," Janko says, "I think we should pay the apartment a visit tomorrow and hopefully meet this Michael Schwarzer,"

GRADUATION DAY

Sunday, 4 May 1986

It's another bright day in Berlin, the sun is bouncing off the Ku'damm pavements outside the hotel. Yesterday's sausage seller is nowhere to be seen but it doesn't matter, I can't eat today. Nervous energy is beginning to build. It's not only me either. I can see Gunari is anxious too, he couldn't keep still in the hotel and now we are outside on the street he is pacing around.

Janko is the only one of us keeping his cool. Or at least the pretence of cool. Both men know that they can't afford to mess this up or Tremmick may evade justice forever. The news of the artwork discovery at Christmas means he will already be on his guard.

Gunari has a big rucksack, I daren't ask what is inside there. Janko carries a briefcase while I only have my polaroid camera slung around my neck.

"Are we ready?" Janko asks us both. Neither of us speak but simply nod, "Let's go then, lead the way Ana,"

I retrace yesterday's trip, taking us on the U-bahn to Moritzplatz. Despite it being the underground train, most of the journey is on raised rails above the roads. West Berlin passes in a blur of tidy apartment blocks and new-build offices.

By the time we reach Moritzplatz, the sun has almost disappeared. The sky is the colour of dirty dishwater and a soft drizzle almost imperceptibly lands on my arms. It is still disagreeably warm and very muggy now. It is nearly eleven o'clock when we reach Eighty-

Seven Sebastianstraße. The men check the door and within seconds Gunari has managed to open it.

We head up the stairs towards the top floor and I seem to be the only one making noises on the steps. Gunari prowls, his feet as soft as a tiger on the hunt. Janko also makes little noise, probably due to his Parisian loafers. We reach the top floor. I eyeball the door on the left - Flat Seven. According to the information outside this is where Frau Zaimoğlu lives, I hope she is a deaf old Turkish lady who minds her own business.

To our right is the door to Flat Eight. I point to it and both men nod their assent. They both stand with their backs to the wall next to the door.

I creep to the door and I still haven't finalised what story I intend to use. I knock hard three times. I hear a noise and a lock turn, my stomach drops to my feet. The door opens and a handsome blond man of about fifty fills the frame. It is the same man I had the staring contest with yesterday which unsettles me.

"Yes?" he says. His voice is gruff. It's pretty much how I sound when I wake up.

"Hello, good morning," I say, my voice faltering. Initially, my plan was to stutter a bit however I aren't putting this on.

"What do you want?" he says, in a direct but not aggressive manner.

"I was looking for Mrs Zaimoğlu's house, I'm her niece," his face turns from cautiously polite to disgust now he thinks that I'm Turkish.

"Over there," he says, pointing at the door. He pulls away and prepares to close the door when a big hand slams open the door. The force puts him on his arse in his hallway and his facial expression has now turned to shock as he sees Gunari looming over him and pointing a pistol at him.

"What is going on?" he says looking at me. I turn to Gunari who is moving towards the man I assume is Schwarzer, the gun now centimetres from his face. His handsome face is now a picture of shock, eyes darting around.

"Do not say anything," Gunari whispers in a growl.

"Who do you think you are..." Gunari whips the pistol across Schwarzer's face with shocking swift brutality. A spray of blood flies off and speckles the wall next to the door. Schwarzer is now lying on the floor holding his face and moaning.

Janko walks in now and closes the door. He takes the gun off Gunari who lifts up Schwarzer and drags his body from the hallway into the living room. Connected through a small archway is a dirty kitchen and dining area. Gunari tells me to grab a chair from the kitchen which I do and place it in the living room. Gunari sets down Schwarzer and takes out some rope from his rucksack. Gunari ties the rope tightly around Schwarzer's chest and subsequently ties his wrists to the chair arms.

I search the house along with Janko looking for evidence. There is a bedroom which is virtually empty except for a mattress with blood stains all over it. In blood on the walls is smeared a slogan: *Blut und Boden.*

"What does that say?" I ask Janko.

"Blood and soil," Janko is intrigued by it, "You don't see that too often these days. Before the war..." Janko simply shakes his head and doesn't continue talking.

There is nothing of note in here so I head back to the living room. I notice a telephone on a table by the window. Is that the one they use? I sincerely hope he doesn't make or receive the calls from his own house. But why else would he come here?

The house itself is unlikely to be a permanent residence. Barely any clothing hangs in the wardrobes, nor is food stocked in the cupboards. It is dirty due to inaction rather than the behaviour of a messy person. A coating of dust covers most surfaces.

"Who are you?" Schwarzer's shock still registers on his face. His eyes constantly dance between the three intruders in his house. A light scar runs across his left cheek which actually makes him look more good-looking.

"I can't believe you are asking that," Gunari says.

"Who sent you?"

"We sent ourselves, as is our right as the appointed representatives of one of your shareholders," Janko says and a look of incomprehension passes over Schwarzer's face.

"None of this makes any sense,"

"Maybe that's because the big guys keep you out of the loop,"

Schwarzer looks very confused. Perhaps he's wondering why Mrs Zaimoğlu sent her family to rough him up.

"We represent the heir of Dr Mengele," Janko opens his arms and points towards me, "Her grandfather didn't lose his share of IMFG because he died,"

This is the big moment, our big risk. Will he swallow our lie?

"We...we didn't forget you. Your family receive

their fair share,"

"Not all of his family, clearly," Gunari says, "We are here to discuss the details of moneys owed to us."

"She doesn't look like the daughter of anyone but a filthy Turk." With a speed that if I hadn't seen it with my own eyes I wouldn't have believed it, Gunari flashes the gun across Schwarzer's face. He had barely finished speaking when his head was snapped laterally and more blood spurted out.

I feel my stomach lurch with disgust at the sheer explosive violence. Schwarzer starts laughing which makes me feel even worse. I can't look at him and I have to turn away. I sense Janko looking at me but I am unable to acknowledge him.

"If you pardon my coarseness, Mr Schwarzer but Dr Mengele was a busy man in Brazil. He was very close to the lady who cleaned his house and eventually in nineteen-seventy she gave birth to the young lady stood next to me, Hannah,"

"I would have heard about it," Schwarzer juts his jaw out in a gesture of idiotic defiance.

"Unfortunately, you didn't hear about it which has placed us all in the difficult situation we are currently in. When Dr Mengele fell ill a couple of years after Hannah was born her mother looked after him until he passed on. He made certain promises about his new family being looked after but these turned out to be lies."

"So what, she's a bastard. Look at her, a hybrid mongrel. She isn't German and she never will be. I don't care if her father was the Führer himself,"

"I feel like you are misunderstanding us. We are the ones in the position of power here. It took many years of searching to obtain your address Mr Schwarzer. You are not an easy man to locate."

"You'll receive nothing from us," Schwarzer's resistance continues, I glance at Gunari who is checking his watch.

"Us?" Janko says. Schwarzer doesn't say anything but his arrogant facade begins to crack, "If you mean Mr Paul Beckermann, our friends will be paying him a visit later today in Munich. And, after seeing the size of him now, I doubt he will be running away so fast,"

Silence descends on the room, Gunari is not allowing Schwarzer out of his sight. I notice I have picked up a bread knife, I can't remember picking it up. I scan the kitchen and I can see the void in the rack from where I lifted it from.

"You are making a big mistake," Schwarzer says softly, a line from a bad thriller movie.

"Will Mr Beckermann be happy to discover that you supplied us with his address?"

"I didn't. I..." Schwarzer realises the trap he has walked in to.

"What will he do, do you think?" Gunari this time has stepped in to the conversation, "If it's anything like his reputation, the future isn't looking so rosy for you eh?"

"His reputation," Schwarzer snorts, his bloodied nose makes it sounds strangely bunged up, "He's never hurt anyone before. He is a businessman, like myself,"

"We shall see. Now, what time will he call today? This is very important," Gunari says. Schwarzer simply chuckles in response so Gunari punches him low in his gut. Schwarzer begins retching horribly, blood and mucus spewing out of his face.

"We can wait all day, but it would make more sense for you simply to tell us. Beckermann calls you at what time?"

"I will not tell you anything, filth,"

"Pass me the hammer from my bag, Janko," Gunari is truly fearsome, a dark and brooding malevolent presence. Schwarzer is trying to keep his emotions under control and exude arrogance but he isn't fooling me. He won't be fooling Gunari either. He should tell us what we need to know, save himself the pain that is inevitably heading his way.

Janko pulls out a rustic builder's hammer out of the rucksack and hands it to Gunari. Janko steps away and pulls me back a little bit further even though I am a good few metres away anyway. Gunari stands in front of Schwarzer and says:

"I will ask you questions. If I need to ask each question more than once it will result in me; causing you; immense pain. Let us begin: What time will Mr Beckermann telephone you today?"

Schwarzer doesn't speak, I don't think he can summon the voice to say anything. His intransigence is yet to be overwhelmed by self-preservation. Schwarzer looks pleadingly at Gunari and simply shakes his head.

"My hand takes hold on justice, I will render vengeance on my adversaries," Gunari whispers this in Schwarzer's ear, raises his hand up and brings it down with tremendous force upon Schwarzer's right hand. A crunchy squelch as it lands and shatters bone and ligament. Schwarzer is so shocked he can only scream without any sound coming out.

"Midday, midday," Schwarzer barks out the

words, the pain possibly not as awful as it will be once the adrenalin dissipates. The colour has drained from his face and his eyes are wide open.

"Mr Beckerman calls you up and says the daily code. What do you reply with?"

"I...I...I say the next day's code and that's it," Schwarzer has begun to cry, his body retching in rhythm with the sobs.

"What time will Dr Tremmick telephone you?"

"Twelve-thirty, every...every day,"

"Good man," Janko says, "if you carry on in this manner, you should be able to see your family today. Perhaps after a trip to the hospital to fix your broken hand of course. Where is the letter from Dr Tremmick?"

Schwarzer nods towards the kitchen, so I walk over to have a look around. I can't see a letter only a small waste bin with a crumpled envelope.

I pick the envelope out of the bin and take the letter out. It is pretty much the same as Beckermann's letter with the same combination of numbers. One thing I notice is the postmark in the corner stamped with *Principauté de Monaco*. I hand the letter to Janko back in the front room.

"What is Dr Tremmick's address?" Janko asks.

"I don't know," Schwarzer mumbles. Gunari raises the hammer up again and Schwarzer wails, "Nooo, I don't know,"

"Wait a second Gunari," Janko says while walking to Schwarzer. He shows the bloodied man a photo, "Mr Schwarzer, these are your children I believe?"

Schwarzer nods meekly.

"They are currently safe and well in America. If you do not listen to our instructions their safety will be compromised. Am I making myself completely understood?"

"Yes," Schwarzer strains out the word like pouring treacle through a plug hole. His head is bowed. Janko turns to Gunari and says:

"We need to clean him up and sort his head out so he can answer the calls,"

"OK, I'll untie him and we can take him to the bathroom," Gunari says in response. He walks over to the stricken Schwarzer, head flopping in semi-consciousness. I walk over to join Gunari and check the man's condition.

Gunari unties the rope around Schwarzer's chest and lets it drop to the floor, he moves on to untie the left hand keeping his eyes firmly on the barely-responsive German. Gunari unties the right hand and then moves around the back to lift him up.

As he edges around the chair, Schwarzer suddenly lunges head-first into Gunari and knocks him off balance. Schwarzer pulls the gun away from Gunari and tries aiming with his broken hand. I am frozen watching him line Gunari up in his sights. I hear Janko shouting, I can't tell what he is saying.

My training kicks in and an injection of adrenalin stings my heart, the breadknife is in my hand still so I pounce like a lioness protecting her cubs and plunge the knife straight through the back of the neck of Schwarzer. The skin immediately yields and then I can feel jagged resistance as it grates across his spine.

Schwarzer utters a gargle and collapses immediately, dropping the gun on the floor. His crumpled body lands and knocks over the chair he was previously sat on. I look in his eyes but there is nothing there. He focuses on me for a split second then the life drains out of him.

I drop to my knees and every emotion one could feel hits me at once. Or to be more accurate, hits the character that I am watching from afar. Nothing is me anymore.

Silence envelopes me, the room is not real. The bloody knife is in my hand, I look down at it and drop the repulsive object. There is no blood on my hands but it feels like my hand is covered in it and I swear the sensation is real.

"I can't stay here," I say, "I have to leave,"

"Ana, you need to stay, we will sort everything out," Janko says, Gunari is sat on the floor, still shell-shocked. His eyes are empty of emotion. Janko is holding his hands up imploring me to stay.

"This isn't me, this isn't me," I run out of the house, down the stairs and then walk off out of the apartment and into the grey heart of Berlin.

DEFEAT IS OPTIONAL

Sunday, 4 May 1986

The anonymity of the city is my shroud, the endless apartment blocks and arboreal avenues. The hum of traffic and the chatter of children fills the air. The incongruousness of daylight after the events of today further unnerves me.

I need to keep walking. If I don't, I honestly don't know what I'll do. After a few hours of aimless wandering I reach the river and there's nowhere else to go so I do decide to stop and sit on a concrete bench. The tears flow, sobbing the shame out of my system.

I've deprived a wife of her husband and three children of their father. It was so easy to perform the action, one fluid movement and he was soon keeled over like a burst balloon. In a few minutes, a normal day transformed into a ferocious snuffing out of his life.

Over the course of the last few months I have spent time thinking about what it would mean to take a life. I have talked myself into thinking I possessed the mental fortitude to kill a person, especially one who deserved it.

Now all I can reflect upon is that I murdered a man in cold blood, not a war criminal but a businessman. A man with faults, obviously, but not a man who has hurt me or my family. His pitiful look as his life ebbed away didn't make me feel guilty. What made me feel guilty was the flash of superiority I felt after committing the deed.

A second was all it took for me to permanently incapacitate a grown adult. Is this how the monsters feel when they kill? Does the feeling grow with every death ultimately leading to the types of crimes that the Nazis committed? Surely everyone holds themselves accountable for their actions?

The sun is hanging low in the sky giving the Berlin sky a reddish-grey hue. It is quiet on the banks of the river, the water barely making a noise as it laps gently against the stone banks. No one is around and I can feel at ease. How easy will I feel if a policeman speaks to me?

Will it show on my face that I have recently committed a violent murder? I'm in a foreign country with no idea what to do if I am arrested. If I manage to return to Yugoslavia, the same applies - prison for arson and attempted murder.

I begin to cry again, if ever there was a time I wanted a hug from my mum, this is it. A teenage girl in a divided city, soldiers patrolling watchtowers with machine guns. Unreal moments have been a hallmark of my time away from home but tonight will never be surpassed.

Behind me the sound of music is gradually rising. An insistent bassline thumps in time with my heartbeat. Where are those sounds coming from? I rise and try to follow the sound of the earthy beat through the dark streets of Kreuzberg.

Somehow, I take a couple of wrong turns and the sound drops away. I can feel my heart pumping hard still so I retrace my steps and the sound comes back. I end up back on one of the main streets with the U-Bahn train line passing over head again.

I track the sound over the road and I can now hear a voice singing robotically over the music. A train passes overhead, it's lights illuminating my face in the evening gloom. I see in front of me a small lit sign stating "BAR".

There are people outside the bar sat on upturned boxes and beer crates. I walk towards the door, a girl with dyed short white hair dressed in leather trousers and leather jacket mutters something to me under her breath. I give her a stare which she holds.

I try and find the door handle whilst maintaining the staring contest with this bitch when a couple of young lads bound through the door nearly knocking me over. The first one ignores me but the second boy apologises. They both look at what I'm wearing, then at each other and begin to laugh.

I enter the bar and immediately feel eyes upon me, judging me. It must be because of what I'm wearing. A pair of white shorts and a plain blue t-shirt, everyone here seems to have spent the day trying to look a certain way. The girls all have cropped hair and the boys have long hair.

A thought occurs to me, am I covered in blood?

Fear pulses through my body, and I look for a sign indicating where the toilets could be. There's too many people around so I head to the bar and see a man with long brown hair and round glasses behind the counter.

"Where is the toilet?" I ask, sounding more aggressive than I mean to.

"Round the corner," he says pointing behind the bar.

I don't thank the barman but almost run to the toilet. A girl who looks like she is in more of a state than I am is leaving, her eyes are glassy and huge staring out of her haunting pallor.

I enter the toilet and throw up in the sink, the toilet bowl is covered in blood and someone else's vomit. Tears are coming out again but this is in response to my violent heaving.

I close my eyes and try and calm myself down as Gunari taught me. I start by controlling my breathing. Ten long inhalations and exhalations. It actually works so I repeat the method. There is half a cracked mirror above the sink and finally I can take a look at my face.

My eyes are puffy but not too bad, a few blood vessels look to have burst below the eyes near the top of my nose. There isn't any blood but I look dirty so I wash my face using ice cold water.

I tie my hair up on top of my head and tuck in my t-shirt too as the bottom of it is looking grubby and the hem is stained, possibly with blood. I leave the bathroom feeling slightly more human.

"Hurry up," a tall girl, with heavy eye make-up wearing a tiny crop top says to me. I don't engage in a conversation with her but head back to the bar. The barman recognises me and asks if I want a drink.

"A beer please," I hand over a couple of marks in exchange for a bottle of Berliner. I down the beer in one long gulp, something I've never done before. I nod to the barman who hands me another beer.

I spot a seat by the window so I push through the throng of conversation and the fug of cigarette smoke to sit down. I scan the bar, there must be forty people here and virtually everyone is smoking. The chat is loud, a quick look at my watch states it is now nearly nine in the evening.

A man with close cropped blonde hair and moustache wearing a Nick Cave t-shirt comes over and sits in the window sill next to me.

"I've never seen you in here before," he says.

"I've never seen you either," I reply, my tolerance for small talk as low as my tolerance for silly moustaches. The man doesn't immediately reply. Instead he rolls a cigarette, lighting it with a match. He offers it to me and I shake my head.

"You're not from Berlin, are you?" he says.

"Does it matter where I'm from?" I reply.

"No, I suppose it doesn't matter at all. I'm from a town called Karlsruhe originally. Now I work at a university in a medical research department. Some of the discoveries they make are fascinating,"

I close my eyes in the vain hope that when I re-open them this fool will have disappeared. I open my eyes and the man hasn't been eaten by a giant worm which I find very sad.

"I'm guessing you haven't had the best day," he says. I look at him and gently shrug, "I'll buy you a beer to cheer you up,"

The man walks to the bar and he returns pretty swiftly. He hands me another Berliner. I down the remnants of my current bottle and take the gift.

"Thanks," I say and clink bottles with him.

"My name is Heiko, what is your name?"

"I am Ana," I say. I probably should have used a pseudonym but it's too late for that, "I'm in Berlin with work,"

"Oh right, I thought you might be a student, you

look very young,"

"Yes, the opportunity arose for something unique so I took it,"

"And now you're having second thoughts about the job?"

"It's more of a vocation, then a job," I say, I look at the floor as I can feel the tears welling up again. If I cry now I'll set the bar on fire. I'm glad Heiko doesn't say anything more. Well, for a minute anyway.

"There's a party going on upstairs if you fancy joining me? My friend Maik lives there in a WG,"

"What's a WG?" I say.

"Ha, you're definitely not a Wessi. It's a *Wohngemeinschaft*, a shared apartment. A lot of Berliners live in them. Lots of young people want to live here but there aren't many places to live. You have to be able to get along with folk here,"

"Do you live in one?" I ask.

"Nope, I've got a flat near my new job, near Checkpoint Charlie. So are you coming up for a drink, meet some of the guys?"

"OK, why not?" I stand and go off with Heiko holding my empty beer bottle in my right hand. If he tries anything I will put this through the side of his head. He looks at me and I can almost sense him wanting to put his arm around me. I glare at him and he thinks better of it.

We pass by the toilet I vomited in. Next to it there is a closed door. Heiko opens the door and the stairs are immediately in front of us. A girl is sprawled on the stairs with a needle and blood coming out of her arm, her skeletal frame on display through her sheer black dress. The blood is dripping on to the wooden stairs smearing them darker.

"What happened to her?" I say.

"She's fine, she's a *süchtige*," I don't know what the word means but I am more appalled at his blasé attitude to this unconscious girl, I kneel down to see if she needs help when Heiko pulls me up.

"Leave her, she is like this every night. She's on heroin, a type of morphine. Don't you have drugs where you come from?"

"I guess not," I look at the girl, her legs are twitching gently, and continue up the stairs.

There is music but it is much quieter than downstairs however there are a lot of people mulling about. There is a musty odour mixed in with the ubiquitous cigarette smoke. We walk past a bedroom where four lads who are surely in a punk band are sat against a wall and passing around a roll-up cigarette and taking turns puffing on it.

A girl is laid across them all, one of the boys has his hand inside her skirt which makes me look away. I hear them calling out at me but I ignore them and stay behind Heiko.

We arrive at a filthy kitchen, mucky plates and mugs piled around and an open fridge filled with beer. Heiko grabs us two beers and hands me one. He then points at a man sat down at a small table by the door.

"That's the man who helped me succeed in my job application. We call him Doktor Party,"

"That's an interesting name," I say, "Is he actually a doctor?"

"I think he's a chemist by trade. He helps a lot of people in Kreuzberg with their prescriptions," Heiko laughs, presumably at his own joke, "I am a trained chemist too, I graduated last year,"

"So, why are you hanging around in places like this?" I ask, this place is a hovel unfit for human or any other creature's habitation.

"This is where the real people live,"

"All people are real,"

"I mean the people who have character and substance."

"As opposed to who? You make no sense," I say and Heiko laughs again. He is so infuriating, my need to bash his head in is becoming uncontrollable.

"You have a lot to learn about the world Ana. We are being controlled by powerful governments and rampant consumerism. The bourgeoisie are in control and their self-interest is destroying the world. Right now, we are in a great struggle to liberate people's' consciousness,"

"Liberate them from what?"

"Americanism, consumerism. It's time people thought for themselves,"

I finish the beer and take another two out of the fridge, reluctantly giving one to this moron next to me.

"Are you working as a chemist?" I say, "That's a good career,"

"Not as such," Heiko laughs again, the cretinous ball of flesh, "I actually left my job at the university to work in medical testing, it's very interesting, there is so much rapid progress with regard to the human brain,"

"Who is this?" a voice rises from behind Heiko. It is the shaven-headed Doktor Party. He could be any age from twenty to sixty years old.

"Oh, this is Ana, a newcomer to Berlin," Heiko says and one of Doktor Party's hairless eyebrows raises.

"Welcome to the German sector of Free Berlin," Doktor Party says and he laughs loudly with Heiko sycophantically reciprocating. My lack of respect for that man increasing even more. "Are you here to get high?"

"Eh? No," I say.

"Have you ever tried it? A little bit of brown will make you forget all of your worries. You look like you have worries, Ana," Doktor Party says.

"I don't have any worries," I say, not liking where this conversation is going.

"You must be the only one. Apart from Heiko here, but his parents pay for everything for him so it's not a surprise. I'll let you have your first taste for free,"

"I'm not interested in your free samples,"

"I can help find you ways to make some Marks if you are adamant that you want to pay. That is not a problem for me, I am Doktor Party and I can make anything happen,"

"Is this how you free people's minds like the girl on the stairs? To me, it appears more like making them dependent on you," I say, striding towards Doktor Party.

"Heiko, I think you should take your new friend away from me," Doktor Party stands up and he is barely taller than me, an angry short man. If this little bald exploiter thinks he can intimidate me he has picked the wrong girl at the wrong time. A few people have entered the kitchen, emaciated, pock-marked men and a couple of beautiful young girls in long trenchcoats. They are watching this face-off with grim fascination.

"Come on Ana," Heiko says and he has to pull me away from this situation, my gaze not leaving Doktor

Party's until I back up into the hallway. Heiko takes me in to a living room filled with more people - more people on drugs, but outnumbered by people dancing and chatting. An oasis of relative normality. We perch on the arm of a sofa.

"Why did you do that? Doktor Party is only helping people. It's their choice to buy from him. It's the ultimate free choice,"

"I can't believe you need me to tell you how naive you are," I say and Heiko once more laughs - I close my eyes and try to maintain my calm.

"This place here, this city is the definition of freedom. People can be who they want to be. They can create what they want, work where they want,"

"Who has ever told you you can't work where you want, or study what you want?"

"What do you mean?"

"Has anyone, at any point in your life, said you can't do this? You can't do this because of the colour of your skin or because your hair is too dark, or because you have a certain surname?"

"That's not what I mean, I'm on about following dreams,"

"You're an idiot. No offence Heiko but one day you will learn about struggle and it will change your perspective on everything. I can't speak to you anymore or my head will fall off,"

I rise and walk off back towards the staircase, Heiko looks nonplussed. I can tell that my admonishment meant nothing to him. A privileged boy who has gone from a top school to university to a good job and he thinks he represents the underclass.

Is this the Western superiority complex?

Back on the stairs, the girl from earlier is moving and her head is lolling against the wall. I sit next to her and prop her up against the wall so she is pretty much upright. The blood on her arm has dried and the needle is dangling out of her arm which makes me feel sick. I take the needle out and place it on the stairs. The girls eyes are vacant but moistening up.

"Thank you," she says, and then mumbles something else in German I can't understand.

"I'm sorry, I don't understand," I feel bad not being able to make out her words but she is slurring too much. I hand her my beer as her skin looks almost translucent, the girl desperately needs some liquids. She lifts the bottle up to her dry, cut lips. The girl takes her time to take a long drink from the beer.

"My name is Birgit," she whispers, continuing to sip at the beer.

"I am Ana, do you need some help?" I say.

"No, no. I am fine," I don't think I've seen anyone less 'fine' in my life. The girl would be absolutely stunning if she wasn't off her head on drugs. "I need to see Doktor Party,"

"I don't think you need any more drugs," I say. Birgit giggles at me.

"I do some work for him so he owes me some money,"

"What do you do?" I ask, fearing the answer of what relationship would a pretty young girl have with an exploitative drug dealer.

"At the clinic with the good doctor and the bad doctor,"

"Doktor Party is a very bad doctor," I say and Birgit looks confused.

"No, he is the good doctor," Birgit pulls my head close, "You don't want to meet the bad doctor,"

"Why not?" I ask, entranced by this zombified girl.

"He hurts people, but they can't hear the screams outside,"

"Outside of where? Birgit?" I shake her as I can see she is about to doze off.

"The clinic, Dr Beckermann's clinic," My stomach lurches at the name, it has to be a coincidence, it has to be. Oh Jesus, tell me its not true.

"What is the name of the company you work for?" I ask, and time itself seems to turn inside out as I already know her answer. If ever I wanted to be proved wrong, this is the moment.

"I...M...F...G. I don't know what the letters stand for," I can't verbally respond so I offer a smile at Birgit. She smiles back and then lays her head down on the step and is soon sleeping.

I need to escape from here due to the cloying fustiness of this apartment and the realisation that I am near the employees of the boss I have recently murdered. I stand up to leave the party but I stop, take a look at Birgit's sad shell of a body and realise I need information. It's time to speak to Heiko again.

DEEP DOWN THE RABBIT HOLE

Sunday, 4 May 1986

Heiko is coming down the stairs as I walk up. He looks delighted to see me, especially when I start talking to him. Simply catching sight of his face inwardly enrages me. Stupid smug idiot.

"Oh Heiko, where is your new job at? Do you work with Doktor Party?"

"Occasionally I do see him at work. He supplies them with some vital medicines. He's genuinely a top class guy, Ana. Top class,"

"Maybe I misjudged him, I'm not good with meeting new people,"

Heiko takes me back up to the kitchen and grabs a couple more beers. I decline his offer as I need to focus my mind on digging up more information instead of getting drunk.

"Birgit told me that sometimes she works for the clinic," I say. The kitchen is busy now and Doktor Party appears to be doing a great trade. A steady stream of people hand over money to him and in return, he hands something over to them. Occasionally I sense him looking over to me but I purposefully ignore him.

"Yes, it's a great way for some of the younger people to earn some money. There aren't many jobs here in West Berlin,"

"You found a job pretty easy to come by," I reply.

"Yes, but I have an education. I am in great demand," his boasts sound ridiculous coming from a man sat on a filthy worktop in a squat surrounded by drug addicts.

"How would I go about earning some money there? Do you test new treatments?"

"We do a variety of things. Some of it is real cutting edge research, some of it is sponsored by NATO I believe. The American government provide covert funds. It's a top secret place," Heiko says, drunkenly placing his index finger to his lips.

"Top secret? I don't believe you Heiko," he seems to be hurt by my comment then starts laughing loudly.

"Oh yes, we are hidden deep below the city. No one can find us,"

That's interesting, where on earth would that be?

"So you work in a cave?" I say causing Heiko to once again start bellowing laughter. A few people turn to stare at us so I nudge Heiko and shush him.

"A cave? You are very funny Ana. No, not in a cave, it's much cleverer than that,"

"I don't believe you Heiko, I think you are trying to fool me because I'm not a local," I respond. Heiko falls into my trap, which is probably the most predictable trap set in modern times.

"It's true, my parents brought me up to never tell a lie. I don't tell lies," Heiko starts pouting. His childish face is eminently slappable.

"I believe you Heiko," I say and rub his shoulder. His face brightens immediately, again like a child promised a chocolate bar to stop sulking, "Where is it located?"

"I'll whisper it to you," Heiko says in a voice actually louder than his normal level. He pulls my head towards his and whispers in my ear, over-dramatically looking around when he is trying to act surreptitiously, "It's in one of the old underground tunnels,"

"The ghost stations?" I say, remembering my chat with the man who sold me the city map.

"Yes, I believe so. It's close to Stadtmitte station - the entrance is at the Karlsbach office near Potsdamer Platz, do you know where that is?"

I nod my head but in truth I don't know where it is. Suddenly, there is a commotion by the table. Doktor Party is shouting in a young man's face. The young lad is frightened and begins to cower in the nook between the wall and the fridge. Doktor Party stands over the spotty lad but as he does so a punch is thrown by someone behind the Doktor. A sucker punch that deliciously connects and floors the good doctor which is very pleasing to witness.

The situation escalates from unruly commotion to full scale riot. Heiko is scared to death, his face is a picture. That also cheers me up endlessly. Scraps are starting everywhere, I need to get out of here fast. The kitchen is a heaving mass of bodies pushing and punching each other.

I drop off the tabletop on the floor and I slip past two skinny lads who are grabbing each other by the shoulders, a man is blocking the exit so I punch him low in the stomach and he lurches over gasping. A girl who witnesses me do this flashes me a big toothy grin so I respond with a thumbs-up gesture.

On the stairs, some more men are running upstairs to involve themselves. It seems as if every individual in this building is shouting. I press myself against the wall and gradually make my way downstairs. The man I punched is at the top of the stairs and he maniacally throws himself down towards me but the men coming up stop him and straight away start raining blows on him.

I make it through the door back into the bar. The screams can still be heard from upstairs and a couple of men bundle through the doors ungainly throwing crap punches at each other. The bar itself is still very busy although everyone is either looking in the direction of the stairs or actively making their way up.

A pretty blonde girl runs in from outside and shouts: "The police are coming!"

No one except for me heeds the cry. I walk out of the bar in to the street. I can hear the sirens and I casually saunter off back from where I came originally. It's not the time for me to be hanging around here.

I arrive at a U-Bahn station that looks like a cross between a castle and a market hall. The sign says it is called Schlesisches Tor. I head inside the station where a few homeless drunks are chatting. I'm not sure if it is safe here but I sit down on a bench to regain my bearings. I pull out my U-Bahn map and it isn't far back to Moritzplatz.

It is too noisy in here, the boisterous drunks are talking nonsense. There are probably six or seven men and one woman, She has a black eye and virtually no teeth. The sight of this pitiful woman is making me queasy. She is drinking from a litre bottle of beer. I can't understand a word of what she is saying despite her being less than five metres away. A couple of staff members chat between themselves and ignore the homeless people.

An old man breaks off from the crowd and sits down next to me. He reeks of booze and I have to turn away from his noxious breath. I know he is going to speak to me no matter what.

"You look like a girl with problems," he says to me in a good-natured manner.

I turn to him to respond and consider a sharp response but he is smiling at me and I suddenly feel sorry for the poor old fool.

"Sometimes it's good to talk," he continues, "I remember when Berlin was not a divided city. I was thirty years old when they began erecting that infernal wall,"

The old man looks to the heavens despite the only view above being of the station ceiling. He is holding a small bottle of spirits. I can't tell what it is but if I ever need to strip paint off a fence I'll purchase a couple of gallons of it.

"I was finally released by the British after the war and I couldn't wait to return to my home in Berlin. I could visit my friends in Wedding and I even started working there at a hospital. My mother lived in Treptow and I told her when they started building that wall that she needed to move out of there. She should have moved in with me in West Berlin. But she was adamant that she wouldn't leave her home. After nineteen fifty-five I never saw her again,"

The old man is now in tears, hunched forward with his head in his hands. I rub the old man's back, his coat is sticky. I want to take my hand away but I keep rubbing, the man is so upset.

"She died, she died, she died," the old man says, "And I never saw her again,"

Again, I don't respond. I think if I speak I will cry and maybe never stop crying. This man must be in his seventies now and his life is wasting away. Returning home after the war with positive hopes and then things not working out how you want. Some people are able to deal with these problems. Others find a way of blotting it out such as this guy drinking away his demons night after night.

"It's a dangerous city, little girl," the old man says.

"I can protect myself," I reply.

"Even the doctors here try to hurt you. They hide us away in their tunnels and do the most unspeakable things to us,"

The drunken shenanigans have calmed down now and everyone in the station who doesn't work here has sat down and started drifting off. A heavy feeling falls over my eyes and I sense I am drifting away far, far underground.

TRAGIC OVERTURE

Sunday, 4 May 1986

One last slug of scotch before bed. Today has been a strange day. My head has been swirling with past remembrances. I knock back the whiskey and it catches the back of my throat and I stifle a gag. Dark memories poison my mood.

Oh my, I must be drunk. It's not often I am in this state. What was it that set me off today? I can barely remember but something infiltrated my thoughts and has been causing ruminations ever since. A phone call? I'm not sure. Oh, my accursed brain is once more letting me down.

I catch a smell of cooked meat and for a few moments I think I'm having a stroke. Did I cook *Brathendl* today? I try and remember, I close my eyes and my head spins. I'm trying to piece together my day and recall what I cooked for dinner.

Instead, a memory stirs from my final days before I left Germany, in the final knockings of the Greater German Reich. It was a muggy late autumn day and the air hung heavy with the threat of rain and the stench of burnt flesh. Most days I wouldn't notice the malodour after a morning scotch or two followed by a brisk walk to my office.

This day was different, the camp itself was

strangely quiet. The numbers being pressed into work parties had declined over the last few months. News was flying around the officers' quarters about the Russian recapture of Tallinn.

My research assistants Werner and Klaus had failed to turn up to work on time yet again citing illness. A hangover was more likely, they spent more and more days in a state of inebriation with the SS guys. The stench would not escape my nostrils. I knocked back a couple more drinks and felt myself beginning to drift away to sleep.

To prevent this, I stood up, downed another scotch and walked back out into the camp. I saw Werner walking in to camp and ordered him to follow me to find the girl I had worked with last week. After the last experiment had finished, the young girl I was testing had the impertinence to speak to me. A little, filthy gypsy girl dressed in clothes that were no more than rags. I ordered Werner to bring her in to the treatment room and tie her down and cover her mouth.

He asked me to repeat what I said. I lost my temper and shouted at him that if he didn't do what I asked, I would personally arrange for him to return to the Eastern Front. Werner finally tied the girl to the trolley using soiled gowns. The miserable little creature was constantly muttering "*Proszę nie, proszę nie,*". I still couldn't evade the smell of cooked flesh, it was clinging to my nostrils and sending me crazy.

I told her to shut up and not to speak her backward language in my presence. I demanded Werner tell me what she was saying. He spoke Polish and I am sure his mother was a Pole but he never admitted it except for one evening after we had been drinking. Ever since that night, he avoided being in my presence as much as possible. I had Werner in the palm of my hand and recently it had taken all of my energies not to bring the Gestapo in to have a quiet word with him.

"She is saying 'please, no', Herr Doktor," Werner's face was pallid. I ordered him out of the room and he was reluctant to leave until I once again bawled in his face. I could see tears in his eyes as he failed to summon the courage to defy me. Werner left the room wiping his eyes.

I was alone with this quivering, feral child. My recent experiments had failed to yield any results regarding the shapes of brains at different life stages. My theory had disintegrated in the last year. After my tests at Dieselstrasse, I was sure that Jews had a much higher frontal bone than other races. I was also convinced that a much smaller occipital bone was a gypsy trait, a sign that they were nearer to our simian ancestors than other races.

But my tests at the camp had shown absolutely nothing to indicate my aspersions were correct. I had examined living people and the bones of the dead and nothing indicated that I was right. In the last few months I had been examining children's skulls with an almost religious fervour. However the lack of viable subjects was severely impacting my work.

My frustration at the army's constant murder of the prisoners was at its peak. If they donated more people to my studies we could have made some real breakthroughs. Instead those damn ovens were being used constantly.

To me, it always seemed such a waste of manpower and resources. I didn't become a doctor to butcher people like cattle. I had no problem with the Poles or the Jews having their own living space like the Americans did with their native populations. Once the Germans had reclaimed our rightful lands there would be plenty of room for the lesser races to live and breed in controlled communities.

I was astonished by the logistical resources that went in to transporting whole populations from Eastern cities to the camps. The war in the East was going terribly and the Führer was continually compounding his errors on the battlefield. Scores of troops were being injured every minute yet thousands of soldiers were involved in moving thousands of Jews across Europe simply to slaughter them.

Idiots like Werner worshipped Hitler and hung off his every word. I recognised straight away that he was a jumped-up prissy fool. I was surprised that his coarse rhetoric struck such a chord with middle classes, in addition to the proletarian masses. The man had no statesmanlike gravitas. He was simply an angry rabble rouser. I never knew fury could be harnessed to such a powerful effect.

Although I have to admit that I had never been so happy at being German when the word arrived that our glorious armed forces had taken Paris. My spine shivered watching those newsreels of our heroic troops parading past the Arc de Triomphe. Like many others, I accepted Hitler's common schtick in return for bringing the glory back to Germany. I didn't think he would achieve what he did but like all megalomaniacs what he had was not enough to satisfy his gargantuan ego.

Hitler overstretched and the Soviets, Americans and British were attacking from every angle. The SS were moving hundreds of prisoners a day out of our camp to other camps within Germany. It was inevitable that the Red Army would be at the gates of Auschwitz within weeks. Thanks to Dr Mengele and my new friend Paul, I had a little escape planned. I had to leave this godforsaken place as soon as I could get away with it.

The little girl's face will haunt me forever. She was repeatedly saying *'nie'*, her eyes were streaming. The tears cleaning a valley down her grimy cheeks. She had a large scar running from the entrance to her right ear down to her collarbone and another circular gouge in the base of her skull. That was the only way I could accurately measure her occipital bone and the size of the foramen magnum. The experiment has once again proved my theory needed more work.

She was a pitiful sight. Her existence was an exercise in futility. It was then that I realised that my work in the war years was a complete waste of time. Ineffectual experiments on subhuman peasants masquerading as serious research.

The girl sat in front of me on the table like a poor imitation of Pinocchio. Her sobbing would not cease. This couldn't go on, I had to stop the noise. It was almost like someone else had taken control of my body. I didn't want to hurt the girl but I was affronted by her. I have no idea what perturbed me so much. Her innocence, her courage? I caught a glimpse of my reflection in a mirror behind the girl. At the time, I didn't recognise the man. Now, I can see that I simply refused to acknowledge it was me staring back.

The girl had stopped sobbing and was looking up at me. I lifted my hands and wrapped them around her tiny throat. My fingers easily interlocked and her neck was very warm and slightly wet, the texture of kneaded bread. A cough barely escaped from her chest and I pressed my thumbs deep into her throat and increased the pressure.

The little girl slapped my arms in a pitiful gesture of defiance. Her eyes transformed from sadness to determination. I maintained my grip, my brain was devoid of all thoughts except that this girl needed to die. I could feel her body going limp and seconds later her eyes froze and her life was extinguished.

For a few moments I was unable to remove my hands from around her neck. Gradually I was able to relax my grip. I don't know why but I stroked some hair away from her eyes. I laid her lifeless body on the table and picked up a white sheet and covered her up. I sat in the chair at the desk and poured myself a large scotch. I drank it in one and then repeated the pouring and drinking process two or three more times.

My mind was blank. I sat for hours in a trance. A little Roma girl lay dead across the room from me. Another death in a camp where life has virtually no value. Is the girl's mother already dead? Most likely she has already been incinerated. Her memory extinguished by walking in to a gas chamber. Her offspring killed by me, surrounded by the machinery of daily death.

There was nothing left for me here. My mind became clear once I knew it was time to set my plan in motion. A couple of times in the last year I had visited Salzburg with my old friend Marcus Reutlinger who I knew from university. He had a contact who bought and sold artwork, a South African named Smith.

If rumours were to be believed certain high ranking officers were helping some disillusioned comrades relocate to South America. I knew it was no coincidence when I was sharing a meal with Reutlinger in Salzburg a couple of months and the commander of Auschwitz arrived in the same restaurant. There was an uncomfortable moment as we both greeted the commander. I was puzzled about how they knew each other.

Reutlinger never admitted he was at the heart of the ratline in all our conversations but following the mysterious midnight departure of the Auschwitz commander three weeks ago I realised our mutual friend was definitely involved. I knew he would help facilitate my escape.

I walked to my desk and telephoned my friend Reutlinger:

"Reutlinger speaking," his gruff Swabian accent came through the line clearly.

"It's Tremmick," I said, staring across at the covered body of the little girl, "It's time for me to leave,"

"OK, we can meet in Prague in two days," I could almost hear the cogs whirring in Reutlinger's brain, "You know the hotel we need to meet at?"

"Yes, I'll be there,"

"Good," he hung up the phone and my time as a tool of the Nazis was over.

The ratline rumour was true.

It was on that previous trip that I called in to Smith's shop in Salzburg and took the painting of what I was virtually certain was of Venice. Smith confirmed that it was by Canaletto and its value would be very high if sold on the open market. This was great news and I relayed the information to Paul via a telegram later that evening.

Following the phone call, the onus was on me to gather my belongings and leave the camp. Paul and I had been planning our post-war plans ever since he arrived. Now he was back to full fitness and eating copious amounts of my food. We had purchased a bakery in Munich in the name of Paul and Horst Beckermann. Horst was Paul's late brother who had been killed at the start of the war in the invasion of Poland. Wilhelm Horst von Reichardt was an infantry officer and one of the first Nazi soldiers to be killed in the war.

Paul travelled back to Munich to run the bakery which was paid for by the inheritance received by his young nephew. Paul took the Canaletto with him for safe keeping. I didn't tell Paul the details of how valuable it was. I kept hold of the modernist painting for my passage out of the Third Reich.

Remembering the day I left Auschwitz, my work and my legacy makes my stomach roil and I have to stumble to the toilet to be sick.

As I hang my head over the toilet boil, feeling partly ashamed and partly exuberant for expelling the sickness, I recall the telephone call from Schwarzer earlier this afternoon. I stated today's code word and he seemed to take an age in responding with a stammer and the next day's code. At the time I thought nothing of it but for some reason it didn't sound like the Michael Schwarzer I know.

Tiredness strikes me and I hobble back to my bed with a bitter taste in my mouth and a pounding headache. I lay in my bed and bring my bedsheet close to my face and I know that I need to reassess that phone call when I'm back to sober tomorrow.

SANCTIFICATION

Monday, 5 May 1986

I wake to a pair of rough hands shaking my shoulders. I open my eyes and instinctively bat the hands away.

"Hey, you need to leave," a gruff female voice says.

I attempt to gather my thoughts. My head is hurting from all the beer last night. A woman in a dark uniform is stood in front of me. At first, I assume it's a cop but I then realise she works for the railway.

"It's time to go, sleeping time is over," she says.

"OK, OK," I reply and stand up and walk out of the station. I anticipate a blinding, blazing sun as I walk out rubbing my eyes. Instead the skies are grey and the air is thick and muggy. A few seconds of walking and I can feel myself sweating.

I double check the map and Moritzplatz isn't too far from here. I can't face seeing Gunari or Janko but I have to tell them about the IMFG clinic. I don't know what to do. I amble around and find a small bakery where I pick up a coffee and a pastry. I sit on the kerb consuming my food and I decide I have to return to Schwarzer's apartment.

After I finish eating and drinking, I follow the elevated U-Bahn line back towards the big roundabout at Kotbusser Tor and head up to Oranienstraße and in a few minutes I am outside Schwarzer's block on Sebastianstraße where the door has been wedged open with a package. I climb the stairs and reach Schwarzer's front door.

I knock three times against the door, heart hammering in my chest. There is no answer. I wait for one minute, counting the seconds and fearing a cardiac arrest. I knock again, three more times. They probably think it's the police. It is times like this I wish we had agreed a secret knock.

Finally, the door opens a crack and I see Janko's grey hair and an eye pop in to vision. His eye stares at me, through me and the door opens. I instinctively harden my body ready for an attack.

I am ambushed, not by violence but by love. Janko grabs me and hugs me tightly. I don't respond, in shock at his response.

"Come in, girl," he says and he grabs my hand and pulls me inside Schwarzer's flat. The apartment smells strongly of bleach and I start to cough. Janko grabs me again in a bear hug and this time I reciprocate and hold him close.

I bury my head in his neck. Janko smells of sweat and bleach, his hands are stroking my hair. We hold each other for a while and let go, my eyes had been closed the whole time. When I reopen them Gunari is stood in the doorway with a serious look on his face.

"Hi Gunari," I say, feeling foolish. Gunari strides over and places me in a bear hug, he relents and holds me by the shoulders, bringing his calloused right hand up to my cheek and stroking it gently.

"I'm sorry Ana," he says and once more puts me in a big hug resting his chin on the top of my head and he keeps apologising. I don't know why he is apologising when it was me who walked out of here. After a few minutes, Gunari finally releases me from his animalistic grip and we all stand around awkwardly.

"Welcome back, Ana," Janko says, "We weren't sure if you were going to come back,"

"Neither was I," I say and I can tell Janko has a lot of questions ready. Now is not the moment to answer interminable questions about my disappearance, "Where is Schwarzer?"

Janko and Gunari look at each other, neither saying anything.

"I'm guessing he didn't come back to life as a zombie Nazi? I'm back, you need to tell me,"

"I dismembered his body which is now wrapped up in the bath in bed sheets," Gunari says. He's not one for poetry or euphemisms, I appreciate that now more than ever.

"That explains the smell of bleach," I say, I consider visiting the bathroom for a cheeky pee but I decide against it.

"You did the right thing, Ana," Janko says, putting on his 'avuncular grandad' voice.

"Maybe I did, maybe I didn't," I don't need sympathy, I need clarity, "Has the phone rang?"

"Yes," Gunari responds, "I answered the telephone. Presumably it was Beckermann who confirmed today's code. I replied with tomorrow's code as Schwarzer said to do and the phone was hung up. I sincerely hope I did it right,"

"Did they both call up?"

"Yes, Beckermann initially. Tremmick phoned up at exactly half twelve,"

"You spoke to him? What did he say?"

"Only the codeword, I grunted the response and he said 'goodbye' and ended the call," Gunari says.

"We can't afford to let him believe Schwarzer is...no longer with us," Janko says, needlessly euphemistically, "They both rang again before you arrived today, and used the correct day's codeword so at the moment we don't think our mission has been jeopardised,"

"Ana," Gunari speaks and looks pained, "It was my fault what happened, my concentration slipped and...and it should never have resulted in that situation,"

I nod and smile at Gunari. I know he will have been dwelling on it since I left and there is nothing to be gained from talking any more about it. Especially with my news.

"I know where we need to go next," I say, Janko's eyes sparkle.

I spend the next half hour talking in the kitchen with the two of them about where I had been and what I had heard about Stadtmitte station.

"You mean, there's an actual laboratory at the station?" Gunari says, his face betraying incredulity.

"Under the station, would be more accurate. But yes, that's what I heard. There's only one way to find out properly." Gunari and Janko share a glance at each other, "I'm ready to end this all,"

Silence descends on the table, the awkwardness that surrounded my return has been replaced by deep thought. I look at the two men on either side of me, one a frighteningly large hulk of a man with a permanent stubble. The other, an elderly, scruffy man with an open, friendly face.

My colleagues? Perhaps.

My friends? Probably.

My family? Most definitely.

"Is this taking us away from our main task, finding Tremmick?" Gunari says, possibly rhetorically as he is looking out of the mucky window.

"If half of what Ana told is correct, surely it is our duty to stop them?" Janko replies. Gunari turns to face him across the table. He looks unconvinced by the proposal.

"I'm not sure it is," Gunari says. He doesn't add any more substance to his response.

"Performing experiments on people, this time for money rather than for twisted beliefs. Is this now acceptable?" I say, anger rising in my voice.

"I'm not saying that, Ana," Gunari says, "I want to know what is happening in there but I wonder if this is our job. If the experiments are illegal it may be better to inform the authorities,"

"You want to call the police?" I shout, I look at Janko in disbelief and he simply shrugs his shoulders, "What do you think Janko?"

"The number one mission is finding Tremmick," Janko replies, "We know he is in Monaco but we don't know where. That has to remain our top priority,"

I can't quite believe these two. After what they have told me about Dieselstrasse, to find out that similar experiments are going on in West Berlin in the nineteen-eighties is astonishing.

"You didn't see this girl, Birgit," I say, "She was barely human. Her body was simply wasting away. And at the centre of it all are sick, rich men exploiting the desperate for their own ends. If you won't go in there, I will," I make this bold statement without realising what it means in practice but it sounded good.

"The Beckermanns are our last remaining link to

Tremmick," Janko says, "Maybe we should pay them a visit,"

Gunari stands up and circles the table in an exasperating fashion. Finally he stops and sits back down. As I wonder what those laps of the kitchen table achieved he addresses us both:

"We need to know what is going on in there before we decide on the best course of action. If we go in there behaving like we are the stars of an action film anything could go wrong,"

"So what do we do?" I say.

"It's your time to shine Ana, it's time you went undercover,"

"Like James Bond?" I say.

"Yes, but try not to get kidnapped by a mad scientist," Janko says, smiling.

"I'll call Heiko and find out the exact location of the entrance,"

WONDERLAND

Monday, 5 May 1986

"Before they built the Wall this was the heart of Berlin for hundreds of years," Janko tells me, "In the twenties and thirties this was the centre of the world. Cabarets and cafes, dancefloors and theatres, Potsdamer Platz was famous around the globe, the beacon of Weimar Germany,"

"It's not looking so good now," I say, casting my eyes across a grey square harshly bisected by a long wall topped with barbed wire. The square is deserted. Virtually no lights are on in any of the buildings on either side of the wire. The setting sun bathes the concrete in a hazy red light, the whole place feels otherworldly, a concrete limbo.

"By the time the Communists erected the wall it was already a sad place, I saw it after the war ended before the wall was constructed. It was a shadow of its former self. It was the convergence of the four sectors so the Americans and the Russians, the French and the British mixed in with the locals. What a shell shocked bunch. What a difference a humiliating defeat in war does for a population.

"I actually was pleased at the time to see so many unhappy Germans, the enablers of the Nazis. Looking back now, I feel guilty about my smugness. It's not good for the soul, revelling in other people's misery,"

A young couple, only in their teens, walk by holding hands and sharing a large bottle of beer. They appear to be the only people around here. From the centre of Europe to an abandoned no-man's-land in five decades.

"It's a shame, Ana," Janko says and he looks genuinely sad at this glimpse of Potsdamer Platz, now a faint heartbeat smothered by ideologies, "A real shame. So where is the entrance?"

"Heiko said it is through a door next to the entrance to a big office building, the sign above the office should say 'Karlsbach',"

Around the square, spotlights have come on in the burgundy gloom. I spot the office with an unlit sign saying 'KARLSBACH'. I point to my destination and it takes Janko a while before he sees where I need to go.

"Are you ready?" Janko is giving off the air of a concerned grandparent, "This is very risky,"

"It will be fine Janko," I say, feeling confident in my undercover skills, "I'll be out as soon as I can - if I'm not out by morning then I'll let you two come and find me,"

"We won't be doing that Ana," Janko says, he moves his hand to my head and strokes my hair.

"What?" I reply, feeling puzzled.

"You're on your own in there, we can't break you out if you find yourself in trouble,"

Now I understand, the mission to kill Tremmick cannot be compromised. I nod my comprehension and my confidence ebbs away slightly.

"Don't worry Janko, I'm tougher than I look," I say, attempting to keep it light-hearted. Janko has the look of a man told he is dying. He attempts a smile but his face barely moves. I give him a kiss on the cheek and walk off to the door.

At the door I tap in the code Heiko told me on the phone: 1-9-3-3. The door unlocks and I push it open, strip lighting immediately fills the foyer with dirty yellow light. The lift is on my right as expected and I hit the 'down' arrow button. After a few seconds the lift arrives and I am startled when the doors part and a man in a full business suit pops out of the lift.

"Oh hello," he says, he is younger than I first thought, probably only about twenty years old, "Where might you be going?"

"Good evening. My friend Heiko told me I could come and make some money at the lab for some medical testing," The man grins at my response. He has an off-putting aroma and he is standing way too close to me.

"You've come to the right place, we are always looking for volunteers,"

"Do you work at the laboratory?"

"Not at the lab, I'm a salesman for IMFG so I'm usually travelling around Germany trying to sell our products. I'm about to catch a flight to Munich now,"

"I was in Munich recently, it's very beautiful,"

"I don't like it there, the Bavarians are too stuck up for my liking. I prefer Hamburg, the people there are real,"

"Everyone is real," I say. I am sure this is the exact conversation I had last night with that silly man Heiko. I am beginning to believe that every young man in West Berlin lacks a good fifty percent of the brain cells required for intelligent reasoning compared to the rest of Europe.

"So how do I find the lab?" I ask. I wish he would

stand further back, his breath is a disgusting mixture of stale cigarettes, strong coffee and mints.

"Take the lift all the way down and then follow the corridor. It's a good fifteen minute walk,"

"Thank you, I best go now," I say and he leans in even further.

"Maybe I will see you again some day, I always pop in and visit the new starters. You know, see how they are settling in,"

"Settling in?"

"Oh yes, some of the volunteers have been here a while now. They love the money, for many of them they are as addicted to hard cash as they are to vodka," the smelly man starts laughing and then walks to the door, "I'm off to the airport, I'll see you soon, beautiful,"

I respond by staring at him with barely concealed loathing. He doesn't notice, he begins laughing again and exits the room. I enter the lift and press the button stating '-1' and it starts descending. The lift is surprisingly quiet for something in such disrepair.

The doors open on a dark corridor with only occasional dim lights glowing every few metres on the ceiling. The corridor seems to go on forever. I inhale deeply and begin walking along the infinite passage.

The minutes pass with no break in the monotonous corridor, No exit doors or decoration, simply walls, floor and lights. A sense of foreboding rises in me as I realise I have no idea what I will be walking in to.

GHOST IN THE MACHINE

Monday, 5 May 1986

I walk for a long time, the squeak of my trainers the only noise in the corridor. It's impossible to say how long I travel down the corridor but eventually it comes to an end. A simple door on the left hand side with no signage. I turn the handle and walk through the door. A gust of wind temporarily unbalances and unsettles me. I am stood on a filthy underground station platform.

Directly opposite is a fading sign on the wall declaring this is 'STADTMITTE'. As I look around, I can see the tracks and an abandoned kiosk on the island between the two tracks. The walls are grubby but there is no litter about. Leaning on the kiosk is a security guard who is startled by my presence.

I wave at him and he waves back. I amble towards him and he puts on his most authoritative pose which I find deeply unimpressive and pathetic. He is another kid, barely out of his teens - his security officer uniform is oversized making him look even sillier.

"Excuse me, Miss," he says in a high-pitched voice, even before he spoke I knew that was how he would sound, "This is a restricted area,"

"I'm not surprised, aren't we in East Berlin?" I reply and he blushes and panics. He doesn't know what to do with his hands. His boss probably banned him from putting his hands in his pocket so he is caught between dangling them by his sides and gesticulating with only his fingers visible.

"No...no I mean, it's restricted for...for business reasons," the boy is talking nonsense but I decide not to torment him any further.

"I'm looking for the IMFG laboratory. Can you tell me where it is?" the guard can barely regain his composure. His fingers barely stick out of his outsized coat arms.

"Yes...yes. I'll show you, I'm the guard,"

"I guessed that, you're doing a great job," I say, deciding I will torment him a little bit more.

The guard opens the kiosk door and points to a staircase going down. I nod and the guard leads the way downstairs.

"Close the door on the way down," he says as we descend deep into the bowels of Berlin. I hear a train rumbling past nearby and I make a strange yelping sound, the guard chuckles at me and tells me: "That's the old U2 line, the East Germans run it, this one is the U6 line which no longer runs obviously."

"Don't the East Germans check on this side?" I say and the guard laughs uneasily.

"They don't check these days, I think the management have an agreement with the *Ossis*,"

I can imagine what type of arrangement this is, probably involving wheelbarrows of US dollars and eyes that don't see anything.

The guard walks in first, I follow him in to a bizarrely normal looking reception area. I could be in a high street accountant's office or industrial park lobby anywhere in Germany. Instead, I am way underground in an entirely different nation to where I entered from. There is another young lad on reception who greets the guard in a jocular manner.

"Hey Fredi, you found yourself a girlfriend at last?" the boy on reception says to the guard. This only inspires more flushed cheeks from the guard.

"What? No, this...lady is looking to volunteer," the guard, Fredi replies.

"Oh, welcome to the asylum," the receptionist says, cackling loudly, "Where are you from?"

"I've recently moved to West Berlin," I reply.

"But where are you from? You don't speak German very well,"

"Why do people keep asking me where I'm from? I'm here to earn money, not tell you my life story. I presume you don't need to see a passport,"

The receptionist snorts nastily, stands and points to the double doors to the right of the reception desk. I stay standing. What does he want me to do, wander in there by myself? The receptionist stands and pushes his chair back aggressively so it bounces back off the wall behind him. He walks over to the double doors and gestures for me to follow.

"Right, come on. You can have a talk with the doctor and see what tests are available. Maybe they'll let you take a shower, you smelly bitch,"

I'm taken aback by his words but I bite my tongue. Now is not the time to create a disturbance. His words have actually hurt me, the more so because it is true. I've not washed since the morning we left the hotel to visit Schwarzer. We walk through the door and the receptionist gives me an unfriendly but mild shove in the back.

We head along a corridor which has the unmistakable appearance of a rundown hospital. A line of stretchers lie parallel to one wall with bedding at various levels of yellowing. Distantly, I can hear shrieking, the sound's remoteness cannot disguise the anguish in the voice. I don't realise but I must have slowed down as I feel another shove in my back. I turn around in silent annoyance at him and the receptionist returns my scowl.

The corridor reaches a T-junction and the receptionist grunts "Right". I turn right and head down the corridor, on the left are large rectangular windows with lab technicians at work inside. I'm not an expert but I think they are performing scientific experiments as there are microscopes and test tubes visible on the worktops.

On my right there is an open door. Peering in, I can see a skeletal girl lying on a bed with a drip attached. Her face is a grey blank and her vacant eyes are unable to meet mine as I walk past.

The next room on the right also has an open door. Another skinny girl lays on a bed sobbing quietly, I slow down and the receptionist barks "Keep moving, junkie,". Once more I avoid responding either verbally or in a 'punchy' manner.

At the end of the corridor are another set of double doors. I turn to the receptionist once we reach there and he nods blankly and I push the doors open.

We enter a large, dark expanse that resembles a field hospital from one of those Vietnam War movies. The cavernous space is filled with shouts and wails. Makeshift wards filled with dirty beds and torn curtains sadly holding on to flimsy rails. The floors and ceilings are dark which enhances the feeling of filthiness. The only light seems to becoming from spotlights crudely affixed to the walls.

There are probably over twenty beds in this room which is probably the size of a sports hall, although half the beds are empty and a couple have been turned over. Everyone in the beds looks bony and desperate apart from a couple of grubby, well-fed men with blotchy red faces who are probably alcoholics.

One of them is sat on the edge of the bed nearest to me and he is holding his head in his hands and crying loudly. I start to veer towards him to check if he is alright when I feel a hand firmly grab my neck and guide me towards the central corridor between the lines of beds.

"Do not speak to any of our volunteers, do you understand, you animal?" the receptionist whispers to me, his mouth only centimetres from my right ear.

Most of the people on the beds have the appearance of detainees from a concentration camp. I feel revulsion at how thin some of the people are. And how young too. A few metres away there is a girl who must surely be in her teens who has bruises all over her body and I can see the definition of every bone. Her skin is pulled over her skeleton like a stretched balloon. She is sat up with her legs up by her chin. She looks at me but conveys no emotion, only emptiness.

"What type of testing do you do here?" I ask the receptionist knowing full well he won't tell me.

"Why do you care? You'll receive some Marks so you can feed your addiction,"

"These people need to be in hospital,"

"You can forward your comments to the Complaints Department at a later point," the receptionist says and starts laughing to himself, he finds it so amusing he says it again.

I notice that on three sides of the hall there are smaller rooms but mostly they are unlit and I can't see what is happening in them. Suddenly a huge cry of pain fills the room. I can't tell where it came from but the sound is incredible, a scream from the very bottom of the soul.

The volunteers, as we are called, begin making noises of their own. Some are whimpering, a few I hear saying prayers. I check my arms and despite the warmth in this deep cavern I have goosebumps. I want to cry and I realise what I am feeling is terror, the same as everyone in here. Pure terror of what is happening in this hellish facility.

"Next time, it will be you screaming, you foreign dog," the receptionist is whispering in my ear again. I close my eyes and try to remain calm. Fear is coursing through my body and it takes all my strength to withhold the tears.

The receptionist clutches my neck again and directs me to the only lit room at the far end of the room. He knocks on the door and opens it without waiting for a response. We walk into a typical GP's diagnosis room and there is a chubby doctor with drooping eyes and a large mouth. Without doubt, I know it is Paul Beckermann's son.

"Ah, who do we have here then?" he says in a cheery manner.

"Some girl from the street looking for money," the receptionist says, he is on the verge of saying more but I can see that he fears the doctor.

"Well, come on in young lady, let us see how we can help each other," I walk in and sit on the edge of the bed as directed by the doctor. The doctor turns to the receptionist and says: "Thank you Thomas, you may leave us now,"

The receptionist scurries away and the doctor turns his gaze towards me.

"My name is Dr Karl Beckermann and I am in charge of this medical facility. I hope Thomas treated you well?" I shrug my shoulders and don't say anything.

"He can be a bit tough sometimes on young girls, especially ones he thinks are on drugs," Beckermann continues, "His mother died of an overdose when he was thirteen and ever since then he has developed his own theories on addiction. I tell him it is an illness but he doesn't believe me. Young people these days find it hard to listen to the older generation,"

Beckermann walks over to me and asks me to stand up. He is very tall, which must be a family trait. He is easily over two metres high. He lifts my arms up and inspects them, then moves to checking out my neck, lifting my hair up. I swear that he pulls my long hair towards his nose and smells it but that could be my imagination.

"You are not a drug addict," Beckermann says.

"I never said I was," I reply.

"So why are you here? You have the body of an athlete,"

"I'm new to the city, I have no money for rent and I met a boy called Heiko. He said I can make money for medical trials,"

"Ah Heiko, he always falls for the exotic arrivals.

Why are you in West Berlin, where are you from?"

"Yugoslavia," I reply, no point in trying to fool him.

"You're very far from home, young girl," Beckermann says, a leer crossing his face. He is very close to me and I realise that he is a big man who could easily overpower me. It takes all my willpower to withstand the trepidation and maintain steady eye contact.

"I wasn't welcome at home so I had to leave. I bought the cheapest flight out of Yugoslavia and that was here,"

"Welcome to Berlin, where dreams come true," Beckermann stifles a laugh and then sits back down in his worn-out chair. I'm amazed it bears his weight as he falls back into it but it manages to hold.

"It's a strange place," I say, attempting to keep the conversation as light as I can, "It's not like Yugoslavia,"

"No, I suppose it isn't." Beckermann replies, he is gazing at me intently. It's hard to gauge in what manner. His demeanour is not aggressive, nor friendly. But it is unnerving. Simply by not overtly showing emotion he has an undeniably ominous aura.

"What tests do you perform here? Some of the people don't look well at all," I say, I know this could provoke a negative reaction but I can't resist asking him.

"Are you a medical professional?"

"No,"

"Well, you wouldn't understand what we do here. We are at the forefront of cutting edge research at this facility, helping to save countless lives."

"Why is the work done underground?"

"You ask a lot of questions don't you? We are

funded by the government and a lot of the science is top secret so they don't want other nations discovering it. Some people may call the volunteers here national heroes. I would be one of those people,"

A silence descends upon the room. I'm puzzled at why he gave me that over-the-top explanation. This place is seriously unsettling me.

"You are in very good shape," Beckermann says, "Many of our volunteers arrive in a very disordered fashion, they have abused their bodies with narcotics and alcohol. Some people have done this for many years, their addictions have taken over their lives,"

Beckermann stands again, moves close to my body and begins examining me once more.

"Yes, you would make an excellent base line sample for our new trial we are due to begin this evening. We would be happy to pay you five thousands Marks too,"

This evening? When I used to sit and watch the cartoons on the television you used to see a character gulp in nervy situations. I do exactly the same and feel the panic rising. The dank humidity is enveloping me and I sense my window of opportunity to escape is beginning to recede.

Beckermann walks away towards the door and I am momentarily glad that he isn't about to start touching me again. Sweat beads are sliding down my face, how does the obese Beckermann keep looking as calm as Lake Bled on a summer's day?

"Come, come," Beckermann gestures to me to follow him.

Beckermann stands outside his office and calls out "Daniel!". One of the orderlies, a burly sandy-haired man of about thirty comes running over, "We have our other volunteer ready for the new study, please show her to the main trial room,"

Daniel puts his arm around my waist and says "Good evening," which is a strangely formal way to direct someone towards a possibly inhumane medical test. I walk off with the big orderly and try and work out if I can escape if necessary.

As we walk around the back of the hall opposite to the side I originally entered, an old man wearing what looks like a filthy loincloth runs up to me. He grabs my arms and is in my face shouting what sounds like "*Folterer! Folterer!*"

I don't know what the word means, I ask Daniel what it is. Daniel blanks me and grabs the old man, another orderly seems to appear from nowhere and also becomes involved.

The old man displays surprising strength and at first manages to fight off the two muscular guys. After a few seconds, with raised voices and screams echoing all over the hall the two orderlies pin the old chap to the floor. A third orderly arrives and plunges a syringe in the old man's neck and he instantly subdues.

Daniel turns back to me, with a look of shock on his face. He grabs my arm and drags me away.

"He nearly beat you up," I say, "The old man was winning until your mate turned up,"

Daniel doesn't say anything, grimaces and drags me away to a nearby door. He pushes along a short corridor at the end of which Daniel takes out a key and unlocks the door.

"Go through the door," Daniel says in a level voice. I ponder whether to fight him, after his exertions with the old man he might be tired. On the other hand he looks in tremendous shape and I'm not sure how far away his back up could be.

The room I enter looks like a traditional hospital ward with three beds lined up to the left and three on the right of the room. In the farthest two beds, curtains are placed at the nearest side of the beds. I see a couple of bony legs poking out of the ends of the beds.

A female nurse is sat down at a desk writing something on a chart. A middle-aged male doctor is stood behind the nurse and talking to her. She doesn't seem to be listening and is concentrating on her notes. The ward is not clean in any respect and has a rather pungent smell of bleach.

"Dr Beckermann sent this one for you, Dr Hansen," Daniel calls out to the doctor who was so caught up in his monologue that he has only now noticed us enter.

"Oh, that is great news, I have been waiting two days for a new subject," the doctor replies, he is of medium build with a dark head of hair and moustache, so dark it looks dyed. He jogs over to me and starts inspecting me like Beckermann did.

"That muscle tone is superb, Beckermann has done it again. What a superb professional he is," I don't know why he is sucking up to him when he is not even here. Daniel doesn't respond to him.

"Please, take a seat," Hansen gestures towards the nearest bed.

"What tests am I doing, the other doctor didn't mention it?" I say walking off towards the other beds. The doctor tries to stop me from walking down the ward but I push him off. Daniel stays stood in the doorway too, unmoved.

"Please, Miss, come and sit down and I can explain it all in great detail for you. Please,"

I pass by the nurse in the centre of the ward who simply smirks at me. As I reach the end of the bed I see the feet of what I thought was an old man. It is actually a young girl, her pink legs have the shrivelled texture of dried fruits.

My eyes move up her body, she is completely naked. Purple bruises and scratches cover a lot of her surface area. Blood is dripping out in isolated spots and running down her body onto the bedsheet. Her arms are fastened securely to the bed bars.

I look up to her face and where her eyes should be. What I see is the most frightening thing I have ever witnessed. Her right eye looks at me with dread. Her left eye is missing, the socket held open by what appears to be a steel clamp. Metal prongs are sticking in the gap where her eye should be. The prongs are holding a huge syringe in her eye.

The syringe has the diameter of a rolling pin with about half the length. The girl is not moving except for her right eye. It is her only communication method but I can feel her right eye conveying agony. She is pleading for release from this ghastly condition.

This is repugnant. Who on earth would do this to a fellow human being, especially in the West where they preach about human rights? If someone told me this place existed I would never have believed them.

I turn round to the doctor who has the appearance of a boy caught stealing a chocolate bar from a shop. Mild embarrassment. I have never felt so much revulsion in my whole life.

"What are you doing to this girl?" I say, attempting to keep my voice from sounding too shrill.

"This is vital scientific work, we are going to save many lives," the doctor says.

"Her eye, did you take out her eye?" I say walking up to him with fists balled.

"She had lots of problems with her eyes so we... we said that we can help her out,"

"You ripped out a girl's eyeball as part of an experiment," I face the doctor and I know I am about to punch this man in to next week. As I prepare to strike I feel hands on either side of me. Daniel has grabbed one arm and the nurse, who I notice has the build of an Olympic shot-putter now she has stood up, has caught hold of my other arm.

The doctor's face has turned from fear to smugness and he directs his colleagues to sit me down. My anger is swelling and I know I will have at least one moment where I will give my all to escape from here. I may not be successful but I will go down fighting either way.

"So, young lady, your little act of rebellion has ended," Dr Hansen says, "It is time for the experiment to begin. You are lucky, we won't be needing to remove your eyeball. Instead we can identify how effective the drugs are when injected directly into the cornea,"

Dr Hansen stands over me, he holds the hypodermic needle in his hand, I know once he injects me there will be nothing I can do. I start shouting in the vain hope that someone, somewhere will rush in and save me. I suppose that is what every volunteer does here. Now I am about to become another shrieking banshee hidden a mile underground. My limbs are fighting and the nurse and Daniel are working hard to suppress me.

"There is no good and bad in nature. Stop putting emotions at the forefront of your thoughts. You are helping us to erase defects and imperfections in humans,"

"You are butchers," I spit at him which riles him immensely.

"Unfortunately for you, I may be the butcher but you are the diseased pig, oink oink," Hansen moves his arm to inject me when I hear a familiar voice from directly behind him.

"One more movement and I blow your head off,"

The doctor freezes. Behind him I see Janko's face. He is holding a pistol directly at the back of Dr Hansen's head. Daniel lets go of me and spins around - straight into Gunari who floors him with one punch. He crumples to the floor.

The nurse is in shock so I grab her head and simultaneously move it towards my fast rising left knee. Her nose explodes on my kneecap and she falls to the floor too.

I admire my two saviours.

"Impeccable timing, boys,"

THE ART OF PROBABILITY

Monday, 5 May 1986

"What is going on here?" Dr Hansen says, his body as still as one of his subdued volunteer medical trialists.

"Exactly my question to you, doctor," Janko says, "Turn around,"

The doctor turns around slowly and comes face to face with Janko's gun. Janko gestures with the gun towards the chair and desk in the centre of the ward. The doctor skips across and sits down obediently.

"Are you OK Ana?" Gunari says to me whilst rubbing my back.

"Of course I am, I was about to escape when you burst in," I say and Gunari smiles in a silly manner. I pop up off the bed and give him a peck on the cheek and then decide to give him the biggest hug I may have ever given anybody. I take Gunari by the arm and lead him to where the one-eyed girl is laying.

Gunari stops in his tracks and walks behind the curtain and begins dry retching. It takes him a few seconds to compose himself and he makes his way back to see the girl.

"Can you speak?" he says to her. Her one remaining eye begin to water. No voice escapes her mouth. Gunari remains close to the girl but he doesn't speak. It could be because of the shock of seeing her or maybe he has no plan. How does anyone plan for this scenario?

I turn around and see the patient in the bed opposite. I paid them very little heed when I initially came in. I stand beside their bed and I cannot tell what gender they are. Short hair, feminine features and a long, thin body. Their gown is wet from sweat. They also have one eye but thankfully the socket is covered by an eye patch.

"Hey," I say to her and I place my hand gently on their upper arm, "Can you hear me?"

"Yes," a weak, reedy voice comes out of dry lips, their eye remains closed, "Where am I?"

"Berlin," I reply, unsure on where exactly they mean.

"Berlin, Berlin. West or East?"

"I'm not completely sure," I say, "You're at the IMFG medical centre. Do you remember coming here?"

"I don't remember anything," the volunteer opens their remaining eye and it is a piercing blue, "I don't remember who I am,"

I continue stroking their arm and face. I don't have a clue what to say to them. I look around to Gunari and he too is stroking the young girl's hand in the opposite bed. Janko is questioning the doctor but I can barely hear his questions or the answers supplied by the petrified Hansen.

Janko calls out to Gunari and I. We both reluctantly leave the two volunteers and stride over to Janko.

"The doctor claims this facility is paid for by the government," Janko says.

"That's what someone else told me, they probably think that is true," I say.

"Treating people no better than farm animals, performing degrading experiments on them," Gunari is quietly seething and he delivers a huge punch to the side of the doctor's head. He says something that I don't understand, possibly in French. The doctor is now barely conscious.

"How did you find me?" I say.

"After you left, we stood around unsure what to do," Janko says, "The more we stood around at Potsdamer Platz we realised that we might have sent you to your death. After the last few days we knew we couldn't do that,"

"Then we met that security guard at Stadtmitte station," Gunari says, "It didn't take long for us to obtain information from him about what goes on in this place. I don't think either of us expected to find this,"

"We saw you being taken away and the old man shouting 'Torturers!' to you and then the big fight, we were hiding behind one of the curtains,"

"So that's what he was shouting, I didn't understand the word he was using," I say. Torturers is exactly the right word.

"Did Dr Beckermann see you?" I ask and both men look surprised.

"He is here?" Gunari says.

"We didn't know, I doubt he will have seen us," Janko adds.

"He has an office at the back of the main hall," I say, "We should pay him a visit,"

"Let's tie these three up first," Gunari says and he is already on the move ripping up bed-sheets. He ties Daniel, the nurse and Hansen to a bed each and also fills their mouths with smaller bed-sheet rags.

"I hope I don't need to use this," Janko says, raising the pistol up, "Especially considering it has no bullets in it,"

I pause for a moment and then burst out laughing, a hearty laugh I needed so much.

"You have no bullets," I repeat, thinking back to when he pointed at Hansen's head.

"No, I found it at Schwarzer's house and I searched everywhere but I couldn't find any ammunition at all,"

We are about to leave the ward and head to find Beckermann when the door opens and Dr Karl Beckermann, of all people, walks straight in. His face is a picture of shock. Janko points the gun directly in his face. The arrogance he displayed to me earlier has vanished. The face reminds me of Schwarzer when we first captured him.

Dr Beckermann looks around and sees the bizarre sight of three of his staff members haphazardly tied to the furniture. Words want to pour out of his mouth but the surreality of the situation silently overpowers his urge.

"Take a seat, please," Janko says, and in a carbon copy of ten minutes ago gestures to the newly arrived doctor to sit down at the nurse's table. The big doctor forlornly slumps into the chair and again I am surprised it supports his bulk. After a minute or two of hanging his head he finally raises it up. Gunari uses more torn bed-sheets to tie him to the chair.

"You are making a big mistake gentlemen," Beckermann has regained his composure, much more convincingly than Schwarzer did in similar circumstances. Janko says nothing, Beckermann turns to Gunari who also remains silent.

"We are a medical facility sponsored by the democratically elected West German government with additional support from certain powerful NATO allies. Whatever organisation you represent, please be aware that you are undermining the progress of cures for diseases such as cancer," Beckermann, in the same pompous manner he did in his office, is preaching, "You may believe your cause is righteous and I have a lot of sympathy for people against this type of testing. Why don't we discuss it together like adults back in my office. I promise you won't find yourself in trouble,"

"I've spent my whole life in trouble," Gunari says with a laugh, "I think it may be yourself who is in major difficulties this evening, Dr Beckermann,"

Beckermann's face betrays panic, the intruders know his name. I'm not sure he expected that.

"What do you want? If you are looking for money you are in the wrong place,"

"I thought this was the right place for money?" Janko says, "Your colleague was seconds away from removing the eyeball of my friend Ana. Why would you rip away the sight of a healthy young girl?"

"I don't know where you people come from but in advanced capitalist societies humans are sovereign entities. If your friend wanted to make some money she is allowed to sell her assets and be very well rewarded,"

"Let's be frank, Dr Beckermann," Gunari interjects, "All this talking is wasting time, all we need is for you to answer one simple question or else you will find yourself in a comparable situation to your friend, the late Mr Schwarzer,"

"My late friend?" Beckermann says. The colour drains out of his face. His bloated red face is now as white as the sheets should be in this facility.

"Yes," Janko says and leans close to the doctor's face, "Unfortunately, Mr Schwarzer was reticent with regards to our questioning. One thing led to another which led to another thing which led to Mr Schwarzer ceasing to be a sentient part of our world. Now Doctor, let me be explicit, if you do not tell us what we need to know we shall kill you right here in front of your staff,"

I look around and see Hansen and the nurse are awake. They are utterly terror-stricken. Daniel the orderly is still having a snooze.

"We visited your father in Munich, Paul Beckermann. I have to say you look very much alike. Your father is friends with Dr Albert Tremmick," Janko says the name and it hangs heavy on our side and on Beckermann too who has once more lowered his head. Beckermann has the air of a man who probably knew at one point in his life, associating with a war criminal would come back and haunt him.

"Now regarding Dr Tremmick," Janko continues, "He is responsible for the mutilation and murder of many of our loved ones in the Roma community. Understandably this is not something we can tolerate. All we require from you is to confirm his address."

"I don't know where he lives, Argentina I think," Beckermann says. The atmosphere becomes even thicker. I shake my head at what I have heard. A very clever man making such a stupid comment.

"We know that is a lie and that Dr Tremmick departed Buenos Aires soon after we encountered him in the Café Tortoni," Janko says.

"Why did you lie to us?" Gunari says, "According to the Gospel of Matthew 'If your right eye causes you to sin, tear it out and throw it away.' Is that why you tore out these peoples' eyes?"

"No, no, no. What are you talking about?"

"Some people may say it caused you to sin. I am tempted to agree considering you lied to us when we asked you a question. Now, one more time, where does Tremmick live?"

Silence hangs over the room like soil over a fresh grave. Seconds pass and I see he is about to reply.

"I would never tell you, *Zigeuner*," Beckermann's bigoted defiance is remarkable. He even starts to smile at Gunari. In response Gunari lifts his hand in which he clasps a sharp medical knife. Gunari plunges the scalpel straight into Beckermann's right eye. The watching nurse squeals, as does Beckermann.

In a matter of seconds Gunari is holding Beckermann's eye up to face the remaining eye still housed in his head. Beckermann vomits down the front of his white coat. Blood courses down his face from the mangled socket and merges with the vomit to create a mottled orange mess.

I can't believe my own reaction. I simply stare at Beckermann and feel nothing for him. I'm not glad he has had impromptu eye surgery but nor do I feel any sympathy. This man is a monster.

"Shut that nurse up," Gunari says and I walk over to her. I am prepared to knock her out but she quietens as I approach and mumbles prayers to herself. On the other side of the room Hansen is staring at the floor. He is wonderfully portraying a man hoping that no one notices his presence, especially Gunari. He appears to be whispering something, possibly a prayer. Funny how the most immoral people find God at these times.

"A life of breaking your oath to help people. Why do people like you do the bidding of demons?" Janko says.

Beckermann fails to respond, he is now convulsing in the chair. The front of his coat is completely covered in the viscous blood-vomit cocktail.

"I would like to see you in this state for ever but as we mentioned earlier, we have so little time. Do you know where Dr Tremmick lives?"

Beckermann continues convulsing, he raises an arm up slightly. Is he pointing? No words come out of his mouth, globules of some sticky substance come out of his mouth.

Janko looks up at Gunari who is stood behind the doctor. Gunari uses the de-eyeballing knife and brings it across the throat of Beckermann. The fine cut is almost imperceptible but eventually a line of blood advances into a torrent that soaks the floor where Beckermann is sat.

"Let's get out of here," Gunari says.

"I think we should check his office," I say, "I think he was pointing back that way when you asked him where Tremmick lived."

The three of us walk back in to the main hall. The scene of half-chaos has continued. Two orderlies are trying to pin down an irate middle aged woman on a bed. Screams can be heard constantly, a macabre choir of the undead singing their hymns of horror.

I lead us through the hall back to Beckermann's office. Out of the corner of my eye, I am sure I see

Doktor Party. He is stood against the wall and doesn't look comfortable at all. Sadly I don't have the time to knock him out.

We enter the office and start looking around. Janko is searching through filing cabinets. Underneath a desk lamp I spot a black address book on his desk. I scour the book page by page, there doesn't seem to be a normal order to it and many of the names are written in initials.

Halfway through the book I see an interesting entry:

A T - IMFG
Więźniów Oświęcimia 20
32-603 Oświęcim
Polen

"Janko, take a look at this," I say, handing the book to him, "AT, could this be him?"

"Yes, Ana, I think it is," Janko snorts, "At least I think it gives us the best clue to find him,"

Janko hands the book back to me.

"Is this Poland? Where is Oświęcim?" I say. I have no idea if I'm pronouncing it right, "I'm confused, I thought he was in Monaco,"

"I have a feeling that the address is hidden at this location here. A sick joke by sick people,"

"How do you mean, where is it?"

"Oświęcim is the Polish translation of Auschwitz. I believe they the information we need can be found there. It is in Auschwitz where we will discover where Tremmick now lives,"

ODE OF THUNDER

Tuesday, 6 May 1986

The sultry heat has finally excised the pain in my joints. Quite honestly, I feel like I am thirty again and imagine myself taking an evening stroll around the gardens of Palermo or Recoleta. If I close my eyes, I can feel the cool breeze against my face as though I was sitting on a bench at Carlos Thays Park. The young Argentine girls would daringly wear their skirts above their knees, sometimes they would whisper to their friends and look at me. What a dream it would have been for them to be charmed and cared for by a powerful European businessman.

Those lingering glances remain seared into my mind. The dark haired girls with their lascivious hazel eyes were unlike anything I experienced as a young man in Germany. The fatherland prized homely, upstanding women who were fine as companions to social gatherings and for raising children. But they never looked at men in that sultry manner like the Latin girls did where one could feel the stirrings down below within seconds.

It would be an interesting study to see if the Southern European obsession with crudity and vulgarity was caused by a brain defect. The more I reflect on it I think it could be related to the weather. Without exception, the Mediterranean peoples are uniformly lazy and hot-headed. They struggle to focus on tasks for long periods and they are unable to work together to accomplish anything of note.

For example, the Spanish had a tough, morally conservative leader for four decades and achieved barely nothing of note compared to the glory of the Spanish empire in centuries long gone. Now Spain is nothing but a cheap holiday destination for the hardworking people of the North. It wasn't war that resulted in the Spanish existing to serve the industrious Northern Europeans but pure economics.

Europe would have no economy if it wasn't for the entrepreneurial, daring spirit of the Germanic tribes. It's not a coincidence that the greatest nations in modern history have been built on the Germanic and Scandinavian races. Anglo-Saxon is the word experts use to describe the economic revolutions that occurred in the United Kingdom, Germany and the United States. All three nations achieved greatness on the back of the same genetic code.

The phone rings. It startles me out of my reverie and I drop the glass I'm holding. The glass clanks off the top of the table and splashes me with scotch across my pale grey trousers and then rolls sadly from the table onto the floor, and cracks into a few large pieces. I pick the empty shards off the floor and place them back on to the table and cut my hand on the final piece.

"Shit!" I exclaim and pick up the telephone receiver, "Yes? What is it?"

"It's Paul," his voice sounds frail.

"How many times do I have to tell you to not ring this number? For the love of God Paul, how stupid can you be?" That's it, this is definitely the time to remove this excess baggage from my life.

"They killed Karl, Albert. They killed my boy,"

Paul says and caves in to sobbing. What is he on about, who killed Karl?

"I don't understand what you mean. Paul, calm down and tell me what has happened," I reply. Beckermann takes a few seconds to respond. I can picture him in his grubby apartment wiping tears away with his chubby fingers.

"I don't know much, I'm going to travel over there now. Two men have breached security at the clinic and murdered my boy,"

"Who was it?" I say.

"I have no idea, all I know is that they both spoke German and French. Dr Hansen phoned me up and told me a few things but he said he is going on leave Berlin today. He refused to answer my questions. He...he said that they...they ripped his eyeball straight out of the socket." Beckermann bursts into tears once again. Which is understandable if what he is saying is true.

"Who are the two men?" Beckermann doesn't respond, "Mossad agents? Homeless people? *Ossis*? Tell me Paul!"

Beckermann continues sobbing quietly. The man needs to get off the phone if he isn't going to speak. This is no way for adults to work out a productive solution. The most likely explanation is that the attackers are Mossad agents. But if they were at the clinic then that would indicate they don't know where I am or they would have come straight to me. Compared to me, the rest are small fry.

Worst case scenario is that it will take them a couple of days to discover where I am. Karl didn't have a clue where I am living so he will not have been able to give me up. Neither does Paul. Only Schwarzer knows my address and he hasn't said anything amiss on the daily phone call, although he has sounded a bit hoarse for the last couple of days.

The Israelis bandits will come hunting within a day or two. Thus, it is finally time to leave Monaco and put my exit strategy in place over the next few days. If I leave by Sunday at the latest that leaves me time to put my affairs in order.

Paul continues sobbing and I tell him that I will telephone him later on. I can't bear to listen to him crying. Each sob feels like a stabbing pain in my ear. I hang up the phone and wander to the kitchen to clean my hand up. The blood is congealing around the wound at the base of my palm. How I detest the dark kitchen with its tiny window overlooking the street. It has always reminded me of an *Einliegerwohnung*, somewhere to park an unavailing elderly relative until they die.

Times like this are a reminder that I should have emulated Verschuer and become a respectable part of the establishment. I could have made a name for myself as an internationally renowned scientist spending my life researching and writing books. I could have travelled the world and felt the spotlight upon me as the main man at conferences giving speeches and signing books. People would be hanging off my every word and politicians would be wanting photographs taken alongside me. Dr Tremmick, Germany's greatest living scientist.

Instead, I devoted my life to radical, unpopular research and kept a low profile. Some of my acquaintances said I was a madman to take so many precautions regarding my personal safety. Yet, once more, maniacs have hunted me down. And once again I will have to make an escape, hopefully with less danger than when I hurried out of the Café Tortoni twenty-five years ago. I can't help but laugh out loud at the escape I made that night.

My heightened sense of self-preservation that I possess was on high alert the moment we entered the *Peluqueria* bar. The two men from FrancoPharm were wearing the same suits as they were the day prior. They appeared surprised to see me, possibly because I was so late. A man of high esteem such as myself would never have arrived early for a meeting with a couple of up-start French braggarts.

I could smell stale sweat and it was hot inside the small room. The room felt even smaller due to the walls being covered with posters, multiple mirrors and almost-black wood panelling. I was puzzled that there was only three chairs in the room. One, at the head of the table and one on either side. Presumably I was obliged to sit in the middle with the Hernández boys by each side of me.

It meant the two men had no seat of their own. What had they been doing for the last hour? Standing around waiting for me or possibly something more sinister?

"Good evening, gentlemen," I said to the men in Spanish. They nodded in response and gestured to the three of us to sit down. The big man was very edgy, his hand touched the large scar on his neck and I became certain that I had met this man before. I could not remember where though but I knew that there was no legitimate reason for me to stay here. We took our seats and I ensured I kept my chair pulled quite far back from the table. The room was narrow and Federico and

Miguel would hopefully be able to block off any potential attacks.

The table contained a few empty boxes of drugs and a few leaflets. I stared right at the old man who simply smiled at me so I fixed my gaze on the big man. He avoided eye contact and his edgy demeanour further deadened the heavy atmosphere.

"Are you not sitting down?" I said to them in French. The two men looked at each other and started chuckling. The older man made a remark about preferring to do his business standing up. I stood up and examined the scene. My mind was very clear, this was a set up.

"No business will be completed here today," I said and sat back in the chair. The strange men glanced at each other and for a moment I could see desperation etched on their faces. At that moment Miguel must have sensed the danger as he leapt out of the chair in the direction of the bigger man.

As the fight began, I took my chance to escape. I reached the door and heard a piercing yelp. In the doorway I turned to see the scarred beast stabbing a syringe in to Miguel's neck. Miguel collapsed in to the table headfirst and on to the floor. After witnessing that, I ran out of the barbershop and back in to the main room. A couple of tango dancers were moving around in front of the stage and the male half looked annoyed as I streaked past them both.

I was aware that the music had stopped. Whether that was literally at that second or when Miguel shrieked I cannot determine. I turned around and saw the two men appear in the hall with blood dripping from their hands. The two men Federico had hired went over to attack them along with a few regulars. Staying at the cafe would be madness so I stepped out into the street.

I had the option of running towards Plaza de Mayo or Avenida 9 de Julio. I heard footsteps running towards my direction from the direction of Plaza de Mayo which caused me to hesitate. Instead of running away in the opposite direction I spotted the sign for the Piedras underground station.

Leaping down the stairs four at a time brought me to the bottom where I jumped over the ticket barrier. A train was already pulled up in the station and I boarded with seconds to spare. A man and a woman with tanned skin and a Jewish look about them were face to face with me as the doors closed. The train began to depart and the two Jews said something to each other and then ran back out upstairs out of the station.

God only knows how many agents were involved in this situation. The next station was Avenida de Mayo and I made the decision to disembark and attempt to catch a taxi. My flat in Recoleta was nowhere near any *Subte* stations and I had to return home as soon as possible. I was caught in two minds about heading back to my residence but based on the balance of probabilities the Israelis probably didn't know my actual address. Ultimately it was a risk I would have to take.

I disembarked and left the station and came out on to the immense, wide Avenida 9 de Julio. I spotted a couple of taxis not twenty metres away. Upon opening the car door I glanced behind me. What I saw could be classed as the most surreal moment in my life. The couple I had been staring at through the train window had ran up to their car which was parked directly behind the taxi I was about to enter. As they began getting in to their car they looked at me and their faces betrayed as much surprise as mine. It would have been darkly amusing if they weren't on a mission to end my life.

"Shit," I said which summed up the situation. I irrupted the taxi and ordered the driver to drive as fast as he could, and threw a large amount of pesos at him. A picture of Juan Perón had been taped on the dashboard.

"The Israelis are chasing me," I said. A risky phrase to say out loud but as he was a Peronist it seemed like a good call, on balance. The driver nodded but didn't say anything as he drastically increased his speed. I stared behind and the Israelis were attempting to stay in contact.

The taxi driver weaved in and out of traffic, horns were blaring and traffic was still heavy for nine o'clock in the evening. The nerves I felt were as bad as the night I abandoned my position at Auschwitz. The taxi driver was driving in an excellent manner, a Fangio impersonator on the streets of Buenos Aires.

"Left on Juncal!" I shouted to the driver, much louder than I wished for. As we approached the junction he swung the wheel round and narrowly missed a passing *Correo Argentino* postal van. We headed onto Juncal and then I pointed to the right. The driver heeded my instruction and turned right towards Plaza Carlos Pellegrini. I looked behind and somehow the other car was right behind us. We approached the plaza and the driver brought the car around the junction turning back on ourselves.

The Israelis saw us spin around the junction but

due to their speed they were unable to adjust and the female driver lost control. The Israelis' car pulled off the road and crashed into the side of the statue of Pellegrini. After clipping the statue the car rotated and ended up on its roof. For what seemed like the first time since entering the taxi, I took a breath. The driver then took me back home.

I arrived back at my apartment building. I handed over a huge tip to the driver, probably equal to a month's salary for the man and I bade him farewell. He firmly shook my hand and I exited the car. Even though I was still in danger I felt relaxed which was concerning to me. The adrenalin had run out since the initial attack followed by the chase through the streets of Buenos Aires.

How do you build your energies up again after that? The thought of being simply shot dead on my doorstep after escaping multiple assassins via a car chase would be rather galling. The streets were relatively busy as many of the Recoleta bars were located near my apartment. I spotted the entrance to my apartment building and it was quiet. I briskly walked to the entrance and the concierge recognised me and quickly left his desk to allow me to enter. I nodded my thanks and took a ride in the lift up to the top floor where my home was situated.

There was no one killer waiting for me at the door so I entered and checked every room. No one was lurking under the bed or in the bath so I packed my belongings I needed in a small black suitcase. My savings were safe in a bank in Switzerland and my mission was to make it there and set plans in motion for a new start in a new country. A surge of nausea struck my belly and

I ran to the bathroom and hurled into the sink.

The pain of the heave was nothing in comparison to the anguish I was feeling about my departure. I was unable to fight the tears back and within seconds I was howling. A mixture of tears and wailing. For how long was I to be punished for my past? Fifteen years of building a new life and helping people in the city and this is my reward. To be chased around my home city by a bunch of worthless Middle Eastern vermin.

My telephone started ringing so I cleaned my mouth up and jogged back into the living room. I picked the phone up but I refrained from speaking.

"Albert? Albert?" a voice spoke. I recognised the voice but I was too afraid to respond, "Albert, it's Federico,"

"Federico," I exhaled, it was rare for him to call me Albert and not Alfonso. A sure sign of the severity of the night's state of affairs, "Where is Miguel?"

"He's dead, they killed him,"

"I'm sorry Federico, this is all due to me,"

"Don't talk like that. It's the fault of the killers and nobody else. Where are you?"

"I'm at home, I was pursued through the city by more Jews. They ended up flipping their car over. I'm leaving tonight, Federico,"

"Leaving where?"

"Buenos Aires. Argentina. I cannot remain here anymore,"

"Don't say that Albert, we can work it out,"

"Unfortunately, young man, we can't fight the resources that our opponents have. My time here in Argentina is drawing to a close. Can I ask a favour Federico?"

"Of course Albert, I owe you everything,"

"Can you drive me to Brazil?"

"I'll be there in twenty minutes,"

Federico hung the phone up and it took a massive effort to re-start packing. In my bedroom I had a set of clothes ready for this situation so it took little time. Above my drawers was a photograph. A picture of Sebastián and I along with Federico and Miguel at the park. We are all about to go rowing together. That was a great day, one where I had no remembrance of the past, only thoughts of the future.

It was the only photograph I took with me. The boys were my family and now Miguel had been slain. My only hope then was that Federico would not be next. For the one and only time in my life I was ready to place my body on the line to protect somebody else. At that point I would have killed every single person in South America to keep Federico safe.

Fifteen minutes later, I looked out of my window and saw the Carabela parked outside. I could see Federico in the driver's seat smoking a cigarette. For a moment I can't peel my eyes away from the young man, a man whose brother had been slain an hour before. I am sure there father did not tell them the truth about where I came from, although no doubt they would have ideas about my origins. Yet they both showed unfailing loyalty to me. I loved those boys so much. I slammed my hand down on the table by the window then composed myself.

I was dressed in a generic workman's overalls and cap. It wasn't much of a disguise but it could have potentially bought me a vital minute. I smudged a small amount of shoe polish above my upper lip, only a tiny dab to give me a slightly dark hue. I departed from my home carrying a suitcase and a briefcase. A decade and a half of labour and this is all I had to show for it.

The concierge looked at me oddly as I walked past and I took my things out into the street. Federico got out of the car and helped put my belongings in the back of the car. Federico sat back in the car while I waited for a moment savouring the nighttime ambience of Recoleta. A couple of men walked past me and made eye contact. Were they Mossad? I was ready to strike back at them but they continued walking towards my apartment building. I had no idea then or now if they were neighbours or enemies.

I was seeing everything as a threat, a souring of the most wonderful moments of my life. My time in Buenos Aires was up. I sat in the car beside Federico and we began the long drive along the route of death past Zarate, over the *Puente La Balsa* and then towards Concordia. It was morning by the time we crossed the border into Brazil. After a night spent at a cheap hotel in Uruguaiana, Federico drove me to Porto Alegre where with help from friends in the German community I arranged flights back to Europe and bade farewell to South America.

JEITINHO
Wednesday, 7 May 1986

"On the way to Berlin I was speaking to Gunari about Nuri," I say, the traffic jam outside Wrocław shows no sign of abating. Four lanes of traffic edging forward at a semi-glacial rate of one metre a minute. Janko maintains an impassive forward gaze.

"What did he tell you?" Janko finally speaks after a couple of minutes and metres.

"He told me about how you helped her and her mum. She became your new recruit. The one I replaced,"

Janko is keeping his eyes on the car in front of us. His eyes are watering, his cheeks reddening. Janko's face is a picture of pure sadness.

"Do you miss her?" I say.

"Every day, Ana. I think about her every day," Janko is now smiling which alleviates the uncomfortable feeling in the car. The car in front creeps forward a few more metres. Janko refrains from following and he sighs.

"Nuri was a formidable woman," Janko says.

He is looking out of the driver's side window. Whether he is watching the passing tram or thinking about some point in the past it is hard to tell, "She was in charge pretty soon after she arrived in our group. I think she had found her *raison d'être* with us and she thrived."

"The boss of you two?" I say and giggle, "I find

that hard to imagine,"

"Oh yes. Věštec died in sixty-nine following complications from pneumonia. Towards the seventies most of the Nazis has been eliminated. We spent most of our time correcting the behaviour of small town bigots all over the place. She was tremendously organised and Gunari and I learnt a lot from her in that respect.

"She even helped recruit members for another cell of Roma, based in Northern Europe and Britain. By the late seventies we had eleven members in three groups across Europe, the most since before Napoleon's time.

"It was coming up to ten years since we eliminated our last Nazi. It was a decade since Nuri had sliced Luburić's throat open in Spain. Have you heard of Otmar von Verschuer?"

I shake my head and even though Janko isn't looking directly at me, he understands that I have no idea who this guy is.

"Along with Mengele, Verschuer was the big brain behind the Nazis eugenics programme. He was descended from European nobility, he had that innate sense of superiority that defines those people. I've seen it a lot in my time. Arrogance and entitlement - not a good combination.

"Josef Mengele was a student of his for a time and during the war Verschuer was firmly involved in the experiments that were going on at Auschwitz. He was a strident advocate of forced sterilisation of people with mental illnesses, epilepsy, the blind and the deaf and other so-called 'undesirables'.

"And after the war, do you know what happened

to him?" A stiff laugh comes out of Janko's mouth.

"No," I reply.

"He was fined six-hundred old Reichsmarks for his part in the war. Verschuer attempted to destroy the records of his activities. He subsequently became a professor in West Germany specialising in the study of genetics. A much more palatable title for the distinguished scientist. He was lauded everywhere for his contributions,"

"That's shocking,"

"It's true, we knew that the Israelis had been contemplating killing him for years but the Americans had dissuaded them. Ultimately, we felt we had to take action. We had received reports on his wartime work from trusted sources. It was not pleasant to speak to people who had been maimed and scarred as part of his trials,"

"So what did you do?"

"He had retired as a professor in nineteen sixty-five but he was still living in Münster not far from the border with the Netherlands. In all honesty he wasn't difficult to find and spy on. One evening in sixty-nine I believe, we headed to his house. A warm summer evening, not unlike the night when we met you, Gunari tampered with his brakes and that was all it took.

"The morning after, Verschuer sped out of his driveway on to the main road. By the time he hit the ring road his BMW raced off. We followed at a distance which was all we could do considering the speed he was going. He had virtually disappeared out of sight when we heard an almighty smash.

"Seconds later we saw that his car had veered straight off the road on a curved incline. The car had slammed into a tree not twenty metres from the road-side. The front was horribly compressed. I couldn't believe it. Most likely, he died on impact, no one could have survived that crash. The speed he hit the tree at must have been phenomenal.

"We pulled over, Nuri ran to check he was dead. He was as dead as anyone would be after ploughing in to that tree. Nuri tossed a letter in the car which stated '600 Marks is not justice' and threw in six one-hundred Mark notes.

"When the story hit the media there was no mention of the note and nor was there any mention of Verschuer's Nazi past." Janko turns to me and shrugs.

"How old was he?" I ask.

"Seventy-three I believe," Janko replies, "There is no statute of limitations for crimes against humanity,"

Is killing old men a worthwhile exercise? It does seem as though we are picking on an easy target, even one with a dubious background. But, if you look at his old pal Tremmick, they were both behind gruesome research. And in Tremmick's case it is still ongoing.

Finally the traffic starts to flow and Janko parks up on a quiet side street. We walk for a few minutes until we enter a large square. Surrounding the square are beautiful tall townhouses in different pastel shades. They remind me of the cover of a book I owned as a little girl which was filled with fairy-tales.

We take seats at one of the many cafes outside on the square. I am ravenous so I immediately start reading the menu. Although the spelling is very different to Slovenian, the Slavic root means many of the Polish words are recognisable.

"I'd recommend *pierogi*, they are filled dumplings. A real speciality here." Janko is now the resident Polish food expert.

I saw it on the menu but I didn't understand what the word meant. We would call them *cmoki* back home. I allow Janko to order for us both.

"So you ran out of Nazis to kill? It's like the cowboys and the buffalos," I say. Talking is helping my stomach from rumbling too much.

"Yes, I suppose we did. What you might label the box office targets disappeared. Nuri maybe became bored and she started to research Dr Josef Mengele after reading an article about the discovery of him living in Argentina.

"It's ironic when you think about it. We were on the verge of killing Tremmick, and failing. At the same time, ten kilometres away in another part of Buenos Aires, an equally vile Nazi, the Angel of Death himself was working as a carpenter,"

"You could have knocked off two for the price of one," I say.

"Wouldn't that have been something? We could have gone public for that!"

Our food arrives, I start shovelling it down my mouth immediately while Janko picks his fork up and then puts it down again.

"The Mossad had been struggling to find Mengele's location after he had been deported from Argentina and moved to Paraguay. He was the most famous fugitive in the world but no one could find his new whereabouts.

"Nuri started investigating and realised that the best chance of finding him would be if there was still a link to Europe. She found nothing from looking in to his family. Eventually, Nuri and I spent a year in Germany systematically researching everything about his life. We looked into the background of hundreds of associates, no matter how tenuous the connection.

"Eventually, we were looking in to an agricultural company Karl Mengele & Sons, the family business based in a town in Bavaria called Günzberg. A name cropped up that rang a distant bell in my head. A man named Hans Sedlmeier who worked for the company. I racked my brain for a while but it came up with nothing. I travelled back to the house in Savoy and literally the first notebook I pulled up, I found it.

"Sedlmeier was part of the Odessa network, in fact I had met the man on multiple occasions. A rustic, rough-spoken man. Tough as oak, and a devout Nazi who felt betrayed by Hitler's failings. He was one of the risk takers for Odessa. He would drive some of the escaping Nazis to various ports to depart for South America.

"I phoned up Nuri who was in Munich and I told her where to go. One evening she broke into the factory and found his office. In an unlocked draw she found sheets of documents showing payments made to a Brazilian bank, and some codes. She noted these down and brought them back to Savoy.

"We took them to an expert in cryptography in Paris. He was a professor, a very distinguished man and he deciphered them. He was almost certain they were a set of coordinates. Further investigation showed that they were in a location near São Paulo in Brazil. We didn't want to become too excited but we knew this was our chance.

"The three of us caught a plane to Brazil in the New Year of seventy-nine. Our experience of air travel wasn't much more advanced since our ill-fated trip to Argentina nearly two decades prior. However Gunari and I were ready to handle anything and with Nuri with us we felt unstoppable.

"We flew from Madrid. It was strange leaving the winter snow of home and arriving in the heat of the Brazilian summer. The contrasts that Gunari and I experienced in Argentina compared to old Europe in nineteen-sixty were ramped up beyond belief. São Paulo reminded me of those American TV shows like Starsky and Hutch. It was beyond glamorous. There were huge skyscrapers everywhere and wide roads filled with cars. You can't comprehend how big Brazil is. Everything was on a scale five times as big as Europe. And the women, oh my, I fell in love more times in the first day than you could count.

"After battling through Brazilian bureaucracy and their almost non-existent public city plans we found out that the coordinates matched a suburb called Eldorado a few miles south of the city centre. Mengele was renting a house from Hunagrian friends and using the pseudonym Wolfgang Gerhard. We located the house which seemed to be surrounded by a rainforest. It was only a small, yellow wooden house,"

"And was he there?" I finish my last mouthful of dumpling and Janko continues:

"No, we waited outside for two days and saw no one. After that we broke in and found a letter from a couple he was friends with, the Bosserts. They had invited him on holiday to a town called Bertioga. We pulled the map out and saw it was a couple of hours away. The Bosserts had helpfully noted the address where they would be staying.

"We drove straight there that day. Gunari was sure that he would probably be driving back past us but Nuri told him to be quiet. We arrived in the evening and spent the night at a hotel. In the morning we found the apartment they were staying at, which was located virtually on the beach.

"We staked out the house under the guise of sun worshippers on the beach. After a few hours we finally caught a glimpse of the three of them having some food on the terrace. We had heard that he had had reconstructive surgery to change his appearance but we knew it was him. All three of us were certain.

"Nuri wanted to kill the Bosserts along with Mengele. Gunari and I vetoed that idea. We were there for Mengele, not for mass murder. Nuri conceded and said she will kill him. As we discussed the best way to kill him Mengele walked past us on the way to swim in the sea,"

"He walked straight past you?" I say.

"It's true, Mengele couldn't have been more than ten metres away. He didn't notice anything strange, he kept walking on confidently to the sea. Nuri spotted her opportunity, she stripped to her bikini and followed Mengele to the water, she hid a syringe in her hand filled with sodium cyanide that we had smuggled in from Europe.

"I wanted to take a closer look but Gunari held me back. Nuri came back to us after a couple of minutes and said 'It's done. We should go'. We packed our stuff up and headed straight for the airport. The news of Mengele's death would not come out for six years,"

"Why would that be the case?"

"The Bosserts had him buried under his new name and the Brazilian dictatorship had no interest in making the news public. It wasn't until last year that the West German police raided Sedlmeier's office in Günzberg and discovered letters from Bossert informing him of Mengele's passing,"

"How did Nuri kill him?" I ask, wondering why Janko would miss out the most vital part of the story.

"It was only when we were on the plane back that she told us what happened. She waded out to where he stood in the water. She said he seemed to be looking into the distance. She swam up right behind him and said to him: 'Dr Mengele?'.

"The man who was known as Wolfgang Gerhard turned round and he once again became the Angel of Death. She said he smiled at her. She knew it was him without a shadow of a doubt, Nuri had done so much research she knew his face better than her own. Even with plastic surgery, she was adamant it was him.

"She jabbed the syringe in to his neck and let the poison flow. Mengele tried grasping at her but it was too late. Nuri easily brushed him off, Mengele ripped out the syringe and tried making his way to shore. Nuri watched him as he struggled in the water, waves were breaking over his body and he wasn't making progress. Finally his body disappeared from view and Nuri headed back to us,"

"There's a chance he might not have died, he may have reached the shore and used an antidote," I say.

"Possibly. His body was exhumed a few weeks before we first met Ana. That's when it was confirmed that he had died in seventy-nine. His acolytes tried to claim he died of a stroke but we knew the real cause of death. We had spread the word in the community that we had eliminated him and this was our vindication.

"And also it spurred a lot more calls to us for help. Meeting you turned in to a happy coincidence,"

"Every cloud..." I say but my thoughts are drifting away to visiting one of the most notorious places in the history of humanity tomorrow.

THE BEAUTY THAT REMAINS

Thursday, 8 May 1986

"I know this sounds silly Janko, but I'm nervous about visiting Auschwitz," I say. I can't help but embarrassingly look out of the bus window. Janko emits a short chuckle.

"There's nothing there now that can hurt you," Janko replies, "but it may lead you to question everything that you believe which makes you human,"

"Why didn't we drive it here?" I say, the chatter on the bus from Polish schoolkids is turning my brain to mush.

"I'm hoping we can find what we need and leave. If we drove we would probably have to stay over as I can't do too much driving these days. The less time I spend there the better,"

"But you have never been before?"

"Without wanting to sound sarcastic Ana but when you have seen one concentration camp before in your life, you don't want to rush back to see another one, even an empty one,"

"Gunari spent time in Auschwitz, didn't he?" I say. I wish I hadn't said it but I have to keep talking.

"Yes," Janko replies, "He was originally in a camp called Marzahn, near Berlin after they seized his family from France. They were all taken to Auschwitz in nineteen forty-four. Gunari managed to escape after a few weeks. He never saw his family again after that,"

That comment finally brings to contemplative silence. For a few seconds anyway.

"So what did he do? He must have been young?"

"Yes, he was only eleven or twelve when he escaped,"

"And he never saw his family again. Poor Gunari, no child deserves that,"

"No child should ever be in that situation. He has only told me little pieces of information over the years, I think he told Nuri in more detail but I don't believe he was able to open his heart like that to another man. He tries to be brave and he is brave but you can't bottle your feelings up inside of you. It's not healthy,"

"How did he meet you?" I ask, I'm not sure why I never asked it before. For some reason I assumed they had always known each other. The time I have spent in Germany feels as long as the previous eighteen years of my life. Funny how you view time.

"Gunari made quite a name for himself over the years in the Roma community. Ultimately he became a bare knuckle prize fighter. He would box all over Europe and gained quite a reputation.

"We knew of him, word travels fast in our community about Roma boxers when they are travelling around. His fights would always attract large numbers of Roma followers. Over three thousand people saw him fight once outside Lyon. I witnessed him fight for over half an hour against a huge African in Marseille. The more he fought, the more his scar on his neck would glow bright red.

"Finally, Věštec and I visited him after a fight in

Turin. A Sinti champion from Hungary had given him quite the beating. His face was a mess when we met him outside his lodgings. He was holding a slab of meat over his right eye so I made a joke asking him if he was eating that steak later. I wasn't sure if he was going to punch me but instead he cracked back about bringing out some peppercorn sauce.

"Gunari spoke to us about his life after the war. Travelling around fighting most nights for a little bit of cash. It was a tough life and even at twenty-six he looked almost forty. In fact he looks the same as he does now, he's finally grown into his lumpy face.

"He is much more intelligent than he gives himself credit for. Our work requires strength and bravery, of course. But most importantly it requires cunning and cleverness. Traits that I see in you too, Ana,"

I blush at the complement and I notice the bus has gone past the road sign indicating we are now in Oświęcim. The sun blinds me through the windows. A beautiful day to visit such an infamous place of darkness.

The town is surprisingly clean and pleasant. I was under the mad assumption that the town would be dour and depressing but it looks like any other normal town. The chatter on the bus is still continuing but quieter than it was for most of the journey.

Janko gives me a slight nudge and says "We're approaching now,"

Green fields are on both sides and ahead I see an austere low-rise brick building topped with a three-storey tower with an archway in the middle. The bus parks up outside and the schoolkids bounce off the bus with the teachers saying hushed words to them. Presumably trying to knock some sombreness into them.

Janko stays sitting after everyone has disembarked. He is holding the headrest of the seat in front, his arm rigid.

"Are you OK, Janko?" I ask. Janko's face has a dreamy look about it.

"Yes Ana, I'm feeling my age a little bit, that's all," the dreaminess of his face has now turned to that of a tired man, "It may be better if you go on ahead. Take it in by yourself. I need a little time to myself for a few minutes,"

I don't think Janko is going to go in at all. I realise that the memories of the Second World War are still incredibly vivid for the people of his generation. I nod and squeeze his shoulder and then hop over him and off the bus.

I didn't notice it on the bus but it grabs my attention immediately: the railway line that goes under the archway only yards from me. I stand under the arch and kneel down to touch the railway.

Hundreds of thousands of people transported along this line to their doom. The wonders of technology used not to better the lives of people but to exterminate them. For the Jews it was the Holocaust. The word used by Gunari and Janko to describe it for the Roma is *Porajmos* - The Devouring. And this is the heart of it where they attempted to remove every Roma from the planet, to destroy our culture, our bodies and our humanity.

Gunari and his family were forced from their lives in the South of France, taken by train to Germany and then to here. I have to sit down for a few moments to prevent me fainting. A couple of the schoolchildren walk past talking excitedly, we exchange looks and they walk off embarrassed.

Until I was taken away my Roma roots were not a defining feature of my personality. I saw myself as an average Yugoslavian kid. Naturally, I knew I was Roma but we were settled, my dad working on the buses. There was the odd incident and the occasional hateful word but nothing that resulted in me fully embracing my Roma identity.

Even after the little incident of burning down my headteacher's house it was an act of defiance for my own reasons. It wasn't an act of political violence, one for all of the gypsies. It was my battle as an individual. My small world, all that I knew.

Now nearly a year later I am here, walking around Auschwitz-Birkenau. Words from text books. Almost swear words. The way that certain place-names evoke a sense of humanity's most destructive impulses: Stalingrad, Hiroshima, Beirut.

I am overwhelmed by it all. The scale of this place is immense, industrial-sized. The sun is blazing down yet the air hangs heavy. The red squat buildings add to the feeling of dread that pushes your shoulders to the floor. It isn't only being here at Auschwitz but everything I have experienced in the last few days. I close my eyes and I see Schwarzer's face at the point his life extinguished. What was going on in his head in those last few seconds?

I don't know how long I am sat on the grass outside of the ruins of Crematorium III. I expected to be shocked by Auschwitz but it is a different type of distress than I first anticipated. It's the extent of the whole enterprise that staggers me. State apparatus used to such a macabre end. How could anyone fight against that?

"Hey, are you OK?" a voice speaks in English to me. I look up and a gangly, bespectacled man not much older than me, is standing over me. He is wearing khaki shorts and a dark green woolen jumper. I don't think it's jumper weather today.

"Hello," I say, unsure what else to say.

"Taking a breather?" he says. I have no idea what 'a breather' is but he is being friendly so I'm guessing it's not an insult, "I guess there aren't many benches to sit on here,"

I laugh a little at the joke, it's not the most cheerful of places so some levity is appreciated.

"No, I'll have a look for a suggestion box later," I reply and the boy finds it amusing enough to laugh. He motions next to me and I wave an open arm, inviting him to plonk himself down.

"My name is Jacob," he says offering a hand to which I shake gingerly, "What is your name?"

"I am Ana, is this your first time visiting here?" I say and straight away I realise it may be the stupidest question I have ever asked.

"No it's not, I'm studying here. The Israeli government pays for Jewish students to research here from around the world. I am from the United States - Philadelphia, Pennsylvania. Have you heard of it?"

"Philadelphia," I almost yell, "That's where Rocky is from!" Once again I embarrass myself with my gaucheness. I'd hate to see how red my face is.

"That's the one!" Jacob laughs at me, again in a friendly way, "He's our most famous citizen,"

"Have you run up the steps?"

"I think everyone in Philly has run up the steps singing the theme music," Jacob says, "But I've yet to punch any hanging slabs of meat in the back of an abattoir. So where are you from Ana?"

"I am originally from Yugoslavia, do you know it?"

"Of course, I was in Zagreb earlier this year when I travelled around Europe. It's very beautiful,"

"It is beautiful," A sharp pang of homesickness hits me and makes me teary. I can't hold back and I begin to cry. I don't know if it is possible for me to be more embarrassing. Jacob puts an arm around me and I sink into the nook of his neck and sob.

"You're not the only person to have this reaction here Ana,"

"It's not that," I say, "Actually, it is a little bit. But, it's everything else. I'm sorry, you've only just met me,"

"Come on, let's go for a coffee. My office is five minutes away,"

We walk off towards Jacob's office and he keeps his arm around me. I can barely hold my snotty head high. I can't face the contrast of the bleak camp with the dazzling bright sky.

WISE GUIDANCE, WAGING WARS

Thursday, 8 May 1986

Jacob pours me coffee into a mug. He hands it to me and he sits on the end of his desk. I sit in his comfy looking chair. Upon sitting down, I realise it's not as comfy as it first appears. One side of the mug says 'How does Moses make his coffee?' One the other, it is written 'Hebrews it'.

"I'm researching the eugenicists and the experiments they performed. It's fascinating but it can be hard going. I have cried more times in the two months since I arrived here than in all of the rest of my life I would say. If I could persuade every teenager to visit here I would do,"

"Maybe," I say, shrugging my shoulders.

"You don't think so?" Jacob's right eyebrow is comically high.

"I don't know. I think you might be an idealist,"

"So young and so cynical," Jacob teases. His eyebrow resets position to neutral, "You seem wired,"

"What does that mean?"

"It means you seem on edge, nervous almost,"

"It's been an interesting few days," I say, raising my own quizzical eyebrow.

"Why, what has happened?"

I refrain from mentioning crashing in to a German postal van, stabbing a man to death and witnessing the grotesque experiments at a subterranean neo-Nazi facility.

"A few ups and downs," I say. Jacob smiles and allows a silence to fall on us. It isn't uncomfortable, in fact it is quite nice to be sitting with someone around my age. Jacob walks around the desk to the visitor's chair and sits down. He's so angular that the act of him sitting down is performed in such ungainly manner it's almost charming.

"I know how you feel," Jacob is smiling and I notice that I am smiling in return. I immediately feel foolish again and put my head down and stare at my coffee, "Are you Jewish, Ana?"

"No I'm not. I am Roma,"

"Oh jeepers, I call the Roma the forgotten victims of the Nazis,"

"We haven't forgotten," I whisper, "We will never forget,"

"No, neither will we,"

Quiet fills the room, conversation has again halted but once more it's not awkward. We both seem to be in contemplation. Behind Jacob, I notice there are photos on the walls of the office. In fact, they are the only real decoration save for the usual office clutter.

I walk over to the photos for a better look. Black and white photos of a young man on his wedding day, a girl riding a bicycle with other children chasing her, a middle aged couple looking uptight on a spotless sofa. It must be a very old photo, you only see that level of pursed formality in the early days of photography. It's almost as if they think if they smile, God will burst out of the camera and zap them for displaying such brazen pride.

"My grandparents," Jacob says, turning round in the chair towards me.

"Were they taken here?" I ask, yet I feel I already knowing the answer.

"Yes, two of my grandparents were gassed to death here at Auschwitz. My mother's parents were taken after Operation Barbarossa that saw the Germans overrun the Soviet Union. They were taken from their house in Minsk in the summer of forty-one only a day after they had told their daughter and her husband to flee. Thus my parents made the decision to leave the city.

"On my father's side, his parents were living in a village on the outskirts of Minsk. They hid for months before being discovered by the *Einsatzgruppen*. They were both executed on the spot and thrown into a mass grave along with hundreds of other Jews. They shot everyone, old people, pregnant women, children. Everyone,"

Another long silence falls over the room. Once more these horrific moments are reduced down to single sentences. Words can never convey the fear his grandparents must have felt wondering when the Nazis would show up. Or those moments when they were discovered. What must have gone on in their heads when they were lined up to be shot? Was it the same things spinning through their brains as Ginesty in Lyon?

"That is terrible, I never knew my grandparents. They had all died before I was born. Although my dad's father died when my mum was pregnant with me."

"My mother and father could never overcome what happened here. They grew up in Minsk. The Jewish population was very large at the time. Many of the cities in Eastern Europe had majority Jewish populations but you don't hear much of that history in schools in those places now.

"My folks escaped to America after reaching St Petersburg. Only eighteen years old and not speaking a word of English. It's amazing that they were allowed in. The U.S. didn't recognise what was happening in Europe as genocide. Only a few thousand Jews were allowed in during the War itself. But, somehow they managed to make into the United States which they were forever grateful.

"Minsk was always at the centre of their hearts. They never called Philadelphia home, it was always Minsk. They worked so hard to make ends meet. Initially, they relied on charity after arriving in New York. The two of them began working in a hotel on the Lower East Side where they lived. My father worked as a porter and my mother was a cleaner. A year or two later they heard that a distant cousin had opened a hotel in Philadelphia. They moved there and worked their way up and eventually my father co-owned the hotel.

"I think they always assumed they would return to what they called home. My mother passed away last year and her last words were 'the trip is never too hard, if you know you're going home.' At the time I didn't know what she meant but after spending time here I am beginning to understand.

"They were never convinced by the concept of the Israeli state. My father has always held the belief that people can live together in harmony,"

"But you don't feel the same way?"

"No."

"As simple as that?"

"Maybe once I believed it. I don't think the Jews will ever be safe in this world. History tells us that. Things may never be as bad as the Holocaust again but anti-Semitism always rises. A politician needs a scapegoat and he blame the Jews. A politician needs an easy answer to a complex question and he endorses killing the Jews, a politician craves money and he takes it from the Jews. And very rarely does anyone else stand against this."

Jacob is probably right. The powerful will always act in their own interest, no matter how dehumanising or abhorrent that can be. It is a depressing thought, the hopeless human condition.

"I'm sorry Ana, I often start ranting about this to people," Jacob laughs nervously.

"It's OK, I have friends who are exactly like that." I say. I realise that Jacob's research may be linked to our search, "Have you ever heard of a man called Albert Tremmick?"

He raises a delightful eyebrow and beckons me over. Jacob picks up a folder that is lying on the desk. He opens it up and it contains many A4-sized photos inside plastic sheets. He turns to a page with a black and white photo of a smirking man in an overcoat.

His hair is full and dark, a hint of lines are developing on the forehead. A square jaw and chubby cheeks. He could be mistaken for a neighbourhood barber if it wasn't for his eyes. They are round balls of emptiness, conveying zero compassion. Jacob clears his throat and begins talking:

"Dr Tremmick, alumnus of Ludwig Maximilian University of Munich worked at Auschwitz after spells at Dieselstrasse and Ravensbrück concentration camps. He was obsessed with the human brain. Many of his experiments were incredibly cruel and painful. He was known to have performed brain surgery on patients without anaesthetic. He had a bunch of madcap ideas relating to ethnicity and brain shapes. His brand of eugenics quickly fell out of favour after the war.

"Josef Mengele was known as the Angel of Death and the head of the programme but Verschuer and Tremmick were both big hitters. Our research in recent years has brought to light a lot more about the last two. We call the three of them the Unholy Trinity here at the museum,"

"Only one out of three left," I mutter to myself. Jacob looks at me quizzically. I hold his gaze and he doesn't look away. I'm not sure what is happening here. Is this that moment you see in the movies when a couple realise they fancy each other? I doubt that generally happens whilst chatting about genocide but I'll take what I can get.

"Mengele died in Brazil and Verschuer was killed in Germany. Tremmick is the last to survive,"

"If he's still alive,"

"He's alive," I say, "His work hasn't finished. Not yet,"

Jacob continues to peer at me in a very strange way. I have said too much already, I need to meet Janko and find that address.

"I know the Mossad heard he was in Berlin in eighty-one, he would be in his seventies by now,"

"His age doesn't absolve his sins,"

"Oh, I agree Ana. One hundred percent,"

"How did you know the Mossad were aware he

was in Berlin?"

"Do you think I'm an Israeli spy?" Jacob finds the notion very amusing, "It was leaked in the Israeli press, I think they thought that because he was on the run it might shake a few apples from the tree,"

"OK," I'm unsure about the relevance of the trees and apples, "That makes sense. So they don't know where he is now?"

"Well I've read nothing in *Haaretz*. Maybe the Mossad are keeping it quiet. Do you know where he is? Is the Romani Mossad chasing him?"

"Who knows, maybe they already caught him?" I say and wink at Jacob. Jacob laughs and pours us both another cup of coffee.

"My mother told me to not drink more than one cup of Joe a day. Oh boy, if she knew how many mugs a day I knock back now! So tell me Ana, how did a young Yugoslavian girl find her way to Poland?"

"By bus," I say, "I've been travelling around. I came from Berlin yesterday,"

"Wow, you must be sick of the border checks in the Eastern Bloc. I was questioned a few times for being American,"

"It's OK. All my documents appear to be fine. Talking of documents, do you have any documents about the Roma and Albert Tremmick?"

"I do. In fact, I have quite a lot of information," Jacob walks to a filing cabinet, opens the middle drawer and pulls out a couple of large books. "Are you looking for something in particular? A family member perhaps?"

"I'm looking on behalf of a friend."

"The second book was compiled by Rachel, who

used to work here. She was an expert on Tremmick and his experiments. I mentioned before he had a thing for brains. I hope you don't mind me going into detail about what he did?"

"No, it's fine," I reply, despite my massive misgivings.

"He was truly obsessed by the brain. He had a theory of brains that ethnicity and nationality affected the size and shape of brains. He thought gypsies had the smallest brains. I hope I don't offend you Ana,"

"It's fine," I wave an impatient hand, "Tell me please,"

"His belief was that the Roma were intrinsically criminal. He thought he would find some evidence that would support it. Similarly he had a belief that Jews were congenitally preconditioned towards dishonesty and deceit. His hypothesis was that Jews would have some odd part of the brain shaped differently to ethnically 'pure' Germans. That gypsies would have something similar poking out or poking in,"

"It's crazy," I say. This man was clearly insane.

"At the time, these theories weren't too outlandish. Even in America the study of eugenics was commonplace. Lots of states practised sterilisation to prevent certain undesirables from breeding,"

I start leafing through the pages from Rachel's book. One of the books underneath is an index of names. It appears to be photocopied pages of the actual Nazi files for when people were taken here.

I flick to nineteen forty-four and start scanning for names. It takes a couple of minutes and I find out what I was hoping for. Or maybe I was hoping not to see it.

A registration document about Gunari's family. A black triangle has been coloured in the corner. It lists his parents Marie Daniel and Michel Daniel and their children and ages: Claire, age three; Pali, age six; Duriya, age nine; Gunari, age eleven and Nadia, age thirteen.

A gasp escapes me. It's strange seeing this all written down. I compare the details to Rachel's book on the off chance that I can find a link.

If ever I wanted to remain in ignorance, it is now. I see that Tremmick performed an experiment on Pali Daniel, the younger sister of my friend Gunari. The experiment consisted of electrical shocks being applied to the little girl's brain to see if it would stimulate brain function. The girl lasted five hours of shocks and mental acuity tests before the largest shock proved too much for her.

I begin crying and Jacob puts his arm around my shoulders and tells me everything is going to be OK. The total opposite seems more likely. I'm not sure I'll ever feel OK again. I continue weeping in to Jacob's chest. This monster Tremmick is going to hell and I will be the one to put him there. After a few minutes I manage to compose myself.

"Do you have a photocopier?" I pull away from Jacob despite a great internal urge to stay in his arms forever and attempt to suppress the tears.

Jacob nods and helps me to copy some of the files. He doesn't tell me it's forbidden to copy the documents. At the copier my hands shake putting paper in the machine. Jacob puts his hand on mine and gives it a quick squeeze. A small gesture but a reminder of the humanity available to all if we choose it.

REBELLION AND RESURRECTION

Thursday, 8 May 1986

I take the documents from Jacob and we stare at each other. Something rolls in my belly, whether it's cramp or lust I can't tell. Jacob isn't conventionally good looking, he is pretty much what I would expect a postgraduate history student to look like. But his gawky face with its big ears and nose is very endearing.

"Thank you Jacob," I say. I can't say anything else. The only other things I could mention would sound trite or stupid. He smiles broadly, flashing his shiny American teeth and rubs my shoulders. I walk towards the door to depart the office.

"Do you actually think Tremmick is still alive?" Jacob says.

"I'm ninety-nine per cent sure he's still around," I say turning back round to face him. Jacob is caught up in thought, a frown creasing his forehead.

"Hopefully someone will catch up with him one day and give him what he deserves," Jacob says.

"I wouldn't mind reading that headline in the newspaper. I'll keep an eye on the Israeli press for updates,"

"Goodbye Ana," Jacob says, his frown deepening. I nod and head out of the office and a few seconds later I am back outside in the blazing heat of the camp. It doesn't take long to find Janko, I didn't think he'd stay on the bus all day.

Janko is stood on a path seemingly looking out to nowhere. I join him in contemplating endless nothingness. The sun is now resting as low as the buildings. Janko notices my arrival and raises his hand slightly. He seems so frail today, I want to take him away from all of this. We stay looking at the great void for quite a few minutes.

"Have you seen Gunari's tattoos on his arms?" Janko says.

"Yeah, they're a bit messy. I think he changed his mind halfway through and got new designs,"

"In a way Ana, that's what he did. When Gunari and his family and the rest of the Roma arrived by train they were forced to take a communal bath. They were forced to sew black triangles in to their clothing to indicate their 'asocial' status. Finally, they were tattooed on their left forearms. The letter 'Z' for *Zigeuner*, the German word gypsy, preceded his number, 10625. I can still remember it.

"He was only a child when he arrived so as he got older the tattoo increased in size. He kept the tattoo as a reminder during his boxing career but when he joined our cause the first thing he did was obliterate it. You may not have noticed it but it's a Romani translation of a bible quote,"

"That doesn't surprise me," I say, "What does it say?"

"'The memory of the righteous is blessed, But the name of the wicked will rot.'" Janko turns towards me and fiercely hugs me. I am taken aback by the spontaneity and vehemence of the gesture.

"Are you OK Janko, are you tired?" I say.

"I'm fine Ana. I'm thinking about Gunari and his escape and that is giving me strength,"

"How did he escape from here?"

"Take a look at this place today Ana. Everything is still, like a photograph. I see it as a place beyond history, beyond time. If you came here during the war, this whole camp was a hive of noise and activity from early morning to late at night. People would be taken off to forced labour from four or five in the morning until the evening. These camps held thousands of people living in enforced squalor.

"In the May of forty-four, there was an attempt by the SS to exterminate everyone in the *Zigeunerfamilienlager*, the Gypsy Family Camp. The guards were not prepared for the ferocity of the response from prisoners. Our people resisted with everything they could find to hand: Spades, iron bars, anything they could lay their hands on.

"They fought off the SS and barricaded themselves in their camp until the Germans pulled out. During the melee Gunari told me what happened. He was battling the SS alongside his father. His father told him that reinforcements were coming from all over the camp. Now was his chance to escape. His dad told him to run.

"And that is what Gunari did. He ran and ran, he told me he still hears the bullets that passed by his head. Guards were taken aback as more and more people from the camp followed Gunari out of the camp. The sounds of gunfire and shouts kept Gunari going.

"He continued running and at some point, he isn't quite sure when he realised it but he was out of the camp. A few other people had made it too, including some Jewish prisoners who he said were in such a state of emaciation they looked dead already. Somehow they had summoned the courage and stamina to burst out of there.

"Gunari said they looked virtually like corpses. They were wandering around unsure what to do next. Gunari considered taking them with him but his father had told him that if any one of his children escape they have to look after themselves first.

"He escaped into the surrounding fields. Gunari spent weeks travelling south foraging from local farms and sleeping in barns or sometimes he would climb up trees and nap there. Eventually he made his way south to Budapest where he stayed until the end of the war before making his way back to France. Not even a teenage boy and he managed to survive all of that,"

"What happened to everyone left in the camp?"

"The SS held back for a couple of months. Eventually at the start of August they moved in and after another huge battle they killed every remaining Roma and Sinti prisoner,"

"Janko, I was speaking to someone who works here. A boy called Jacob. And I read a document about Gunari's sister," I say, I feel myself becoming emotional again. Janko appears surprised.

"I don't need to know Ana. I can imagine what it said. Keep that in your thoughts Ana, whenever you're feeling hopeless. Remember that you are not without hope, that you can bring justice to these people, and avenge those we have lost,"

"He is evil," I say.

"Pure evil. We don't have long, Ana. Tremmick

will be aware of the laboratory incident sooner rather than later. He may already have fled. We need to find his address and travel there as soon as we can,"

I hug Janko again and we hold each other for a few minutes. I think he needs it more than he would be willing to admit. In all honesty I am in desperate need of some tenderness too.

"Jacob told me that there is a guestbook for visitors. I think that will be our best shot,"

"Come on, let's waste no more time,"

We walk off back towards the museum entrance to locate the visitor books. Janko is speeding ahead of me, the hint of a mission and he has re-found his mojo. Janko arrives at the main entrance first and enters. I follow him and I am glad it is virtually empty. The schoolchildren have departed. It is only Janko and I and a couple of staff members counting down the minutes until their shifts end.

Janko starts flicking through the pages of the visitor book. It is a huge book, large white square pages filled with words. Some of the dedications are very long indeed.

"There's so many entries, how do we know what we are looking for?" I say.

"I'm checking the dates, I have an idea," Janko keeps his eyes on the pages, quickly scanning the dates. After less than a minute he stops leafing through the pages and scrutinises the open book.

"The date is from last year, the twentieth of April - Hitler's birthday," Janko says.

"I've found it!" I almost scream, Janko puts his hand on my arm to keep me calm, as the staff have looked over to us "This is it. Look at what he wrote,"

My colleagues and I felt that our time spent at Auschwitz-Birkenau was very educational and instructive. I would love to have spent more time here but, alas, I am called away to pastures new. However I will use the lessons I learnt here to further strive towards creating a more harmonious society
A. Tremmick (Dr)
Apartment 4, 13 Rue des Roses, Monte Carlo 98000 Monaco

"Found you, you bastard," Janko whispers. I hold his hand and we leave together.

REQUIEM

Friday, 9 May 1986

Yet again, the time approaches to make another disappearance. These last few years I have wondered whether my continued existence has been worthwhile. The clinic in Berlin failed to complete the radical advancements I anticipated and has been aborted. Along with our head of business development Michael Schwarzer too, according to Paul.

Beckermann called me up earlier today and told me the news. The body of Schwarzer was found in a bathtub filled with bleach and water at one of the company apartments in Kreuzberg. Beckermann swore that someone called by the flat this morning and tried turning a key in the lock. They must have run away once they found out the door was already unlocked.

Paul kept an eye out of the window and saw a man of about forty with brown hair and leather jacket walking out of the apartment and down the street. It would explain who has been answering the phone every day. This interloper has been impersonating the man running the day-to-day business. Now it's all over, once this leaks in to the press the scandal may bring down both German governments so it may not be all bad news.

"Schwarzer is dead," Paul said to me over the phone. "They killed my son and now they kill my nephew,"

"They are cowards," I said.

"My poor boy. A son every father would be proud of. A doctor in my family, we were so proud of him. And these pigs murdered him in cold blood. Do you know they sliced his throat open like he was a dumb cow in an abattoir?"

Over the course of the last three days, Beckermann has transformed from a distraught parent to a man intent on revenge. Emotion was scrubbed out of his voice. I told him that he should consider putting his escape plan into action and that we should cease communications for ever.

"I don't have an escape plan," he told me.

"What?" was all I could reply.

"There is nothing for me outside of Munich. This has been my home for over three decades. All I want now is justice for my boy,"

"Don't be stupid, Paul. You…"

"I don't care, Albert," Beckermann interrupted me, "I am coming for their blood. If it is the Jews that did this I will kill them all if I can. I will be flying to see you on Saturday."

"Stop this intransigence," I cried out, "You need to leave Germany and find somewhere safe,"

"There is no discussion now Albert, I have instructed Joachim to pick me up on Saturday at the airport in Nice. It will probably be the final time we meet Albert so I will say goodbye on Sunday,"

Beckermann hung up on me and left me wondering what kind of life this is for an old man. I am too old for this game, it's not like when I left all those Israelis in the trail of my dust when I triumphantly fled from Argentina. Or the time I managed to leave ravaged Europe, the disintegrating continent. Or five years ago when I escaped from another dicey situation with that lunatic woman on that winter's night in Berlin.

Oh Albert, running away is your one true skill isn't it? Yes, it is. Even if you take an extreme view and believe that I did things in the war that may not be considered ethical, is that a reason to spend four decades hunting me? It is a mighty waste of misdirected resources. To murder Schwarzer whose father died in the first week of the war and committed no crimes, that is a sin. And Paul's son Karl, to treat them like disposable vessels is reprehensible. I thought I was supposed to be the evil madman? I never scooped out a man's eyeball or stabbed a man and threw him in a bath of bleach. Who is actually the monster?

The only monstrous act I perpetrated was that little girl in Auschwitz. In my defence, I have a strong belief that what I did was perform a mercy killing. The little girl was on the verge of passing away within days anyway. All I did was prevent her agony being prolonged. After I committed the deed, my mind was all over the place.

As I departed Auschwitz the promised storm arrived, it was like a tropical storm in Indochina rather than autumn in Eastern Poland. I arranged to meet Reutlinger in Prague before we both travelled together by train to Salzburg.

Before I had departed, I phoned Paul who confirmed the Canaletto was safely locked up away in Bavaria. I took the second picture, a modernist piece that Paul claimed was valuable but he didn't know who painted it.

We arrived in Salzburg and the city was subdued, almost a ghost town. The realisation that the end of the

Nazi regime was imminent could be felt everywhere, it was palpable. We were both dressed in civilian clothes which I was glad about. German soldiers walking the streets were being subjected to stares and barely concealed remarks.

Smith's shop was a dusty compact shop on Getreidegasse. Sculptures and old engineering antiques were packed in to the shop. The two men I recognised from my last visit were in the store. Two handsome, well-toned blonde men. Smith and a man with a name that I forgot the moment he told me last time.

"Ah, gentleman. A pleasure to see you in Salzburg as always," Smith said throwing his arms wide in the air. Reutlinger shook his hand and I nodded a curt welcome.

"My friend is looking to do some business today, Mr Smith," Reutlinger said. He attempted to be charming but he couldn't quite remove the smugly sinister tone in everything he said. Since he joined the Gestapo I can't deny that I was afraid of him and the power he wielded. He never spoke about anything to do with his work but I knew he was of a high rank.

"That sounds excellent," Smith replied, "Money makes the world go round. Herr Reutlinger, it is rare that you disappoint me so what have you got to show me today?"

I removed the modernist piece from the wooden tube that it was resting in and unfurled it on the counter. Smith's eyes lit up when he saw it. It wasn't my kind of picture but I had a feeling that for a collector it would be very appealing.

"What do you think, Mr East?" Smith said. The younger man leant over the painting and examined it.

"It looks like a work of one of the major cubists, the colours and lines are so striking. Especially in contrast with the nautical theme. Do you know who painted it?" the man who Smith called East, said. Reutlinger and I both shook our heads.

"It is by Jean Metzinger," Smith said, nodding his approval at the work, "It's a masterpiece. I would put Metzinger second only to Gleizes in terms of the consistency of his work,"

"What about Picasso?" East said.

"I'm never convinced by his sincerity, he's not for me," Smith replied. It felt like these two were playing in a game. I felt out of my depth so I went for a direct question.

"How much would you buy this off us for?" The two employees shared a look, Smith rubbed his chin and stared at me:

"I can offer you sixteen thousand reichsmarks today to purchase this artwork,"

"What, it must be worth twenty times that amount?" Reutlinger bawled. The two men flinched and even I was placed on edge.

"You can always take the painting to another dealer and I'm sure they would be happy to pay more, they may be a little more discerning regarding the provenance of course but I'm sure that won't be an issue to you fine gentlemen,"

Clever bastard, I thought. I could see Reutlinger considering shooting Smith right now. I needed the money right now, my savings weren't insignificant but not enough to start a new life.

"We'll sell for thirty thousand and no less," I said. Reutlinger looks at me, initially with anger but then I could feel his emotions turning to respect. I had acted with authority and it had impressed him. It also impressed Smith who accepted my offer and he went off behind the back to sort out the money.

As we were waiting, I spoke to the younger man regarding another artwork.

"Do you remember the Canaletto I showed you last month? It is currently safe in Germany. I am protecting it from destruction while this madness goes on in Europe. What do you think it's value would be?"

"It's hard to tell, selling a Canaletto is a risky business due to his popularity. I could take down your details and potentially we could organise a price in the next few months?"

The man wrote down an enormous figure on a piece of paper. I could sell the painting or hold on to it for a rainy day. I supplied a few details and told him I would be in touch soon. I would have to tell Paul to ensure the painting is secure due to its immense value. I knew it was valuable after the first visit but the figure Smith wrote down took my breath away although I managed to maintain an unruffled demeanour

Smith returned from the back with a stack of Reichsmarks and US dollars. He had divided the payment between the currencies. He really was a clever bastard.

After he handed the money over there was a passing underwhelming moment. I don't know what caused it but it seemed too easy. Perhaps it was a rare feeling of guilt that I was deserting my country at war. However, the moment passed, and Reutlinger and I left the shop and drove out of Salzburg and out of the Third Reich. With help from the Italian Black Brigades we were in

Genoa within twenty-four hours. Within a couple of days I was on an ocean liner heading towards a new life in South America.

DOVES AND RAVENS

Saturday, 10 May 1986

It has been forty-eight hours since we discovered Albert Tremmick's address in Monaco at Auschwitz. I'm astounded at the sheer gall of the man to write it the visitor book. It would be farcical if it wasn't so abhorrent. It was the dramatic flourish of a man revelling in his own misdeeds.

My brain struggles to comprehend Tremmick's motivation. Decades of inflicting misery upon the weakest members of society. His lackeys consistently claimed medical breakthroughs without providing any specific examples. Only sweeping generalisations and bold declarations of advancement.

However, how are they funding the clinic in Berlin? Perhaps their covert operations are actually paid for by Western governments. Maybe radical treatments are being developed and helping people around the world. I guess I'll never find that out and I'm not sure I want to. My soul is disintegrating due to the knowledge I already hold.

Tremmick is a man who isn't constrained by ethics which isn't a desirable trait for a doctor. In my opinion there is no cure for an illness that is worth the suffering of young girls being maimed and violated. Anyone who believes otherwise needs to question their own beliefs and what the sanctity of human life means in the real world.

Surely there is a limit to what society deems acceptable for medical research. I know there are laws in place for that type of thing. It's bad enough when you see monkeys being tormented on a daily basis in the hope for cures. But when you come face to face with a young woman with a metallic instrument protruding from her eye like a robotic insect proboscis it is more than I, or any right-thinking person, could bear.

I can almost see the motivation in people like Tremmick in that type of behaviour. An egotist drowning in his own intellectual grandeur, unable to comprehend the sickness that lies at the heart of it. But what about the orderlies and the nurses? Did the nurse who was complicit in my so-called treatment tell her family what she did at work each day? I can't see how you could tuck your children up in bed at night after you've spent a day blinding other peoples' children for no discernible reason.

All the way through medical school was Dr Hansen thinking about how miserable an existence he could create for his patients? I am fascinated to know the stories of these people and what drove them to abandon their dignity and ethics and work in that lab.

Janko and I arrived in Nice to meet Gunari a couple of hours ago. Janko drove us back to Berlin and then we actually caught a plane. It was incredible. Janko's thoughts were solely related to Tremmick and he was barely communicative. Which made quite a change for Janko and it was quite refreshing as it gave me a chance to go exploring around an airport.

Despite the false passport, I couldn't stop smiling going through passport control. Janko at one point told me to "stop grinning like an idiot,". The West German checks were quite intensive and the female officer asked me a couple of questions about my East German and Polish stamps. A mention of Auschwitz was enough for her to hurry me along.

Janko sat in a cafe with a coffee and his musings. I explored every square centimetre of the departures section. I was fascinated by the gleaming high windows and ceilings that seemed to reach up to the sky itself. I spent one hour simply staring out of the window and watching the planes take off from the runways.

When it was time for us to fly, the super glamorous Air France hostesses welcomed us on to the plane. Janko had finally lightened up, possibly reminiscing about Amina when he flew to Buenos Aires. I clambered into the window seat and I didn't stop looking out of the window until we broke the cloud cover. From the air you could see the Wall dividing the city like a jagged ribbon of concrete.

I could feel my heart racing as Brandenburg became a toytown region, the houses and roads suitable only for ants. Wisps of cloud became thicker and thicker and all of a sudden we were above the clouds. My insides immediately calmed down and all I could see was endless blue sky. It was a most humbling experience. I wonder if pilots are religious people?

Janko and I are now sitting outside a bar opposite the train station in Nice. We expect to see Gunari any moment, he flew from Berlin to Geneva last night. He stopped off at the cottage to pick up supplies for us and then headed to a hotel nearby. Our flight only landed at Nice an hour or so ago and we arranged to meet near the station. After we had dropped our stuff off at the hotel, Janko said he needed some fresh air, so he left a message for Gunari at the front desk.

Gunari must have driven the Argento at a pace it hadn't seen in years if he was ever going to arrive here this morning from the Alps. I'll be surprised if it made the journey without setting itself on fire. Janko would clearly see it as a vindication of his belief in the supremacy of Italian automobile engineering. Janko is staring at his watch and maintaining surveillance over the station concourse.

We are both nursing coffees. The taste is creamy but I am deriving no joy from it. My stomach is cramping. Whether it is due to my period or nerves I can't tell. I am exhausted. When this is all over I need a break. It's funny, as this would be the perfect destination for a beach holiday.

The rain that greeted our arrival in the south of France has disappeared and has been replaced by a muggy warmth. Flies buzz around the next table and their barely eaten fruit platter. The passing traffic sounds like one insistent press of the horn. My stomach cramps again and the pain shoots up to my head. I place my head in my hands and try to relax. I feel Janko poking a finger on my head. The man clearly has a death wish.

"What are you doing?" I say, somehow restraining myself from swearing.

"It's Gunari," Janko says. I scan around and I can see Gunari crossing the road and delivering a mean look to the driver of a mucky Peugeot van who braked strongly in front of him. The driver wants to say something but he wisely chooses against that course of action.

Gunari spots us and offers a wave which Janko returns. I jump out of my seat and give him a hug and a peck on the cheek. Gunari looks shyly surprised. He returns the hug and ruffles my hair. A sense of pride comes over me which is then swamped by another cramp which makes me hunch over slightly.

"Are you two ready?" Gunari says, remaining on the pavement, "I've already bought the train tickets,"

"Yes," Janko replies and places a few Francs neatly on the table, "Let's go see how the other half live,"

THE FLOWERS
OF MONACO

Saturday, 10 May 1986

The three of us cross the road and head directly in to the station. Our train is about to leave from the nearest platform so we hop on and take a seat on a new-looking red and white carriage. The train pulls away quite literally as I take my seat. It is about three-quarters full but there is very little chatter on the carriage.

None of us speak as the train trundles through the resort towns of the Riviera. I absorb the exotic-sounding names from the signs at the platforms - Ville-franche, Beaulieu, Èze, Cap d'Ail. The train occasionally passes very close to the sea. I watch children frolicking on the beach in a cove, lovers in the cafes enjoying lunch. A different world from my own.

The grey blockiness of Berlin was barely a day ago yet travelling along the Côte d'Azur makes it seem a lifetime ago. We enter a tunnel and Janko nudges my elbow knocking me out of my hazy state, and nearly knocking my head face first in to the table. I shoot a 'What-the-hell' glare at him.

"We are approaching the station in Monaco," Gunari whispers.

"I left my passport at the hotel," I say, panic rising. Why does he tell me these things at the last minute?

"You don't need it to enter Monaco but technically you should have some form of identification in case the police request it,"

"But I don't have any identification,"

"Neither do I." Janko winks and then points out of the window. I notice we are entering a dimly lit train station. We disembark and it looks like we are in one long curved tunnel with spotlights across the soaring ceiling each emitting an ugly orange illumination.

The two men set off through the railway station at a furious pace and I initially struggle to keep up. We step out of the station into a dazzling summer's day. The sun is blinding and I hunt in my bag to find my sunglasses which I fail to locate. Gunari stops suddenly and consults a page torn from a travel guide containing a Monaco street map.

After a good while searching in my rucksack I finally grab my sunglasses. I put them on and I can actually open my peepers without my eyes watering. Straight ahead in the distance I can see the famous port lined with yachts. The closer out towards the sea the yachts become bigger and more ostentatious. I cross the road to catch a better look, some of the yachts are huge. I wonder who owns them? Maybe if Janko sold that van Gogh in the cottage he could buy one for my summer holiday. I'll advise him of my idea later on.

All around, I see apartment blocks everywhere. The roads are quiet despite Janko's warnings that the place is renowned as the world's most expensive car park. Gunari calls out to me and points to his left so I skip over the road again and have to jog to catch them up.

The pavements are so narrow that we have to

walk in single file. We pass by various businesses catering for the rich: solicitors' offices, art galleries and estate agents with the occasional palm tree popping out of the concrete. A couple of workmen are stood admiring a big hole in the road and casually abusing each other in industrial French. It's interesting that even somewhere as rich as Monaco still needs working class tradesmen to keep the place running.

We turn left, I see a sign indicating we are now on Avenue Berceau. The road rises on a sharp gradient. We reach an odd shaped junction with three roads veering off in different directions and elevations and a pedestrian staircase striking out even higher. Gunari instructs Janko and I to halt.

"Rue des Roses is at the top of the steps," Gunari says to us, "I will wait here, you two check it out. If you see him Janko you know what to do,"

Janko nods, he is carrying a briefcase. I know it contains his SIG P220 pistol, bought from a former Swiss soldier in Geneva last winter. Janko's face looks drained of colour. So does Gunari's and I'm guessing I do too, considering how sick I feel.

"Let's go," I say, standing around in the sun is making me feel even worse.

"Take a walk along Rue des Roses then you can continue around the parallel street and meet me back here. If I hear a shot I will depart back to Savoy. Hopefully I will see you both there,"

Janko nods to Gunari and then gestures to me to head upstairs.

I head up the stairs and Janko follows. Rue des Roses is a narrow one-way street which has the now-typical Monegasque narrow pavements on either side.

Four-storey apartment blocks line our path on either side. Janko walks in middle of the road while I stick to the tiny pavement on the left. Occasional cars drive towards us so Janko keeps moving to the side and then back to the centre of the road.

I am surreptitiously holding a photo of Tremmick taken by Gunari in Argentina along with the copy I took from Jacob at Auschwitz. Will I recognise Tremmick if I see him? What a nightmare it would be if he simply walks right on past and I don't realise until I'm bed tonight.

We cross a junction and arrive outside number thirteen. It is a splendid apartment block in comparison to the indistinguishable buildings at the start of the street. Ornate decoration surrounds the door. The road is only wide enough for one line of traffic although there are about twenty mopeds parked up in a bay opposite.

"Keep walking," Janko whispers to me as I prepare to inspect the front door. I'm not sure what has triggered him to say it in this manner but I know to listen to him.

We carry on striding down the street and pass a man in his twenties. He is wearing a light coat and dark jeans. He stares at me as I walk past. I hold his gaze until we pass. A scooter whizzes by and the driver honks the horn which makes me jump.

A busy crossroads awaits us and Janko guides us right onto Avenue Sainte-Cécile and almost immediately we turn right again on to Rue des Lauriers. Bang in front of me is a huge tower, I nearly trip over gawping at it. It must be thirty storeys high.

"What's that?" I say to Janko.

"The tallest building in Monaco, the Millefiori apartments. It's a bit two-dimensional for my tastes. It's like it was designed by a child,"

We continue walking down the road in the shadow of the tower. It is nice not to be burning up in the full glare of the sun. I wish this nauseous feeling would pass, the cramps are only making it worse. The last thing I want to do is call in sick on such an important day.

"Why didn't we stop at the apartment?" I ask.

"I didn't trust the guy on the street. I think he was carrying a weapon," Janko says, his face ghostly white.

"Maybe," I say, unsure of Janko's thinking. This heat is probably making him paranoid.

"We have to be careful. If Tremmick knows we are onto him he may have enlisted help. They will be dangerous people if that is true."

So we have to kill another man in addition to Tremmick? This plan doesn't look like it is going to work. We are supposed to be silent shadows not creating a bloodbath. Something inside tells me that I may not be leaving Monaco any time soon.

A minute later we arrive back at our starting spot. I see Gunari standing against a wall in the shade and smoking a cigarette.

"We saw the entrance to the apartment and possibly an armed accomplice," Janko says. Gunari whistles softly and takes a drag of the cigarette before scowling and throwing it on the floor.

"There may be other guards too that we don't know about, especially in his apartment,"

We stand around and I feel utterly useless. What am I doing here? I don't feel like I am contributing anything and in all honesty I'm not sure the other two are offering anything practical too. Perhaps Tremmick will never be caught, too well-defended for us to strike.

I glance up at the top of the steps and I can't speak. I try to nudge Janko and end up nearly knocking him over. I point up towards Rue des Roses.

Janko stares up and sees what I see - the man we saw in the street is walking past accompanied by a silver-haired man.

"It's the guard," Janko says what I couldn't say, "with a man who could be Tremmick,"

"Let's go and take them out," I say. I'm ready for action and start to move off towards the stairs.

"No, no," Gunari says holding back my arm, "The guard has seen you. I will follow them at a distance. You two follow me,"

Gunari pulls out his Glock 17 from the inside of his jacket, cocks it, and places it in the outside right pocket of his coat. He jogs up the stairs with his hands in his pockets to follow the duo. Janko and I stare at each other for a few seconds then slowly make our way up the stairs in ambling pursuit of Gunari.

I reach the top and wait for Janko who is struggling with the steps. He looks out of breath which is worrying me.

"Can you continue, Janko?" I'm seriously concerned about him.

"I'll be fine. Come on, Ana - Gunari is nearly out of view," Janko grimaces and sets off at a strong pace. I speed up to catch him and I can see Gunari about thirty metres away. He takes a left turn and disappears from view.

We increase our stride and as we turn left I see

Gunari ahead taking a right. We reach the street where he turned and I check the street-sign which informs me it is Rue Bellevue. In the far distance I see the two men we are hunting walking along the narrow street. Apartments are on our left and a high stone wall covered in climbing plants commands the right side.

The two targets head left down a staircase, Gunari follows them and eventually me and Janko reach the steps and go down as well. I reach the bottom, look around and see Janko is still with me. At the last moment I see Gunari vanishing down steps about twenty metres to my left. I motion to Janko telling him where they went.

The bottom of this set of steps brings us back to the street near the station. Gunari turned right, so we follow him. I can't see the two men anymore but I presume Gunari can. Outside the train station Gunari walks through the entrance. As Janko and I are about to follow him into the station Janko tells me to stop.

"We can wait here," Janko says.

"He might need our help,"

"Maybe so, but he needs to handle this himself. A public area like this, all three of us can't become involved,"

I pace outside the station, a sweaty mess. The heat and the sickness is driving me insane. I pull out my bottle of water from my bag, take a swig and within a second I throw up against a wall. I notice a few strangers watching me, I turn to Janko and he seems embarrassed.

I heave again but barely anything except a trail of saliva comes out. I sit on the concrete and drink some more of the warm bottled water. I await the sound of a gunshot.

Instead I hear Gunari calling to us:

"Hey! Quick, I have an idea,"

I stand up and have to fend off a dizzy moment. Once it passes, I join Janko in entering the station.

"Where are they?" I say.

"They have left via the other exit," Gunari says.

"Why aren't you chasing them?"

"He bought a train ticket from the woman over there, it's definitely Tremmick," Gunari has a manic look in his eyes, "He's here in Monaco,"

"I think I know what your idea is. Very clever, Gunari," Janko says. He grabs my hand and walks with me over to the ticket window where a middle-aged woman sits ready to serve us. Her craggy face is heavily made up and heavily bored too. Janko puts on his most friendly manner.

"Good afternoon Miss, I hope you are well today?" Janko says. The woman doesn't respond, "I hope you can do me a favour. My brother has bought a ticket from you a few minutes ago. I am meant to be driving him to the station but he has forgotten what time his train departs. Could you be a darling and confirm what time the train leaves?"

The woman couldn't be more bored of Janko's tale:

"Your brother bought a ticket for the 0610 train from Monte Carlo,"

"Oh my, what a helpful response. He is so forgetful these days, he can't drive anymore as he forgets where he is living,"

The woman sits back in her chair impressively dismissive of Janko's sugary chat. Janko turns away then stops, holds a finger up and spins back round to the woman:

"Just one more thing, I should check he bought the right ticket. Which destination did he book for? I hope he didn't choose Moscow again," Janko laughs softly.

"He bought a ticket to Barcelona. You can tell him there are no refunds if he has purchased it for the wrong destination," the woman replies. Janko smiles at her and then turns back to join me and we walk out of the station to see Gunari.

"Do you know Columbo?" Janko asks me. He is grinning like a madman.

"No, is he friends with Bavarian Boris?" I reply and Janko shakes his head and chuckles.

DISLOCATION

Saturday, 10 May 1986

"What happened to Nuri?"

The two tired-looking men eyeball each other and then back to me in amusing synchronicity.

"She took matters into her own hands. She stopped working as part of a team," Gunari says.

"Like Icarus, our Nuri flew too close to the sun," Janko adds, "If you don't work together, your chances of success greatly diminish,"

The three of us are eating a very late lunch at a restaurant in Nice. Janko has already called it the last supper much to Gunari's annoyance. Our food has arrived but we are mainly pushing it around the plate, even me. My stomach cramps are affecting my appetite which makes me very sad as my *pasta Provençal* smells delicious.

"She found out that Tremmick was living in East Berlin. By the time we found out what she had discovered it was too late," Janko's face is hard, the past has painted a harsh lesson.

"Why didn't she tell you what she had found out?"

"I think she underestimated us," Janko replies. "She was blinded by righteousness. She was impatient, always demanding action straight away,"

"Unfortunately, she underestimated Albert Tremmick too," Gunari says, accompanied by a frustrated snort. Janko motions to the waiter to bring another bottle of wine to our table.

"I honestly never thought we would be provided with an opportunity to take out Tremmick again," Janko says, taking a big gulp of his wine, "After the Argentinian fiasco I thought that would be it. Even now, I assumed he would have vanished already after what happened in Berlin,"

The waiter returns and places a bottle of Château Cos d'Estournel down on the table. I wish we had sat in the shade. I can feel my head start to burn even though it's about four in the afternoon.

"What did Nuri find out about him?" I ask. No one responds for a minute or two, both men sip their wine and look almost guilty.

"Oh Nuri, if only you had told us what you had found out," Janko says, I see tears falling down his face. Gunari notices too and he stops looking and stares at the table, "We could have ended his existence there and then and also stop that dreadful underground lab from being set up,"

Janko wipes the tears away and laughs uncomfortably. I place my hand on his and give it a little squeeze, his hand is soft and puffy.

"When she joined us, she was immediately a voracious reader. She read everything in my library within a year or two. She would read newspapers from around the world every single day. It was where she occasionally found anti-Roma discrimination that we would take action against.

"One day in January eighty-one she disappeared. She told us that she was researching something and that she may be gone for a while,"

"It wasn't out of the ordinary, she had done it a

few times previously. She would come back in a few days, a week at most, and everything would be back to normal." Gunari says.

"Only this time she was gone for two weeks with no letters or telephone calls." Janko says, "That was when we started researching the scant notes she had left behind. All we could see were some newspaper cuttings about a child with a rare abnormality. The child had been born with two brains,"

"What?" I say, I've never heard such nonsense. Gunari throws a withering look at Janko and intercedes:

"The child was a conjoined twin. In the womb something strange happened and the other one died and part of its brain fused with the one who survived, the child was being taken from Bulgaria to East Berlin for treatment,"

"I'm sure that's pretty much what I said," Janko says, "the child was only six months old. Funding had been found from a South African private medical clinic to treat the child,"

"Nuri had looked in to the company," Gunari continues, "She discovered that one of the suppliers to this South African company was an Argentinian firm. The director of the firm was Federico Hernández. The same Federico Hernández who was in business with Tremmick and whose brother I had put to sleep in Buenos Aires,"

"The work she had put in to find this out was staggering," Janko says, "I went in to her room and found directories of businesses in dozens of different countries. She was looking for a needle in a haystack and she was lucky enough to stab her finger with the needle.

"We presumed she had headed to East Berlin and we made plans to follow her there. But the newspaper cuttings were from three months prior. There was nothing else there except a cutting from two weeks before she left. It stated that the child had passed away during treatment,"

"Oh, the poor little guy," I say, although it may have been a blessing for him if he was very ill.

"Yes, indeed," Janko says, "Gunari said let's go there and see what we can find. That evening we made some calls, managed to sort out our papers and then headed to Zurich to fly to Berlin Schönefeld.

"I was freezing to my bones when we stepped out of the airport. You know how fresh it is by the lake in Savoy in winter? It feels lovely on your skin. But in Berlin, the wind whips you while the drizzle soaks you. I couldn't shake the ominous feeling inside. A deep sadness in my soul that told me this was not going to work out how any of us hoped.

"Everywhere we seemed to go the police asked us questions. Two shady men in East Berlin looking lost. We used the classic Jewish refugee story which they would invariably believe. East and West Berlin, the police were both sensitive of offending Jews. If we had mentioned we were Roma they would probably have deported us immediately.

"We were staying in a seedy hotel on Alexanderplatz. Not a curved line in sight there. Blocks of concrete rectangles everywhere, a palette of greys. We went straight to bed that night and I felt more hopeless than at any point in my life.

"I woke up and the despair hadn't abated. I hate

going anywhere without a plan or even any idea on what to do next. The only clue we had was the East Berlin office of the South African company. We headed there." Janko waves his hand but I'm not sure what the gesture is meant to convey. Gunari take over the story as Janko's hope appears to have deserted him once more.

"Outside of our hotel we saw the TV Tower, do you remember seeing it?" Gunari asks, I nod my head in agreement, "It's a huge tower halfway to heaven with a giant ball at the top that contains a viewing platform and restaurant. It's the tallest building in either part of Germany. I really don't know how Janko missed seeing that the night before but like he said, we were out of our depth.

"It's not often we would admit that," Janko says, "Perhaps Nuri was right and we were the ones who had become complacent. But, not telling us what she was up to and where she went. She failed us, all of us.

"The office was on a street two blocks from Unter den Linden. We saw the Brandenburg Gate with the wall behind it and East German guards in front of it preventing people walking up to it. The symbol of the city reduced to an embarrassing afterthought. Berlin really is a strange place,"

"The office was in a grand old building," Gunari says, "According to the sign outside they were on the second floor. We weren't sure on what to do. Janko decided to go up and claim to be a salesman."

"I walked up the stairs," Janko says, "Hope had not yet returned. Desolation was in my heart, my brain empty of ideas. I reached the top of the stairs. An open door welcomed me in. I saw a bored young girl on reception, the rest of the office was empty. I could see rooms that looked like they had been vacated quickly, documents lying on the floor.

"My mind snapped to action and I told the receptionist that I worked for the company that owned the building and I was performing a check before their lease expired. She barely looked up when I said I was going to take a look around. I could have told her I was attaching explosives to the walls and she probably would have carried on painting her nails.

"I went through each room methodically. I was back in my element investigating. I found what I was searching for. Alas, in retrospect, I missed the bigger picture. I found documents that linked the South American supplier with another firm who were participating in the reconstruction of the Deutscher Dom on Gendarmenmarkt.

"If she had told us what she knew we could have helped a lot of those people in that clinic," Janko says, "Everything is now beginning to fall into place. The company was responsible for building some of the underground infrastructure around the church,"

Janko stops speaking and I don't really understand what he's on about. Gunari too, looks intrigued.

"We were there, at the church, you must remember Gunari?"

"Yes, I remember us looking around below the church that night," Gunari says, "Creepiest night of my life,"

"It was rather ghostly," Janko emits a chuckle, "It was deserted but there was odd noises coming from everywhere. Things clanging on the floor, rattling pipes. I thought Gunari was going to run out of there at one point,"

"I didn't take you for Scooby Doo, Gunari," I say.

"It was a very odd experience," Gunari concedes, "And not one I would like to repeat,"

"But after what I've seen this week there might be a more sinister explanation," Janko opens his hands out, "Ana, can you guess which U-bahn station is nearest to Gendarmenmarkt?"

Now I see what he is saying, I nod at Janko. I turn to Gunari who is now smiling bitterly.

"Stadtmitte is a minute away on foot, the noises we heard..." Janko leaves the ending to us to interpret.

No wonder Janko looks devastated. They were almost able to stop Tremmick's clinic right at the beginning.

"Did you find anything of use at all?" I say.

"A letter from Tremmick to a man with initials P.B.," Gunari replies, "It stated that he had been in a meeting with a potential investor, a female former soldier from Yugoslavia. I read the letter and knew he meant Nuri. I've no idea how she organised it,"

"At the end of the letter," Janko says, "It said another meeting had been arranged at the TV tower where final details were to be ironed out, the meeting was organised for the very night we were in the church. Tremmick, Nuri and P.B. - now we know that was Paul Beckermann.

"We headed across East Berlin in a taxi back to Alexanderplatz. It was nearly midnight. I had an ominous feeling about everything. Why had Nuri not told us what she was doing?"

"She had nothing to gain from not telling you," I say, equally puzzled.

"Exactly," Janko replied, "We threw a few Ost-marks at the driver and jumped out of the taxi by the Neptune Fountain. There was no one around and snow was dropping out of the crisp sky like you see on a Christmas card. As we ran towards the tower in front of us, we heard the noise first. The scream of a woman falling from above,"

Both men are shaken from the memory. Janko speaks robotically and closes his eyes.

"I looked up and saw her. Nuri, plummeting from the tower. She didn't look real. It can't have been real; I still tell myself that today. It had to be someone else,"

"The sound," Gunari says, "I still hear the sound of her hitting the ground in my dreams,"

"We ran over to her body which had landed on the steps outside the entrance," Janko says, "A few people seemed to come from nowhere to see what had happened. A teenage girl started screaming like a maniac. The body on the floor. It was Nuri, our Nuri,"

"I'm so sorry," I say for some reason, "Did Tremmick push her out?"

"I guess we'll never know," Gunari replied, "We had to leave her body and try and find him. Janko ran in to the TV Tower and I ran around to the other side where the other entrance is. I made my way around when I saw an old man jogging away from the building. I started to run and the guy turned around. It was Tremmick,"

"My God,"

"He was panicking, and he stumbled as he saw me running towards him. He continued in the direction of the S-Bahn station when a big West German Mercedes pulled up at the side of the road. Tremmick entered in the passenger door and the car sped away. Tremmick looked at me and smiled as he drove away. If only I had a gun I would have taken a shot at that creature,"

Gunari is exhausted from telling the story. Janko is holding back tears.

What a way to die, falling from the top of one of Europe's biggest buildings. I mull over what went through Nuri's head as she headed towards the concrete. Was her head full of regrets for not telling Gunari and Janko her plans or was it thoughts of her mother alone in a flat half a mile up in the sky in Belgrade?

FALLEN ANGEL

Saturday, 10 May 1986

Falling from the sky like a doll dropping off a table. The ghost of Nuri has haunted me since I left Yugoslavia. In some ways what Nuri represents has plagued me all my life. That need to do more and more to make an impact is intrinsic to my character. I have always prided myself on my independence and hard work. I've never found it easy to ask for help or to admit I'm struggling. Undoubtedly, I'm toiling at the moment with the pressure but I can't face saying this to Gunari and Janko.

"We need to be ready for any eventuality," Gunari says. His rugged hands are rotating the beer mat continuously and speedily. I'm clearly not the only one burdened by our duty. Janko remains placid but I keep catching him staring off into the distance.

"Does Tremmick know we are here?" I ask. Gunari and Janko look at each other then shrug at the same time. It is now after nine in the evening and we are sat outside at a bar opposite to the place where we ate. I'm now hungry even though I spent three hours finishing my pasta at the restaurant.

"I don't think he knows that we are here specifically but he will know that people are on his tail. He will be extra careful now," Janko says, "We need a back up plan in case Gunari isn't able to finish him off,"

"Once he walks in the main entrance I will follow behind him and shoot him in the back of the head. That is my plan," Gunari says.

"It's a solid plan. Have you called Bavarian Boris today?" I ask.

"Yes, he didn't receive a call from Tremmick, so we know that the train he is taking tomorrow will mean he won't be returning to Monaco any time soon," Gunari answers.

The beer mat continues spinning in his big paws.

"I wonder where he will be going to," I say.

"He will have a contingency ready to go," Janko says, "But it could be anywhere. Oh, before I forget Ana, we bought you a gift as part of Plan B,"

"Plan B," I say, "You make Plan A sound very ill-fated, Jank,.."

Janko hands me a black bag with a distinctive gold logo of interlocking C's. I open the bag and pull out a piece of folded red material. I unfurl it and hold it to the side of the table and I can see it is a stunning red dress. It is a thing of beauty which even I can appreciate despite not knowing the slightest thing about fashion.

"It's by Coco Chanel," Janko says, "Gunari picked it up for me before he left West Berlin. He is well known for his knowledge of Parisian haute couture," Gunari chuckles uncomfortably. I would have paid money to have seen him make this purchase.

"Why have you bought me this?" I ask, I'm not sure this is the time or place for gift-giving.

"Plan B involves preying on the basest of male instincts," Janko reclines in his chair, then sits back up again after he notices how disagreeably uncomfortable it is, "A lot of men allow their guard to drop when they notice a young, attractive girl. Tremmick is no different, we spotted that in Argentina,"

"But he's really old," I say, I'm astonished that old

men could be into that kind of thing still.

"Old men often have the same urges they did at sixteen," Janko says. That sounds appalling. I was finally feeling better but this conversation is turning my belly upside down again. I turn to Gunari who is smiling and he winks conspiratorially at me.

"A second can make a lifetime of difference, Ana. All we are doing is maximising our chances of success,"

"It is a nice dress, it's a shame I don't have any shoes to go with it," I've only got my filthy Adidas Lendls which have floppy soles coming off at the front.

"We'll take a look back at the hotel, I've brought a few of Nuri's old shoes," Gunari says.

"Following quite literally in her footsteps eh Ana?" Janko says. Considering she fell from a very large height to her death this isn't the most reassuring news to hear. He almost looks pained after saying it out loud. I'm sure it sounded wittier in his head.

"Yes, you are really helping my nerves Janko," I reply, "What is Plan B?"

"Plan B may be a little more…" Janko searches for the correct word, "Improvised. Plan A should be sufficient, no messing about this time. One bullet from Gunari and then we race out of there.

"I will stay in the car with you Ana. Any problems from Gunari's side and we will have to respond. I have put supplies in the car for a week. Potentially this may not be over by tomorrow. Our passports should be fine for most places you can reach her in a day or so,"

"There are two exits at Monte Carlo station," Gunari says, "I will be responsible for the entrance we went through earlier today. You two will be watching the second exit. Janko is in charge and you both need to be ready to leave me here. I will return to the hotel in Nice and stay there for seven days before returning to the cottage. You have the phone number of the hotel if you need to contact me,"

"Try and sleep tonight Ana, I know it will be difficult but the wine should help," Janko adds.

We all amble back to the hotel together, Gunari and Janko say they are both going for a walk before bed. I am actually very tired so I go straight to my room. I pack my rucksack up with my belongings. On the table next to my bed I leave out my Casio watch and bagh nakh.

I lie in bed thinking about my mother and father. I look at the telephone in the room and I consider phoning them up. I push the thought out of my head, I'm not going to start going rogue like Nuri. I wonder what they are doing now? It has been nearly a year since the two men took me away from them. I hope they are both doing well and not missing me as much as I am missing them.

It's the little things that you take for granted. Coming downstairs and seeing your breakfast laid out by my Dad before he headed to the depot. Or when you open your drawers and see some new socks that you know you didn't buy yourself. All-encompassing little acts that show that my parents loved me every moment of the day.

I miss the evenings when Mum would brush my hair and sing '*Što te nema*' to me, which means 'Why aren't you here?'. At the time I never fully appreciated our time spent together but now thinking about my mother and her love of Jadranka Stojaković's music makes me unbearably upset.

Always intruding on my thoughts is the image of Nuri, a woman I have never met. A woman I have never even seen in a photograph. But I can see her etched in my mind, falling like lightning from heaven.

POTESTATEM DISSOLVIT UT GLACIEM

Saturday, 10 May 1986

Sometimes I surprise myself with my level of invent-iveness. I am sat nursing a glass of whiskey at the air-port in Nice confident that my final escape may very well be my finest hour. This will be my final drink be-fore the plan is set in motion tomorrow morning. I will need a clear head for my departure. I am feeling almost gleeful about the future.

All we are waiting for now is the arrival of Paul and what will be our last ever meeting. I moulded the man and all in all, it was a pretty successful job. Four decades have elapsed since we made a pact to stick to-gether and try and build a better world, a world shaped by my own radical vision where all of the complexities of the human brain are completely understood.

I am not a man to sing my own praises but to have governments of many nations seek my help is a badge of honour. What I am most proud of is uniting the two Germanys to work together under my banner. Obvi-ously, if it ever became public they would both pretend to know nothing but eventually the history books will add the footnotes.

At midday Joachim had burst into the living

room with limbs flailing madly around as I ate my breakfast and said he had seen two suspicious looking men. He was certain they were Israeli agents. I think I have passed my paranoia on to him. The poor chap is obsessed with the thought that Jewish spies are hiding behind every lamp-post.

"How can you be so sure?" I asked, half-concerned and half-amused.

"I don't know," Joachim replied, calming down, "There was something about them I didn't trust,"

"Was it their horns?" I said.

"Their horns?" Joachim was puzzled and I decided I should cut out the jokes, especially if they actually were Israeli operatives. Despite his over-suspicious nature, Joachim has a good antenna for trouble even though I was sceptical that they would have found me so soon after what happened in Berlin.

"Keep a watch today, circle the streets around here. It's probably nothing," I said, trying to reassure him. Joachim is most effective when he has a task in hand. It's when he has nothing to do that he frets. And I can't abide his ceaseless worrying. I'm convinced his anxiety is contagious, when he starts carping I feel myself sharing phantom worries.

Joachim followed my instructions which helped me complete my final preparations without his fussy intrusions. If the Jews are here already then they most likely know where I am located. I needed to set a trap so when Joachim arrived back a couple of hours later I informed him we needed to head to the train station.

Joachim told me he had to take a shower, the boy washes three times a day. His sweat glands must be faulty. It's probably linked to his nervous disposition. I can take solace that this aids his attention to detail. His idiot brother could learn a lot from him.

Even though my plans were in hand, Joachim's agitation led me to bear a shortness of breath. A sure sign of the onset of a panic attack. I tried some breathing exercises to relax. A walk to the station through the spotlessly clean streets should be a pleasurable experience but this could potentially be the riskiest trip of my life. I pushed out the negative thoughts from my brain and imagined tomorrow evening beginning a new life.

Finally Joachim came out dried and dressed following his shower. I gave him an even stare. It always helps to keep him on his toes.

"Are you sure you want to leave the house today?" Joachim said as he slipped on his shoes, "I told you about the two suspicious men outside earlier,"

"If they were here watching me, they would have already paid me a visit. Stop worrying so much. All we are doing is walking to the train station,"

This must be what it would have been like to have been married. Constantly fretting about me. What a nightmare that would have been to have spent my life with a person like that. Someone whose life was so insignificant that their only self-worth was garnered from constantly worrying about their significant other.

I came close a couple of times I must admit. There was a girl at university whose name I could never remember. I always called her Katerina but her name was actually Katja. She used to become so annoyed with me when I called her the wrong name. Eventually I turned it into a joke which she would laugh at but I only did it because I genuinely forgot her name.

When I graduated and told her I was relocating to Frankfurt she was astonished and greatly upset when I didn't invite her to come. After days of incessant arguing she had coerced me into asking her to come along. It was the first time that I was made to feel guilty about my behaviour even though I had done nothing wrong. It would be the last time I allowed that to happen.

A day before I left I visited her at her parents house and told her that I would be going alone and that I had no interest in seeing her again. I listed many valid reasons why this was the case. I talked about her lack of intellectual rigour compared to me. I said that she may feel insecure about the gap between our social standing. I told her that I could have my pick of many powerful women and she should be happy for me. I thought she would rationally accept the straight truth and respect me for not sugar-coating it.

I couldn't believe her response. She was so angry that she shouted a string of filthy curses at me. I rose out of my chair and pulled a fist back to put her back in her place when Katerina actually feinted. Her father had come upstairs when he heard the commotion and saw me about to strike his daughter. When her father and I roused her, she simply sat on the edge of her bed rocking silently.

 I made my excuses and went to leave. Her father, a rotund elderly bank manager, grabbed onto my arm and said: "You're a cold bastard,"

I reciprocated the gesture by clutching his wrist and standing eye to eye with him. I batted away his arm from mine and he did nothing in return, so I called the man an embarrassment and headed out of the house. I never saw the girl or her father again.

I frequently chuckle out loud at the thought of that pathetic old man trying to stop me. A man with no plan about what he was actually going to do after he seized my arm. It is symptomatic of the general population that they are unable to plan ahead, slaves to their own primitive desires.

My plan now was clear and I nodded to Joachim that we should start moving. We headed downstairs and into the street. The two of us both looked in each direction and no-one ran up and stabbed me in the back and no sniper shot my brains out. I curtly mentioned this to Joachim who disdainfully shook his head.

It was a lovely day in Monaco, my last full day I would be spending there. The walk was pleasant and I managed to set a solid pace, I was feeling very fresh. Joachim was edgy and I had to tell him to keep calm and stop his head veering off all over the place. I'm glad this was my final day with him.

We entered the train station and the icy blasts from the air-conditioning were a joyous feeling. My back was clammy with sweat and stuck to my white shirt. I spotted an empty ticket desk and headed over to the woman who appeared utterly disinterested.

"Excuse me madam, I would like to purchase a ticket to Barcelona on the earliest train tomorrow," The woman scarcely concealed her disdain, a typical example of Mediterranean customer service. That is one thing I won't miss here. Southern Europeans have such an unwarranted sense of their own self-importance. She flipped through a few pages of her timetables and after a pointless and, dare I say it, deliberately long wait she made eye contact with me for the first time.

"At ten past six the train departs Monaco, stopping at Èze, Cannes, Marseilles, Montpellier, Girona and arriving at Barcelona at ten o'clock in the evening. The price is six hundred and seventy francs for one ticket."

I handed over the money to the woman in fresh one-hundred Monegasque franc notes. The woman printed out the ticket card and listlessly handed it to me along with my change. I did not thank the woman as she was clearly unworthy of my gratitude.

After picking up the ticket and joining Joachim we travelled out of the back entrance and enjoyed a walk around La Condamine. We sat at a cafe and I took in the view of the yachts thanking my stars that this escape was going swimmingly compared to my previous acts of escapology.

It was a close call in Buenos Aires and in some ways an even closer call in Berlin five years ago. In Argentina I was almost paranoiacally obsessed with self-preservation. By the time I landed in Berlin five years ago I have to confess to being blasé with my precautions.

After a decade of keeping on the move around Europe and the Americas I had finally made my home in the South African city of Bloemfontein, thanks to the favourable BJ Vorster regime. I opened medical research clinics in many of the townships across the country.

As South African sanctions began to bite my business. I decided to cut our ties with the country and close the clinics. Under the cover of bringing a sick Bulgarian child to our Berlin clinic I managed to bring back large amounts of currency. This comprised not only my savings, but also money from Afrikaaner Apartheiders who were being stung by the sanctions from Western regimes.

I arrived in Berlin ready to start a new chapter in my life. I was hoping it may be the last place I would reside but it turned out I would be gone within weeks. And it was due to some psychotic woman who had discovered the links between Federico Hernández and my South African interests and then worked out the link to Berlin.

Berlin in January can be an oppressive place, the cosmetic glamour and lights of West Berlin couldn't hide the fact that it was hemmed in by a concrete monolith. East Berlin is aesthetically and morally, utterly rigid and bland. And this influenced life in West Berlin. The people in West Berlin gave the appearance that their Western lifestyles were making them happy. In truth they were as miserable and spiritually dead as their Communist brethren over the wall.

Flattery opens doors. I claimed to be Andre Hester, a South African who lived in Austria for many years. I exchanged large sacks of US dollars to purchase a fifty years lease on the land underneath the old Stadtmitte station from the East Germans and agreed to contribute towards the rebuild of the Deutscher Dom. The East German government were glad of the money we gave them in exchange for a nice office and rental of a few underground areas that were no longer in use. I set up the facility and used my contacts in West Germany to source the equipment and funding. Occasionally, we would take custody of some of the Stasi's more troublesome citizens.

Within a few weeks of my arrival in the city, the woman telephoned our office. She called herself Aleksandra Nuričić and we arranged a meeting at our office a short walk from Unter den Linden.

She told us that she had been serving as a soldier in Yugoslavia but had recently been discharged. She had read about little Bulgarian baby Kalin and she let it be known that she could access children with similar complicated health issues. She said that her cousin worked at an orphanage in deepest Yugoslavia where state funding had been drastically cut in the last couple of years.

We were swayed by tales of gypsy children being born with wild deformities. Conjoined twins, clubbed feet, hunchbacks. A whole cavalcade of disfigurement that we could investigate. She knew my weakness and she exploited it ruthlessly.

In return for a hefty cash reward she would be able to supply children for us to help with our testing. The orphanage would be fully funded again so it was a win-win for everybody concerned. I was enamoured by the soldier, she was incredibly intelligent and someone that I began to see as almost an intellectual equal and potential business partner. Paul and Michael were suspicious but, to my eternal shame, I dismissed their fears as fanciful and grounded in jealousy.

The final meeting with the Yugoslav woman would be held at the TV Tower. We had received word that the restaurant had been closed for two weeks for refurbishment. No one would be there on an evening so we arranged with the security staff that we would be able to host a discreet meeting there.

The weather was dreadful and Paul and Michael's constant suspicions were weighing on my mind. By the time of the meeting I was almost convinced that the woman was not who she said she was. I had been blinded by her intelligence and potent charm.

My nerves were on edge waiting for her. Decorators' tables and temporary walls were dotted around the restaurant. Snow was tumbling down outside, Berlin was an awe-inspiring blanket of white. I was staring out of the window entranced by the snow-covered city when I heard a voice calling my name. I quickly spun around and was momentarily confused.

"Mr Hester?" Aleksandra Nuričić said, if that was her real name.

"Ah good evening, Aleksandra," I said, laying the charm on thick. I greeted her with a kiss on each cheek and she seemed embarrassed by the closeness. A week earlier, I would have put this down to her military bearing. I held a hand on her lower back and guided her to a chair in which she sat down dutifully.

"My colleagues are under the impression you are not who you claim to be," I said while maintaining an upbeat manner. I could see her shift in her seat. She didn't respond, she simply continued to stare at me. That was my final confirmation that she was an imposter. Butterflies tingled in my belly and I strived to maintain my composure.

"Perhaps you are also not whom you say you are, Mr Hester. Or should I say Dr Tremmick?"

"Why are you here this evening? Tell me the truth,"

"Why do you think you I am here?"

"I would hazard a guess that you're not here for altruistic reasons unlike myself,"

"Altruism?" the woman snorted, a face now filled with hatred, "You do not know the meaning of that word,"

"Oh, so you are the moral arbiter now? A lying opportunist who doesn't realise she has made the biggest, most fateful decision of her life,"

"On the contrary Dr Tremmick, this is the night when fate selects you for judgment,"

The woman prepared to stand up to attack me when Paul's giant hands clamp down hard on her shoulders. He had crept through the restaurant earlier and had been hiding behind a wall a few metres away. For him, the stealth brought back memories of travelling through fields in Poland avoiding partisans and Soviets.

Schwarzer, who had also been hiding came out and grabbed the woman's feet. The two men lifted her up so she was helpless. She was writhing and managed to unloose one of her hands where she raked it down the face of Schwarzer. He screamed and punched her hard in the gut. She now had all but one limb free.

I was stood still, I couldn't react. Violence has never been my strong point, I leave that to other people who enjoy those kind of primitive urges.

The woman was on the floor flailing around trying to free her other hand, she was repeatedly striking Beckermann's chubby paw that was clamped around her collar-bone. At the moment it seemed that she was going to succeed, Schwarzer delivered a sickening stamp into the guts of the woman. She was incapacitated from the blow and curled herself up in a ball, she began coughing blood up when Paul shouted. I can't recall what it was but I knew it was related to the final journey for this woman.

Before the meeting we had unfastened one the big windows that look out across the city. I moved to the window and pulled the window from its pane. A huge gust of snowy wind hit me and knocked me over. Paul shouted something again, I turned around and he was dragging the woman towards the window. She was screeching like an animal, it was a primal sound. I was on my knees in a state of disbelief.

Schwarzer joined Paul at the window, gusts of white wind powering through the gap. Schwarzer kicked the assassin viciously in the ribs and the noises emanating from her became even more disgusting.

Paul clubbed her across the face with his right hand and her head snapped back and bounced off the window frame. She began to wail at this point and my mind was taken back to the little gypsy girl in Auschwitz begging for her life. In one smooth motion, Paul lifted her up and hurled her through the snow-filled breach, a howl of anguish trailing behind her.

I jumped to my feet and ran to the window. The three of us watched as her body plummeted through the air and crash to the floor metres away from the eyeline of Neptune and her fountain.

For a second or two we stand around in complete shock until Schwarzer tells us we need to leave.

"Albert, Karl is in the car outside the North entrance. Get in the car and leave the city now," Schwarzer said.

"What are you two going to do?" I said.

"We will leave later, I know the way out of one of the emergency fire escapes. Quick man, go!"

And I did run, I reached the lift in record time. As the doors parted on the ground floor I was ready for the police but there was no one there. I ran out of the TV Tower and I could see Karl's car a hundred metres away.

He must have seen me running as he started the car and accelerated towards me at great speed. He pulled up and I rushed into the passenger seat. I kept an eye out to see if I could see any police. I didn't see any police but I did see a familiar face. The man with the scarred neck who tried to murder me in Argentina.

As Karl drove away I could not resist smiling at my opponent, once more vanquished and impotent. It was only a small spanner in the machinery of the Berlin clinic but it did mean I was once again forced to leave my new home and leave Paul and Michael in charge.

In a funny turn of events this was the airport I landed in after departing East Berlin on that night. I arrived in Nice airport and began a new life yet again. I assumed that would be for the final time. Fate has selected one more departure for me.

MONTE CARLO
OR BUST

Sunday, 11 May 1986

A fitful sleep causes my mind to repetitively spool back to a moment from my childhood when my mother would sit on my bed reading to me. In reality, she would read me children's stories but in the dream she is telling me about the experiments in Berlin. Her face is as serious as it was on the rare occasions she would tell me off. She is recounting every detail of that terrible place.

My mum is explaining that the girl with the hole instead of an eye was the daughter of abusive parents. Alcoholics who only cared where their next drink came from rather than ensuring their little girl ate her breakfast on a morning. She ran away from home at age sixteen and made her way to Berlin. Her parents didn't report her missing to the police. They simply allowed their child drift away, pulled down by treacherous currents of their own self-hatred and exploitative, powerful men.

She is telling me that the old man shouting 'torturers' at the orderlies was a teenage conscript at the back end of the war. His only battle was in the defence of Berlin as the Soviets closed in. A young boy who developed in to a man during the glories of the Nazi regime. When he finally seized the chance to represent his nation on the battlefield, his unit surrendered within hours without firing a single bullet from his rifle. He tormented himself for years by labelling himself a coward, a betrayer of the values of his nation. Decade after decade of alcohol abuse followed and his weakness preyed upon by underground vampires.

How does my mother know these things about these people? I am confused. I know it is a dream but I am so upset. I start crying and my mother's face doesn't change. Tears relentlessly flow and blur my vision. A voice I don't recognise fills my ears as though it is coming from every angle, saying my name. Finally my eyes begin to clear and I see who is speaking to me.

The woman in the dream isn't my mother; when I examine her face I know it is Nuri.

My watch starts beeping which tells me it is half past four. Vile images from the IMFG facility in Berlin are at the forefront of my head. The pitiful girl with the syringe in the hole where her eye should be. Her soul dead but her body technically alive. The grubby old man in his loincloth, like a figure from the bible testifying about the torturers.

I am shattered but I can't face staying in bed if it means when I fall asleep I see those images again. I sit up in bed and open the curtains next to the bed. There is no hint of sunrise and the majority of the street lights outside have been smashed. I pull myself up onto my knees and try and check the street outside. It's too dark to see anything clearly and there is no sign of movement. This is the witching hour. My hands are shaking and I bring them up to my eyes to check. The fingers are gently vibrating. I'm sure they don't normally do that.

It's a surprise I haven't taken up smoking to relax myself. Although if that results in my speaking in a grizzled voice like Janko I'll put that idea on the back-burner. I peel myself away from the blackness and the window and jump off the bed. I pop in the shower, tie my hair up away from the water and turn it on. I hear a knock at my door which I presume is one of the men. I ignore it and there isn't a second knock so I can assume they heard the shower running.

After exiting the shower and drying off I put on the Chanel dress and I laugh out loud thinking about Gunari at the shop buying this. The dress is out of this world, or at least my world. It makes me look less like a scruffy tramp like I normally do and someone who could fit in lounging around on a yacht. Although when I put my dirty trainers on, it slightly mars my glamorous new look.

Another knock at my door. I open it and it is Gunari.

"Ready?" he says. I pick up my things and leave the room. We walk off and Janko comes out of his room, tells me I look like a million dollars and hands out some *pains au chocolat* to Gunari and I, which we eat on the way down the stairs.

It is five minutes to five when the three of us enter the Argenta and pull away from the hotel in Nice. It only takes fifteen minutes of racing along the deserted main road to reach Monaco. Janko takes a quick detour past Tremmick's house but there is no sign of him. The traffic is light at this hour and we are able to drop Gunari off in front of the main entrance.

No goodbyes are said, Gunari is wearing his leather jacket with the Glock 17 hidden in an inside pocket. Gunari walks straight into the station. It is all very low-key. If this is the last time I see Gunari, I would be heartbroken. Janko drives us away through the winding streets of Monaco and a few minutes later we arrive in front of the lower entrance. We park over the road in a shallow car park. To our left and right are tunnels.

I check my watch and it is now a quarter to six in the morning. Tremmick is due to depart in twenty-five minutes. I hope we aren't too late. He's probably at the platform surrounded by burly henchmen like the American president. My ears are tuned waiting to hear a gunshot. Would I even hear it from down here?

"Are you OK, Ana?" Janko asks.

"Yeah, I'm ready," I say despite being utterly un-ready. This is completely surreal, stalking a Nazi war criminal on the spotless streets of Monaco. At least I'm not feeling as ill as I was yesterday. The sun is now rising and the morning traffic is beginning to pick up.

Five more minutes pass and still nothing happens. Janko turns the radio on and slides the dial to a local Monegasque station. Clearly he thinks there may be breaking news being imminently announced. Instead we hear adverts for Loews Hotel Monte-Carlo and Heli Air Monaco.

The waiting is killing me. I check the time again and it is exactly six o'clock. If Tremmick is getting on that train it should be any minute now. Gunari's plan is to wait just inside the upper entrance doors, spot him and then shoot him in the head. He is then due to immediately leave and meet up with us down here to make our escape.

Has Gunari completed the mission yet? I don't think I've seen Janko look so tense, he has his SIG on his lap. Janko is completely still. His eyes are the only sign of movement, darting around trying to spot Albert Tremmick.

The numbers of people entering and exiting the station is beginning to rise. Once more I check the time and it is now seven minutes past six. Janko has started loudly rapping his figures on the steering wheel. I refrain from telling him to stop and he carries on oblivious to my torment.

A black BMW pulls up at the station in front of us, blocking our view.

"I can't see the entrance," I say, stating the obvious.

"Neither can I," Janko says, "Does the driver of that car look familiar to you?"

The windows are tinted but there is something about the man that is escaping my memory. It is there on the tip of my tongue. There may by someone in the back too but the tint on the windows is too dark to see through properly.

"I might have to get out of the car and take a better look. I can't see the entrance because of that car. Pass me that newspaper, Ana,"

I hand yesterday's copy of *Nice-Matin* to him and Janko steps out of the car leaving his gun in the glove box. He walks twenty metres to his left and does an admirable job of pretending to read the newspaper while also peering over the top of it towards the station.

By the time Janko has looked back down at his paper a short old man limps along the road in front of our car. The man crosses the road and then steps into the parked car. That's when it hits me.

The BMW begins to move away. I open the car door and leap out and shout to Janko.

"Quick Janko! That's him!"

I point in the direction where the car has now disappeared to, in to the tunnel to our left. Janko runs over to our car and we both get back in.

"The driver is the guy we saw outside Tremmick's place yesterday." I say, "And Tremmick has just walked past you in to the car. Let's go!"

"Shit," Janko says, he hits the accelerator and we race off on to the Monaco streets, Janko is doing a fair impression of Alain Prost, "Shit, shit, shit,"

"They can't have gone far Janko, step on it,"

"Calm down, Ana, you're not in the A-Team. We will catch up and then stay behind them and see where they go."

"I can't see them,"

We burst out of the tunnel and the road splits into three lanes, all at different levels. Shards of sunlight strike the road. Janko maintains our pace as we enter another tunnel. I squint to get a better look in front, the black car could be about a hundred metres in front.

"I think that's it in front," I say. I'm finally beginning to calm down after the shock of seeing Tremmick getting in that car and driving off.

"Don't worry," Janko says. Is he saying that to me or to himself?

As we approach a roundabout at the end of the tunnel I maintain eyes on the black car. The traffic is steady and I spot the BMW leave the tunnel and head right. My eyes struggle to adjust to daylight as we exit on to a junction surrounded by beautiful four-storey apartments with pretty shops spanning the bottom floors.

Janko turns right and the black car remains in the distance, a good hundred metres away still. The road is narrow with parked cars lining up along one side. The road curves around to the right with the castle walls dominating from above.

"The palace is on our left, we can safely assume he won't be visiting Prince Rainier for a morning cup of coffee," Janko says as we head straight over another roundabout. We are soon surrounded by more utilitarian square residential blocks and Janko speeds up to maintain vision with the black car.

Soon, the big concrete blocks give way to low rise houses on the left and a hefty stone wall on the right. The BMW remains in sight, but only just.

"Should we speed up Janko?" I ask.

"No, no. We're OK, he's driving along the Riviera road. He's not speeding so I don't think they're aware,"

The road is barely wide enough for two lanes, trees are hanging over the road too. The sturdy stone walls don't look too yielding if we spin off the road. I hope Gunari is OK, he's probably wondering where we are.

"Keep your eyes on the car, Ana," Janko says.

"I am, I am," I respond, I've not let it out of my sight since the tunnel in Monaco. We are now in a slightly more built-up area with more holiday apartments. To my left, the Mediterranean Sea occasionally pops into view. I have to fight the urge to take my eyes away from the black car and drink in the scenery.

"I hope he doesn't go up towards the hills," Janko says. Over to our right, the hills rise high above and are heavily dotted with apartments. At the moment the black car remains in the distance steadily travelling along the road.

The road tightens with the outcrop wall barely a metre from the right of our car. All of a sudden the sea comes in to view on our left, the large expanse makes us both look at it. Within a few moments, we are flashing in and out of tunnels again.

"Is there enough petrol in the tank?" I ask.

"I hope so," Janko replies, not filling me with great confidence. What an anti-climax that would be, running out of fuel in the middle of nowhere as Tremmick disappears forever.

The rocks to our right rise straight up for twenty metres. With the sea immediately below us to the left it is almost like we are balancing on a ledge. The sea and sky are almost the same colour making me disoriented. I focus on the black car which keeps leaving my view as the road winds around the edge of the land.

The road curves inland and widens, the black car is a good hundred and fifty metres away. Janko speeds up slightly and within a minute we are in another tunnel. I can't see the end of the tunnel and the car is not in view.

"I can't see it, Janko," I say, desperation in my voice.

"He didn't pull off, we would have seen him," Janko replies and increases the speed again.

We surge out of the tunnel and Janko actually slows down which I find bizarre. The Med is visible again and a railway line runs adjacent to the road as huge hills once again hug us on the right hand side.

Parked traffic begins to dot the sides of the road and a village appears in our eye-line ahead. Janko drops his speed drastically, I can't see the black car. I am checking every single vehicle that we drive past. Trees and climbing plants seem to have sprouted out of the rocks.

On the right is a little cafe and I spot the black BMW parked up outside.

"Janko!" I cry out, "That's it there,"

Luckily I refrain from pointing out of the window like a gormless tourist. Janko maintains his speed and I see him glance out of the corner of his eye. On our left is a train station signed as '*Gare d'Èze-sur-Mer*' and Janko turns the Argenta around in the car park nearby.

Janko pulls the car up and we are about fifty metres away. Parked vehicles and abundant foliage help to disguise us. From what I can see, the cafe owner has just opened as he lets in a queue of about four people, probably regulars buying their morning refreshments.

"What shall we do?" I say impatiently.

"We wait," Janko says with no emotion.

So we wait. I wonder why Janko doesn't walk over and shoot them all. As we went past I had a good look and I am adamant there was another guy in the back of the car. If the driver is the man we saw outside Tremmick's apartment who is the man in the back?

As I keep my eyes on the black car, the passenger door opens and an old man exits the vehicle. The old man looks around, Janko and I are both slumped in our car. I can still maintain eyes on him through a narrow gap in the bush on the driver's side of the car.

"He's looking both ways," I say. Occasional traffic is passing, mainly vans and small trucks. The old man walks around to the back of the car. It looks like he is opening the boot but I can't see for sure.

"What's he doing?" Janko says.

"I think he's getting something out of the back," I say.

Tremmick, the old man, walks towards the driver's door. He appears to be engaged in a feisty conversation with the driver through the window as he suddenly stands up and bangs his hand on the top of the car.

The man in the back of the car also leaves the vehicle. I can't believe it, it's Paul Beckermann. I would recognise that fat lump anywhere. He must have left Munich when he found out about the clinic and his son. His huge frame slowly ambles around the car and he starts speaking to Tremmick. Neither look very happy.

A smile creep on my lips as I can see the impact our work has had on these two vile people. I turn to Janko and his eyes are focused on the target.

"That's Beckermann from Munich," I say.

"So that's what he looks like, it's always nice to put a face to a human rights abuser," Janko stares at the obese man waddling around the car with a look of pure disgust.

Beckermann and Tremmick shake hands and Tremmick starts to walk off pulling a small rolling suitcase. Beckermann gives him a hearty slap on the back, laughs so loud I can hear it in our car and makes his way to the passenger door where he enters the car.

Tremmick walks over the road towards Èze train station. He must be catching a train, maybe the opposite way than to Barcelona. I can't see through the trees to see how busy it is there. If the nearby pavements are any indicator, it is probably deathly quiet.

"Ana," Janko says, in his most gentle voice, "This

is my plan,"

"Go on," I say.

"I'm going to follow Beckermann wherever he goes and take him out. I can't stand that man, an arms-length maniac. No blood on his hands, I will show him what blood is. I need you to deal with Tremmick. Do you understand what I'm saying?"

"I understand, Janko," I say. I understand but I'm unbelievably scared. Janko is basically ordering me to murder Tremmick. I have to follow the orders from my senior officer. Unlike the Nazi troops who slaughtered the populations of entire villages, this is a righteous death. I think about Pali, Gunari's sister, a terrified little girl mutilated to death by this man.

The BMW containing Beckermann slowly pulls off and does a one-eighty turn in the road. I grab my rucksack and get out of the car, the door is still open when Janko speaks to me:

"Ana, remember why you are doing this. For family, for friends, for all of us,"

I don't say anything, the car door remains frozen in my hand. I turn to my right and see the black car driving back off towards Monaco.

"Be strong Ana, and let your heart take courage," Janko says. Finally, my mind snaps back to normal.

"That's a good line, Janko," I say, impressed by his words.

"Yeah, I stole it from Gunari, he says it a lot." Janko smiles and starts the engine. I close the door and Janko drives away. I watch him leave and drive off into the distance.

I am alone and ready to kill Albert Tremmick.

NULLA POENA SINE LEGE

Sunday, 11 May 1986

I stand in the same spot where Janko was parked up for a few seconds. I am dressed in the red Chanel dress and my formerly-white Adidas Lendls. Gunari never did find me any matching shoes. My only possessions are in my rucksack: a change of clothes, Polaroid camera, false passport, a makeup bag full of random currencies and my bagh nakh.

God forbid if any police pull me over and ask me to account for my possessions. Or ask why I'm here at small resort on the French Riviera. Janko said that I should try and charm any cops who speak to me. He says hostility is the worst trait you can display upon initial contact with the police. You should play to their ego. It's only when they take you to the station that you say and sign absolutely nothing.

I can't comprehend that I am obliged to murder an old man in cold blood here in a beautiful village on the Côte d'Azur. Of all the surreal moments in the last couple of weeks this could be the most out-of-this-world. I have a plan which I think will work. However with Janko driving off, I'm not sure on my escape. I'm not sure he needed to leave but I think having borne witness to the clinic in Berlin he holds Beckermann personally responsible. When Janko has the determined look in his eye, he can be a very stubborn man.

The sun is now piercing through the morning cloud. This would be an amazing day to go swimming in the sea or lying on a beach reading a book. Instead I have other plans.

I take off my trainers and put them in my rucksack. I pull out the tiger claws and put them on my hand. The only thing you can notice is the tan-coloured strap around the top of my hand. When my fist is closed the blades aren't visible. I clench and de-clench my fist a few times and make a minor adjustment to the strap.

I place the rucksack underneath a rusty, parked van positioned directly to the right of where Janko parked us up. I am beginning to sweat and my stomach is rumbling from the nerves. I have to urge myself to not simply sit down here and avoid killing Tremmick.

It takes a minute but finally I am able to walk to the station which is a small two storey cube. The station is yet to open and there is no-one around that I can see. The path to the platforms is between the station building and some big, out-of-control rose-bushes.

I pluck a dark pink rose from a nearby bush and place it in my hair. I walk past the sickly-smelling bushes to the platform and the station is virtually deserted save for some high palm trees and a squat old man stood next to a black suitcase. The man is Tremmick and he appears to be reading a magazine.

I am fighting the nerves in my stomach. It is almost as if little knife stabs are pricking my internal organs. I keep telling myself this is for the *Berša Bibahtale*, the unhappy years suffered by the Romani. This man performed terrible, cruel experiments on countless people. He and his ilk killed without compunction nor reason. People like him are responsible for the deaths of half a million Romani.

This man who escaped justice and a trial.

This man who lived in luxury across the world enabled by sympathisers and people who find it easier to look away rather than face up to hard truths.

This man who brought *Kali Traš*, Black Fear, to us. Now, I shall bring him his due punishment. The wind and the rain will wash away his sins.

UNFINISHED SYMPHONY

Sunday, 11 May 1986

They failed to kill me in Buenos Aires or Berlin, they sure as hell won't be finishing the task here on the French Riviera. Knowing that I have once again given them the slip here in Monaco is exhilarating. Every time the Israeli *Banden* have tried to eliminate me they have failed.

The laborious lengths these people stretch to, actually delights me. The money they are wasting to murder an old man in cold blood. I am simply an un-ostentatious, harmless old man who was but a minor player in the crimes of the Nazis. If only they used this wealth to try to improve citizens' lives at home they might see more joy. Surely there must be politicians in Israel who realise that spending taxpayers' money on hospitals and schools is a more worthwhile cause? Is it simply their genetics that propels them towards spite-ful vengeance?

But I can feel the anger rising up. My life has been turned upside down once again. People who can't let the past rest and believe hounding a sick old man is a dignified use of resources. War makes no man proud, I know that better than most. Ultimately, it is a war and terrible things happen in defence of your country.

I didn't gas any Jews or force them into ghettos. I

wasn't responsible for rounding up their families, making them all stand on the precipice of pits and machine gun them to death. I was a doctor, in many cases helping them. I cured countless Jews from illnesses in the camps. You don't see that written in the newspapers in Israel. Some people could argue I was a voice of reason, some may even call me a protector of the Jews.

The Mossad, or Shin Bet, or whoever it is will not be happy when they realise that I am once again one step ahead of them. They think they are trying to catch some bone-headed idealist. However I can be as devious and cunning as any of these Jews. One more time, one last time I hope, it is time to melt away and settle somewhere else.

The fake train ticket idea was my creation. I could sense I was being watched when I was buying the train ticket. Whether it is intuition I do not know but it is good practice to prepare well. If someone was watching me purchase a ticket they would obviously concoct a ruse to find out where I intended to travel. I knew they would ask about where I was going and so it has proved. Joachim was sure he saw two agents boarding the train at Monaco. They will be combing the train searching for me, guns in hand. I wonder if they will disembark before Barcelona when it dawns on them that I have outwitted them.

The time is approaching to catch the real train going eastwards to Genoa where I will change and travel on to Vienna. Once in Vienna, I will change again and head to a little flat I purchased in cash after I moved to South Africa. Totally untraceable back to me or any of my acquaintances. It is located in the upmarket suburb of Hietzing, my new place will overlook Schönbrunner Park. It's no coincidence that it is reminiscent of my place in Buenos Aires. I can look forward to seeing out my remaining years in comfortable surroundings.

Paul wasn't too impressed when I told him a few minutes ago that this was our final meeting. He took on an offended air and immediately tried to ignore what I said.

"Don't be silly Albert, call me when you arrive safely at your next destination," Paul said.

"Do you ever listen Paul?" I slammed my hand on the roof of the car, "This is it now, goodbye Paul. Thank you for giving what you have given, farewell and best of luck for the future,"

Paul walked around the car and I firmly shook his hand. Paul and I shared a look, the last time I will see his face. The most infuriating, yet loyal, man I have ever met. I smiled and turned away pulling my case towards the station. Paul slapped me on the back in that maddening manner of his and I heard his booming laugh. Clearly, he doesn't think this is the last he will hear of me. But I know that was the last time I would ever see Paul again.

I now enter the station and I see roses are growing everywhere. An overwhelming sight of coruscating pinks and reds glowing like a print by the American artist Warhol I once saw in a magazine. Yet it's too intense. The rose-bushes don't look like they are flowering. Instead they remind me of a quickly spreading virus. A wave of nausea stuns me and the smell reminds me a bit of the camps, an intense, sickly smell.

I didn't expect such a sudden feeling of sickness and it takes me a few minutes to compose myself. The train is due in about ten minutes. I can relax here for a while and watch the sun rise. I should sit down but the adrenalin is still keeping me on my toes. I can sit down when the train arrives. I pull out a copy of Der Spiegel and it has a large nuclear warning sign on the garish black and yellow cover alongside a headline about the Chernobyl nuclear meltdown. Those damn Soviets will kill us all. Wouldn't be ironic if I began my new life in Vienna and the city was obliterated by a nuclear warhead a day later?

I glance to my right and I see a young girl walking onto the platform looking lost. She is ravishing. Long dark hair, a pretty red dress and a rose flirtatiously placed in her hair. She starts to walk over to me. As she moves, I notice she is not wearing any shoes and walking unsteadily.

Typical French girls drunk on wine bought by boorish rich men. It's such a common sight on the Riviera. This girl is tantalising me. Maybe there are some things in the south of France I will miss. Beautiful young girls obsessed with men with money and power.

The girl is even more stunning up close, she has dark eyes – possibly of gypsy heritage by the looks of her. And she starts to speak and she sounds Slavic. I'm entranced by her.

"Excuse me sir...." she begins...

ANATOMY OF A KILL

Sunday, 11 May 1986

The cloying warmth of the sun bares down on me. Tremmick is about twenty metres away and I saunter towards him, my bare feet making no sound on the concrete platform.

I keep my eyes on him and I notice he is turning around. I finally see the face of a monster. Initially, he appears troubled by my presence but it doesn't take long before he starts gratuitously eyeing my body up and down. It's such a strange feeling to have this old man staring at my body. He is leering at me, barely disguising his lust. A man without morals. A man unaware of his impending final judgment.

"Excuse me sir," I say in French, surprising myself at how successfully I can conceal my own fear, I say it in the dozy manner of someone who has been drinking alcohol all night, "Do you know what time the next train to Nice is due?"

"About an hour's time, sweetie," the vile creature responds, with a smirk. His eyes are drawn to my legs for an uncomfortably long period and then back to my eyes.

"Thank you," I say, fixing him with my stare. I move closer to him and he begins grinning, his body shape is welcoming. More so when I lean in towards his neck and he slides a soft hand around my waist. In his ear, I whisper in German:

"Thank you Dr Albert Tremmick, the Exterminator of Dieselstrasse,"

I pull back and see the old man's face, it is a picture of incomprehension. I've never seen a face change so quickly from unchallenged arrogance to epic desolation.

Everything is slowing down. I see the shocking recognition on his face of what is about to happen. I open my right hand holding the blade and hold it behind my back. My training has led me to this point, my body is as primed as a coiled snake.

Finally - it feels like minutes but in reality it is milliseconds - the old man tries to lunge at me. He is too slow. Time is not his friend. I skip around the back of him, evading his grasping, pale hands like a Russian ballerina. I grab him by the shirt collar and pull my face up to his sweating neck.

He can't force me off him. I am too strong.

"There will be no more experiments on our children, Doctor," I whisper in his ear. I raise up my right arm and rake the bagh naka across his throat.

Tremmick utters a pathetic yelp and crumples to the floor. He hits the floor hard and utterly without grace, there's no gradual fall to his knees like you see in the movies. Dark red blood spurts lavishly from his shredded throat. There is so much blood it doesn't look real. He grabs his throat but in mere seconds his life passes away.

Within seconds the platform is covered in a circle of rose-red blood. It is dripping onto the tracks painting the tracks burgundy. I stare at the tracks and think back to Auschwitz. There can be no erasing what happened there but the wind and the rain has finally cleansed the world of this malignancy.

A SAFE HAVEN

Sunday, 11 May 1986

What on God's earth do I do now? How do I make my way back? Janko could have parked up and waited for me but instead he drove off like a maniac to catch Beckermann.

I stand on the platform for a few moments. I'm momentarily lost, geographically and mentally. My heart is beating in my chest at a mad rate making me anxious. Gunari's voice plays in my head telling me the cure to anxiety is steadying my inhalation and exhalation.

I close my eyes and try to control my breathing. As soon as I take the first breath, my mind shouts at me to get the hell out of here. And make it quick! But I don't rush off, instead I concentrate on holding my breath, and then taking a long exhalation. I repeat it nine more times and after that, I open my eyes and feel bizarrely calm.

Walking away proves a challenge to my serenity as I stumble trying to avoid the mammoth blood spillage that surrounds me. I manage to hop between the pools and sploshes. I lean on the wall next to a telephone on the wall that must be a hundred years old.

It is unbelievably lucky that no other passengers have come on to the platform. The next one who does is going to get the shock of their lives. No trains are approaching from either side.

If I was James Bond, I would head down to the

beach fifty metres below and steal a speedboat and shoot away. Unfortunately I can't see this as a viable option. I wouldn't know how to turn it on and if there were any mishaps my standard of swimming would be less than 'competent' and more 'can temporarily prevent drowning'.

Will I have to walk it? It's not that far, maybe a couple of hours journey but I'd rather not be on the main road when the police inevitably show up. I have to leave this platform immediately, that much is certain.

I take one last look on the slain Nazi on the platform. His prone corpse reminds me of Second World War photos featuring civilians lying dead in the street. The irony isn't lost on me. I don't feel anguish or guilt, instead my mind is solely focusing on escape.

I walk back around the station and reclaim my bag from underneath the van. I pull out my trainers and slip them on my feet. I take out my sunglasses and as I place them on, I notice something move over the road.

Two men have exited a car and are walking over the road towards the station. Shit. Both men are in their early thirties and wearing jackets despite the morning warmth. One has fair hair and broad shoulders, the other long legs, dark hair and a moustache.

I ready myself to try and take them both out if needs be. I am holding the rucksack in my left hand and I have retained the bagh nakh in my right. I don't want to be using this again if I can help it. If they are police perhaps I should take the consequences. It would provide me with the opportunity to state why I murdered Dr Albert Tremmick on a Riviera train platform. If I go to prison for this it would probably be fair karma in response to burning down my headmaster's house.

The dark haired man calls to me in English from about five metres away:

"Hey, hold on a second," I stand still and hold my right hand behind my back, hoping that my manner appears to be nonchalant. The dark-haired man gestures to his pal and the fair-haired man walks through the passage towards the platform.

"Who are you?" the dark-haired man says to me. He is stood between the station and the road blocking my exit. If it comes to a race, I fancy my chances. The opportunity remains for me to run to the left where we originally parked up and then I can spin back around once I'm on the main road. Although, if they are policemen they could easily call for back-up and it's highly probable that I would be swiftly captured.

"Why are you speaking English?" I say, also in English. It is strange that he didn't address me in French. I'm not sure if it makes him more or less likely to be a cop. I don't even look English or American.

The man doesn't reply but instead he moves his hand inside his coat, obviously reaching for a weapon. My time is running out. Fight or flight. I tense my arm ready to lash out if the guy makes a move.

The fair-haired man returns and whispers something in a language I can't make out. The dark-haired man smiles at me and then gestures to his acquaintance to leave. The two men start walking back to their vehicle. I don't understand what is going on. I follow the men up to the main road and to their car.

The two men get in their car. In the passenger seat, the dark-haired man winds the window down. He is still smiling. This must be the strangest encounter with a policeman ever.

"Fine work Ana," he says. My mouth falls open in shock and I barely manage to utter the word "*Kaj?*" which means "What?" in Slovenian.

The car begins to drive off and the man leans out of the window and says:

"Jacob sends his regards,"

The car drives off leaving me outside the cafe pondering who they were. I can't ponder too long as this is distracting me from scarpering from here. I place the bagh nakh back in my rucksack and contemplate walking it back to Monaco. As I do a bus approaches, I hunt in my bag and find a few French coins.

The bus stops for me and I hand over a couple of francs for a ticket. I casually wander to the back seat. The bus is virtually empty save for a few middle aged men in office wear. The bus begins to weave along the coastal road, the Mediterranean glistening like an impossible jewel and I begin to cry softly.

FINISHING THE RACE

Sunday, 11 May 1986

The bus driver is shouting and it breaks me out of my trance. The bus is parked at a jaunty angle alongside a taxi. The driver's head and neck are hanging out of the window and he is launching a wide variety of insults and is now threatening to shit down the taxi driver's neck. I'll remember that one next time Gunari whacks me in training.

The taxi driver simply shrugs and laughs and the bus driver cuts his losses and pulls the bus away. We are travelling along virtually the same route Janko and I took the other way, barely a couple of hours ago. Never has one morning felt as long as this one. At the big roundabout near the palace on the hillside, the driver takes a different route and it brings us out at the harbour. Gleaming white yachts are on one side of us and apartments of equal white gleam are on the other.

The bus slows to a stop and the driver drops me off at the harbour. The morning traffic has significantly picked up. Honking horns and crowded cafes attack my senses and bring me out of the stupor I have been in since I got on the bus.

I move towards a roundabout and look up and I can actually see the lower and upper train station entrances from this spot. I now have my bearings but I'm not sure where to go. I need to see if Gunari is still hanging around the upper entrance.

I start heading up the winding streets towards the upper station entrance. My pace seems incongruous with the dress I'm wearing. Not many women are speed-walking around Monte Carlo in expensive evening dresses and mucky trainers.

A group of immaculately turned out older women give me filthy glares as I power through the middle of their group. About halfway up the hill, I lean over the metal wall and check out the lower station entrance. I can't locate Janko, Gunari or the Argenta so after a minute or two I continue my ascent.

After only a couple more minutes I arrive at the upper entrance. No sign of Gunari outside so I enter the station and reach an upper level above the tracks. I examine the platform areas which are covered by arches illuminated by golden lights.

Again, I fail to locate Gunari. The station is very busy now with commuters and tourists. I sigh and decide to check out Tremmick's place before heading back here to catch a train back to the Nice and see if the guys are at the hotel.

The giant Millefiori building comes into view as I round the corner. I still can't believe how high it is, it's crazy. I can't help but look up towards the top of it as most people must do. I break my touristy eyeballing and realise Rue des Roses is round the corner.

And then I see it.

The car that Tremmick was travelling in is parked less than ten metres away. I double check the license plate matches the one we followed to Èze, which it does. I quickly go to the car and touch the bonnet which is still very warm. Surely they've headed to Tremmick's place but where is Janko and his beloved Argenta?

My eyes flash towards the turnoff to Rue des Roses. I spot the giant figure of Paul Beckermann going around the corner. I couldn't see the other guy. I jog to reach the end of the road.

I carefully look around the corner and see three men. Beckermann, the driver and Janko too. I can't believe it. Janko is in front of the driver and I don't think he is there willingly. Oh my God, my stomach lurches and I have to battle the urge to throw up and instead I start gasping like a maniac.

My legs have become jelly-filled and I struggle to walk. They are at the entrance to number 13 less than twenty metres away. I move to the row of mopeds that line the street and pretend to be messing about with one of the bikes. I pick up a helmet too to complete the picture.

Beckermann is keeping an eye out. I think he looks directly at me but he pays me no heed and I notice he takes some keys out and opens the door. He holds it open for Janko and the driver to walk through.

WIthout hesitation I run across the street and put my foot inside the main door to prevent it closing. I hear footsteps on the stairs. I enter the block and slowly shut the door. There is a postbox on the wall that lists fourteen apartments so I assume number thirteen will be on the top floor. The address bar simply has the name Müller written on the label, presumably his pseudonym here in Monaco.

I can still hear footsteps above but I decide to go for it. I climb the stairs with the stealth of a Japanese ninja. I use my arm to hold my rucksack tightly against my side. By sticking to the outside of the stairs I hope to minimise any creaky floorboard sounds that can occur on the inner bannister side.

After reaching the halfway point on the second floor, I pause and listen. I overhear a voice, possibly Beckermann speaking in German:

"Keep moving, you filthy Jew. Joachim, if he talks one more time, punish him,"

I can't hear if Janko replies. Knowing him, he won't stay silent. They must be near the top floor now so I resume my upward creeping. Upon reaching the third floor, I hear a door slam.

Helplessness envelops me. Janko faces grave danger. Gunari is nowhere to be seen. I head to the top floor and stop outside the door. My heart is beating so fast it is hurting me. Fight or flight?

THE GREATER LOVE

Sunday, 11 May 1986

I am torn. I know I am duty-bound to try and rescue Janko but every little voice in my head is telling me to run out of here. Run far away from all of this. My heart is beating so fast, it's surely medically impossible, the rhythm of the end of the world.

Janko and Gunari saved me in the clinic in Berlin. It's now my turn to save Janko, I wish Gunari was here too. He must be back at the hotel in Nice. I could leave and try and telephone him at the hotel.

No, there's no time. These monsters could kill Janko at any minute. If they knew what I have done to their pal Tremmick an hour ago, they would murder him right away.

The door in front is not only a physical barrier. I move my arm to touch the handle but it refuses to move. My body is stuck in its fight or flight response. My mind and body are in a fifty-fifty split. Unlike earlier with Tremmick, every fibre of my being is telling to leave this building. My hands are shaking and I can feel a tear dripping down my cheek. I have never been so scared.

Five deep breaths, that's what I need. The voice of Gunari by the lake.

One. Janko needs to be saved.

Two. Be strong Ana.

Three. Remember your training.

Four. They fear you more than you fear them.

Five. Love is more powerful than hate.

I place my hand on the handle and gently turn it. Gunari frequently tells me to keep it simple. I bring the handle completely down and push the door open as softly as I can manage.

The door makes a barely audible whoosh as it slides away from the jamb. I freeze at the sound. I can't envisage how anyone else would have heard it but I hold still for ten seconds before guiding the door open, sneaking in and closing the door equally mindfully.

I am inside a dark hallway, there is no furniture, only a couple of black and white family photographs on the walls. One is of a younger Tremmick with another man who are holding an oar each and two young lads lifting a rowing boat up and grinning. I rest my rucksack down and take out the bagh nakh and strap it to my hand again. A smell of the roses from the train station where I left Tremmick's body hits me and I almost heave.

I silently edge my way along the hallway. Two doors are on either side of the hallway. Only one door is open which is on the far left hand side so I move there. I make it to the open door and I can hear laughter.

I daren't look around the corner into the room. The laughter ceases and I hear a voice that once more has the sounds of a big man, surely it is Beckermann:

"Stay lying down there, if you move we will shoot your friend in the head,"

Your friend? Oh my God, please don't say it is Gunari in there too. My fear has now transformed into abject terror. I don't think I was this scared when I was at the clinic facing a completely different future.

"The Israelis have really started letting things slip sending you two clowns. We spotted this old kike following us in Cap d'Ail. And now we catch you snooping around this apartment. Why are you here, you filthy animal?"

If it is Gunari, he doesn't reply.

I try and work out a plan. If one of them is within striking distance I should try and take them out without delay. I need to try and see what is going on in the next room.

My stomach is lurching desperately and the adrenalin is making my unmoving body tingle. I ready myself and slowly move my head around the door frame so I can assess the scene.

Beckermann is nearest to me, about two metres away with his back to me. Gunari is lying face-down on the floor in front of him underneath where the living room window is situated. Over on my left, Janko is on his knees and Beckermann's acquaintance, the man he called Joachim, is stood over him.

Joachim is holding a pistol to Janko's head although his eyes are fixed on Gunari. The young man looks nervous. He probably didn't realise today day would turn out like it has so far.

Join the club, Joachim, join the club.

"You should allow us to leave," Janko says, his voice is frail but he is speaking each word very clearly, "Our colleagues know where we are and they will be here very soon. If you let us go, you will be able to escape from here,"

Beckermann once again laughs. A hearty boom

around the living room almost as if he had heard a fantastic mother-in-law joke at the bierkeller.

"You stupid, conniving creature," Beckermann's manner has turned cold again, "We know you have no one else, the other two are on the train to Barcelona chasing shadows. This is one time where the Mossad finally receive what they deserve. Now tell me why you are here. Old man, start with you,"

Janko stares up at Beckermann and says nothing. The atmosphere is so heavy, it reminds me of the clinic where my own human instinct told me nothing good was in that place. I sense Beckermann is about to order Joachim to kill Janko.

"Speak, kike," Beckermann spits at Janko, most of the substance hits his shirt, "What are you doing here at this apartment?"

"I was thinking of relocating," Janko smiles at Beckermann, "How is the climate at this time of year on the Côte d'Azur?"

Beckermann nods to Joachim who whips the pistol against Janko's face. I see blood and teeth fly out of his mouth. My heart sags and I know I have to intervene any second now. Janko looks at Beckermann and smiles at him, blood dripping from his mouth.

Gunari then begins speaking:

"Those who hope in the Lord will renew their strength,"

"What did you say?" Beckermann is furious. His focus is pulled from Janko to Gunari.

"They will soar on wings like eagles;" Gunari's voice rises powerfully despite him facing the floor.

"Shut up," Beckermann's fists are balled up like puffy pillows. Joachim is entranced by the raving mystic on the floor.

I shift my gaze to Janko. He sees me, smiles and shakes his head once. He wants me to leave. He must realise I would never desert him. I nod and I hope he understands what I am trying to signify. He nods in response and my courage is building to a crescendo.

"They will run and not grow weary, they will walk and not be faint," Gunari must be channelling the voice of God.

"I told you to shut up, Jew!" Beckermann shouts and steps towards Gunari.

This is my chance. I sprint through the doorway towards the huge mass that is Beckermann and I rake the tiger claws diagonally down his back. He screams in pain, a high-pitched animal howl, and falls to his knees, shaking the floor.

At the precise moment I attacked Beckermann, Janko took the opportunity to barrel his head into the midriff of Joachim. The force knocks down the burly guard and the gun flies through the air. Gunari displays the speed and grace of a man thirty years his junior to raise himself off the floor and burst over to Joachim.

The pistol clatters on the floor and Gunari reaches it first and kicks it away. Joachim has managed to rain a couple of punches down on the top of Janko's head. Before he can unload a third one Gunari kicks Joachim in the throat. Joachim emits a truly awful gargling noise and begins writhing on the floor and clutching his neck.

Gunari moves over to the pistol and picks it up. He aims it at Joachim, who is still making horrible sounds. He sees the gun and holds his hands up. Beckermann remains on his knees, his fat arms are unable to reach the area of his back that I have sliced open. Bloody gore is dribbling on to the flowery carpet, painting it burgundy.

I walk around to his front and Beckermann half-heartedly tries to grab me. I direct a forceful jab straight into his bulbous nose and he once more falls back and howls in pain.

Gunari drags Joachim over to the window and tells him to kneel which he obeys. Joachims turns to Beckermann and says:

"I'm sorry, Grandad," Is he the brother of the butcher who kickstarted this whole crazy chase around Europe?

Beckermann doesn't respond to his grandson. His attitude has spun so fast from hectoring anti-Semitic superiority to a man who knows the time for judgment has arrived.

"Kill us now, Jews. Show some courage for once," Beckermann says.

"We are not Jewish," Janko walks over to Beckermann, "We are Roma, and we are in the process of imparting justice upon you and your friends,"

"Disgusting pigs," Beckermann once more spits bloody saliva at Janko, "You can kill me but you won't stop our work. We are on the right side of history,"

"That's what you think. And we saw the consequences of this at your little clinic in Berlin. We also met your son there."

"That was you? You dirty reprobates?" Beckermann is nonplussed, "You killed my son,"

"Probably," Janko says, "I remember my friend over here ripped out his eyeball with a spoon. I'm not a medical professional but I do believe that may have been a contributory factor in his demise,"

Beckermann is irate and tries standing up, I move over and punch him hard in the stomach and he collapses. Smears of blood are decorating the walls and carpet. His grandson is in tears at the window.

"Your clinic is no more. You are an immoral person Mr Beckermann. You have the same arrogant bearing as another of your late colleagues, Michael Schwarzer."

Beckermann doesn't reply to this. It was probably dawning on him anyway that we had killed Schwarzer.

Gunari then interjects:

"Ana, did you locate Tremmick?"

Everyone in the room turns towards me, including Beckermann. Panic crosses his face which reminds me of the moment his son realised Gunari was going to scoop out his eye in the manner of a Venetian gelato server.

"I killed him on the platform at Èze station," I say. I decide not to elaborate. Janko maintains his eyes on Beckermann, Gunari sends a nod my way.

Beckermann's head sinks as the realisation that everyone in their despicable group has now been eliminated. He lifts his head up to me and speaks:

"Why would you do this?" I ignore him but Janko does speak, his voice now back it's normal, grizzly self.

"We did this for the justice of our people. This is the punishment for anti-Ziganists like you. This is our response to the *porajmos*, people like you committing genocide against the Roma. This is for the people labelled as satanic wizards and for the people mutilated simply for being born a gypsy.

"This is for the people who were told they were a plague or an infestation, no better than the rats in the sewers. This is for the people who are automatically assumed to be criminals, told they are pickpockets or rapists, or that they are scum, that they are dirty. That they are unhygienic and lazy malignant presences in your cultured cities.

"This is for the people marked by the Nazis with a black triangle, for the people murdered in cold blood by the *Einsatzgruppen* or forced into the gas chambers at Treblinka, Auschwitz and Sobibor. This is not only for the million that were devoured by the Nazis but for every Roma who has faced discrimination and hatred simply for their ethnicity."

Beckermann's face is impassive. Janko takes the gun off Gunari and shoots Beckermann square through the nose. Despite the attached silencer, the noise of it snappily reverberates around the room. Beckermann's brain explodes all over the wall. His grandson wails and tries to attack Gunari who is simply too strong for him. In one swift motion Gunari drags Joachim close to him and breaks his neck. Joachim collapses on the floor.

We three survivors all survey the scene. Janko is frozen and Gunari has to physically begin moving him.

"Wait a second," I say and run off to pick up my rucksack. I take out the copies of photos of Tremmick that I obtained from Jacob and place them on the table. I also drop a couple of sheets of paper detailing who lived here and who Beckermann is, along with documents about the underground clinic underneath Stadtmitte station.

The three of us exit the apartment and quickly make our way out of the block. On the street there is the hustle and bustle of Monegasque city life. There are no screams or indications that anyone has heard the gunshot. We walk fast away from the scene and back to Janko's Argenta outside the Millefiori tower. Somehow, I missed spotting the car on my way to the apartment.

Gunari drives us and I sit in the passenger seat. Janko lounges in the back and holds a towel to his bloody mouth.

"You should probably book an appointment with the dentist when we return home," I say.

"That's true," Janko says, "I think this incident may potentially may hamper my chances of marrying Benedetta Barzini,"

"Ana," Gunari says, "I think that was the most heroic thing I have ever witnessed today,"

"Why were you there?" I say, ignoring the compliment.

"Well, I waited for a couple of hours at the station, then headed to where you two were supposed to be and I realised you were gone. So I broke in to Tremmick's apartment to see if there was anything I could find. I thought there may have been a chance that he would return there. The last thing I expected was Janko walking in being held at gunpoint,"

"Probably not the finest moment of my long and distinguished career," Janko says.

"I thought that was the end for me Ana," Gunari says, "I was certain me or Janko would be killed, possibly both,"

"I'll always save you guys," I say my cheeks reddening with pride, "You did the same for me,"

"There is no greater love than laying down your life for your friends. That's what you did for us," Gunari says and grabs my hand and holds it tight. He stares directly into my eyes, deep into my soul and adds, "Thank you Ana,"

THE SCOURING OF THE BALKANS

Friday, 10 July 1992

My passport bears the name of Maria Lawina, citizen of the Federal Republic of Germany. The photograph identifying Maria was taken two Christmases ago. Her eyes are a double abyss, highlighting that it was taken during a low phase. Her eyes are those of a woman who has become trapped after staring deep into a pit of despair.

I have no clue where I first heard the phrase 'pit of despair'. It's one of those expressions you hear somewhere or read about and it sticks with you. It was when I actually read about its origins that it seemed to perfectly reflect my own emotional state.

An American psychologist studied the impact on monkeys of being torn away from their mothers and locked in tiny, darkened cages. Within weeks they would be withdrawn, huddled in a corner of the isolation cage. The scientists forced the females to bear offspring which they would neglect or attack. Sensory deprivation would cause the monkeys to lose their essence of what made them monkeys.

For myself, instead of a cage it was a dark cloud enveloping me in depression. I could almost see the cloud approaching me, wisps of despondency bursting out of the haze and touching me. This sinister cloud would be always be on the verge of intruding into my life.

The trigger, or probably more accurately, the biggest trigger for the dark clouds was the newspaper article that I discovered at the cottage. Janko was at hospital for a routine appointment and Gunari was away visiting family gravestones.

In my usual curious way I was perusing Janko's notebooks and folders. They contained all kinds of articles on a wide range of topics. Not only stories about Mengele or Bormann but innocuous columns on motor racing, North African cuisine and ski resorts. As I casually leafed through the eclectic mix I came across a large folded page. It's size struck me as odd as most of the other articles had been carefully cut out of the newspaper.

However this one was ripped out and as I unfolded it not only did I notice that it was a front page of the paper that my dad used to read, *Dnevnik*, with its distinctive red letter masthead. But also, the front page had a large headline stating '*Kje je?*' - meaning 'Where is she?' and a photo of myself taken from my last school pictures.

The article told a story of how a deranged, gypsy teenage arsonist called Ana Bihari had torched her headmaster's house. It had left the headmaster and his wife with serious burns. Three weeks had passed since anyone had seen 'the trouble-causing teenager with a record of insubordination' and that she faces a possible thirty year prison sentence, once the Yugoslav police catch her.

I read the article dozens of times, examining every word. No mention of any motive, only a litany of slurs against me. They wrote that I was known for outbursts of rage in the classroom. A lie. They wrote that I had once been expelled for a week for trashing a store room at school. Another lie. They wrote that I had missed a term of school due to a pregnancy scare. Yet another lie.

What I didn't expect was the range and intensity of the emotions I felt after discovering the article. Anger coursed through my body and it took tremendous self-control not to rip the cottage apart like wild-haired version of Bruce Banner. Never in my life had I experienced such searing inner fury.

Barely seconds later, the anger drained away and overwhelming shame and embarrassment caused me to burst into shuddering tears. It felt like someone had used a vacuum cleaner to suck up any remaining humanity straight out of my body. All I could think was how disgusting I felt, a wretched creature unworthy to be alive.

The despair arrived, entrenched itself deep into my head and it has never gone away. I am unable to parse gloom from my soul and my past. I struggle to come to terms with the fact that once upon a time I was not consumed with hopelessness.

Sometimes the clouds are out of sight but it is like standing at the top of the nearby hills and I can see the rain-clouds coming. That's when I know the cascading low is heading my way. And for the last few years the rain-clouds have always been in sight or hanging over me, drenching me with torrential misery.

More and more I would listen to Gunari reading from the bible on an evening. Over the years Janko seemed saddened that I was taking such an interest in religion. Gunari's faith was the only thing that sustained him. For Janko, any faith in God was obliterated during the war.

Janko never said anything about it but I imagine many years ago, the two of them will have had debates. At times, the atmosphere was similar to that between two parents after a big argument when no one wants to mention what has happened in front of the children. Gunari didn't preach to Janko who in return would refrain from making his thoughtless barbs.

A bible verse that Gunari once said has grown on me over the years. 'It is the Lord who goes before you. He will be with you; he will not leave you or forsake you. Do not fear or be dismayed.'

I had never known fear until I was taken away by Gunari and Janko. After the events in Berlin and Monaco I learnt the true meaning of fear. I wasn't even sure what I was fearful of. It could have been the thought of being arrested by the police or that someone would gain revenge upon me. Eventually I realised that it was the sense that God was ready to judge me. And that he would not judge me kindly.

So I exist with a shadow of foreboding cast over my heart. I can be performing the most menial of tasks such as slicing vegetables when I break down. I am unable to control the sobbing and my anxiety would only increase if Janko saw me and asked what was wrong.

I never told him about the darkness residing in me. That I was like Jonah swallowed by the giant fish. I couldn't tell him that I saw no way out of the belly of the beast and that I could see no hope for me. All I could do was to hold him and bawl in to his neck. He would stroke my hair and tell me everything was going to be alright. Which only made me feel worse as I was sure that things actually weren't going to turn out OK.

So for the last few years, I have tried to understand my depression. If I can pinpoint exactly what is making me so despondent perhaps I can do something that may alleviate it. Unfortunately, I have come no closer to a cure, or anything at all to alleviate my hurt.

The hopelessness always seems to centred on my departure from Ljubljana and not to the deaths that I am responsible for since I left the city. As the black shroud descends it would often be accompanied by the memories of the final gasps of Michael Schwarzer or Paul Beckermann.

But I would be able to rationalise these actions in the context of their time and place. My teenage arsonism maintains its deathly hold on my conscious. I am unable to separate the frustration that caused me to follow that course and the damage it did to myself, my family and the people I hurt.

Some days I sit by the lake for the majority of the day, even in the depths of winter. Occasionally Gunari will come out with a hot drink which I accept but he doesn't speak to me. He can recognise my hurt, I can only assume he is possessed by the same pervasive anguish. When I come inside, I can barely remember what I was thinking about, as if I was in a trance by the lake.

I'm not sure Janko knew how to handle my moods. I think that ultimately our differing personalities made it hard for us to understand how we both feel. He was of a generation that bore hardship without betraying overt emotion. I believe this was difficult for Janko as he was a naturally open man. It resulted in him becoming a man who wanted to tell you more about his emotional state but he would fear people would disapprove of him if he did so.

Janko said that people shouldn't be scared of expressing their inner feelings. However he could never truly open up as he had been a 'strong' man for too many years for him to be able to change his ways. Perhaps he felt guilty for undermining his own ethical code.

Seven years have passed since I last set foot on home soil. When I left, the country was called Yugoslavia. As I pass through the border at Gorizia and board the bus again I see a sign saying "Welcome to Slovenia". The guards on the Italian-Slovenian border look relaxed, probably more so than the ones guarding the Serbian frontier.

The bus rumbles through the hills and forests and memories flood back of trips away with my parents. Even though this is tens of kilometres from anywhere I actually visited as a child, rising inside of me is a state of belonging. The green lushness and rising mountains evoke a sense of comfort in me that I haven't felt for a long time.

I see the signs for Ljubljana and my heart yearns to go there but that will have to wait as business awaits me in Belgrade. The bus is due to head through Rijeka and Zagreb first.

The one time I visited Belgrade, I couldn't fathom the scale of the city. It was only when our class of schoolchildren were at Kalemegdan fortress and I could see the river that I could grasp the geography of the place. That moment of clarity when the random shapes mould into something relatable and you can make rational decisions again.

The bus arrives in Belgrade and I am struck by how dreary it looks in the evening gloaming. Massive housing blocks dominate the scenery and I am transported to a moment I was never even present at. I can almost feel the presence of Nuri, living in fear of her stepfather in a cramped apartment with her pathetic mother. I wonder if Nuri would have made the same decision to join our organisation with the benefit of hindsight. I have exhausted the 'what if...' scenarios over the last seven years but it is the different endings to Nuri's story that I most ruminate over.

A flash of a memory hits me. I remember back to when Janko made a comment about me stepping in to Nuri's shoes. I laugh out loud at the image of Janko's face after he said it. The stubby old woman next to me on the bus snarls at me so I wink at her. I miss Janko and listening to his stories.

Gunari and I watched Janko pass away comfortably in his sleep at the cottage last winter. There were no 'last words' from him. The last few hours he drifted between lucidity and a dream-like state. He would nod if offered water but he didn't speak. Or couldn't speak. I suppose I will never know.

I'm not sure what the word is to describe how I felt when Janko died. It was not strictly sadness that I felt, nor was it an empty feeling as a dear friend exited my life. I was proud of the man and the life he led. He had witnessed so much over the years. A tough life beyond the comprehension of most people. Yet he managed to pass away as an old man, surrounded by people who loved him in a safe place. I think that was all he wanted in the end. Recruiting me could be seen as his last significant act as a member of our group.

Upon returning to the cottage after the events in Monaco, Janko never really recovered from the emotional toil. He struggled to walk for long distances and increasingly Gunari and I could be classed as his carers. His brain and fixed-up gnashers worked perfectly but his body was beginning to fail him.

After the fall of the Berlin Wall, Janko wanted to visit the city again but his failing health meant he was unable to go. Instead, he sent me to go and photograph the reunited city. It was the strangest feeling visiting Berlin as a tourist. For Berliners under the age of fifty half of the city was a foreign destination. I visited the city in nineteen-ninety and again a year later. Both times when I returned Janko would pore over my photos for hours.

Janko was only an occasional visitor but the Berlin of the Twenties held a romanticism for him. He saw it as the pinnacle of civilisation, in huge contrast with that night in Potsdamerplatz when I infiltrated the IMFG clinic. Knowing that Berlin was once more potentially on the way to becoming the city he loved again perked him up.

Sadly, his spirits were de-perked soon after due to the disintegration of Yugoslavia. I grew up in Slovenia, where most of the people I went to school with were Slovenes but there were significant amounts of Serbs and Croats there too. Whether it is a nostalgic gloss I can't confirm but I don't remember much in the way of deep inter-ethnic rivalries between the people. The only common denominator was a dismissive attitude to Roma and Muslims.

I read about the country falling apart but I

couldn't believe it. I thought that eventually it would all be resolved but when I spoke to Janko about it his face was ashen. It was almost like he could read the signs of impending catastrophe. He characterised Milošević as a man who thought he was fifty per cent cleverer than the rest of the clownish politicians when in reality he was only one per cent cleverer.

He was especially scathing about the Croatian President Tuđman and the hypocrisy and craven disregard for the rights of non-Croats. Janko was aghast that Tuđman, a professor of history, would invoke phrases and symbolism of the fascist Ustaše regime. Janko was sickened that people would not heed the lessons of history.

As the war developed between the Croats, Bosnians and Serbs it didn't feel real. I was stunned by the images being beamed through our television. Slovenian soldiers taking Yugoslavian troops as prisoners. The indiscriminate bombing of Dubrovnik's old town. The dead bodies lying in the street, lives cheaply wasted.

I was miles away in my Alpine cocoon dealing with the war in my head while my compatriots were tearing each other apart. I was scared for my parents and I was relieved that Slovenian independence was gained so swiftly. Not that I wanted an independent Slovenia, I only wanted peace for my family. Whether it is Slovenian or Yugoslavian in charge, I have absolutely no doubt that institutional discrimination against Roma will continue.

Eventually, an uneasy truce developed between the Serbs and Croatians. There had been no issues with my early morning crossing over the border and as I expected, no one had arrested me for the arson seven years ago. How does that even work when the country that issued the arrest warrant doesn't even exist anymore? Do the Serbian remnants of Yugoslavia and the new nation of Slovenia continue chasing felons of a country that no longer exists?

The bus stops outside of the central train station and I disembark. Memories flood back of the school trip I went on we got off here. I'd never seen so much traffic outside the station, Belgrade was almost like New York City in the eyes of the teenage Ana. In comparison to Berlin or Monaco the grey-brown concrete blocks that surround the station look menacing and oppressive. Dirty men immediately approach me for money and an old Roma woman is sat on the floor holding a young girl and begging, next to the taxi rank.

I won't be visiting the park and fortress at Kalemegdan today. I am heading to the bohemian district of Skadarlija. My target is a woman named Yeta Dalmat. She owns a bar in the suburb where traditional Kosovan-Albanian music is played. Last week at the cottage, Gunari received a phone call from a distressed man. The caller told him that his eighteen year old niece who was working in the bar owned by Dalmat had been raped at the end of her shift by the woman's son.

Her family tried to seek redress with the Dalmat clan but were told in no uncertain terms by Yeta, the matriarch, to shut up and never bring up the incident again. She issued severe threats against the family if they dared to speak to the police.

The family of the girl actually told the police about the rape. The police said that ultimately it was her word against the Dalmat family. There was nothing they could do. I know this is untrue and they could act in accordance to the law. But basically the Serb police have no inclination to involve themselves with Koso-van-Roma feuds.

Yeta discovered that the family had spoken to the police, most likely from a paid informant. She gave the family an ultimatum to leave the city or face the consequences. The girl and her parents have now fled the city in fear of their lives.

In addition to running the bar where the rape occurred, Yeta owns multiple properties in the neigh-bourhood. She is well-known in the area as a huge, globulous creature with major links with gangsters in Albania and across Europe. According to local Roma, she possesses an immense ego to match her appetite.

Hearing about her dismissive attitude to the rape of a teenage girl doesn't surprise me. Nothing surprises me now. Watching my country disintegrate and the acts of unwarranted violence that citizens of a sup-posedly civilised country are capable of is bad enough. But all I need to do is think about the clinic in Ber-lin and it is a constant reminder of the inhumanity of powerful people.

I spoke with Gunari and told him I would resolve this one on my own. He agreed with no disagreement, which surprised me. He said this also might be a good time to see my parents and take a break from life in Savoy. At this moment though, I need to put thoughts of home to the side and concentrate on the task in hand.

The Serbs have abrogated their responsibility to one of their citizens. It falls to me to deliver justice.

For a man to rape a girl with impunity in Skadarlija, home of the most historic Balkan Roma community is intolerable. I will not accept this behaviour and I will answer their crime by taking the head of the Hydra.

My initial plan was to act against the son, a man called Ilir but after further discussions with local Roma I decided on an alternative route. My new plan is callous and shocking and it is so brazen that I can't quite believe I am going ahead with it. However I have no hesitancy in taking direct action, the more brutal the better.

I arrive a street away from Skadarlija at the home of Miro, the man who requested our help. Miro's niece was the girl who was attacked. He has arranged to take me to Subotica where I intend to go through the Hungarian border tonight after the mission is completed. Miro is the only one who knows my full plan.

"Isn't it too flagrant?" He said to me on the telephone last night.

"She is a big personality, she needs a big departure for the message to sink in," I replied. It only takes me twenty minutes to walk to Skadarlija from the train station. I arrive at a five-storey brown townhouse which contains Miro's apartment.

At his flat, I drop my bag off and Miro's wife hands me a traditional Roma outfit to wear. I take my jeans and t-shirt off and put on the deep red chiffon dress with gold trim, I then put on a white long-sleeved top that shows off my shoulders and cleavage. I tie my hair up and place on it my own golden *dikhlo*, a gift from my mother when I was twelve in case I ever get married. I think it would be fair that I won't be requiring the headscarf for that occasion. Finally, I wrap a long burgundy shawl around my shoulders. It is long enough for me to wrap it around and tuck it into my skirt.

I examine myself in the mirror and I am satisfied with the impression I have generated. The image of a vengeful mysterious gypsy woman, the stereotype for centuries around Europe.

I reach in my bag and pull out Janko's old Glock 17. The plain, unprepossessing weapon has been mine for a few years now. Gunari has been training me with increasing regularity with firearms and I am confident in my abilities. I tuck the gun into my skirt, covered by my shawl.

Some of Miro's friends have arranged to aid my escape, they will be waiting for me to kill her. A few people will create a blocking move to prevent people trying to accost me as I escape. Miro and a pal will direct me to the car where we will hopefully flee the scene.

I am walking up to the area alone, Miro is a few metres behind with his friends. The bars of Skadarlija are reasonably busy, a mix of the Friday post-work crowd and groups of people out for the evening. Many of the bars have live bands playing music and I can hear multiple songs from different angles as I stride through Skadarska, the main street of Skadarlija. Smoke rises above each section of outside seating and it is a very warm, muggy evening.

My breaths are long and deep, many of the men working as door security are carefully watching me. My outfit is not a commonly seen thing here in Belgrade, even in this suburb. Most Roma don't dress like this in day to day life in the cities, maybe once in their lifetime when they marry. I see Yeta's bar around fifty metres away. It's as busy as the other bars in the neighbourhood, I can't see the devil-woman herself.

I stand ten metres in front of the outside seating area. I can sense the eyes of many of the patrons checking me out. They probably think I am playing music here later. There are currently a couple of old men playing music, one on the violin and the other playing the çifteli.

I remain staring towards the entrance, the atmosphere is turning a touch queer as people are pointing at me. The musicians' concentration has floated off towards me and they are now going through the motions. That's when I see her, holding a platter of meats. She is sweating and her dark hair is matted across her forehead. She notices me and gives me a strange look.

"Yeta Dalmat!" I call out. I hope it sounded as commanding as I wished. The woman continues watching me with curiosity. She places the platter down and begins to walk over in my direction. She isn't angry but still appears puzzled at my presence.

"Are you Yeta Dalmat?" I say loudly.

"Yes, I am," the woman replies, "Who on earth are you?" Her Serbian is heavily accented, almost like a parody of an Albanian yokel. Her little arms are waving comically around at the side of her body and she is now beginning to get riled. I do not respond to her, I simply stare at her. The thirty or forty people sat outside are virtually silent. The musicians may have stopped playing but I don't notice.

"Who are you, bitch?" Yeta spits out the words and I can see why so many people fear and despise her. I simply smile at her and she emits a screech. A bizarre sound coming from this round lump of flesh.

A much younger man comes outside from the bar

entrance and stands beside her.

"Mama, what is happening?" he watches me with caution.

"It's OK, Ilir, go back inside. I will deal with her," So that man is the rapist. A handsome guy with an easy manner and terrible moustache. Guilt is not weighing down on this man.

I reach in to my skirt and pull out the Glock. I cock the hammer in a smooth, easy motion and point it at Yeta. There are no screams from the customers but I hear multiple intakes of breath.

"Yeta Dalmat," I begin, "Your son is a rapist and you have not allowed him to face justice,"

Yeta's face turns into a snarl and her hands are now balled up and held up near her chin like a boxer. She attempts to set off to confront me when I pull the trigger. The bullet flies straight into the left eye of Yeta and the impact knocks her back in to her son, Ilir. He is astonished, he allows the body to slump to the floor and his eyes dart from his mother to me.

My mission is complete but the very sight of this rapist animal is too much for me to take. Bar patrons and pedestrians are screaming and I notice a couple of Miro's friends closing in. I take my chance and step on the front foot and fire another shot straight into the temple of Ilir. He is brought down and the commotion grows louder.

I back away and walk off as planned to the left of the bar, people aren't trying to stop me as I reach an alleyway where I see Miro. I run off to see him and we make our way through the back streets of Skadarlija. We reach his car, a worn out Peugoet and I clamber into the back and lay down.

"How did it go?" Miro says breathlessly as he steps on the accelerator and the car doesn't exactly speed off but chugs off because it's a rusty lump of metal.

"Two for the price of one," stripping off my clothes in the back, "*Bavol i brushíndo,* Miro," Once more, the wind and the rain roars through Europe, ruefully I concede necessity demands it will not be for the last time.

HOMEWARD BOUND

Sunday, 12 July 1992

The night train from Budapest was crowded, noisy and the passport checks were cursory yet disruptive. No one questioned me, or Maria Lawina, about where I came from or if I murdered two people in cold blood less than forty-eight hours ago in Belgrade. The train arrived at Ljubljana's bare train station on time at exactly eight o'clock.

At first I couldn't force myself to stand and leave the train. It was only when the guard came along the train and told me it was the end of the line that I finally disembarked with jelly legs and a dismal sense of foreboding.

Now I stand outside Ljubljana train station, The trees sprouting around the streets and arboreally camouflaged apartments bring back so many memories. It isn't as warm as the morning I left the city but the scent of summer is unmistakable. Traffic is light and the grass verges are beginning to yellow.

The thought of seeing my parents again makes my stomach turn. I haven't eaten since yesterday lunchtime but I know if I eat now then I will be sick. I stand around like a fool for what seems like an age. Eventually I begin walking to my old home. I reach the Dunajska cesta junction and it reminds me of directing

Gunari out of the city when I was a scared little teenager. Cranes rise above the city and billboards celebrate recognition of Slovenia's independence by the European Union.

Now I turn right on to Dunajska cesta, a group of young girls no more than ten years old wander past me on their way to the swimming pool at Tivoli Park. It is strange hearing my language being spoken again. I walk past a cafe and listen to some old timers chatting away about some illness their friend is suffering from. As the years have gone by my thoughts and dreams have come to me more frequently in French than Slovenian. The streets of Bežigrad are familiar yet don't feel like home.

I check my trusty Casio watch which states it is nearly nine o'clock. I have subconsciously taken a circuitous route back to my parents' house. I finally arrive and I see the house I grew up in, the house I left in shame. It seems so much smaller than I remember, it is strange clapping my eyes on it after so long.

It's time to stop standing around outside the house and face my past. I make my way to the door when I notice it is being swung open even though my eyes are facing downward, boring holes into the garden path. I reach the door and finally raise my head. Standing in the doorway is my mother. I was worried that I wouldn't recognise her but when I see her face, a torrent of memories flood my brain like a music video. Images flash around and my eyes are watering, my senses deserting me.

I can see nothing and I feel my mother grab and hug me tightly.

"Ana," Mum is stroking my hair and I can't stop sobbing, "My Ana,"

My mother keeps repeating my name and I would happily die in this embrace. Despite all the homesickness over the years, I have underestimated how much I have missed my mother.

"I've missed you Mum, you wouldn't believe how much," I say, pulling away from her and rubbing the snot from my nose with the sleeve of my sweatshirt. Mum continues to stroke my cheek and I remain standing awkwardly unsure what to do next.

"Is Dad at work?" I say, peering over her shoulder to see an empty house.

"Come inside Ana, off the street," my mother replies and holds my hand and walks us both inside. I allow my bag to slump off my shoulder onto the floor and walk around the front room. It has barely changed in the seven years since. The carpet is the same, as are the curtains and the dining table.

Suddenly I notice that there is something slightly amiss. My dad's slippers are not in front of his leather armchair where they normally would be. I glance at the coat-stand and I see none of his jackets hooked up. I move to the fireplace where on the shelf above is a picture of Dad holding me on his shoulders at the top of the castle when I was about five years old. I pick up the photograph and I see my hands wrapped around his neck and Dad grinning.

"Can we go see Dad?" I say. Mum turns me around and nods towards the door. We walk in comfortable silence for twenty minutes, towards the end of the journey I hold my Mum's hand. I don't care how old I am and how stupid I look. We arrive at the ornate two-storey stone gate and enter Žale cemetery.

As I see the lines of gravestones I once more feel

the tears welling. I force myself not to cry and holding them back makes my throat hurt. Eventually, we arrive at my father's gravestone. It is a simple rectangular block with clean gold-coloured etchings of angels.

"He died two years ago?" I say, stating the obvious as it is written on the headstone in front of me.

"Yes, it was a heart attack when he was coming home from work," I meet my mother's eyes, I'm lost for words. I'm lost for a father. Once more, I do the only thing I can do, or want to do. I fall into my mother's embrace and I allow her to comfort me.

"Was my Dad ashamed of me?" I ask, as my mother hands me a cup of coffee and a big plate of *funšterc*. I tuck in immediately to the omelettes and it makes me feel like I'm twelve again sat at the kitchen table overfeeding myself. Mum walks over to me and strokes my hair. If I wasn't so voraciously hungry, I would cry again.

"I don't think he ever understood why you did what he did. It's not a matter of shame,"

"You understood, didn't you, Mum?" Mum's eyes are kindly looking down on me. She smiles and sits back down at the dining table opposite me.

"Oh yes, I understand," Mum says, her eyes focusing away at a point in the past, "Your father wanted an easy life. He wasn't a man who could confront difficult subjects. We nearly split up before I fell pregnant with you. We were spending a day at the park, like young people in love do. It was such a beautiful day but after we had stopped for an ice cream, a drunk man shouted some very offensive remarks towards me,"

"What, really?" I reply, I've never heard this story

before.

"Yes. It was such an unexpected and jarring moment. Your father shied away from confronting the man who abused us, he tried to drag me away and walk off. I responded to the drunkard with choice words of my own. This made your father even more embarrassed. He was more concerned that I was the one standing up for myself,"

"Some people aren't able to face bad things and bad people,"

"Your father never grasped the reasons behind what you did. He thought it was about not being able to go to university but I knew that it was much deeper than that. Maybe you have only now fully understood what it means to be a Roma woman in this world."

"Did we do the right thing in letting you leave home?" Mum says, "This was my biggest concern. Every day, I have thought about you and I question whether I let you down,"

"It was probably for the best. I only wish we'd been able to stay in touch, things haven't been easy since I left,"

"I know," Mum replies and looks hesitant. She wants to broach a subject but doesn't know how to. It reminds me of being a kid, I can read her so well after all these years. I smile at her and sit back in my chair putting down the cutlery.

"What happened to Janko?" she says, almost in an embarrassed manner.

"What are you on about?"

"I had a feeling you were going to show up here again Ana. I've been waiting for this moment for the last few months,"

"Janko died in January at the cottage, I don't understand how you knew something had happened to him?"

Mum walks to the living room and returns to the kitchen with what looks like a square wooden jewellery box. She pulls one of the kitchen chairs around to my side of the table so she is seated next to me and opens the box which is full of photos and letters.

"Janko wrote to your father and I every couple of months updating us on your wellbeing,"

"I can't believe it," I say as my mother passes me the box. There are a bunch of letters written in German from that silly, sweet old man to my parents detailing my time in Savoy. There are photos too. One of me outside a cinema in Lyon holding an oversized tub of popcorn waiting to go in and watch Rocky IV, another one of me in a tracksuit about to go for a run. There is one that Gunari took of Janko and I by the lake taken before everything with Tremmick. I am beaming wildly with my hair all over the place and Janko is foolishly grinning, I remember that he was telling me a story about how he invented Polaroid cameras.

I always wondered what happened to it as I could never find it. For some reason I assumed Janko threw them away. There are photos that I took of Berlin, Munich, Monaco and all the other places I've visited over the years. An archive of my life, the letters also allude to the type of work I did.

I read an snipper of an article from *Le Monde* describing the bloody death on a train platform on the French Riviera of a man they believe to be Nazi eugenicist Albert Tremmick. In the weeks following the

murder Janko had walked to the shop to pick up newspapers and it appears he was removing articles about
Tremmick from the paper.

"I can't believe it," I say again. My heart is breaking in half thinking that I will never see my Dad again
or Janko, who was as close to a father as I could have
wished for.

"This was the final correspondence we received
Ana. It was a note from Janko stating he wasn't in great
health and asking us to pass this letter to you, in case
you came back. I haven't read it Ana," My mother passes
me the letter, I see my name written in his spidery
handwriting and I open the letter:

Dear Ana,

*If you are reading this then I am very much likely to be dead.
Gunari will say I am in heaven, I will only say I that I am
at rest. Where the location will be, I have no clue! Gunari
has his beliefs and I have mine. Neither of us can claim the
other is wrong. And neither of us would enforce their opinion on the other.*

*I have found it hard to prepare for the end of my life. I am
not fearful of what it means for me. I am more concerned
with you, my princess. The struggle to convey what you
mean to me has consumed me for weeks. I have failed time
after time to speak to you in the manner I wished to. Please
do not think less of me for putting these words on to paper,
rather than uttering them to your face.*

*Everything you do is subjective, everyone is a judge. All you
can do is live your life true to your beliefs and by the time
you come to the end if you believe you have a positive tally,*

then that is all you can do. I am content that when my time comes I wasn't a complete write-off as a human being.

Nothing can erase your good deeds in life, not the wind or the rain or burning fire. Your accomplishments will outlive you, our community will speak of your name for decades to come. The tales of your life will be spun into myths where only the underlying truth will remain.

Ana, I want you to know that I have been in the place where you are now. The aftershocks of the war turned me to nihilism. I was forced to sink to the very depths of my soul to confront what kind of man I was.

Ten years after the war ended, things became too much for me. I wrote a note stating my intentions and drove off to the South of France. I arrived in Marseille and headed for the building known as the Madman's House, a very apt name. I stood atop the massive concrete Unité d'habitation *building in Marseille. I could see the whole city unfurled. The suburbs, the factories, the beach, the basilica, the stadium, Parc Borély, the Mediterrenean Sea. It was all spread out before me, overwhelming me, enchanting me to end it all.*

I thought about my family, the family I abandoned age twenty-one and never saw again. I never found out if they lived or died during the war. By the mid-fifties I was too much of a coward to find out the truth.

So I travelled to Marseille with the firm intention of killing myself. I don't know how long I stood on the edge of that tower block. I was on the verge of allowing myself to fall when a thought simply popped into my head. "Your time is not now Janko". Whether it was the voice of God, or crea-

tures from outer space, or my conscience, I will never know.

However, I knew that it was my choice to step down from that ledge. I accepted that one day I would die, but it would not be that day falling from a concrete behemoth in Marseille.

There is a famous quote that says "Death never takes the wise man by surprise, he is always ready to go".

You will be ready when your time comes, Schatzi but that time is not quite yet. This is your life, embrace what that means. Savour every morning you wake up at the cottage, as the sun rises above the mountains and reflects upon the lake. Thank the Lord, if that is what you so wish.

All I ask is that you don't close yourself off from the vibrancy of life. If you lose your ability to empathise, it can tempt you down the darkest path. Take heart from the love of your parents, the love of Gunari and the love I hold for you. You are the closest I will ever have to a daughter and seeing you in pain hurts me to my very core.

Remember what we have achieved together. Remember that your actions were a response to the iniquitous actions of people who voided their humanity. Remember that moment when you burst through the door and saved Gunari and I.

Gunari said it was the most heroic thing he had ever seen. I'm not one to quote the Good Book but at that moment you ran straight into the valley of the shadow of death and you feared no evil. I told you to leave us, to allow fate to decide what happened to Gunari and I. But you chose to save our lives, to sacrifice everything for others. You made that choice. You always have a choice, Ana.

My sleeping beauty, it is time now for me say me to say fare-well. I am relieved that I have written this letter. Take care of Gunari, take care of your parents and equally importantly, don't let Gunari crash my little Fiat in to any postal vans.

Forever, your eternal friend,

Janko

I re-read the letter and I can almost hear Janko's voice saying it back to me. My mother is stroking my back as the tears fall out of my eyes in large drops. I turn to my mother, smile and ask: "Mum, am I OK to stay here for a few nights?"

THE END

Printed in Great Britain
by Amazon

65692965R00241